Resounding praise for
DAN SIMMONS
and *DARWIN'S BLADE*

"A LITERARY THRILLER LIKE NO OTHER.... The pace of this novel speeds along like the lead car of the Indy 500....*Darwin's Blade* exemplifies Simmons's skill at delivering novels that are different from anything else in the market today, while still managing to tell a hard-charging, edge-of-the-seat tale."

— *Milwaukee Journal Sentinel*

"SPELLB............................. ....-HRILL-ER.... A breezy writing style, rollicking humor, and ingenious descriptions of weird accidents make this action-packed thriller a real winner."

— *Publishers Weekly* (starred review)

"ALTERNATELY HILARIOUS AND SUSPENSEFUL.... Simmons is not one to disappoint.... His readers already know that he will keep them on the edges of their seats; that his gift for descriptive writing will make them feel as if they are right there, and that he will make them feel as if they are old friends (or enemies) with his characters. This time, though, they may be

surprised to find themselves laughing out loud while reading this tale....Another tasty treat from Mr. Simmons. Savor it."
— *Rocky Mountain News*

"HARROWING....Not since J. G. Ballard's *Crash* have automobile wrecks been so compelling.... Simmons throws a light on a whole new murky subculture for thriller fans....He has mastered whatever genre he's chosen to write in....With a simple, unadorned style backed up by massive amounts of research, intricate plotting, and well-rounded characters, he isn't hemmed in by formulas." — *San Antonio Express-News*

"THIS IS AN EXCITING NOVEL, full of shootouts, computer-aided investigations, duplicity, and humor. The humor...is the black kind, common to cops, reporters, and accident investigators—where you laugh to keep from crying."
— *Houston Chronicle*

"A SMART, WELL-RESEARCHED THRILLER."
— *Kirkus Reviews*

"A BORN STORYTELLER....Simmons has over the last decade repeatedly shown himself to be one of the most versatile, intelligent, and unpredictable novelists around." — *Locus*

"ONE OF AMERICA'S FINEST WRITERS.... Dan Simmons is, in many ways, the reincarnation of Robert Louis Stevenson."
—*Des Moines Sunday Register*

"A HIGH-TECH, HIGH-VOLTAGE ACTION THRILLER. Offering an appealing hero and heroine, deadly villains, zippy dialogue, and high-tech weaponry and expertise, this is, most of all, a hair-raising adventure to satisfy the most discriminating reader." —*Library Journal*

"IF DONALD WESTLAKE, JOHN IRVING AND ROBERT PARKER had sat down to collaborate on a novel, *Darwin's Blade* would have been the aftermath.... Simmons manages to juggle tragedy and comedy with uncommon skill.... This off-beat thriller will have readers wondering whether to laugh or cry in their headlong rush to see how it all ends." —*Denver Post*

"A STRONG, THOROUGHLY INTELLIGENT NOVEL — welcome relief from thrillers that offer nothing more than action scenes strung together.... Don't be surprised if you come away from this book with what might appear to be an unhealthy interest in accidents." —*Booklist*

DARWIN'S BLADE

DAN SIMMONS

MULHOLLAND BOOKS

LITTLE, BROWN AND COMPANY

LARGE PRINT EDITION

Copyright © 2000 by Dan Simmons
Excerpt from *The Abominable* © 2013 by Dan Simmons

Mulholland Books / Little, Brown and Company
Hachette Book Group
237 Park Avenue, New York, NY 10017
mulhollandbooks.com

First Mulholland Books Edition: September 2013
Originally published in hardcover by William Morrow, November 2000

Mulholland Books is an imprint of Little, Brown and Company, a division of Hachette Book Group, Inc. The Mulholland Books name and logo are trademarks of Hachette Book Group, Inc.

The publisher is not responsible for websites (or their content) that are not owned by the publisher.

The Hachette Speakers Bureau provides a wide range of authors for speaking events. To find out more, go to hachettespeakersbureau.com or call (866) 376-6591.

ISBN 978-0-316-21349-3 / 978-0-316-40364-1 (large print)
Library of Congress Control Number 2013942927

10 9 8 7 6 5 4 3 2 1

RRD-C

Printed in the United States of America

This book is dedicated to Wayne Simmons and Stephen King. For my brother Wayne, who is involved with accident investigation every day, admiration that your sense of humor has survived; for Steve, who felt the cutting edge of Darwin's blade via someone else's lethal stupidity, gratitude that you're still with us and willing to tell us more tales by the campfire.

Occam's Razor: All other things being equal, the simplest solution is usually the correct one.

—*William of Occam, fourteenth century*

Darwin's Blade: All other things being equal, the simplest solution is usually stupidity.

—*Darwin Minor, twenty-first century*

DARWIN'S BLADE

1

"A IS FOR HOLE"

The phone rang a few minutes after four in the morning. "You like accidents, Dar. You owe it to yourself to come see this one."

"I don't like accidents," said Dar. He did not ask who was calling. He recognized Paul Cameron's voice even though he and Cameron had not been in touch for over a year. Cameron was a CHP officer working out of Palm Springs.

"All right, then," said Cameron, "you like *puzzles*."

Dar swiveled to read his clock. "Not at four-oh-eight A.M.," he said.

"This one's worth it." The connection sounded hollow, as if it were a radio patch or a cell phone.

"Where?"

"Montezuma Valley Road," said Cameron. "Just a mile inside the canyon, where S22 comes out of the hills into the desert."

"Jesus Christ," muttered Dar. "You're talking Borrego Springs. It would take me more than ninety minutes to get there."

"Not if you drive your black car," said Cameron, his chuckle blending with the rasp and static of the poor connection.

"What kind of accident would bring me almost all the way to Borrego Springs before breakfast?" said Dar, sitting up now. "Multiple vehicle?"

"We don't know," said Officer Cameron. His voice still sounded amused.

"What do you mean you don't know? Don't you have anyone at the scene yet?"

"I'm *calling* from the scene," said Cameron through the static.

"And you can't tell how many vehicles were involved?" Dar found himself wishing that he had a cigarette in the drawer of his bedside table. He had given up smoking ten years earlier, just after the death of his wife, but he still got the craving at odd times.

"We can't even ascertain beyond a reasonable doubt what *kind* of vehicle or vehicles was or were involved," said Cameron, his voice taking on that official, strained-syntax, preliterate lilt that cops used when speaking in their official capacity.

"You mean what make?" said Dar. He rubbed his chin, heard the sandpaper scratch there, and shook his head. He had seen plenty of high-speed vehicular accidents where the make and model of the car were not immediately apparent. Especially at night.

"I mean we don't know if this is a car, more than one car, a plane, or a fucking UFO crash," said Cameron. "If you don't see this one, Darwin, you'll regret it for the rest of your days."

"What do you..." Dar began, and stopped. Cameron had broken the connection. Dar swung his legs over the edge of the bed, looked out at the dark beyond the glass of his tall condo windows, muttered, "Shit," and got up to take a fast shower.

* * *

It took him two minutes less than an hour to drive there from San Diego, pushing the Acura NSX hard through the canyon turns, slamming it into high gear on the long straights, and leaving the radar detector in the tiny glove compartment because he assumed that all of the highway patrol cars working S22 would be at the scene of the accident. It was paling toward sunrise as he began the long 6-percent grade, four-thousand-foot descent past Ranchita toward Borrego Springs and the Anza-Borrego Desert.

One of the problems with being an accident reconstruction specialist, Dar was thinking as he shifted the NSX into third and took a decreasing-radius turn effortlessly, with only the throaty purr of the exhaust marking the deceleration and then the shift back up to speed, *is that almost every mile of every damned highway holds the memory of someone's fatal stupidity.* The NSX roared up a low rise in the predawn glow and then growled down the long, twisty descent into the canyon some miles below.

There, thought Dar, glancing quickly at an unremarkable stretch of old single-height guardrail set on wooden posts flashing past on the outside of a tight turn. *Right there.*

A little more than five years ago, Dar had arrived at that point only thirty-five minutes after a school bus had struck that stretch of old guardrail, scraped along it for more than sixty feet, and plunged over the embankment, rolled three times down the steep, boulder-strewn hillside, and had come to rest on its side, with its shattered roof in the narrow stream below. The bus had been owned by the Desert Springs School District and was returning from an "Eco-Week" overnight camping trip in the mountains, carrying forty-one sixth-grade students and two teachers. When Dar arrived, ambulances and Flight-For-Life helicopters were still carrying off seriously injured children, a mob of rescue workers was handing litters hand over hand up the rocky slope, and yellow plastic tarps covered at least three small bodies on the rocks below. When the final tally came in, six children and one teacher were dead, twenty-four students were seriously injured—including one boy who would be a paraplegic for the rest of his life—and the bus driver received cuts, bruises, and a broken left arm.

Dar was working for the NTSB then—it was the year before he quit the National Transportation Safety Board to go to work as an independent accident reconstruction specialist. That time the call came to his condo in Palm Springs.

For days after the accident, Dar watched the media coverage of the "terrible tragedy." The L.A. television stations and newspapers had decided early on that the bus driver was a heroine—and their coverage reflected that stance. The driver's postcrash interview and other eyewitness testimony, including that of the teacher who had been sitting directly behind one of the children who had perished, certainly suggested as much. All agreed that the brakes had failed about one mile after the bus began its long, steep descent. The driver, a forty-one-year-old divorced mother of two, had shouted at everyone to hang on. What followed was a terrifying six-mile Mad Mouse ride with the driver doing her best to keep the careening bus on the road, the brakes smoking but obviously not slowing the vehicle enough, children flying out of their seats on the sharp turns, and then the final crash, grinding, and plummet over the embankment. All agreed that there was nothing the driver could have done, that once the brakes had failed it had been a miracle that she had kept the bus on the road as long as she had.

Dar read the editorials proclaiming that the driver was the kind of hero for whom no tribute could be too great. Two Los Angeles TV stations carried live coverage of the school board meeting during which parents of the surviving children gave testimonials to the driver's heroic attempts to save the bus under "impossible circumstances." The *NBC Nightly News* did a four-minute special profile piece on this driver and other school bus drivers who had been injured or killed "in the line of duty." Tom

Brokaw called this driver and others like her "America's unsung heroes."

Meanwhile, Dar gathered information.

The school bus was a 1989 model TC-2000 manufactured by the Blue Bird Body Company and purchased new by the Desert Springs School District. It had power steering, a diesel engine, and a model AT 545 four-speed automatic transmission from the Allison Transmission Division of General Motors. It was also equipped with a Federal Motor Vehicle Safety Standards (FMVSS) 121-approved dual air-mechanical, cam-and-drum brake system that had front axle clamp type-20 brake chambers and rear axle clamp type-24/30 and emergency/parking brake chambers. All of the brakes had 5.5-inch manual slack adjusters.

The driver seat was lap-belt-equipped; the passenger seats were not. Dar knew that this was standard design for school buses. Parents who would never allow their children to ride unrestrained in their family vehicles happily waved goodbye to their children each morning in buses carrying fifty children and no passenger belts or harnesses. The estimated gross weight of this bus, the passengers, and their camping baggage was 22,848 pounds.

The driver had—as the newspapers and TV reports had put it—"a perfect safety record with the district." Blood tests taken at the hospital immediately after the accident showed no evidence of drugs or alcohol. Dar interviewed her two days after the accident, and her account was almost word for word the same as the deposition she had given the CHP the evening of the crash. She reported that about one mile from their starting point, on a slight downhill grade, the bus brakes had "seemed weird and mushy." She had pumped the brake pedal. A warning light had come on, indicating low brake pressure. At that point, the driver told him, the grade had changed from the downhill grade to a two-mile uphill climb and the bus began to slow. The automatic transmission had shifted to a lower gear and the brake warning light went off and then blinked a few times. The driver said that she assumed the problem had fixed itself at this point and that there was no reason not to continue.

Shortly thereafter, she reported, they entered the long downhill grade and the brakes "just failed completely." The bus began picking up speed. The driver said that she could not slow it by using either the service or emergency brakes. Brake odor was strong. The rear wheels began smoking. She said that she had overridden the automatic transmission and shifted down to second gear, but that did not help. She said that she had then grabbed the radio to call her dispatcher, but had to drop the microphone in order to wrestle the wheel to keep the bus on the road. For six miles she succeeded, shouting at the students and teachers to "lean left!" and "lean right!" Finally the bus had contacted the outside guardrail, run along it, and gone over the embankment. "I don't know what else I could have done!" said the driver during the interview. She was weeping at that point. Her report agreed with the interview testimony Dar had taken from the surviving teacher and students.

The driver—overweight, pasty-faced, and thin-lipped—seemed stupid and somewhat bovine to Dar, but he had to discount his own perceptions. The older he got and the longer he worked in accident investigation, the more stupid most people seemed to him. And more and more women tended to appear bovine in the years since the death of his wife.

His people checked the driver's record. The TV stations and papers had reported that she had "a perfect safety record with the district," and this was true, but it was also true that she had only worked for the district for six months prior to the accident. According to DMV reports from Tennessee, where the driver had lived before moving to California, she'd been issued one DUI citation and two moving violations in five years. In California the bus driver held a school bus certificate (passenger transportation endorsement) issued two days before her employment by the district and had a valid California class B (commercial driver) license restricted to conventional buses with automatic transmissions only. The California DMV records also indicated that ten days before the accident, the driver had two violations: failure to provide financial responsibility and failure to properly display license plates. CHP records showed that because of these violations, her regular driver's license had been suspended. It had been reinstated the day before the accident after she had filed an SR-22 (proof of financial responsibility) with the DMV. She had no outstanding traffic warrants at the time of the accident. She had received 54 hours of instruction that included 21 hours of behind-the-wheel training in a bus similar to the crash vehicle, but the curriculum had no requirement for mountain-driving training.

Dar's report on the physical damage to the bus ran to four single-spaced pages. Essentially, the bus body had separated from the chassis, the roof had collapsed and crushed inward from just behind the driver's seat to the third row, the left side had crushed inboard, buckling and fracturing all of the window-frame supports and popping the glass out all along the left side, and the bumpers were missing. The fuel tank had been damaged in several places, one rubber fuel line had been cut, but the tank hadn't been breached and its guard remained securely fastened to the chassis.

Dar reviewed the inspection and repair orders for the bus and found that the brakes had been adjusted every 1,500 miles and that the vehicle was inspected on a monthly basis. Although the last inspection had been only two days before the accident and the mechanic had stated that he found the brakes slightly out of adjustment and had ordered them to be adjusted, there was no record of the mechanics' having adjusted the brakes. Safety Board tests of the accident vehicle's brakes showed that they had been out of adjustment on the day of the crash. Further investigation showed that the school district had only recently switched over from the CHP California Code of Regulations inspection form to a company-developed form (1040-008 Rev. 5/91), and the chief mechanic had checked both the "OK" box and the "Repair" boxes on the form, initialing the "Repair" boxes. But unlike the older inspection form on which the order for further service was written in a space under the "Repair" box, the chief mechanic's written work order had been scrawled on the back of the new form. The five mechanics working under him—there was one mechanic for every eighteen buses, as per school district and industry guidelines—had missed the handwritten work order.

"Well, that's it, then," said the superintendent of the Desert Springs School District.

"Not quite," said Dar.

Three weeks after the accident, Dar staged a reenactment of the accident. An identical 1989 model TC-2000 school bus, loaded with 5,000 pounds of sandbags to simulate the weight of the students, teachers, and their luggage, was brought to the summit of Montezuma Valley Road at the national forest area where the classes had carried out their "Eco-Week" overnight camping trip. The brakes of this TC-2000 had been misadjusted to precisely the degree of error found on the accident vehicle. Dar designated himself as driver of the test vehicle and accepted one NTSB volunteer to ride along to videotape the reenactment. The California Highway Patrol closed the highway for the duration of the test. School Board members were present at the exercise. None volunteered to ride in the test bus.

Dar drove the vehicle down the first grade, up the two-mile uphill section, and then down the long canyon road—the worst grade was 10.5 percent—finally bringing the vehicle to a full stop at a pull-out ten yards beyond where the accident vehicle had plunged off the highway. He turned the vehicle around and drove it back to the summit.

"The brakes worked," said Dar to the assembled School Board members and CHP patrolmen. "There was no brake warning light. No smoke or smell of burning brake linings."

He explained what had happened on the day of the accident.

The bus driver had left the national forest campsite with both of her emergency parking brakes set. After the first downhill stretch where they could smell the brakes burning, the next two miles had been uphill. "Brakes give off an odor," explained Dar, "when the brake drum and shoes reach temperatures above approximately 600 degrees Fahrenheit." The teachers, students, and driver had smelled the burning odor during both the first couple of downhill and uphill miles on the return journey. The driver had ignored the smell.

The brake warning light had gone off briefly and then started blinking again as the bus approached the top of the last rise before the long descent toward Borrego Springs. The surviving teacher, sitting in the first row on the right side, had seen it blinking.

"There's only one engineering explanation for the brake warning light to signal brake overheating during this portion of the trip," said Dar. "The emergency brakes had been applied continuously from the time the bus had left the campsite parking lot." In addition, he explained, the surviving passengers told of the bus "handling poorly" and "surging slightly" during the first two uphill miles of the trip. The driver had ignored all of these warning signs and had begun the long, downhill section of the canyon road.

Dar explained that on the day of the accident, he had noted that the front wheels of the bus were freewheeling but that the rear wheels were locked. He explained further that this type of bus had automatic brakes that would be applied without driver input when air pressure in the system drops below 30 pounds per square inch. The locked rear wheels had told him that low air pressure in the brake system had caused the automatic brakes to be applied, and their Safety Board tests had shown that the system had not leaked and that the air compressor was sound. But the automatic brakes could not stop the bus because they had been overheated prior to their application.

At this point Dar got back in the bus, set the parking brake, and drove away from the campsite again. A convoy of CHP vehicles and private cars followed.

The bus surged slightly going uphill. Both Dar and his assistant manning the video camera commented on tape that they could smell the brakes burning. CHP vehicles trailing the bus reported over their radios that they could clearly see smoke coming from the rear wheels. The brake warning light came on. Dar paused briefly where the accident-bus driver had paused, pumped the brakes as she had, and then started down the long incline.

The brakes failed 1.3 miles down the steep canyon road. The automatic brakes deployed but then also failed due to overheating. The bus began to accelerate.

When the bus reached 46 miles per hour, Dar shifted from D-3 to D-2, slowing it, and then shifted to D-1, causing the bus to lurch but also to slow quickly. Still moving 11 miles per hour, he selected a sandy patch of hillside on the inside stretch of the next curve and nosed the bus into it, bringing it to a halt with only the smallest of bumps. A second later, the armada of

CHP cruisers and School Board members' cars converged on the bus. Dar got in one of the highway patrol cars and they drove down to the accident site.

"The driver left the campsite with her parking brake on, which meant that both emergency brakes were set, thus overheating the entire system for the first two miles and dropping the air pressure below thirty psi," he said to the crowd gathered around the point where the bus had left the highway. "The automatic brakes deployed, but their efficiency was low because of the overheating. Still, that should have been enough to slow the bus to below twenty-eight miles per hour. It did in this reenactment."

"But you were going faster than that," said the superintendent of schools.

Dar nodded. "I manually shifted from second gear into third gear and then to fourth," said Dar.

"But the driver said that she shifted *down*," said the president of the School Board.

Dar nodded. "I know. But she didn't.

When we inspected the transmission after the accident, it was locked in fourth gear. The Allison automatic transmission is programmed to automatically shift *down* in the event of such sudden acceleration. The driver overrode the automatic transmission and shifted into fourth gear."

The crowd stared at him.

"The road marks here showed five hundred and fifty feet of striated, curved tire marks on the day of the accident," he said, pointing. The marks were still visible. All eyes followed his pointing finger. "The automatic braking system, although degraded by loss of air pressure due to overheating, was still trying to stop the bus when it hit the guardrail up there." Everyone turned to see the bent and battered guardrail. "The bus was going sixty-four miles per hour when it contacted the guardrail," said Dar. "It was doing approximately forty-eight miles per hour when it left the road and became airborne about *here.*"

All heads turned back.

"The bus was in fourth gear when it hit

the guardrail because the driver had selected that gear," said Dar, "not because the transmission had failed or automatically upshifted. She was in a panic. After burning out the brakes, ignoring the burning brake odor and the unusual handling of the bus going uphill, then after ignoring the brake-pressure warning light and deciding to continue down the steep grade despite the fact that the brakes felt 'weird and mushy' at the top of the pass, the driver overrode the automatic transmission at approximately twenty-eight miles per hour and shifted into fourth gear by mistake."

Two months after the accident, Dar had read in the back pages of a local paper that the driver had been found guilty of reckless driving resulting in the wrongful death of seven persons. She had received a one-year suspended sentence and her class B commercial driver's license had been suspended indefinitely. None of the Los Angeles TV stations or newspapers that had hailed her as an unsung hero covered this aspect of the story in anything more than a passing mention, perhaps out of embarrassment at their earlier enthusiasm.

It was light enough to drive without headlights when Dar reached the accident scene. Cameron had been slightly off in his location; it was a little less than a mile from where the canyon opened out into desert. The twisting road showed all of the accoutrements of modern highway death: highway patrol cars parked along the shoulder, flares sizzling, cones set up, patrolmen herding what traffic there was up and down the left, uphill lane, two ambulances, even a helicopter buzzing above. Everything except wreckage.

Dar ignored the patrolman's waving baton and pulled off on the broad right shoulder where the official vehicles were parked. Red and blue lights painted the canyon walls with pulsing light.

The patrolman strode over to the NSX. "Hey! You can't park there. This is an accident scene."

"Sergeant Cameron sent for me."

"Cameron?" The officer was still pissed off at Dar's disregard for his baton. "Why? You from Accident Detail? Got ID?"

Dar shook his head. "Just tell Sergeant Cameron that Dar Minor is here."

The patrolman glowered but pulled a radio from his belt, stepped a few paces away for privacy, and spoke into it.

Dar waited. He realized that the CHP cops on the shoulder were all staring up at the canyon wall. Dar got out of the NSX and squinted up at the red rock. Several hundred feet higher, on a broad setback up there, lights glared and people and machines moved. There was no road or trail up that steep cliff to the setback, no way down from the cliff top hundreds of feet higher. A small, green and white helicopter lifted off from the ledge and dropped carefully into the canyon.

Dar felt his stomach sink as he watched the chopper land in a cleared area along the shoulder. *LOH*, he thought. Light Observation Helicopters, they had called them in Vietnam, lo those many years ago. Dar remembered that the officers loved buzzing around in them. Now they used this type for traffic reports and police work. Probably a Hughes 55.

"Darwin!" Sergeant Cameron and another patrolman jumped out of the helicopter and moved out from under the whirling blades in a half crouch.

Paul Cameron was about Dar's age, in his late forties. The sergeant was large and quite black, barrel-chested, and sported a neatly trimmed mustache. Dar knew that Cameron would have retired years earlier if he had not started late in his police career. He had joined the Marines just when Dar was leaving the Corps.

There was a younger patrolman with him: white, in his early twenties, baby-faced, with a mouth that reminded Dar of Elvis.

"Dr. Darwin Minor, this is Patrolman Mickey Elroy. We were just talking about you, Dar."

The younger patrolman squinted at Dar. "You really a doctor?"

"Not a medical doctor. A Ph.D. Physics."

While Patrolman Elroy thought about

that, Cameron said, "You ready to ride up and see the puzzle, Dar?"

"Ride up." Dar didn't bother to hide his lack of enthusiasm.

"That's right, you don't like to fly, do you?" Cameron's voice only had two tones—amused and outraged. He was in his amused mode now. "But hey, you have a pilot's license, don't you, Dar? Gliders or some such?"

"I don't like to be *flown*," said Dar, but he grabbed his camera bag out of the NSX and followed the other two men toward the helicopter. Cameron sat in the front copilot's seat and there was just room on the back bench for Dar and the young patrolman. They buckled in.

The last time I flew in one of these goddamned things, thought Dar, *it was on a Sea Stallion leaving the Dalat Reactor.*

The pilot made sure that they were all strapped in and then twisted one stick and pulled up on another. The little chopper lifted, fluttered, and then tilted forward, climbing for altitude at the mouth of the canyon before buzzing back, hovering a minute over the wide shelf of stone and sagebrush, and then settling down carefully, the rotors no more than twenty feet from the vertical rock wall.

Dar walked away from the thing with shaky legs. He wondered if Cameron would let him rappel down the canyon wall back to the highway when it was time to go.

"So is it true what the sergeant says about you and the space shuttle?" said Patrolman Elroy with a slight twist of his Elvis lips.

"What?" said Dar, crouching and covering his ears as the chopper took off again.

"That you were the one that figured out what made it blow up? *Challenger,* I mean. I was twelve when that happened."

Dar shook his head. "No, I was just an NTSB flunky on the investigatory committee."

"A flunky who got his ass fired by NASA," said Cameron, tugging on his Smokey hat and securing it.

Elroy looked puzzled. "Why'd they fire you?"

"For telling them what they didn't want to hear," said Dar. He could see the crater here on the ledge now. It was about thirty feet across and perhaps three feet deep at the deepest. Whatever had struck here had burned, flared against the inner rock wall, and started a small fire in the grass and sagebrush that grew along the ledge. A dozen or so CHP people and forensics men stood and crouched near or in the crater.

"What didn't they want to hear?" asked Elroy, hurrying to keep up.

Dar stepped at the edge of the impact crater. "That the *Challenger* astronauts hadn't died in the explosion," he said, not really paying attention to the conversation. "I told them that the human body is an amazingly resilient organism. I told them that the seven astronauts had survived until their cabin hit the ocean. Two minutes and forty-five seconds of falling."

The kid stopped. "Jesus Christ," he said. "That isn't true, is it? I never heard that. I mean…"

"What is this, Paul?" said Dar. "You

know I don't do airplane accidents anymore."

"Yeah," said Cameron, showing strong
white teeth as he grinned. He crouched,
rooted around in the burned grass, and
tossed a scorched fragment of metal to
Dar. "Can you ID that?"

"Door handle," said Dar. "Chevy."

"The guys think it was an '82 El
Camino," said Cameron, gesturing toward
the forensics men in the smoldering pit.

Dar looked at the vertical rock wall to
his right and at the highway hundreds of
feet below. "Nice," he said. "I don't suppose there are tire marks at the top of the
cliff."

"Nope. Just rock," said the sergeant.
"No way up from the back side, either."

"When did this happen?"

"Sometime last night. Civilian reported
the fire about two A.M."

"You guys got right on it."

"Had to. The first CHP boys here
thought it was a military plane down."

Dar nodded and walked to the line of
yellow accident-scene tape around the pit.

"Lot of shards in there. Anything not belonging to an El Camino?"

"Bones and bits," said Cameron, still smiling. "One person, we're pretty sure. Male, they think. Scattered because of the impact and explosion. Oh, and fragments of aluminum and alloy casings that don't have anything to do with the El Camino."

"Another vehicle?"

"They don't think so. Something that was in the car, maybe."

"Curious," said Dar.

Patrolman Elroy was still eyeing him suspiciously, as if Dar were a joke the sergeant was pulling on him. "And are you really the guy they named the Darwin Award after?"

"No," said Dar. He walked around the crater, making sure not to get too close to the edge of the cliff. He did not like heights. Some of the Accident Investigation men nodded and said hello. Dar took his camera out of the bag and began imaging from different angles. The rising sun glinted on the many thousands of pieces of scattered, scorched metal.

"What's that?" said Elroy. "I've never seen a camera like that before."

"Digital," said Dar. He quit shooting pictures and video and looked back down the highway. The entrance to the canyon was visible from up here, directly in line with the highway stretching out east toward Borrego Springs. He looked at the tiny viewfinder monitor on the camera and shot some stills and video of the highway and desert lined up with the crater.

"Well, if the Darwin Award isn't named for you," persisted the young patrolman, "who is it named for?"

"Charles Darwin," said Dar. "You know, survival of the fittest?"

The boy looked blank. Dar sighed. "The society of insurance investigators gives the award to the person who does the human race the biggest favor each year by removing his or her DNA from the gene pool."

The boy nodded slowly, but obviously did not understand.

Cameron chuckled. "Whoever kills himself in the dumbest way," he translated, and looked at Dar. "Last year it was that guy in Sacramento who shook the Pepsi machine until it fell on him and squashed him, wasn't it?"

"That was two years ago," said Dar. "Last year it was the farmer up in Oregon who got nervous shingling the roof of his barn and tossed the rope over the peak of the roof and had his grown son tie it to something solid. Turned out the something solid was the rear bumper of their pickup truck."

Cameron laughed out loud. "Yeah, yeah. And then his wife came out of the house and drove to town. Did the car insurance people ever pay the widow?"

"Had to," said Dar. "He was attached to the vehicle at the time. Under policy rules, he was covered."

Patrolman Elroy quirked his Elvis smile, but he obviously did not understand the point of the story.

"So you going to solve this one for us, or what?" said Cameron.

Dar scratched his head. "You guys have any theories?"

"Accident Investigation thinks it was a drug deal gone wrong," said Cameron.

"Yeah," said Elroy, eagerly. "You know. The El Camino was in the back of one of those big military, freighter kind of planes…"

"C-130?" said Dar.

"Yeah." Patrolman Elroy grinned. "And the dudes had a falling out, shoved the El Camino out the back…bingo." He gestured toward the crater like a maître d' awarding patrons a table.

Dar nodded. "Good theory. Except where would drug runners get a C-130? And why haul an El Camino in it? And why shove the whole vehicle out? And why did it explode and burn?"

"Don't cars always do that when they go off cliffs and things?" said Elroy, his twist of a smile fading.

"Only in the movies, Mickey, my boy," said Cameron. He turned to Dar. "Well? You want to get started on this before it gets hot up here?"

Dar nodded. "On two conditions."

Cameron raised his heavy eyebrows.

"Get me back down to my car and loan me your radio."

Dar drove the NSX out of the canyon and into the desert, stopped, looked around for a while, drove farther, looked a bit longer, drove back to his first stopping point, and walked out into the desert, gathering pebbles and other small items and putting them into his pocket. He shot some images of the Joshua trees and the sand, then walked back to the car and took a few more images of the asphalt road. It was still early and the traffic was light—a few vans and pickups—so there was no backup from the single-lane closing in the canyon. But it was already eighty degrees in the desert and Dar took off his jacket and kept the air-conditioning going as he sat in the idling black Acura on a gravel turnout two miles from the entrance to the canyon.

Dar powered up his IBM ThinkPad, downloaded the stored images from the Hitachi digital camera via a flash card, and scrolled through them for a few minutes. He ran the short video segments he had shot. Then he enabled his numeric keypad and tapped in equations for several minutes, exiting once to activate map software and the GPS unit he carried in the glove box. He double-checked distances, angles, and elevations, and then finished his arithmetic, shut down the computer, stowed it away, and called Cameron on the radio he had borrowed. It had been thirty-five minutes since he'd left the ledge.

The green and white chopper buzzed by once and landed five minutes later. The pilot stayed inside his bubble while Cameron got out, adjusted his hat, and walked over to the NSX.

"Where's young Elvis?" said Dar.

"Elroy," said the sergeant.

"Whatever."

"I left him behind. He's had enough excitement this morning. Besides, he was being disrespectful of his elders."

"Oh?"

"He called you an arrogant A-hole after you left," said Cameron.

Dar raised one eyebrow. "A-hole?"

The fellow ex-Marine shrugged. "Sorry,

Darwin. It's the best the boy could do. He's never been in the military. Generation Xer and all that. And he's white. Linguistically deprived. I apologize for him."

"*A-hole?*" said Dar.

"What do you have for me?" Cameron was obviously tired and edging out of his amused mode into his more habitual pissed-off attitude.

"What do I get for having anything for you?" said Dar.

"The eternal gratitude of the California Highway Patrol," growled Cameron.

"I guess it'll have to do." Dar squinted at the little helicopter that seemed to shimmer as heat waves rose from the highway between it and the NSX. "As much as I hate to get in that goddamn thing again, I think it'll be easier to show you if we go back up for a couple of minutes."

Cameron shrugged. "Crash site?"

"Uh-uh. I'm not flying in that canyon again. Just tell your man to follow my directions and to keep it under five hundred feet."

* * *

They hovered above the highway half a mile east of where the NSX was parked. "Did you see that scorched, rippled pattern on the asphalt here near the turnout?" said Dar through his headset microphone.

"Yeah, sure, now I do. Not when I drove this way in the dark this morning. So what? Highway's fucked up like that in a thousand places. Shitty maintenance out here."

"Yes," said Dar, "but stretches of the road here look as if they've been melted and then resolidified."

Cameron shrugged, "Desert, man. Going to be what today?" He turned to the pilot.

"A hundred and twelve," said the pilot, never moving his sunglasses in their direction, his attention on the instruments and the horizon. "Fahrenheit."

"OK," said Dar. "Let's head back toward the NSX."

"That's *it?*" said Cameron.

"Patience."

They hovered three hundred feet above the highway. A station wagon rushed past headed west, kids' heads poking out of both rear windows, goggling at the helicopter. The Acura looked like a black, wax candle that had melted in the heat.

"Notice those skid marks?" said Dar.

"When we flew down, sure," said Cameron. "But they're a mile and a half from the canyon. More than two miles from the crash site. You saying that some-body ran out of control, left skid marks here, and crashed almost three miles away, two hundred feet up a canyon wall? Fast motherfucker." The sergeant was smiling, but he was not amused.

"Long skid marks," said Dar, pointing to the parallel tracks heading off west.

"Kids burning rubber. Find tire marks every few hundred meters out here. You know that, Dar. Just lucky if we don't find the kids in the wreckage the next morning."

"I measured them," said Dar. "One thousand eight hundred and thirty-eight feet of nonstriated road marks. If it was a kid doing peel-outs, he did one hell of a long wheelie and left most of his tires on the asphalt. If it's skid marks…"

"What are you saying?" said Cameron.

"Simple matter of friction coefficient. Our El Camino tried to stop here and couldn't. Brakes melted." Dar fished in his pocket and handed Cameron several tiny pellets and spheres of what looked to be melted rubber.

"Brake pads?" said Cameron.

"What's left of them," Dar said, and handed the sergeant several more tiny droplets. These were tiny pellets of metal. "These are from the surfaces of the actual brake drums melting," he said. "The Joshua trees along this stretch are dusted with both powdered rubber and melted steel."

"El Caminos never had brakes worth shit," said Cameron, shifting the pellets in his dark palm.

"No," agreed Dar. "Especially when you're trying to haul your speed down from somewhere around three hundred miles per hour."

"*Three hundred miles per hour!*" said the CHP sergeant, his jaw dropping slightly.

"Land this thing," said Dar. "I'll explain outside."

* * *

"I think he did it after dark because he didn't want anyone seeing him attach the JATO units back at that turnout," said Dar. "And then—"

"JATO units!" said Cameron, taking his hat off and rubbing the sweat liner with his fingers.

"Jet Assist Take Off units," said Dar. "They're essentially just large, strap-on, solid-fuel rockets that the Air Force once used to get heavy cargo planes off the ground when the runway was too short or the load was too—"

"I know what the fuck JATO stands for," snapped Cameron. "I was in the Corps, man. But where would some dickweed with an '82 El Camino get two of those?"

Dar shrugged. "Andrews Air Force Base just north of here. Twelve Palms just down the road. More military bases around here than any other comparable patch of real estate in the United States. Who the hell knows what military surplus they sell for scrap or whatever."

"JATO units!" said Cameron, looking at

the endless skid marks again. They weaved in several places, but recovered and then headed straight as a double-shafted, black arrow for the distant canyon. "Why'd he use two?"

"One wouldn't have done him much good unless he sat on it," said Dar. "If he lit off just one and it wasn't positioned perfectly on the El Camino's exact center of mass, the vehicle would've just spun like a Catherine wheel until the rocket dug or melted him a hole in the desert."

"All right," said Cameron. "He strapped or bolted or cinched on *two* of these Air Force surplus rocket fuckers. Then what?"

Dar rubbed his chin; he had neglected to shave in the rush to get going. "Then he waited for a break in traffic and lit them. Probably a simple battery circuit. Once they're lit, you can't shut them off. They're essentially just oversized skyrockets, like miniature versions of the two strap-on boosters that the space shuttle uses. Light 'em and go. No turning back."

"So he turned into a space shuttle," said Cameron, his expression strange. He looked at the mountains two miles away. "Airborne all the way into that rock wall."

"Not all the way," said Dar, turning on the ThinkPad and pointing to some delta-v estimates. "I can only guess at the thrust those things put out, but the rocket flare melted those patches of the highway back there and probably got him up to about two hundred and eighty-five miles per hour at just the point these skid marks begin, about twelve seconds after ignition."

"Helluva ride," said Cameron.

"Maybe the kid was going for a land speed record," agreed Dar. "About this point, with the telephone poles flashing past in the dark like a picket fence—the rocket blast would've illuminated them—our boy had second thoughts. He slammed on the brakes."

"Lot of good it did him," said Cameron. The sergeant was almost whispering now.

"Brake linings melted," agreed Dar. "Brake drums melted. Tires started coming apart. You notice that just the last hundred meters or so of road marks are intermittent."

"Brakes going on and off?" said Cameron, his voice filling now with the future pleasure of telling and retelling this story. Cops loved roadkill.

Dar shook his head. "Nope. These are just tire-melt patches at this point. The El Camino is taking thirty- and forty-foot hops before becoming completely airborne."

"Holy shit," said Cameron, sounding almost gleeful.

"Yes," said Dar. "There's a final melt point just beyond where the tire marks cease. That's where the JATO units were burning down at a nice healthy thirty-six-degree takeoff angle. The El Camino's climb ratio must have been impressive."

"Fuck me." The sergeant grinned. "So those candles burned all the way to the cliff wall?"

Dar shook his head. "My guess is that they burned out about fifteen seconds after takeoff. The rest of his ride was pure ballistics." He pointed to the GPS map on the ThinkPad's screen, with the simple equations to the right of the arching trajectory from desert to canyon wall.

"The road turns and starts climbing where he impacted," said Cameron.

Dar winced slightly. He hated the verb-use of nouns such as *impact*. "Yeah," he said. "He didn't make the turn. The El Camino was probably spinning around its own horizontal axis at this point, giving it some flight stability during the descent."

"Like a rifle bullet."

"Precisely."

"What do you think his...can't think of the word...high point was?"

"Apogee?" said Dar. He looked at the computer screen. "Probably no less than two thousand and no more than twenty-eight hundred feet above the desert floor."

"Holy shit," whispered Cameron again. "It was a short trip, but it must have been one hell of a ride."

Dar rubbed his ear. "I figure that after the first fifteen seconds or so, our guy was just a passive bystander, no longer a participant."

"What do you mean?"

Dar touched the screen again. "I mean that even at the lowest boost rates I can plot to get him from here to there, he was pulling about eighteen g's when he left the asphalt. A two-hundred-pound guy would have..."

"Had the equivalent of three thousand four hundred extra pounds sitting on his face and chest," said Cameron. "Ouch."

The sergeant's radio squawked. "Sorry," he said. "Gotta take this." He stepped away to listen to the rasping and squawking while Dar turned off his computer and stored it in the cabin of the NSX. The car was idling again to keep the air-conditioning going.

Cameron stepped closer. His expression was a queer mixture of a grin and a grimace. "Forensics boys just excavated the steering wheel of the El Camino from the crater," he said softly.

Dar waited.

"Finger bones were embedded in the plastic," finished Cameron. "Deeply embedded."

Dar shrugged. His phone chirped. He flipped it open, saying to the CHP sergeant, "This is what I love about California, Paul. Never out of a cell. Never out of touch." He listened for a minute, said, "I'll be there in twenty minutes," and flipped the phone shut.

"Time to go to work for real?" said Cameron, grinning now, obviously phrasing the telling and retelling of this for future days.

Dar nodded. "That was Lawrence Stewart, my boss. He's got something for me that sounds weirder than this shit."

"*Semper Fi,*" said Cameron, to no one in particular.

"*O seclum insipiens et inficetum,*" said Dar, to the same audience.

2

"B IS FOR BUD"

It took Dar less than fifteen minutes to drive to the crossroads truck stop–cum–Indian casino to which his boss, Lawrence Stewart, had asked him to hurry at all possible speed. In the NSX, with radar detector pinging fore and aft and sideways, all possible speed meant 162 miles per hour.

The truck stop was west of Palm Springs, but was not one of the major Indian casinos that rose up out of the desert like giant adobe fake-pueblo-style vacuum cleaners set there to suck the last dime out of the last Anglo sucker's pocket. This was a rundown, seedy little truck stop that looked as if it had hit its heyday about the same time Route 66 was booming (even though this one was nowhere near Route 66), and the "casino" was little more than a back room with six slot machines and a one-eyed Native American dealing blackjack on what seemed to be a twenty-four-hour shift.

Dar spotted Lawrence right away. His boss was hard to miss—six two, about 250 pounds, with a friendly, mustached face that at the moment seemed quite flushed. Lawrence's '86 Isuzu Trooper was parked away from the pumps and the open garage doors, on a heat-rippled strip of concrete just catty-corner from the truck-stop diner.

Dar looked for some shade to park the NSX in, found none, and pulled it into the shadow of Lawrence's sport utility vehicle. One glance showed him that something was odd. Lawrence had taken out the Isuzu's left "sealed beam unit" or SBU— car-guy talk for headlight assembly—and carefully laid the bulb and other pieces on a clean work cloth on the Isuzu's high hood. At the moment Lawrence's right hand was deep in the empty headlight socket, his left hand was fussing with his right wrist as if the truck had grabbed him, and he was on his cell phone—his ear pressed heavily to his shoulder so that the phone wouldn't drop. He was wearing jeans and a short-sleeved safari jacket that he had sweated through in the chest area, under the arms, and down the back. Dar looked again and realized that Lawrence's round face not only looked flushed, it looked red to the point of impending coronary.

"Hey, Larry," said Dar, slamming the NSX door behind him.

"Goddammit, don't call me Larry," rumbled the bigger man.

Everyone called Lawrence Larry. Dar had once met Lawrence's older brother, a writer named Dale Stewart, and Dale had said that Lawrence-Don't-Call-Me-Larry had been fighting that losing battle over his name since he was seven years old.

"OK, Larry," agreed Dar amiably, walking over to lean on the right fender of the Isuzu, careful to keep his elbow on the work cloth and not the burning-hot metal. "What's up?"

Lawrence stood upright and looked

around. Sweat was running down his cheeks and brow and dripping onto his safari shirt. He nodded slightly toward the plate-glass window of the diner. "See that guy on the third stool in there—No, don't turn your head to look, damn it."

Dar kept his face turned toward Lawrence while he glanced at the long window of the diner. "Little guy with the Hawaiian shirt? Just about finished with... what?...scrambled eggs?"

"That's him," said Lawrence. "Bromley."

"Ahh," said Dar. Lawrence and Trudy had been working on a stolen-car-ring case for four months. Someone had been stealing only new rental cars from one of their corporate clients—Avis in this case—and then repainting the vehicles, shipping them across state lines, and reselling them. Charles "Chuckie" Bromley had been under surveillance for weeks as the ring's number-one car thief. Dar had had nothing to do with the case until now.

"That purple Ford Expedition over there with the rental plates is his," said

Lawrence, still holding the phone to his shoulder by force of jowl. Dar heard squeaks coming from the cell phone and Lawrence said, "Just a minute, honey, Dar's here."

"Trudy?" said Dar.

Lawrence rolled his eyes. "Who else would I call *honey?*"

Dar held up both hands. "Hey, your personal life is your own, Larry." He smiled while he said it because he knew no other couple as committed to each other and dependent upon one another as Lawrence and Trudy. Officially, Trudy owned the company, and the couple worked sixty- to eighty-hour weeks, living, breathing, talking, and evidently thinking about little other than insurance adjusting and the ever-mounting caseload they were carrying.

"Take the phone," said Lawrence.

Dar rescued the Flip Phone from between Lawrence's sweaty cheek and shoulder. "Hey, Trudy," he said to the phone. To Lawrence he said, "I didn't know Avis rented purple Expeditions."

Normally Trudy Stewart sounded pleasantly businesslike and very busy. Now she sounded very busy and very irritated as she said, "Can you get that idiot free?"

"I can try," said Dar, beginning to understand.

"Call me back if you have to amputate," Trudy said, and hung up.

"Damn," muttered Lawrence, glancing over at the diner where the waitress was taking Bromley's plate away. The little man was sipping the last of his coffee. "He's going to be leaving in a minute."

"How'd you do that?" asked Dar, nodding at where Lawrence's right hand disappeared into the headlight opening.

"I've been tailing Bromley since before sunrise and I realized that I only had one headlight working," said Lawrence.

"Not good," agreed Dar. People noticed one-eyed cars in their rearview mirrors at night.

"No," snarled Lawrence, tugging at his wrist. It was firmly stuck. "I know what the problem is. These SBUs have a cheap little fuse connector that comes loose. It's behind the headlight assembly rather than under the dash. Trudy fixed it the last time the thing joggled loose."

Dar nodded. "Trudy has smaller hands."

Lawrence glared at his accident reconstruction specialist. "Yeah," he said as if biting off a dozen more pertinent and violent responses. "The opening's funnel-shaped. I got my hand in there all right, even reconnected the damn fuse clip. I just can't...it just won't..."

"Let go of you?" prompted Dar, looking over at the diner. "Bromley's calling for the check."

"Damn, damn, damn," muttered Lawrence. "The diner was too small for me to go in without being spotted. I pumped gas as slowly as I could. I just figured that if I worked on this awhile, it would look normal enough..."

"You look like somebody with his hand trapped in a headlight socket," said Dar.

Lawrence showed his teeth in what was definitely not a friendly smile. "The inside of the circular flange is razor-sharp," he hissed through those teeth. "And I think my hand has swollen with the last half hour's attempt at pulling it out."

"Couldn't you get to it from under the hood?" said Dar, ready to roll up the work cloth and pop the hood open.

Lawrence's grimace remained. "It's sealed. If I could have reached it under the hood, *I wouldn't have gone in through the headlight.*"

Dar knew that his boss was an amiable sort, easy to joke with and kindhearted, but he also knew that Lawrence had high blood pressure and a rare but fearsome temper. Noting his boss's beet-red face, the sweat dripping from his pug nose and mustache, and the murderous intensity of his voice, Dar guessed that this might not be a good time for further banter.

"What do you want me to do? Get some soap or grease from the mechanics in the garage?"

"I didn't want to draw a crowd…" Lawrence began, and then said, "Oh, shit."

Four of the mechanics and a teenaged girl were walking toward them from the garage. Bromley had paid his check and was out of sight, either in the men's room or headed for the door.

Lawrence leaned closer to Dar and whispered. "Chuckie is meeting his boss and several of the others in the stolen-car ring somewhere out in the desert this morning. If I can photograph that, I've got them." He tugged at his right hand. The Isuzu Trooper held its grip.

Dar nodded. "You want me to follow them?"

Lawrence made a face. "Don't be stupid. Across desert roads. In *that?*" He inclined his head toward the black NSX. "You've got a front clearance of about six millimeters there."

Dar shrugged in agreement. "I wasn't planning any off-road work today. Shall I drive your truck?"

Lawrence stood upright, his hand firmly embedded. The grease monkeys and the teenaged girl had arrived and were forming a semicircle.

"How could you drive *my* truck while I'm attached like this?" hissed Lawrence.

Dar rubbed his chin. "Strap you on the hood like a deer?" he suggested.

Chuckie Bromley came out of the diner, glanced over at the small crowd around Lawrence, and climbed up awkwardly into his purple Ford Expedition.

"Hey," said one of the teenaged mechanics, wiping his black hands on a blacker rag. "Stuck?"

Lawrence's basilisk stare made the boy take a step back.

"We got some grease," said the second mechanic.

"Don't need grease," said an older mechanic with missing front teeth. "Just spray some WD-40 in there... Course, you're still gonna lose some skin. Maybe a thumb."

"I think we oughta take the grill apart," said the third mechanic. "Remove the whole damn headlight assembly. It's the only way you're going to get your hand out of there, mister, without tearing ligaments. I have a cousin who got trapped by his Isuzu..."

Lawrence sighed heavily. Chuckie Bromley drove past them and turned west onto the highway. "Dar," he said, "would you get that file off the passenger seat? It's the case I need you to work on today."

Darwin went around and picked up the file, glanced at it, and said, "Oh, no, Larry. You know that I hate this sort of—"

Lawrence nodded. "I was going to do it on the way home after photographing the desert meeting, but you're going to have to cover for me. I may be getting stitches." Lawrence looked at the huge, purple Expedition disappearing down the highway. "One more favor, Dar. Would you get my handkerchief out of my right back pocket?"

Dar complied.

"Stand back," said Lawrence to everyone. He tugged hard at his hand, twice. The sharp metal ring had a firm grip in there. On the third tug he pulled hard enough to make the Isuzu rock forward on its springs.

"Aaayargh!" cried Lawrence, sounding like a black-belt karate expert preparing to break bricks. He grabbed his right forearm with his left hand and threw all 250 pounds of himself backward. A spray of blood spattered across the asphalt and almost hit the teenaged girl's sneakers. She jumped back and stood daintily on her tiptoes.

"Arrrrrurrrr," said the assembled crowd in unison, an orchestrated groan of disgust and admiration.

"Thanks," Lawrence said, and took the kerchief from Dar with his left hand, wrapping it around the bleeding meat of his right hand just above the joint of thumb and wrist.

Dar put the cell phone in Lawrence's upper left safari-shirt pocket as his boss got behind the wheel of the Trooper and started the ignition.

"Want me to go with you?" asked Dar. He could imagine Lawrence getting weaker from loss of blood just as the band of felons noticed the light glinting off his boss's long lens documenting the stolen car scene. The chase across the desert. The shooting. Lawrence fainting. The terrible denouement.

"Naw," said Lawrence, "just do that

retirement-park interview for me and I'll see you at our place tomorrow."

"Okay," said Dar, his voice dull. He would rather have had the desert chase and gun battle with stolen car thieves than to go do this damn interview. It was the kind of thing that Lawrence and Trudy usually spared him.

Lawrence roared away in the Trooper. The Expedition was just a plum-colored dot on the horizon.

The four men in mechanics' overalls and the teenaged girl were looking at the spray pattern of blood on the white concrete.

"Jeeee-zus," said the youngest. "That sure was a stupid thing."

Dar dropped into the black leather of the heated NSX. "Not even in Larry's top twenty," he said, got the engine and the air-conditioning roaring, and pulled away, also headed west.

The mobile home park was in Riverside just off the 91, not far from the intersection with the 10 that Dar had driven west on from Banning. He found the proper surface street, pulled into the entrance of the mobile home park, and parked in the sparse shade of a cottonwood tree to read the rest of the file.

"Shit," he whispered to himself. From Lawrence's preliminary field report and the data from the insurer, the park had been around for a while before turning into a senior-citizen community. Now one had to be at least fifty-five to live there—although grandchildren and other youngsters were allowed to visit overnight—but the age of the average resident was probably closer to eighty. It looked from the data sheets as if many of the older residents had lived there even before the park had opened as a senior community about fifteen years earlier.

The mobile home park owner was carrying a high self-retention—which was relatively rare—carrying its own risk up to $100,000 before the insurance kicked in. Dar noted that this particular owner—a Mr. Gilley—owned several mobile home parks and maintained a high self-retention on all of them. This suggested to Dar that these parks were considered high-risk, that there had been a high volume of accidents in Mr. Gilley's retirement mobile home parks over the years, and that the insurance companies had been unwilling to provide the usual full coverage because of the frequency of these accidents. Dar knew that this might indicate a careless attitude on the part of the owner, or just bad luck.

In this case, Gilley had been notified four days ago that there had been a serious accident in this park, and that one of his resident tenants had died—the park was called the Shady Rest, although Dar could see that most of the mature trees had died and there was little shade left. The owner had immediately contacted his business attorney, and the attorney had called Stewart Investigations to reconstruct the accident so that the attorney could evaluate the liability of his client. A fairly common case for Lawrence and Trudy's company. Dar hated these cases—slip and falls, negligence cases, nursing home lawsuits. It was one reason why he worked under special contract for the Stewarts to reconstruct the more complicated accidents.

No one in the file's chain of communication seemed to have any detailed facts about this accident, but the owner's attorney had told Trudy there had been a witness—another resident by the name of Henry—and that Henry would be expecting an interviewer at the clubhouse around 11:00 A.M. Dar glanced at his watch. Ten to eleven.

Dar read through the few paragraphs of transcript from the attorney's phone call. It seemed that one of the elderly residents, Mr. William J. Treehorn, seventy-eight, had driven his electric-powered cart over a curb outside the clubhouse, fallen from the cart, struck his head, and died instantly. The accident had occurred around 11:00 P.M., so the first thing Dar did was drive to the clubhouse—a single-story A-frame building that needed maintenance—to check the nearby lighting. He could see the security lights that would have illuminated the walkways directly in front of the clubhouse, and there were three low-pressure sodium street-lights on 35-foot poles visible around the curve of lane. Dar was a bit surprised by the low-pressure sodium lights; they were more common farther south near where he lived, near San Diego, because they were supposed to minimize light scatter for the Palomar Observatory. Still, if all the lights worked, there would have been more than adequate lighting in this accident area. A point in favor of the absentee owner.

Dar drove slowly past the front of the clubhouse. He made a note on his yellow legal pad that there was construction going on in front of the community building: part of the asphalt street had been repaved, there were delineators and cones still in place, yellow tape restricted access to several sections of sidewalk, and some repaving equipment remained parked in the roped-off part of the street. He drove around to a small parking lot at the rear of the clubhouse and walked in. There did not seem to be any air-conditioning in the building and the heat was stifling.

A group of older men was playing cards at a table near the rear window. The view out the window was of a pool and hot tub that looked as if they were rarely used—the cover to the hot tub was lashed down and mildewed, and the pool needed cleaning. Dar approached the game diffidently even though the four were watching him rather than their cards.

"Excuse me, don't mean to interrupt the game," said Dar, "but is one of you gentlemen named Henry?"

A man who looked to be in his late seventies sprang to his feet. He was short, perhaps five five, and could not have weighed more than 110 pounds. His skinny, white, old man's legs emerged from oversized shorts, but he wore an expensive polo shirt, brand-new running shoes, and a baseball cap with an emblem on it advertising a Las Vegas casino. His gold wristwatch was a Rolex.

"I'm Henry," said the spry oldster, extending a mottled hand. "Henry Goldsmith. You the fella the insurance company sent around to hear about Bud's accident?"

Dar introduced himself and said, "Bud was Mr. William J. Treehorn?"

One of the old men spoke without looking up from his cards. "Bud. Everybody called him Bud. Nobody never called him William or Bill. Bud."

"That's right," said Henry Goldsmith. The man's voice was soft and sad. "I knew Bud for—Jesus—almost thirty years, and he was always Bud."

"Did you see the accident, Mr. Goldsmith?"

"Henry," said the older man. "Call me Henry. And yeah...I was the only one that saw it. Hell, I probably *caused* it." Henry's voice had thickened so that the last few words were barely audible. "Let's go find an empty table," he added. "I'll tell you all about it."

They sat at the farthest table. Dar identified himself again, explained who he worked for and where the information would be going, and asked Henry if he was willing to give a recorded statement. "You don't have to talk to me if you don't want to," said Dar. "I'm just gathering information for the adjuster who reports to the owner's attorney."

"Sure I want to talk to you," said Henry, waving his hand and waiving all his legal rights. "Tell you just what happened."

Dar nodded and turned on the recorder. The microphone was directional and highly sensitive.

The first ten minutes or so was unnecessary background. Henry and his wife lived across the street from Bud and his wife in the park, and had since before the trailer park had reopened as a senior-citizen community. The families had known each other in Chicago, and when all the kids were gone, they moved to California together.

"Bud, he had a stroke about two years ago," said Henry. "No...no, it was three years ago. Just after those goddamned Atlanta Braves won the World Series."

"David Justice hit the home run," Dar said automatically. He was interested in no sport except baseball. Unless one considered chess a sport. Dar did not.

"Whatever," said Henry. "That's when Bud had his stroke. Just after that."

"That's why Mr. Treehorn had to use the electric cart to get around?"

"Pard," said Henry.

"Pardon me?"

"Them carts, they're made by a company named Pard and that's what Bud called the cart—his pard. You know, like his buddy."

Dar knew the make. They were small and three-wheeled, almost like an oversized electric tricycle; a regular battery drove a small electric motor which powered the rear wheels. The little carts could be ordered with regular accelerator and brake pedals like a golf cart, or with brake and throttle controls on the handlebars for people without the use of their legs.

"After the stroke, Bud's left side didn't work at all," Henry was saying. "Left leg just dragged. Left arm...well, Bud used to cradle it in his lap. The left side of his face looked all dragged down and he had trouble talking."

"Could he communicate?" Dar asked softly. "Make his wishes known?"

"Oh, hell, yeah," said Henry, smiling as if

bragging about a grandchild. "The stroke didn't make him stupid. His speech was... well, it was hard to understand him... but Rose and Verna and I could always make out what he was saying."

"Rose is Mr. Treehorn's... Bud's... wife?" said Dar.

"Only for fifty-two years," said Henry. "Verna, she's my third wife. Been married twenty-two years this coming January."

"The night of the accident...," prompted Dar.

Henry frowned, knowing that he was being put back on track. "You asked if he could make his wishes known, young man. I'm tellin' you he could... but mostly it was Rose and Verna and me who understood him and sorta... you know... translated to others."

"Yes, sir," said Dar, accepting the rebuke.

"Well, the night of the accident... four nights ago... Bud and I came over to the clubhouse as usual to play pinochle."

"He could still play cards," said Dar. Strokes were strange and frightening things to him.

"Hell, yes, he could still play cards," said Henry, voice rising again but smiling this time. "Won more often than not, too. Told you, stroke messed up the left side of his body and made it hard for him to...you know...form words. Didn't hurt his mind though. Nope, Bud was as sharp as a tack."

"Was there anything different on the night of the accident?" said Dar.

"Not with Bud there wasn't," said Henry, his jaw setting firmly. "Picked him up at quarter till nine, just like every Friday night. Bud grunted some things, but Rose and me knew that he was saying that he was going to clean us out that night. Win big. Nothing different about Bud that night at all."

"No," said Dar, "I meant, was there anything different about the clubhouse or the street or the—"

"Oh, hell, yes," said Henry. "That's the reason it all happened. Those chowderheads who came to repave the street had parked their asphalt rolling machine in front of the handicapped ramp."

"The handicapped ramp out front," said

Dar. "The one in front of the main entrance?"

"Yep," said Henry. "Only entrance open after eight P.M. We like to start our games at nine…generally run to midnight or later. But Bud always leaves so as to be home by eleven because he wants to be there before Rose goes to sleep. She don't sleep well without Bud next to her and…" Henry paused and a cloud moved across his clear blue eyes, as if he had just remembered.

"But Friday night, the asphalt rolling machine had been left in front of the only handicapped access ramp," said Dar.

Henry's eyes seemed to refocus from some distant place. "What? Yeah. That's what I said. Come on, I'll show you."

The two men walked out into the heat. The access ramp was clear now, the asphalt new on the street beyond. Henry gestured at it. "The damn asphalt truck blocked the whole ramp and Bud's Pard couldn't make it up the curb." They walked together the twenty feet to the curb.

Dar noted that it was a standard street

curb, angled at about seventy-eight degrees to be easier on car tires. But it had
been too steep for Bud's little electric cart.

"No problem," said Henry. "I went in
and got Herb, Wally, Don, a couple of the
other boys, and we lifted Bud and his Pard
up onto the walk as smooth as you please.
Then he drove himself into the card
game."

"And you played until about eleven
P.M.," said Dar. He was holding the tiny
recorder at waist level, but the mike was
aimed at Henry.

"Yes, that's right," said Henry, his voice
slower now as he pictured the end of the
evening in detail. "Bud, he grunted and
made some noises. The other boys didn't
understand him, but I knew he was saying
that he had to get home 'cause Rose hates
to go to sleep without him. So he took his
winnings and him and me left the game
and came outside."

"Just the two of you?"

"Well, yeah. Wally and Herb and Don
were still playing…they go way past midnight most Friday nights…and some of

the other boys, the older ones, y'know, they'd gone home early. So it was just Bud and me going home at eleven."

"But there was still the paving machine in the way," said Dar.

"Of course there was," said Henry, sounding impatient now at Dar's slowness. "Think one of them construction knuckle-heads had come by at ten P.M. and moved it for us? So Bud drove his Pard to the curb where we'd lifted him up, but it seemed...you know...too steep."

"So then what did you do?" Dar could picture what happened next.

Henry rubbed his cheek and mouth. "Well, I said, 'Let's go down to the corner there...it's only about thirty feet...' be-cause I thought the curb's not so high there. And Bud, he agrees. So he scoots his Pard down past the useless ramp to the corner...come on, I'll show you."

Dar accompanied Henry to the corner beyond the handicapped access ramp. Dar noted that one of the low-pressure sodium vapor lamps was right next to the cross-walk there. There was no curb cut. Dar stood on the sidewalk while Henry stepped out into the street, his voice becoming more animated, his gnarled hands moving and gesturing as he spoke.

"Well, we get here and the curb doesn't look that much lower. I mean, it isn't. But it was dark, and we figured it was a little lower here, maybe. So I suggested to Bud that we take the front wheel of the Pard and drive it off the curb here 'cause it doesn't look quite as tall as the other parts of the curb along here. Least in the dark."

Henry paused. Dar said softly, "So did Bud drive the front wheel off the curb?"

Henry refocused his eyes, looking down at the curb now as if he had never seen it before. "Oh, yeah. No problem at all. I held on to the right handlebar of the cart and Bud drove the front wheel off the curb. Everything was hunky-dory. The cart wheel went right off and I kind of held onto it a little bit so it wouldn't be a real hard bump. So then we had the front wheel of Bud's little Pard off the curb and Bud looks up at me, and I remember, I said, 'It's all right, Bud. I've got the right handlebar. I'll hold onto the handlebar.' "

Henry pantomimed holding on to the handlebar with both hands. "Bud, he hits the switch with his right hand to activate the motor, but he doesn't give it any throttle, and I say again, 'It's OK, Bud, we'll get that left rear wheel off the curb and get it down on the street and I'll hold onto you here—both hands on the handlebar—and then you can just drive forward and the right rear tire, it'll drive right off the curb, and then we'll be on the street and then it's a straight shot home.' "

Dar stood and waited, seeing Henry's eyes cloud again as he relived the moment.

"And then the cart moved forward and I was holding on to the right end of the handlebar...Used to be real strong, Mr. Minor, worked twenty-six years loading boxes in the Chicago Merchandise Mart till we moved out here but this damned leukemia the last couple of years...Anyway, the left wheel dropped off the curb and the damned cart started to tip to its left. Bud looks at me and he can't move his left arm or leg, and I say, 'It's OK, Bud, I got it with both hands,' but the cart just kept tipping. It was heavy. Real heavy. I thought of grabbing Bud, but he was...you know...strapped into the cart the way he's supposed to be. I did everything to hang on to that cart. I had both hands on the handlebar, but I felt it tipping farther and farther...it's a heavy cart what with the battery and motor and all...and my hands were getting sweaty, and I thought later that I should have hollered for the fellas who were still playing pinochle, but at the time...well, I just didn't think about it. You know how it is."

Dar nodded and held the tape recorder.

Henry's eyes were filling with tears now, as if the full impact of the event was striking him for the first time. "I felt the cart tipping and my fingers starting to slip and I couldn't hold it anymore. I mean, it was just too much weight for me, and then Bud looked at me with his good eye, and I think he knew what was going to happen, but I said, 'Bud, Bud, it'll be all right, I'll hang on. I'll hang onto this. I've got you.'"

Henry looked at the curb for a full minute in silence. His cheeks were moist. When he spoke again, the animation was completely absent from his voice. "And then the cart tipped farther and fell over to its left and Bud couldn't do anything because, like I said, he was paralyzed on his left side. Then there was this crash and this...sound...this sickening sound."

Henry turned and looked Dar straight in the eye. "And then Bud died." Henry fell silent, just standing there with his arms stretched out in the same position they must have been the instant the handlebars had slipped from his grip. "I was just trying to help him get home so he could say goodnight to Rose," whispered Henry.

Later, when Henry had left, Dar used his tape measure to calculate the fall distance from Bud's head location while seated in a Pard cart to the pavement. Four feet six inches. But at that moment he said nothing, did nothing, just stood next to the old man whose arms were still extended, his closed fists slowly opening to splayed fingers. The hands shook.

Henry looked back at the pavement. "And then Bud died."

Dar called it a day and drove down the 91 to the 15 and then headed south, toward his condo outside of San Diego. *Fuck it*, he thought. He'd started the day at 4:00 A.M. *Fuck it all*, he thought.

He would type up the transcript of the tape recording and hand it in to Lawrence and Trudy, but he'd be damned if he would follow up on this case. He knew the drill. The manufacturer of the electric cart would be sued, no doubt about that. The park owner would be sued—there would be no doubt about that. The construction company that had blocked the ramp would be sued by everybody, no doubt about that.

But would Rose sue Henry? Probably. Dar had very little doubt about that either. Thirty years of friendship. He was trying to get his friend Bud home in time to kiss his wife good-night. But after a few more months…perhaps a second lawyer…

Fuck it, thought Dar. He would not inquire. He'd never check the file again.

Traffic on the 15 was relatively light, which was one reason that Dar noticed the Mercedes E 340 that had been keeping pace with his left rear quarter panel. Also, the Mercedes's windows were tinted, front and side, which was illegal in California. State and local cops had helped push that law through—none of them wanted to approach a car with opaque windows. Also, the Mercedes was new and modified for speed, with eighteen-inch wheels and a raised rear end with a tiny spoiler. Dar had a thing about people who bought luxury cars—even autobahn cruisers like the Mercedes E 340—and then hopped them up into performance cars. He thought such people were the worst kind of idiots—pretentious idiots.

So he was watching in his left mirror as the Mercedes accelerated to pass him on the left. There were five lanes along this stretch, three of them empty, but the Mercedes was whipping around the NSX as tightly as if they were on the last lap of the Daytona 500. Dar sighed. It was one of the drawbacks of owning a serious performance vehicle like his Acura NSX.

The Mercedes pulled alongside and slowed, matching speeds. Dar glanced left and could see his own face, sunglasses and all, reflected in the dark window of the big German car.

The instincts of two decades earlier took over and Dar ducked even as the black window rolled down. He glimpsed the barrel of something industrial and ugly and very full-automatic—an Uzi or a Mac-10—and then the firing began. His left window exploded glass onto his ear and hair, and bullets began tearing through the aluminum NSX.

3

"C IS FOR CAREERING"

The shooting seemed to go on interminably, but almost certainly lasted no more than five seconds. An eternity.

Dar had thrown himself flat across the low center console, burrowing his head into the black leather of the passenger seat as glass shards filled the air like parade confetti, his left hand still on the bottom curve of the steering wheel, his right heel lifting to the brake and pressing hard. There had been no one but the Mercedes in sight behind him. His left foot hit the clutch as he used his left hand, which was higher than his head, to slam the little shift lever from fifth to third. The noise of the bullets slamming into the aluminum of the door and front end of the now rapidly decelerating NSX sounded like someone riveting in a huge barrel.

The NSX slid to a stop on what Dar hoped and prayed was the highway's shoulder—he had not lifted his head to check—and he kept his head down after the shooting stopped. He slithered across the glass-covered console and passenger seat, hearing and feeling other shards fall from his head and back, set the stick in neutral, and pulled up on the parking brake as he crawled over it and then he was out the passenger door, on his belly on the pavement and peering under the low-slung sports car, trying to see if the E 340 Mercedes had stopped alongside him. It would be bad news if it had; it was thirty yards to the fence that bordered the interstate, and no trees or other cover in sight beyond that.

No wheels visible. He heard the roar of the Mercedes accelerating and he crawled on his elbows to the front right wheel of the NSX, catching a glimpse of the gray vehicle rocketing away.

Dar stood up shakily, feeling the adrenaline surging, suppressing the urge to vomit, and only then wondered if he had been hit. He touched his left ear and his fingers came away bloody, but he realized in an instant that it was only a small glass cut. With the exception of a few other slices from the broken safety glass, he had not been touched. A Honda Civic drove by below the speed limit, the round-faced male at the wheel staring wide-eyed at Dar and his car.

Dar inspected the NSX. They had shot high and they had used a lot of ammunition. The left and right windows were gone, the A-pillar had a bullet hole in it—the aluminum bright around the jagged indentation—and there were three holes in the driver's-side door. One bullet would have hit Dar dead center in the ass if the steel side-impact strut had not deflected it, and two others had struck on the B-pillar part of the door where the handle was.

The front of the car had also taken half a dozen hits as the NSX had decelerated, but a quick inspection showed that all of the bullets had missed the wheels—running scars across the low, sloping hood or entering between the wheel and the passenger compartment or between the wheel and the front bumper. If the Acura NSX had been a front-engined vehicle, the damage would have been quite dramatic, but the engine in the sports car was set amidships, just behind the driver, and it was still idling with its usual ready purr. This—and the fact that the wheels were untouched and there didn't appear to be any suspension or structural damage— decided Dar.

He ripped off his shirt, used it to brush the broken glass off the driver's seat, got in, slammed the NSX into gear, and accelerated down the shoulder. The gray Mercedes had just disappeared over a dip in the interstate perhaps two miles ahead. The vehicle had been moving fast—Dar had estimated that it was passing the few other cars on the interstate at twenty-five to thirty miles per hour above the limit of seventy.

Dar was doing a hundred in third gear

when he swung off the shoulder back onto the right lane of the interstate, blowing past the Civic whose round-faced driver was still staring.

This is crazy, he thought, and slammed the NSX into fourth gear, hearing the roar of the normally aspirated six-cylinder performance engine just behind his seat as he let all of the snakes out of their cage, bringing the sports car close to the 7,800-rpm red line.

But he was angry. He was very angry. Dar could not remember being this angry in a long, long time. He shifted into fifth and floored it.

He passed two cars and a semitrailer on their left, the sound of the passed vehicles actually Doppler-shifting down in tone because of his speed. As he came over the rise, he caught sight of the gray Mercedes about three miles ahead on the next long hill climb of the interstate. It was in the far left lane and still doing about a hundred. He reached for his shirt pocket to grab his cell phone—realized that he'd taken off the shirt and thrown it as a crumpled

ball onto the passenger seat after cleaning out the glass. He patted the shirt, but
there was nothing in the pocket. He had
dropped the phone somewhere during his
ducking, slithering, sliding out, crouching,
elbow crawling, or glass dusting. *Shit.* He
told himself that it didn't matter—that
the howling wind noise coming through
the two shattered side windows would
have drowned out any call to the police. At
least the windshield was intact except for
one two-inch stress fracture at the upper
left where a slug had hit the top of the A-
pillar.

Eyes on the road and on the tail of the
Mercedes, he glanced down for the
briefest second at his speedometer: 158.
He accelerated, leaning over as he did so
to grab his camera bag from the floor of
the passenger side. *Please, God—whoever's
in charge of all this—just don't have let any
of the slugs hit my cameras.* Through a combination of quick pats and even quicker
glances Dar ascertained that the bag was
unhurt, unsnapped the top, and unceremoniously dumped the contents onto the

passenger seat. He didn't want the digital camera; he wanted the Nikon and the long lens.

Dar set the Nikon between his legs, fumbled for the telephoto, and began changing lenses as he accelerated up and over the next hill at 165 miles per hour. Changing lenses was usually a two-handed job—one had to depress a button to release the lens before screwing the new one on—but he had done it one-handed before. Just never at this speed.

Out of the corner of his eye he saw a CHP patrol car coming the other way on the westernmost northbound lane, and glanced at his mirror in time to see the black-and-white CHP vehicle slewing through the median, its lights beginning to swirl and flash as it reversed direction to give chase. If the siren had come on, Dar couldn't hear it above the wind noise in the tiny cockpit.

It was just his luck that this CHP car was one of their pursuit Mustangs—a '94 model from the look of it—decked out with one of their usual 302 V-8 engines.

Dar's quick glimpse of the driver and his partner had told him that they were both young, and the speed of their pursuit showed him that they were both gung ho. *Just my luck*, thought Dar, focusing on the Mercedes ahead of him.

Somehow he had kept his Serengeti driving glasses on during all of his flopping and crawling antics, and without these keeping the worst of the wind from his eyes, Dar didn't think he could have seen well enough in all the wind to keep up the pace. But he was. The Mercedes was only twenty car lengths ahead now. It had slowed to about eighty-five—but the driver must have just glanced in his mirror and glimpsed either the NSX or the police flashers or both, because suddenly the gray Mercedes shifted lanes and accelerated up the next long stretch of hilly interstate, passing cars on the left and right, using all five lanes, hunting for open spots and then surging ahead.

Dar followed lane to lane. He knew that the normal Mercedes E 340s were electronically governed to keep their top speed down to 130 mph, but this window-tinted, spoilered, fat-tired, modified son of a bitch was now doing at least 155 as it dodged through the thickening traffic.

Goddammit, thought Dar. He had the long two-hundred-millimeter lens on now and the Nikon in his left hand as he whipped past traffic on his left and right. But the Mercedes was still a quarter of a mile ahead, too far for a clear shot at the license tag. And Dar had no idea how he could hold the camera steady enough to read the plate even if he got closer.

He didn't care. He dropped the Nikon back in his lap, gripped the perfectly sized steering wheel with both hands, and swerved from the far right lane to the far left to stay behind the Mercedes. His speedometer read 170 and he was above the red line. Dar desperately did not want to blow this Acura engine: it was a hand-crafted work of art, assembled by one man at the Japanese factory. Somewhere on that mostly aluminum engine block was the man's name engraved in Japanese symbols. In an age of superchargers, turbochargers, and every other prosthetic breathing aid, this was a normally aspirated V-6 that derived speed from perfection. It would be a desecration to blow such an engine. Nonetheless, Dar kept the perforated pedal to the metal—or in this case, to the luxurious black rubber mat that ran up the firewall above the luxurious black carpeting—and let the tach creep further into the red. The little six-cylinder screamed and the gap began to close.

What if they just slow down and shoot me again? asked the still sane part of Darwin's mind. He had no weapons in the car. He had no weapons at home. He hated handguns. *What if I slow down and the cops shoot me?* riposted the adrenaline-driven part of Dar's brain. *Might as well catch these fuckers first.*

The Mercedes shifted from the far left lane to the far right lane, cutting off two vehicles as it did so. One of them—a Ford Windstar van—braked too quickly and spun four times before coming to a halt with its nose pointed back the way it had come. Dar noticed the pallor on the man's and woman's faces in the front seats as he passed them at 168 miles per hour.

This is how it'll end, you asshole, shouted the sane part of Dar through the adrenaline-filled Dar's thick skull. *In the movies these car chases are always excitement and close calls. In real life, it's a dead family—innocent people killed—and you're not even a cop. You don't even have the right to do this.*

The driving Dar theoretically agreed with the sane Dar—he glanced at his mirror and saw the flashing lights as the CHP Mustang almost showed clear air under the wheels as it came over the rise less than a mile behind him—but the part of him that was driving was angrier than he had been for many, many years. And the Mercedes was only a hundred yards ahead now, back in the far left lane again with little traffic around it. Dar held his foot to the floor and leveraged the Nikon onto the slivered sill of the NSX door, keeping the long lens inside so the wind wouldn't catch it and pull the expensive camera out of his hand. *This is going to be tricky*, he thought, deciding that he should shoot through the windshield with both hands on top of the wheel to prop and steady the Nikon, helping to steer with his left knee, just snapping away at full auto and hoping that one of the photos would be readable.

The Mercedes braked and changed lanes so quickly that it crossed five lanes in a long, controlled slide, barely missing a delivery van and recovering just in time to fire down an exit ramp like a bullet down a barrel.

Fuck, Dar prayed, and braked to fall behind a Greyhound bus, braking again and skidding across the last three lanes toward the exit. He made it with the NSX's rear wheels spinning at gravel on the shoulder, two corrections, and he was accelerating down the ramp, just catching sight of the exit sign as he passed—*Lake Street*.

All right. He knew where he was. This road he was broadsiding onto now, following the fishtailing Mercedes, went nowhere except through the little bedroom community of Lake Elsinore along Lakeshore Drive. It used to be the old Alberhill exit, but that non-town was already behind them. Dar looked ahead to his left and saw two county sheriff's cars—both black and white, both Chevys—one a Monte Carlo, the other an Impala—and both heading west from the town to intercept them. Both the Mercedes and the NSX blasted past the intersection before the sheriff's cars got onto Lakeshore Drive, but Dar could actually hear the sirens as the two Chevys skidded onto the street and accelerated only a hundred yards behind him. The CHP Mustang was close behind them and trying to pass.

If I pull up to the E 340, Dar thought coolly, working it out as if it were a minor chess problem, *the guys inside will shoot me.* He glanced in his mirror. *If I slow down, the cops probably won't shoot me, but it's possible that they'll be so busy arresting me that they'll let the Mercedes get away.*

The Mercedes's brake lights flashed on. Dar had no choice but to brake himself, the big seventeen-inch disk brakes hauling the sports car down from speed so abruptly that he was pressed forward with three g's as the inertial reel locked and his harness held him in place.

Incredibly, the Mercedes swung out of control to the left, fishtailed to the right, then bounced across an empty corner lot—Dar could see three feet of daylight under the E 340—landed on asphalt, corrected itself perfectly, and then accelerated up a street headed west. Dar couldn't read the street sign as he brought the NSX through a controlled slide onto the same narrow road, but he knew it from previous jobs that had brought him this way—*Riverside Drive.* Actually the beginning of Highway 74, it was a narrow two-lane road that crossed the mountains through the Cleveland National Forest and emerged on I-5 at San Juan Capistrano about thirty-two miles west. Dar had used the shortcut many times.

The Impala did not make the turn, and Dar caught a glimpse of it in his left mirror as it spun through a gas station entrance, just missing a Jaguar that was fueling up at the outermost pump, and then disappeared in a cloud of dust behind a line of vehicles in a used-car lot. The CHP Mustang and the other sheriff's car both made the turn and came barreling up Riverside Drive, less than a quarter mile back now as the winding road slowed the chase.

This is where I should stop and let them handle it, thought Dar, knowing that no claim of attempting a citizen's arrest was going to keep him out of jail. Suddenly a helicopter buzzed low over him, passed the Mercedes, and then circled around away from the hillside, preparing to make another pass.

Police helicopter, thought Dar, knowing that L.A. County had sixteen of the things while all of New York City used only six. But then he saw the markings. *Wonderful.* He'd be on Channel 5 KTLA in time for the six-o'clock news. Actually, he realized, he was probably on *now*. There were so many police automobile pursuits televised live in Southern California that there was talk of a cable channel that showed nothing else.

Dar roared up the increasingly steep and winding road, trying to keep the roof of the

Mercedes in sight. It had been years since he had raced sports cars, but everything felt very, very right as he hit the apex of each decreasing radial turn exactly on the money, accelerating out of the turn with a roar, tapping the brake, setting up the next turn, shifting down, allowing just enough drift of the rear end, and coming out again at full throttle. Very few supercars in the world could outhandle the Acura NSX in this sort of situation. By the time they were nearing the top of the steep grade, the police had fallen out of sight behind them and he was within three car lengths of the E 340.

It had been two miles up the winding, twisting road above Lake Elsinore and the men in the Mercedes had obviously decided it was time to get rid of him. They slowed during a right-hand uphill hairpin, the passenger-side window came down, and a man with dark hair, a dark suit, and a dark metal Mac-10 leaned out.

Dar got off five or six photos with his Nikon, held one-handed, as the automatic weapon blazed away at him. Something banged metal near the right rear of the sports car, but the handling stayed good and Dar dropped the camera into his lap, shifted down, roared around the decreasing radial, uphill right turn and accelerated until he was almost on the Mercedes's bumper. He noticed that it had Nevada tags and memorized the numbers.

The shooter leaned out again, but Dar was too close; he dodged into the left lane and accelerated almost even with the Mercedes. The gunman fired through his own tinted left rear window, sending bronzed glass flying, but Dar had already accelerated ahead and then dropped back next to the Mercedes. The driver's window hummed down and Dar looked to his right directly into their faces, memorizing them, as both vehicles approached the last hairpin turn at eighty-five miles per hour.

Dar knew that beyond this point he would be in trouble. There was a long straight stretch along the ridgetop of the mountain before the curves started again. But on this last left-hand curve before the summit, directly ahead, was an old restaurant–turned–biker-bar called The Lookout. Dar had stopped there for lunch once, but the ambience—there were generally twenty to thirty "hogs" parked outside and as many guzzling and fighting inside—had not been to his liking.

The Lookout was on the right side of the road with outdoor patio seating on the south side of the restaurant. The patio consisted of little more than some rotting two-by-fours supported by wooden beams extending directly from the sheer cliff face of the hillside above Lake Elsinore. Dar could see a dozen or more bikers sprawling around a few old tables. Their hogs were parked directly in front of the patio.

Dar looked right just in time to see the passenger lean over and extend the muzzle of the Mac-10 out the driver's window behind the driver's head. It was aimed directly at Dar's face.

Dar hit the brakes, the automatic weapon fired over his hood, and then he cut hard right and accelerated, catching the heavier Mercedes amidships. The Mercedes's left-side door air bag deployed as designed, smashing the shooter's hand into the top of the doorframe and causing the Mac-10 to fly out of the man's hand and bounce off Dar's hood. Dar's NSX was a '92 and had only a driver's-side air bag, but after years of investigating and reconstructing air-bag accidents, he had long since disconnected his.

Now he stood on the brakes, first forcing the heavier car to its right and then falling behind the still-racing Mercedes, the tires of the NSX screeching and smoking, but the ABS working hard, the brake pedal pounding against Dar's foot as he drove through the skid, slammed into second gear, and almost made the hard hairpin turn to the left, leaving the shoulder but missing the restaurant, scraping boulders and low brush before finally crunching and sliding to a stop a hundred-some feet farther up the road.

When the door-side air bag had deployed, the gunman had fallen forward onto the driver, whose own shoulder harness kept him from falling against the steering wheel, but who was having little luck steering. The new Mercedes E 340 barreled straight ahead through the apex of the left hairpin, hitting the first row of the parked Harleys. Both of the E 340's front air bags deployed while its driver, still pinned by his partner and now blinded by the air bag explosion and unable to reach the steering wheel, the shooter unable to move because of the air bag deployed into his own seat area, did all he could—standing on the brakes while driving straight ahead, knocking more Harleys left and right and causing a dozen bikers to leap for their lives as the heavy car drove straight onto the rickety patio, smashed tables to splinters, skidded across the rotted boards, tore through the creaky handrail, and used the patio as a ramp to launch itself off the mountain.

Dar caught a last glimpse of the gray Mercedes, its front windows down and both men's faces quite visible, mouths opened wide, air bags deflating even as the two-ton car seemed to pause a moment in midair à la Wile E. Coyote—barely missing the bubble nose of the Channel 5 KTLA chopper that had its gyro-stabilized cameras zoomed in on the screaming faces and hurtling car—and then the vehicle went nosedown and dropped out of sight on its way to the valley floor seven hundred feet straight down.

The NSX's frame had been bent, the driver's door wouldn't open, and Dar's passenger door was lodged against a boulder, so he clambered out of the window just in time to become the focus of the skidding CHP Mustang and the overheated sheriff's Monte Carlo. Doors flew open. Guns were drawn and aimed. Commands were shouted.

Dar leaned against the NSX, spread his legs as directed, linked his fingers behind his head as suggested by the officers' screams, and tried to breathe slowly so as not to be sick. The adrenaline surge of anger was receding like some mad tide, leaving just flotsam and jetsam of emotions behind.

The CHP officers, young, with high badge serial numbers Dar noticed in his one glance over his shoulder, were not men he'd worked with before. He understood from their shouts and barks that they would blow him fucking away if he made a single fucking move. Dar did not move. One of the state troopers and the sheriff held guns on him, and the third—the older of the two CHP men, a grizzled veteran who looked to be about twenty-three years old—approached and frisked him quickly, jerked his arms down and back, and slapped cuffs on him.

A couple of the bikers wandered over with beers in their hands. The one with the longer beard was showing yellow teeth in a wide grin. "Hey, man, that was the coolest fucking thing I've ever seen. Almost took out fucking Channel Five, man. Definitely awesome."

The sheriff's deputy told the bikers to get back inside The Lookout Restaurant; several other bikers wandered over to explain that they'd never been *in* the fucking restaurant—that they'd been on the patio—and it was a fucking free country, man. Like, where else but America could you see a new Mercedes drive off a seven-hundred-foot drop and almost take a fucking news chopper with it, man?

"Snotty Eddie's gonna have to rename his fucking bar, man," said a biker with a shaved head and a tattoo of a skull on his bare chest. "Change it from the fucking Lookout to the fucking Launchpad, man."

Dar was glad when the two highway patrolmen dragged and pushed him to the CHP Mustang.

"He's gotta go to Riverside, you know," the sheriff was saying. He still had a long-barreled Colt in his hand.

"We know, we know," said the older of the two young state troopers. "Why don't you or your deputy get on your radio and get some backup here—and tell them we need a forensics team—before there's a fucking riot. OK?"

The sheriff looked at the milling bikers now as they began assessing the damage to their hogs and cursing more imaginatively, nodded, put away his big pistol, and walked back to the Monte Carlo.

Only the sheriff's deputy had walked out

onto the flimsy, damage-strewn, shaky patio to stand nervously at the edge, peer through the wide gap in the railing, and stare down toward Lake Elsinore where the Mercedes had disappeared. From somewhere far below came the buzz of the news helicopter. Part of Dar's mind was calculating the time it had taken the Mercedes to free-fall the distance even as the state troopers shoved him into the backseat of the Mustang. It would be one hell of a news video.

The last thing Dar heard before being driven away was the deputy on the patio edge softly repeating, "Holy shit, holy shit, holy shit," as if it were his private mantra.

4

"D IS FOR DICKWEED"

The car chase and Dar's arrest were on Tuesday afternoon. Freed on bail that evening, he attended a meeting on Wednesday morning in the deputy district attorney's office in downtown San Diego.

When he was booked on Tuesday, Dar had been shirtless, wearing only his sneakers and the now soiled and bloody jeans that he had pulled on at 4:00 A.M. With the scratches from flying glass, no shirt, wildly mussed hair, two days' stubble, and what his fellow grunts in Vietnam had long ago called a "postcombat thousand-yard stare," his mug shot looked classically and fiercely felonious. He could picture it hanging in his study, right next to an old color photo of him receiving his robe and scroll symbolizing his Ph.D. in physics.

At 9:00 A.M. Wednesday morning, sitting at the long table with more than a dozen other people who had yet to be introduced, Dar was shaved, showered, and dressed in a crisp white shirt, striped rep tie, blue linen blazer, tropical-weight gray pants, and polished Bally black shoes that were as soft as dance slippers. He wasn't quite sure if he was a guest at this meeting or still a prisoner of the state, but he wanted to look decent in either case.

The deputy district attorney's assistant's assistant, a nervous little man who seemed to embody every gay stereotype in the culture—from his hand-wringing and nervous giggles to his overwrought wrists—was busy offering donuts and coffee to everyone. Set on the table opposite Dar was a line of Smokey hats and badged caps behind which sat at least eight police captains and sheriffs; on the same side of the table but at the far end, substituting briefcases on the tabletop for hats, were two plainclothes officers, one with the haircut of an FBI special agent. All of them except the FBI man accepted at least one donut from the deputy DA's assistant's assistant.

On Dar's side of the table, besides Lawrence and Trudy and their lawyer, W.D.D. Du Bois, was a motley assortment of bureaucrats and attorneys, most of them wrinkled, rumpled, jowled, and slouched, all in sad contrast to the starched, silent, stern-jawed crispness of the cops on the other side. Most of the attorneys and bureaucrats just accepted coffee.

Dar took his Styrofoam cup with thanks, received an "Oh, you're welcome, you're welcome" and a pat on the back from the deputy DA's assistant's assistant, and sat back to wait for whatever came next.

A black man dressed in a bailiff's uniform stepped into the room and announced, "We're almost ready to start. Dick-weed's on his way and Sid's just leaving the ladies' room."

The previous afternoon, still handcuffed, Dar had been driven to the county jail in downtown Riverside. In the car, the older of the state troopers had literally read him his rights from a frayed three-by-five card. Dar had the right to remain silent, anything he said could and would be used against him in a court of law, he had the right to an attorney, if he could not afford an attorney, one would be appointed for him. Did he understand?

"You're *reading* it?" Dar asked. "You must repeat it ten thousand times a year."

"Shut the fuck up," explained the trooper.

Dar nodded and remained silent. He had been Mirandized. And a perfectly good adjective had been made into a verb.

At the Riverside County jail, a low, ugly structure right next to the tall, ugly Riverside city hall complex, the young CHP officers reclaimed their cuffs and officially handed him over to the Riverside sheriff, who gave him to a young deputy to book. Dar had never been arrested before. Still, all of the procedures—emptying the pockets of personal possessions, fingerprinting, and mug shot—were familiar from TV and the movies, of course, and it all combined to give him a strange sense of disembodied déjà vu that added to the unreal quality of the last hour or so.

He was put in a holding cell, alone but for the company of a few sullen cockroaches. About fifteen minutes later, the deputy returned and said, "You got a call coming. Want to call your lawyer?"

"I don't have a lawyer," Dar said truthfully. "Can I call my therapist?"

The deputy was not amused.

Dar called Trudy, who had dealt with so many legal issues that she could have passed the bar exam with half her brain tied behind her back. Instead of handling legal issues herself, however, she and Lawrence kept one of the best lawyers in California on retainer. It was necessary given that Stewart Investigations occasionally got dragged into one of the broad lawsuit nets cast out by hopeful litigants plying the fraudulent-insurance-claim waters as diligently and daily and doggedly as New England fishermen.

"Trudy, I—" began Dar when she picked up the phone.

"Yes, I know," she interrupted. "I didn't catch it live, but Linda taped it for me. The commentators are going on about road rage."

"Road rage!" shouted Dar. "Those bastards tried to kill me and then I—"

"You're at Riverside, right?" interrupted Trudy again.

"Right."

"I've got one of W.D.D's associates on the way. You'll give a deposition there at Riverside with the associate present and he'll have you out in an hour."

Dar stood and blinked at the phone. "Trudy, bail's going to be about a billion dollars. Two men are dead. Dead live on Channel Five. Riverside County's not going to let me out of here without—"

"There's more to this than meets the Insta-Cam," said Trudy. "I've been on the phone. I know who the two guys were and why the CHP and county mounties aren't releasing your name to the media. And why W.D.D. will be able to—"

"Who were they?" said Dar, realizing

that he was shouting again. "Did they say on TV?"

"No, it wasn't on TV and we're all going to be further enlightened tomorrow morning at the San Diego deputy district attorney's office," said Trudy. "Nine A.M. You'll be out on bail...the San Diego County DA already has a writ from one of his judges asking the Riverside County judge to be lenient. Don't worry about media following you home...Your name isn't going to be leaked until at least tomorrow."

"But..." Dar said, and realized he did not know what else to say.

"Wait for W.D.D.'s associate," said Trudy. "Go home and take a hot shower. Lawrence just called in and I let him know what's going on. We'll give you a call tonight and then you'll get a good night's sleep. It looks like we'll all need it for tomorrow."

W.D.D. Du Bois, pronounced "du-boyz," was short, black, and brilliant, with a Martin Luther King mustache and a Danny DeVito personality. Lawrence had once said that in the courtroom W.D.D. could suggest more with his mustache than most people could with their eyebrows.

Du Bois was not the attorney's real name. Or, rather, it had not been at birth. Christened Willard Darren Dirks in Greenville, Alabama, W.D.D. had been born in the early 1940s with everything working against him—his race, his family's rural poverty, the state he was born in, the IQ and attitude of most of the state's white inhabitants, his parents' illiteracy, the lousy segregated schools he attended—everything except his IQ, which was higher than most professional bowlers' average score. When he was nine, young Willie Dirks discovered the writings of W.E.B. Du Bois (pronounced "du-boyz") and had his own name legally changed by the time he was twenty. By that time he had gotten himself out of Alabama and through the University of Southern California and into UCLA's law school. He was only the third Negro to graduate from that esteemed institution and he was the first to run a major law firm in Los Angeles consisting only of other black lawyers, associates, and staff.

The fact that this coincided perfectly with the Civil Rights Act of 1964, a blizzard of new government-backed civil rights legislation, and Lyndon Johnson's legislative steps toward a Great Society that required no-holds-barred legal battles on all fronts, helped W.D.D.'s practice but did not define it. His firm handled mostly civil cases, but W.D.D.'s first love was criminal law, and these were the few cases he still argued personally in court—the stranger the case, the more the appeal to Attorney Du Bois. It was well known—at least in legal circles—that Attorney Robert Shapiro had tried to bring Du Bois into the O. J. Simpson case before Johnnie Cochran got involved, but that W.D.D.'s only comment to Shapiro had been, "Are you kidding? That brother's guilty as Abel's brother Cain. I only represent innocent killers." Stewart Investigations had offered him some deliciously weird cases over the years, and Du Bois showed his appreciation for that by representing Trudy's company when things got complicated. This appeared to be just such a moment.

The deputy district attorney entered and took the chair at the head of the table. The politically ambitious Richard Allen Weid was sensitive about his last name, which was pronounced "weed." His father had been a famous judge, so Richard could not just change his name, but he told people not to call him "Dick" even more frequently than Lawrence objected to "Larry." Which guaranteed that—at least out of earshot—everyone in the DA's office, in the downtown San Diego Justice Center, and in Southern California called him "Dick," and more commonly, "Dickweed."

"Sid" was a bigger surprise to Dar. The woman was attractive, in her late thirties, a little overweight in a nice way, professionally groomed but with an expression that seemed to suggest high intelligence filtered through restrained amusement at life. She reminded Dar of some character actress he really liked, but he could not for the life of him recall the actress's name.

Dar guessed this woman spelled her name "Sydney" with two *y*'s, and since she took the only other "power seat" at the table—the empty chair at the opposite end of the table from Dick Weid's—she was obviously someone with serious clout.

Deputy DA Weid brought the meeting to order. "You all know why we're here today. For those of you who may have been on duty and missed the news yesterday or this morning, a copy of Mr. Darwin Minor's statement should be in front of you...and we've got this tape."

Shit, thought Dar as the assistant's assistant pulled the standard media cart with a half-inch VHS VCR and old monitor out of the corner and moved it to a place of pride next to the deputy DA's chair. The assistant popped in the tape and Dick Weid wielded the remote.

Dar had not seen the news video the night before. Now he watched the Channel Five live coverage of the chase from the interstate exit, up the winding road above Lake Elsinore, ending in amazing footage as the news chopper—hovering a hundred feet out from The Lookout Restaurant's patio—was almost hit by the Mercedes E 340 as it came barreling out into midair as if trying to leap to safety onto the skids of the helicopter. Mercifully, Deputy DA Weid kept the reporters' wild narration muted. Unmercifully, the Steadicam zoomed in on the faces of the two men—both their heads and shoulders protruding now from the driver's-side window as if they were trying to climb out to safety—and Dar could clearly see the shooter's lips moving in a shout, although he could not make out the words.

When the Mercedes fell out of the camera's view, the Channel Five pilot immediately put the chopper into a spiraling dive so that the gyro-stabilized camera could unblinkingly and unmercifully stay on the plummeting vehicle all the way down until the E 340 struck the hillside, upside down, at least five hundred feet below The Lookout's patio. The wreckage bounced through trees and shrubs for another hundred feet, the body of the Mercedes staying amazingly intact but with wheels, bumpers, mirrors, axles, muffler, hubcaps, windshield, suspension, catalytic converter, and the humans inside flying amazingly apart, until finally the wreck disappeared into its own cloud of dust, rubble, and smashed trees in a steep ravine on the cliffside.

Deputy DA Weid used the reverse control on the remote to run the wreckage backward. The pieces of car leaped together and the car levitated back into the air, and then Weid stopped on a freeze-frame of the two men's faces, one of them in the act of shouting at the helicopter in what appeared to be a cry of supplication. Dar saw every head in the room swivel toward him—even Lawrence's and Trudy's—and he felt the weight of every gaze. He considered asking, *Didn't their air bags save them?* but decided to keep his mouth shut. Besides, three of the four front-seat air bags had deployed and deflated by the time the vehicle was airborne, making the front of the passenger compartment all the more pitiful in the video, as if it were draped inside with huge, empty condoms.

Two men were dead and he had caused it. Dar felt the vertigo of the video leave him and a heaviness descend again on his spirit, but it was not regret. He clearly remembered the sound of the Mac-10's slugs shattering his driver's-side window and whizzing by his head. He remembered the anger from yesterday as a distant thing, but he remembered it clearly enough to know that if those two bastards had survived the fall, he would have happily climbed down the mountain and beaten them to death with a stick. He kept his mouth shut and his face neutral, and eventually the others at the table turned their gazes away from him.

"Before we go any further," said Deputy DA Weid into the thick silence, "I should say that we've had expert lip-readers from the San Diego School for the Deaf analyze this gentleman's last cry" — he pointed the remote at the freeze-frame where the mustached shooter was still frozen in time, mouth wide open in the act of shouting his final words — "but as close as our lip-reading experts can determine, the man was saying...ah... 'gave nooky.' "

Everyone stared except for Sydney, who laughed out loud. *"Gavnuki,"* she said, still chuckling to herself and pronouncing it quite differently than Dick Weid had. "It's Russian for 'shitheads.' I think the guy was stating his opinion of Channel Five."

"All right," the deputy DA said, and clicked off the TV image.

"That would confirm the Bureau's identification of the two men," said the handsome man in the FBI haircut. "The Mercedes was stolen in Las Vegas two days ago. We have identified the two deceased occupants of the stolen vehicle as Russian nationals. The driver, Vasily Plavinksy, has been in the country for three months on a temporary visa. The other man—"

"The one who tried to kill my client with an automatic weapon," interjected Attorney Du Bois smoothly.

The FBI man frowned. "The other man, also Russian, entered the country through New York just five days ago. His name is Kliment Ritko."

"That might be an alias," said Dar.

"Why do you say that?" asked the FBI

special agent, his voice tinged with condescension. "In your deposition, you claimed you had never seen these two men before. Are you now saying that you have some personal knowledge of the identity of these two...ah...victims?"

"Would-be murderers," said W.D.D. Du Bois instantly. "Hired killers."

Dar said, "I just suggest it might be an alias because there was an infamous Russian painter named Kliment Ritko. His 1924 painting *Uprising* foretold Stalin's reign of terror. He even painted Lenin, Stalin, Trotsky, Bukharin, and the rest of the Bolshevik leaders against a blood-red background, surrounded by troops shooting defenseless people in the street."

There was a full thirty seconds of silence—an embarrassed silence—as if Dar's display of pedantry had been equal to him jumping up and peeing on the table. Dar resolved to keep his mouth shut through the rest of the proceedings unless asked a direct question. He turned his head slightly and saw Sydney, whoever she was, give him a frank stare of appraisal.

"Let me introduce everyone at the table," said the deputy DA quickly, trying to take control of the meeting again.

"Most of you know Special Agent James Warren, agent in charge of the San Diego branch of the Bureau. Captain Bill Reinhardt is LAPD, their liaison with Operation SouthCal Clean Sweep. Captain Frank Hernandez is from our own San Diego Police Department. Next to Captain Hernandez...and thanks for coming in today, Tom, on such short notice, I know you had a conference to attend in Vegas...is Captain Tom Sutton of the California Highway Patrol. Next to Tom is Sheriff Paul Fields from Riverside County, whose cooperation has been fantastic in this operation. Most of us know Sheriff Buzz McCall from right here in San Diego County. And at the end there...hi, Marlena...is Sheriff Marlena Schultz from Orange County."

Deputy DA Weid took a breath and turned to his left.

"Some of you have met Robert...Bob, isn't it?...Bob Gauss from the State Division of Insurance Fraud. Welcome, Bob. Next to Bob is Washington-based attorney Jeanette Poulsen from the National Insurance Crime Bureau. To Ms. Poulsen's left is Bill Whitney from the California Department of Insurance. And beyond Bill is...ah..." Deputy DA Weid had to glance at his notes. It had been a flawless performance up to that point.

"Lester Greenspan," said the rumpled, bureaucratic-looking man. "Chief attorney for the citizen's group Coalition Against Insurance Fraud. Also out of Washington, officially liaising with your Operation SouthCal Clean Sweep."

Dar winced. *Liaising.*

"Next to Mr. Greenspan is someone whom we all know and love," said Deputy DA Weid, obviously intending to inject some energy and bonhomie into the sagging proceedings. "Our deservedly renowned and very lucky Los Angeles–based defense counselor W.D.D. Du Bois."

"Thank you, Dickweed," said Du Bois with a wide smile.

Weid blinked as if he had not heard correctly, and smiled back. "Ah...next to W.D.D....most of you law enforcement people know these two...are Trudy and Larry Stewart of Stewart Investigations out of Escondido."

"Lawrence," said Lawrence.

"And beyond Larry there," continued the Deputy DA, "is someone else whom a lot of us have met in the line of business, Mr. Darwin Minor, one of the best accident reconstruction specialists in the country and the driver of the black NSX we saw on the videotape. And at the end of the table—"

"Just a minute please, Dick," said Riverside County's Sheriff Fields. He was an older man with gunslinger eyes, and when he turned his gaze on Dar, the effect was obviously meant to be both freezing and wilting. "That was the most reprehensible and cold-blooded example of vehicular homicide that I have ever seen."

"Thanks," said Dar, returning the sheriff's electric stare amp for amp. "Only *they* tried to kill me in cold blood. My blood was very, very warm when I drove them off the road—"

"Just a minute!" commanded Deputy DA Weid. "Let me finish. And at the end of the table, I'd like to introduce Ms. Sydney Olson, chief investigator for the state's attorney's office and currently the leader of the Organized Crime and Racketeering Task Force's Operation South-Cal Clean Sweep. Syd...you have the floor."

"Thank you, Richard," the chief investigator said, and smiled again.

Stockard Channing, thought Dar.

"As most of you know," said the chief investigator, "for the last three months, the state has been carrying out a major investigation—Operation SouthCal Clean Sweep—in an attempt to crack down on the startling rise in insurance fraud claims in this part of the state. We estimate that insurance fraud this year alone is costing Californians about seven point eight billion dollars—"

Several of the sheriffs whistled respectfully.

"—and is driving up insurance rates at least by twenty-five percent."

"More like forty percent," interjected Lester Greenspan from the Coalition Against Insurance Fraud.

Sydney Olson nodded. "I agree. I think the state's estimates are far too conservative. Especially after the last six months or so."

Special Agent James Warren cleared his throat. "It should be noted that Operation SouthCal Clean Sweep is modeled after the Bureau's very successful 1995 Operation Clean Sweep in which we made more than one thousand arrests."

And probably four convictions, thought Dar.

"Thank you, Jim," said Chief Investigator Olson. "You're right, of course. We're also basing our operation on Florida's probe, Crash for Cash, where state officials arrested one hundred and seventy-four suspects, many of whom were found working in a single ring linked to fake accidents."

"Mostly slip-and-falls?" asked Trudy Stewart. "Or heavier stuff?"

"A lot of the suspects were repeat offenders on slip-and-falls," said Sydney. "But the big catch was a Miami attorney and his son who headed up an organized ring. They staged more than one hundred and fifty auto crashes, paying low-income individuals to collide with each other on the Florida highways and then filing spurious claims against the insurers through collaborating chiropractors or their own law firms."

"Nothin' new about that in Southern California," said Riverside County's Sheriff Fields in his gunslinger drawl. "Deal with that almost every damned day. 'Bout one out of every eight or ten of the accidents on I-15 through our county is staged. Not a damned thing new."

Chief Investigator Sydney Olson nodded in agreement. "Except for the fact that in the last few months there's been some sort of turf battle for control of organized insurance fraud."

"Groups?" said Sheriff Fields, squinting suspiciously.

Deputy DA Weid spoke. "In Dade

County, Florida, they discovered that it was largely the Colombians—the former drug runners—who were organizing the insurance fraud. We're running into the same thing with some of the organized Mexican or Mexican-American gangs in East L.A. and elsewhere."

"Figures," grumbled Sheriff Fields.

Captain Sutton of the CHP shook his head. "The majority of staged crashes aren't being headed up by our Latino gangs," he said quietly. "They tried to get into the action and got their butts kicked. Quite a few top *hommes* in body bags."

Sheriff Schultz from Orange County cleared her throat. "We've seen the same thing with organized Vietnamese crime. They want to dominate, but someone is muscling them out."

Special Agent Warren said, "And whoever it is that's been most successful in this turf war is bringing in Russian and Chechnyan mafia enforcers...all along the West Coast, but especially down here."

All eyes turned back toward Dar and those seated near him.

Lawrence made a coughing noise that usually preceded a longer statement from him. "Our company's hired Dar...Mr. Minor...Dr. Minor...to reconstruct several accidents that were obviously staged. He's been an expert witness in half a dozen cases and so have I."

Trudy was shaking her head. "But we haven't seen any sign of a highly organized ring in these fraudulent claims," she said. "It's just the usual assortment of losers and second- or third-generation insurance-claim parasites. They depend on it the way welfare addicts used to depend on their checks."

Deputy DA Weid looked at Dar. "There's no doubt that these two men in the Mercedes were not only Russian mafia imported as part of this turf battle, but that they were tasked to kill you, Mr. Minor."

Dar winced slightly at the use of the noun *task* as a verb. Aloud he said, "Why would they want to kill me?"

Sydney Olson turned sideways in her chair and looked Dar in the eye. "That's what we hoped you'd tell us. What happened yesterday represents the best lead we've had in several months of investigation."

Dar could only shake his head. "I don't even know how they could have *found* me. The whole day was crazy…" He quickly and concisely told of his 4:00 A.M. JATO-unit wakeup call, the meeting with Larry, and the interview with Henry at the Shady Rest Senior Mobile Home Park. "I mean…*none* of that day was planned. No one could have known that I'd be coming south on I-15 at that time of day."

Captain Sutton of the CHP said, "We found a cell-phone frequency scanner in the wreck of their Mercedes. They must have monitored your calls."

Dar shook his head again. "I didn't make or receive any cell phone calls after my meeting with Larry."

Trudy said, "Lawrence called in after he'd gotten the photographs of the stolen-car ring to say that you were covering the mobile home park interview."

Dar shook his head again. "Are you suggesting that the stupid JATO thing or the seventy-eight-year-old man falling from his Pard is part of a massive insurance-fraud conspiracy? And that someone would import Russians to kill me over it?"

Again Captain Sutton of the CHP spoke. For such a big man—he was at least six five—his voice was very soft. "The JATO thing, we cleared. The human remains in the wreckage—teeth—were ID'd as nineteen-year-old Purvis Nelson from Borrego Springs, who lives with his uncle Leroy. Leroy buys metal in job lots from the Air Force. Evidently someone at the Air Force base didn't notice that those two JATO units hadn't been used. Purvis did, though. He left his uncle a note..."

"A suicide note?" someone asked.

The Highway Patrol captain shook his head. "Just a note dated eleven P.M. that night saying that he was going to break the land speed record and that he'd see his uncle at breakfast."

"In other words, a suicide note," muttered San Diego County's Sheriff McCall. The sheriff looked at Lawrence. "The deposition mentions that when you and Mr. Minor met just before the shooting, you were on your way to document a stolen-vehicle transaction. A car-theft ring targeting Avis vehicles. Could this have been the cause of the attack on Mr. Minor?"

Lawrence laughed softly. "Sorry, Sheriff, but the Avis-theft thing was a strictly hillbilly family operation. You know, one of those good-old-boy Southern families where the family tree doesn't have any branches?"

None of the sheriffs, police captains, nor the FBI man smiled.

Lawrence cleared his throat. "Anyway, no, this bunch I was following wouldn't have any dealings with the Russian mafia. They probably don't even know Russia *has* a mafia. It was an inside job. Brother Billy Joe worked at Avis and, as part of the usual checkout procedure, got the address where the car renters were staying locally. Then brother Chuckie would take one of the agency's duplicate keys out and steal the vehicle—they liked sport utilities—that night. They'd meet in the desert with cousin Floyd, cleverly repaint the vehicle at a shop they had out there, and Floyd would drive it up to Oregon as soon as it was dry and resell it at a lot they legally owned up there. They'd change the license tags, but not the registration numbers on the vehicles. They were morons. I turned the photographs and notes over to Avis yesterday and they've given the info to local and Oregon police authorities."

Chief Investigator Olson raised her voice slightly to bring the conversation back on track. "Which means that none of yesterday's incidents were connected to the attempt on your life, Dr. Minor."

"Call me Dar," muttered Dar.

"Dar," Sydney Olson said, and made eye contact again.

Dar was struck again by how she blended professional seriousness with that hint of amusement. *Is it the sparkle in her eyes, or in the way she moves her mouth?* he wondered, and then shook his head to clear it. He had not slept well the night before.

"You've done *something*, Dar," she continued, "that's convinced the Alliance that you're on to them."

"Alliance?" said Dar.

Chief Investigator Olson nodded. "It's what we've been calling this fraud ring. It seems to be very extensive and well connected."

Sheriff Fields pushed back from the table and flexed his cheek and jaw muscles as if he were looking for a spittoon. "Extensive fraud ring. Operation Clean Sweep. Missy, you've got a bunch of the usual losers out there on the highway deliberately fender-bending other people's cars and then screaming whiplash. Nothing new. All this task force stuff is a waste of the taxpayers' money."

Chief Investigator Olson's face reddened slightly. She gave the old would-be gunslinger a stare that might have come from Bat Masterson. "The existence of the Alliance is a reality, Sheriff. Those two dead Russians in the Mercedes—ruthless mafia members who, according to Interpol, killed at least a dozen hapless Russian bankers and businessmen in Moscow and probably one overconfident American entrepreneur over there—those two dead Russians are real. The Mac-10 slugs in Dr. Minor's automobile are real. The ten billion or so extra dollars that fraud tacks on to the cost of California insurance...that's *real*, Sheriff."

The old man's gaze broke away from Sydney Olson's and his Adam's apple worked as if he were swallowing rather than spitting his chaw. "Yeah, no argument. But we all got pressing things to get back to. Where does this...Project Clean Sweep...go from here?"

Deputy DA Weid smiled. It was a good smile, a reassuring smile. A once and future politician's smile. "The task force is temporarily moving its headquarters to San Diego because of this incident," he said happily. "The media's screaming for the identity of the driver of the black NSX. So far we've actually kept a lid on the story, but tomorrow..."

"Tomorrow," said Sydney Olson, looking at Dar again, "we're going to release the official story. Some of it will be accurate, such as the fact that the two dead men were Russian mafia hit men. We'll say that their attempted target is a private detective—Dar's real identity and occupation will be kept secret from the press for obvious reasons—and we'll announce that we believe the killers were after him because he's close to uncovering their conspiracy. And after that announcement, I'll be spending quite a bit of time with Dr. Minor and Stewart Investigations."

Dar returned her challenging gaze. Suddenly she did not look as cute as Stockard Channing to him anymore. "You're staking me out like that goat in the dinosaur movie... *Jurassic Park*."

"Exactly," said Sydney Olson, smiling openly at Dar now.

Lawrence raised his hand like a schoolboy.

"I just don't want to find my friend Dar's bloody leg on my moon roof someday, okay?"

"Okay," said Sydney Olson. "I'll insure that doesn't happen." She stood up. "As

Sheriff Fields said, everyone has important duties to get back to. Ladies, gentlemen, we shall keep you all informed. Thank you for coming this morning."

The meeting was over, and Dick Weid looked nonplussed at not having wrapped it up himself. Sydney Olson turned to Dar. "Are you going home to Mission Hills now?"

He was not surprised that she knew where he lived. On the contrary, he was sure that Chief Investigator Olson had read every page of every dossier ever opened on him. "Yeah," he said. "I'm going to change clothes and then watch my soap operas. Larry and Trudy gave me the day off and I haven't had any other calls."

"Can I come with you?" asked Chief Investigator Olson. "Will you bring me along to your loft?"

Dar considered ten thousand obvious sexist responses and rejected them all. "This is for my own protection, right?"

"Right," said Sydney. She moved her blazer aside slightly, just enough to show the nine-millimeter semi-automatic tucked in the quick-release holster at her hip. "And if we hurry," she said, "we can grab some lunch on the way and still not miss any of *All My Children.*"

Dar sighed.

5

"E IS FOR TICKET"

We've only known each other a couple of hours," said Syd, "and already you've lied to me."

Dar looked up from where he was grinding coffee beans at his kitchen counter. They had grabbed a bite to eat at the Kansas City BBQ—Syd's suggestion, she said she'd been staring at it from the Hyatt for two days and just the sign made her hungry—and then he'd driven her up to his old warehouse building in Mission Hills. He'd parked his Land Cruiser at his spot on the open ground floor, just a huge, dark room with a maze of pillars, and they had taken the large freight elevator—the only elevator in the building—up to his sixth-floor apartment.

Now he just looked at her as she wandered through the living area between the tall bookcases that delineated areas in the loft.

"So far I've counted…what?…about seven thousand books," continued Syd, "no fewer than five computers, a serious sound system with eight speakers, and eleven chessboards, but no TV. How do you watch your soaps?"

Dar smiled and spooned ground beans into the filter. "Actually, the soaps usually come to me. It's called 'taking statements from witnesses or victims.' "

Chief Investigator Sydney Olson nodded. "But you *do* have a TV somewhere? In the bedroom, maybe? Please say you do, Dar. Otherwise I'll know I'm in the presence of the only real intellectual I've ever met outside of captivity."

Dar poured water into the coffeemaker and turned it on. "There's a TV. In one of the storage closets over there near the door."

Syd cocked an eyebrow. "Ah…let me guess…the Super Bowl?"

"No, baseball. The occasional night game when I'm home. All of the play-offs and the Series." He set mats on the small, round kitchen table. Bright light came in through the eight-foot windows.

"Eames chair," said Syd, patting the bent wood and black leather chair in the corner of the living-room area where two walls of bookcases came together. She sat in it and put her feet up on the wood and leather ottoman. "It feels comfortable enough to be a real one ... an original."

"It is," said Dar. He set two white, diner-type mugs on the tablemats and then poured coffee for both of them. "You take cream and sugar?"

Syd shook her head. "I like James Brown coffee. Black. Rich. Strong."

"Hope this suffices," said Dar as she reluctantly got out of the Eames chair, stretched, and came over to join him at the kitchen table.

She took a sip and made a face. "Yeah. That's it. Mr. Brown would approve."

"I can make a new batch. Weaker. Saner."

"No, this is good." She turned around to look back across the room and into the other areas of the loft that were visible. "Can I play chief investigator for a minute?"

Dar nodded.

"A real Persian carpet delineating your living area there. A real Eames chair. The Stickley dining room table and chairs look original, as do the mission-style lamps. Real artwork in every room. Is that large painting in the open area there opposite the windows a Russell Chatham?"

"Yeah," said Dar.

"And an oil rather than a print. Chatham's originals are selling for a pretty penny these days."

"I bought it in Montana some years ago," said Dar, setting his coffee down. "Before the big Chatham stampede."

"Still," said Syd and finished her mental inventory. "A chief investigator would have to conclude that the man who lives here has money. Wrecks an Acura NSX one day but has a spare Land Cruiser waiting for him at home."

"Different vehicles for different purposes," said Dar, beginning to feel irritated.

Syd seemed to sense this and turned back to her coffee. She smiled. "That's all right," she said. "I'm guessing you're about as interested in *making* money as I am."

"Anyone who discounts the importance of money is a fool or a saint," said Dar. "But I find the pursuit of it or the discussion of it boring as hell."

"Okay," said Syd. "I'm curious about the eleven chess boards. Games being played on all of them. I'm only a duffer at chess—I know the horsie from the castle thingee—but those games look like they're master level. You have so many chess master friends drop in that you need multiple boards?"

"E-mail," said Dar.

Syd nodded and looked around. "All right, that wall of fiction. How are those books shelved? Not alphabetically, that's for damned sure. Not by publication date, you've got old volumes mixed in with new trade paperbacks."

Dar smiled. Readers always gravitated to

other readers' bookshelves and tried to figure out the system of shelving. "It could
be random," he said. "Buy a book, read it,
stick it on the shelf."

"It could be," agreed Syd. "But you're
not a random kind of guy."

Dar sat silently, thinking of the chaos
mathematics that had made up the bulk
of his Ph.D. dissertation. Syd sat silently
studying the wall of novels. Finally she
muttered to herself, "Stephen King way
up on the upper right. Truman Capote's *In
Cold Blood* a couple of shelves below, still
on the right. *To Kill a Mockingbird* on the
second shelf from the bottom. *East of Eden*
way the hell to the left over by the window.
All of Hemingway's crap—"

"Hey, watch it," said Dar. "I love Hemingway."

"All of Hemingway's crap on the bottom
right shelf," finished Syd. "I've got it!"

"I doubt it," said Dar, feeling his feathers
ruffled again.

"The bookcase is a rough map of the
United States," said Syd. "You shelve re-
gionally. King's up there freezing his ass off

near the ceiling in Maine. Hemingway's down there near the floor heating vent, comfortable in Key West…"

"Cuba, actually," said Dar. "Impressive. How do you shelve your novels?"

"I used to do it according to the relationship between the authors," she admitted. "You know, Truman Capote right next to Harper Lee…"

"Childhood friends," added Dar. "Little, weakling Truman was the model for Dill who visits every summer in *Mockingbird*."

Syd nodded. "With the dead authors it worked all right," she said. "I mean, I could keep Faulkner and Hemingway the hell apart, but I always had to keep moving the live ones around. I mean, one month Amy Tan's tight with Tabitha King, and the next thing I read, they're not talking. I was spending more time reshelving my books than I did reading, and then my work started to suffer because I was frittering away my days worrying if John Grisham and Michael Crichton were still good buddies or not…"

"You're so full of shit," Dar said in a friendly tone.

"Yep," Syd agreed, and lifted her coffee mug.

Dar took a breath. He was enjoying himself and he had to remind himself that this woman was here because she was a cop, not because of his devastating charm. "My turn," he said.

Syd nodded and sipped.

"You're about thirty-six, thirty-seven," he said, starting with the riskiest territory and rapidly moving on. "Law degree. Your accent's fairly neutral, but definitely devoid of back east. A little midwestern left in the corners of your vowels. Northwestern University?"

"University of Chicago," she said, and added, "And I'll have you know that I'm only thirty-six. Birthday just last month."

Dar went on. "Chief investigators for even local district attorneys are some of the best enforcement people around," he said softly, as if to himself. "Former U.S. marshals. Former military. Former FBI." He looked at Syd. "You were in the Bureau for what? Seven years?"

"Closer to nine," said Syd. She got up,

went to the coffeemaker, and came back to pour them both more of the thick, black stuff.

"Okay, reason for leaving…" Dar said, and stopped. He did not want to make this too personal.

"No, go ahead. You're doing fine."

Dar sipped coffee and said, "That glass-ceiling sexism thing. But I thought the Bureau was getting better."

Syd nodded. "They're working on it. In ten more years, I could have been as high as a real FBI person could get—right under the political crony or career pencil-pusher that some president appoints as director."

"Then why did you leave…" Dar began, and then stopped. He thought about the nine-millimeter semi-auto on her hip and the quick-release holster. "Ahhh, you enjoy *enforcement* more than…"

"Investigation," finished Syd. "Correct. And the Bureau is, after all, about ninety-eight percent investigation."

Dar rubbed his cheek. "Sure. And as the state's attorney's chief investigator, you get to investigate to your heart's content and then go kick the door in when it comes time."

Syd gave him a dazzling smile. "And then I get to kick the felons who were hiding behind that door."

"You do a lot of that?"

Sydney Olson's smile faded but did not disappear. "Enough to keep me in shape."

"And you also get to run interagency task forces like Operation SouthCal Clean Sweep," said Dar.

Her smile disappeared instantly. "Yes," she said. "And I'd be willing to bet that you and I share the same opinion of committees and task forces."

"Darwin's Fifth Law," he said.

She raised an eyebrow.

"Any organism's intelligence decreases in direct proportion to the number of heads it has," said Dar.

Syd finished her coffee, set the mug carefully on the mat, nodded, and said, "Is this Charles Darwin's law or Dr. Darwin Minor's law?"

"I don't think that Charles ever had to sit

on a committee or report to a task force," said Dar. "He just sailed around on the *Beagle*, getting a tan while ogling finches and tortoises."

"What are the rest of your laws?"

"We'll probably stumble across them as we go along," said Dar.

"Are we going to be going along?"

Dar opened his hands. "I'm just trying to find this movie's plot. So far it's fairly formulaic. You're setting me up as bait, hoping that the Alliance will sic more mafia killers on me. But you have to protect me. That must mean you'll be staying within sight twenty-four hours a day. Good plot." He looked around his living room and in toward the dining area. "Not sure where you'll sleep, but we'll think of something."

Syd rubbed her brow. "In your dreams. Darwin. The San Diego PD will be sending extra patrols by at night. I was supposed to take a look at your living arrangements and give a…quote…*security-wise sitrep*…end quote, to Dickweed."

"And?" said Dar.

Syd smiled again. "I can happily report

that you live in an almost abandoned warehouse where only a few units have been converted to condos or lofts. There's no security on the stairways...unless you count sleeping migrant winos as guards. There's little light and zero security on the ground floor where you park your Sherman tank of a sport utility vehicle. Your door's all right—reinforced, with three good locks and a police bar—but these windows are a nightmare. A blind sniper using a rusted Springfield without a scope could take you out. No drapes. No shades. No curtains. Are you a closet exhibitionist, Dar?"

"I like good views." He stood and looked out the kitchen window. "From up here you can see the bay, the airport, Point Loma, Sea World..." He trailed off, realizing how unconvincing he sounded.

Sydney joined him at the window. He caught a faint whiff of some scent she was wearing. It was nice—more like the woodsy smell of the forest near his cabin after a rain than heavy perfume.

"It is a beautiful view," she said. "I need

to call a cab and get back to the Hyatt so I can make some phone calls."

"I'll drive you..."

"The hell you will," said Syd. "If this is going to be a buddies movie, you've got to shelve the chivalry right up front." She used the kitchen phone to call a cab.

"I thought you weren't going to be protecting me twenty-four hours a day," said Dar. "How can it be a buddies movie?"

Syd patted him consolingly on the shoulder. "If the snipers don't get you and the Russian mafia doesn't cut your throat in that killing ground you call a parking area and the crackheads don't kill you just for the hell of it, then phone me the next time Stewart Investigations calls you out on an interesting case. Officially we'll be looking for patterns of collision and accident insurance fraud."

"Unofficially?" said Dar.

"Well, I guess there is no 'unofficially,' " said Syd, hitching up her heavy purse and walking to the door. "Dickweed's given me some office space in the courthouse. I'd officially appreciate it if you'd drop in there tomorrow morning so we can decide how we're going to check through your case files." She jotted her number on a card. "And maybe I'll get a glimpse of something that will explain why our late friends in the former Mercedes thought you were worth taking out."

"They probably confused me with some other guy who owns an NSX and didn't pay his gambling debts at the MGM Grand," said Dar.

"Probably," said Syd, turning back toward him and the apartment as they got to the door. He unlatched it. "How many books *do* you have in here, Dr. Minor?"

Dar shrugged. "I quit counting after six thousand."

"I probably owned that many once," said Syd. "But I gave them all away when I became a chief investigator. Travel light, that's my motto." She stepped into the hallway and pointed a finger at him. "I'm serious about you dropping in at the office tomorrow and then calling me as soon as you get a good case call." She handed him one of her cards with her Sacramento office number written on it and her pager number. The San Diego courthouse office number was penciled in.

"Sure," said Dar, studying her card. It was an expensive one but did not give a home phone number. "But remember, you asked for it." He looked up. She had already walked away and disappeared out of sight around the bend in the corridor, heading for the freight elevator. Her soft-soled shoes had made almost no noise on the concrete floor.

"You asked for it," Dar said again and went back into his loft.

"Olson here," answered her sleepy, almost drugged-sounding voice after the fifth ring.

"Rise and shine, Chief Investigator," said Dar.

"Who is this?" Sydney's sleepy voice ran the last two syllables together.

"How soon we forget," said Dar. "It's one forty-nine A.M. You said you wanted to come the next time I was called out on a case. I'm dressed and ready to go. I'll give you five whole minutes before I pick you up in front of the Hyatt."

There was a pause. Dar could hear her breathing softly. "Dar...you remember that I said an *interesting* insurance case. If this is some jackknifed eighteen-wheeler out on I-5—"

"Well, you know, Chief Investigator Olson," said Dar, "You never really know if something's *interesting* until you go look and see. But Larry's going, too, and he rarely asks me to meet him at a site."

"Okay, okay," mumbled Syd. "I'll be outside in five minutes."

"Four minutes now," Dar said, and hung up.

The highways were relatively empty as Dar took surface streets over to the 5 and then north past La Jolla.

"Have you heard of La Jolla Joya?" said Dar as the washes of light from the sodium vapor highway lights moved across his windshield and both their faces.

"Sounds like a stripper's stage name," said Syd, still rubbing her cheeks to wake up.

"Yes," said Dar, "but actually it's the San Diego area's newest rock concert venue. It's in the hills west of the highway up here…actually it's closer to Del Mar, but I guess the Del Mar Joya didn't have quite the same ring."

"It doesn't have much of a ring as it is," said Syd. Her voice carried the fatigue of someone who had been working eighteen-hour days.

"True. But that's where we're headed. Concert's probably over by now, but there's at least one dead body there."

"Stabbing?" said Syd. "Some Hell's Angels thing like Altamont? Or just someone crushed when the herd stampeded?"

Dar grinned despite himself. "We wouldn't get called for either of those. See, the city ordinances kept cracking down on rock concerts at their usual stadiums and venues—especially the heavy-metal ones—and—"

"Who's headlining tonight?" she interrupted.

"Metallica," said Dar.

"Oh, goody," said Syd with precisely the

same enthusiasm as someone who's just been told he has to take a barium enema.

"Anyway," continued Dar, "a would-be superpromoter bought these hundred and sixty-two acres of scrub gully and fenced it all in. It's sort of an arroyo, plenty of room for parking out front, stage on the flat area, and a gentle hill running up until it's just trees and cliffs. He put in lights, stage, sound towers, and three thousand seats, and there's a nice grassy hillside for umpty-thousand others who want to sit on blankets or whatever. They added a lower fence to keep people off the back twenty acres or so, the woods, after their first concert. Some older patrons complained of fornication going on back in the darkness."

"Which the complainers would have to have sought out with night-vision goggles in order to see," said Syd.

"Yeah. But the promoter thought it would still be safer to separate the audience area from the woods and the rock cliffs. That's why Larry and Trudy's client called them."

"They're on retainer for the promoter?"

"No."

"For the insurance company that covers the concert liability?"

"No."

"For Metallica?"

"No."

"I give up," said Syd. "Whose ass are we rushing out to cover?"

"The fence company's," said Dar.

Most of the concert patrons were leaving as Dar drove the Land Cruiser up the dusty ditch against the traffic flow to get to the concert area. Metallica had long since bussed itself to wherever Metallica dwells when not on stage, but a few score dazed, sleepy, and doped fans still milled around in front of what had been the bandstand. Dar saw the emergency lights at the far rear of the arroyo and headed that way. A California Highway Patrol officer stopped them at a gate in the low fence that separated the grassy seating area from the fornication woods, looked over their credentials in the beam of his six-battery flashlight, and then waved them through.

The emergency vehicles—several CHP cars with their flashers going, two ambulances, a sheriff's car, two tow trucks, and a full fire truck—were gathered at the narrow end of the V of the arroyo. Douglas firs rose thirty and forty feet here, hiding the stars and the top of the cliffs. In the cone of the cruiser spotlights and emergency lights, Dar could see the smashed remnants of an upside-down pickup truck, an older Ford 250 from the looks of it. He parked the Cruiser, pulled a powerful flashlight from the backseat, and he and Syd walked toward the lights, identifying themselves twice more to get past groups of officious cops and bands of yellow accident-scene tape.

Lawrence walked over to them.

"Damn," said Dar. "How'd you beat me here?"

Lawrence smirked under his mustache. "Not so hot now without your NSX, are you?"

"Syd, you remember Larry Stewart from this morning's meeting?" said Dar.

"Lawrence," said Lawrence. "Good evening, Ms. Olson."

"Hi, Lawrence," said Syd. "What do we have here?"

Lawrence blinked in happy surprise for a moment and then said, "Belaboring the obvious, one hellaciously smashed Ford F 250. Driver dead. Was ejected through the windshield and thrown approximately eighty-three feet. I paced it off, so the number's not exact." He pointed his own flashlight toward a mob of people standing and crouching around the corpse of a man at the base of a tree.

"He drove into the cliff face in the dark?" said Syd.

Lawrence shook his head. Suddenly a CHP officer joined them.

"Sergeant Cameron," said Dar, surprised. "You're far from home tonight."

"Well, if it isn't the Mercedes-killer," said Cameron to Dar. He touched his cap in Syd's direction. "Howdy, Ms. Olson. Haven't seen you since the L.A. task force meeting last month." Cameron hooked his thumbs in his belt until the leather creaked. "Yeah, well, I was moonlighting here—working crowd security—and just as the concert was ending, someone found this mess."

"Anyone hear it happen?" asked Dar.

Cameron shook his head. "But that doesn't mean much. During a Metallica concert, with those speakers and amplifiers cranked up, you could set off a Hiroshima-sized tactical nuke back here and nobody would've heard it."

"Alcohol?" said Lawrence.

"We can see about ten empty beer cans in the smashed passenger compartment of the pickup," said Cameron. "There are another eight or nine thrown free...like the driver."

"Could he have driven into the cliff wall?" asked Syd.

Lawrence and Sergeant Cameron both shook their heads at the same time. "See how the truck is mashed down?" said Lawrence. "The thing fell from up there."

"It drove *over* the cliff?" said Syd. "From above?"

"It would have to have backed over to end up in this position," said Dar. "That's why the driver was thrown west...*toward* the concert. The truck landed tail first—you can see how it crumpled—and ejected the driver like a cork out of a champagne bottle before the cab crushed."

Sydney Olson walked closer to the crushed pickup truck and watched as an emergency crew finished attaching two cables from the two tow trucks to the undercarriage. "Stand back," called one of the CHP officers, "we're gonna lift it."

"You have pictures?" Dar asked Lawrence.

Lawrence nodded and patted his Nikon. "This is going to be the interesting part," he said very softly.

"What is going to be..." Syd began, and then said. "Oh, my God."

Beneath the wreckage of the pickup truck was the body of a second man. His head and right arm and right shoulder had been smashed almost flat. His left arm was broken in a compound fracture that looked as if it had happened before the flattening. He was wearing a T-shirt but was naked from the waist down—or rather, his pants were bunched around his ankles at the top of his work boots. A dozen searchlights and flashlights were trained on the corpse and Sydney Olson said, "Oh, my God" again.

The man's legs and exposed torso were scratched in a hundred places. There was a folding knife open and protruding from his thigh. The wound had bled heavily. The man had the end of a length of clothesline tied clumsily around his waist and there must have been a hundred more feet of the clothesline lying on and around the body. Worst of all, three feet of a thick branch—a holly branch—protruded from the corpse's rectum.

"Yes," said Dar. "Interesting."

Photographs and measurements were taken. The police officers and rescue workers milled and discussed, discussed and milled. The medical examiner and a county coroner both pronounced the man dead. This was a relief to some of the onlookers. Debates raged as to how exactly this accident had played itself out.

"No one has a fucking clue," whispered Sergeant Cameron.

"This is crazy," said Syd. "Like some satanic cult thing."

"No, I don't think so," said Dar. He went over to talk to the fire fighters. Five minutes later they had moved the long fire-truck ladder and extended it to the top of the cliff, invisible through the branches to the onlookers below. Darwin, Lawrence, and two of the CHP officers clambered up the ladder with powerful flashlights. Five minutes after that, they scrambled down the ladder—all except for Dar, who stayed twenty-five feet up and waved at the fireman at the controls. The ladder swiveled into the thick tree branches, taking Dar with it, and he ducked the heavier boughs and shined his flashlight back and forth.

"Here," he called at last.

Syd squinted up, but could not make out what Dar was touching and then photographing. Lawrence was looking through small binoculars he had pulled from a flap pocket of his safari shirt.

"What is it?" asked Syd.

"It's the guy's underpants caught on a

branch," said Lawrence. "Sorry," he added, offering her the binoculars. "Want to look?"

"No, thanks."

Fifteen minutes later, the discussions were over, the bodies were being put in body bags and carried by stretcher to separate ambulances, and everyone seemed satisfied. Lawrence walked back to the Land Cruiser with Dar and Syd. His Isuzu Trooper was parked just beyond Dar's truck.

"All right," said Sydney Olson, sounding slightly irritated. "I don't get it. I couldn't hear you talking to the officers. What the hell happened here?"

Both men stopped walking and started talking at the same time. "Go ahead," said Dar. "You tell the first part."

Lawrence nodded. His large hands opened and gestured as he started the explanation. "Okay, basically, these two guys drank their eighteen or twenty cans of beer and tried to crash the concert. No tickets, but they knew about an old fire road and decided they could come in the back way after dark. But the back way is fenced by our client. A ten-foot-high wooden fence up there."

Syd stared back toward the cliff and the darkness. They were lifting the smashed pickup onto a flatbed truck now.

"They accidentally drove through the fence?" she said, her voice thin.

"Uh-uh," said Lawrence, shaking his head. "They backed the pickup right against the fence and the driver—a skinnier guy—boosted his pal over. But it was real dark up there, and when the bigger guy went over, he found that it was a thirty-foot fall. So he came crashing down through those tree branches..."

"And that killed him?" said Syd.

Lawrence shook his head again. "Naw, he hit a big branch about forty feet up. That was probably when he broke his arm. The branch had snagged him by his undershorts and part of his belt."

"He still didn't realize how high he was," added Dar. "Looking down in the dark, he could see the tops of the shorter trees and probably thought they were bushes that would break his fall."

"So he cut himself out of his shorts," said Lawrence.

"And fell another twenty feet," said Syd.

"Yeah," said Lawrence.

"But that didn't kill him," said Sydney, speaking in a tone that suggested she now knew that she was the straight man.

"Nope," said Lawrence. "That just scratched him up something terrible as he fell through the branches. Plus that was also when his own knife was jammed three inches into his thigh and that holly branch got rammed up his ass. Pardon my French."

"And then what?" said Syd.

"Dar, you figured it out first," said Lawrence. "Why don't you tell the finale."

Dar shrugged. "There's not much more. The driver could hear his friend crying in agony down there. He realized what a drop it must have been. The big guy's screams of pain must have been drowned out somewhat by the Metallica concert, but the driver knew he had to do something."

"So he..." prompted Syd.

"So he took the length of old clothesline that was lying in the back of the pickup, threw it down to his friend, and told him to tie it securely around his waist," said Dar. "That's my guess. Actually, it wouldn't have been that easy or succinct. There would have been a lot of drunken shouting and cursing and crying going on, but the bigger guy wrapped the line around his middle twice and tied it off with a granny knot, while the skinny guy tied the other end of the rope securely to the rear bumper of the F 250."

"And then..." said Syd.

Dar tilted his head as if the rest was obvious. It was. "Well, our skinny driver was very drunk and very rattled. He accidentally put the truck in reverse, gunned it, drove backwards ten feet through our client's high fence—the tire tracks up there speak for themselves—and dropped backwards forty-some feet onto his buddy, catapulting himself eighty-five feet out through the windshield in the process."

"E-mail me your report in the morning

and I'll write the official version and send it to our client," said Lawrence.

"I'll have my analysis to you by ten A.M.," said Dar.

Sydney shook her head. "You do this for a *living?*"

6

"F IS FOR FOREPERSON"

The first phone call came in a little after 5:00 A.M.

"Damn," said Dar. He didn't really consider it morning until sometime between 9:30 and 10:00 A.M., sitting over coffee and a second bagel, behind the morning paper.

The phone rang again.

"Hello?"

"Mr. Minor, this is Steve Capelli with *Newsweek* magazine. We'd like to talk to you about—"

Dar slammed the phone down and rolled over to catch a little more sleep.

The second call came in two minutes later.

"Dr. Minor, my name is Evelyn Summers...perhaps you've seen me on Channel Seven...and I was hoping that you would—"

Dar would never know what Evelyn was hoping because he hung up, turned the ringer off on the phone, and walked over to the window. Along with the San Diego Police patrol car that had been parked inconspicuously across the street all night, there were now three very conspicuous TV trucks. A fourth truck with a satellite antenna on its roof pulled up as Dar watched.

He walked back to his phone, and recorded a new message on the answering machine: "Yo, dis is Vito. Dere's nobody home but me an' the Dobermans. You got sometin' to say to me...say it! Otherwise, hang the fug up."

Dar went into the bathroom to shower and shave. Ten minutes later, dressed and holding a steaming mug of coffee in his hand, he looked out the front window again. There were five TV trucks and four vans parked across the street. Well, he thought, it had taken them forty-eight hours to get his name from the DMV based on the tag number from his poor NSX;

somebody at one of the news channels must have a contact in the department. Dar doubted if the reporter had been lucky enough to get a copy of his driver's-license photograph, but he wasn't going to stroll out front to find out. The phone light blinked on and off. Dar started packing his duffel bag, folding shirts and trousers and humming the theme to *The Godfather* as he did so.

Upon arriving at the Justice Center, Dar saw that Deputy DA Weid had been his usual generous self in setting up a temporary office for the visiting state's attorney's chief investigator. Sydney Olson's "office" was in the basement of the old section of the Hall of Justice, not far from the holding cells, a former interrogation room with puke-green and white-faded-to-yellow walls randomly decorated with scuff marks and smashed-mosquito abstract art going back to the 1940s, some folding tables and metal chairs, and no windows except for the bit of reflective one-way glass. But the folding tables were covered with modern machines—a Gateway top-of-the-line laptop, Dar noted, connected to printers, scanners, and other peripherals. There were also two new phones, each with at least four lines. A map of Southern California had been tacked to the filthy rear wall and had already sprouted an array of red, blue, green, and yellow pins. A male secretary, busy at a second computer, informed Dar that Investigator Olson had been called to the district attorney's office, but she had left word that she would be back in an hour and would like to talk to Dr. Minor before he left the building.

The secretary offered Dar some coffee from the inevitable pot scorching away on the table under the one-way mirror. Cop coffee was 180 percent caffeine and the texture of road tar on a hot summer day, and he had long since decided it was the secret weapon that kept America's law enforcement agencies going despite the long hours, miserable working conditions, lowlife clients, and terrible pay. Dar took a healthy swig, feeling tired and grumpy.

"I'll check back later," said Dar.

Finding an empty bench in the basement corridor, Dar fired up his ThinkPad and finished typing his report on the Metallica concert accident. He attached the modem umbilical to his digital cell phone, dialed up Stewart Investigations' dedicated line, and e-mailed the report straight to their fax machine/printer so that they would have a hard copy waiting.

Putting the laptop back in its case, Dar pondered how he could kill another half hour. Making up his mind, he walked to the end of the corridor past holding cells full of prisoners who were howling like mutts in a kennel, and then jogged up the polished steps into the handsome old Gothic courthouse itself. Unlike the efficient and butt-ugly new addition to the Hall of Justice where Dickweed and others had their offices, the old courthouse lacked air-conditioning but made up for it with a regal bearing.

Dar had told Syd Olson the day before that he enjoyed soap operas. While he almost never watched television, he did tune in to the criminal and civil cases being tried in the old courthouse between his own appearances as expert witness. As he slipped into courtroom 7A and took his place at the rear of the room, he nodded at several senior citizens whom he recognized as fellow courtroom addicts.

It took him only a few minutes to get up to speed. This was a sexual harassment trial...a female employee claiming that the owner of the small company for which she worked had been making sexual overtures. About half the jurors looked heavy-lidded and ready for a nap in the stultifying heat as witness after witness droned on about the employer's sexist habits. A receptionist in her twenties testified that the boss had more than once stated in her presence that the plaintiff—a secretary in her midforties—"gave good phone."

Ten minutes later it was the plaintiff's turn to testify. The woman looked like Dar's high-school Latin teacher—old-fashioned glasses on a bead chain, a conservatively tailored suit, a huge bow at the neck of her white blouse, sensible shoes, and dull blonde hair done up in a bun. She seemed to be a truly private and modest person, and her expression suggested that she regretted having ever started this proceeding.

Her attorney led her through a series of questions as the defendant, an oily little ferret in a triple-knit suit, sat slumping and smirking at his table. The plaintiff's answers were so soft that twice the judge had to ask her to speak up to be heard over the creaking of the old fans turning overhead. Several jurors were close to succumbing to afternoon naps. Dar knew the judge—His Honor William Riley Williams—sixty-eight years old and with so many wrinkles and jowls melting into one another that he looked like a wax effigy of Walter Matthau that had been left too close to an open flame. But Dar also knew that Judge Williams had a keen mind behind that somnolent and bored visage.

The plaintiff's attorney closed in for the kill. "And what, exactly, Ms. Maxwell, was the final incident in your employer's established pattern of inappropriate behavior which served as the catalyst in your bring-

ing this long-overdue request for legal relief?"

There was a pause while the plaintiff,
the jury, and the silent onlookers worked
to translate the legalese into English.

"You mean what did Mr. Strubbins do
that finally made me bring this lawsuit?"
said Ms. Maxwell at last, her voice so soft
that everyone in the courtroom who was
awake, including Dar, leaned forward
slightly.

"Yes," said her attorney, switching to
English.

Ms. Maxwell reddened. The flush
started at her neck above the white bow of
her blouse and moved up into her cheeks
until she was a bright red.

"Mr. Strubbins said...made an indecent
proposal to me."

Judge Williams, his chins and jowls
propped on one mottled hand, asked her
to repeat the answer a bit more loudly. She
did so.

"Would you characterize this indecent
proposal as obscene?" asked the plaintiff's
attorney.

"Oh, yes," said Ms. Maxwell, her blush deepening. She looked down at her hands where they were clenched on her lap.

"Would you please tell the court precisely what this obscene proposal was?" asked her attorney, turning toward the jury in anticipatory triumph.

Ms. Maxwell looked down at her hands for a long moment and then said something inaudible. Dar and the few spectators leaned farther forward. Several of the regular geezers turned up the volume on their hearing aids.

"Could you repeat that a bit more loudly, Ms. Maxwell?" requested the judge. Even his voice sounded like Walter Matthau's.

"I'm too embarrassed to say it out loud," said the secretary, blinking rapidly behind her cat's-eye glasses.

Her attorney wheeled around with a startled expression. This obviously had not been part of the game plan. At the defense table, Mr. Strubbins smirked and whispered something to his poker-faced attorney.

"May I approach the bench, Your

Honor?" asked Ms. Maxwell's attorney, trying to regain his courtroom equilibrium and not lose the moment. There was a brief sidebar during which the defense attorney spluttered, the plaintiff's attorney gesticulated and ran on in an urgent whisper, and Judge Williams listened with drooping eyelids and a silent scowl.

After a moment, the attorneys were shooed back to their places and the judge turned to the blushing plaintiff. "Ms. Maxwell, the court understands your reticence to repeat what you have characterized as an obscene proposal, but since your case demands that the court and jury know precisely what Mr. Strubbins is alleged to have said to you, would you write it out on a piece of paper?"

Ms. Maxwell paused, then nodded, still blushing wildly.

The spectators groaned and sat back in their hard pews. Dar watched as the bailiff brought a pen and a stenographer's notebook. Ms. Maxwell wrote on a page for what seemed like many minutes. The bailiff tore that page out of the notebook and handed it to the judge. The judge looked at the page with no change in expression and then beckoned the two attorneys forward. Both lawyers read the page without comment. The bailiff took the piece of paper and carried it over to the jury box.

The juror in the first seat was a woman, also wearing glasses, very tall and thin but surprisingly buxom, dressed in a black business suit and white blouse, her hair also tied back in a bun.

"You may give the paper to the foreman of the jury," said Judge Williams.

"Foreperson," said the woman in the first seat, sitting up even more rigidly than before.

"I beg your pardon?" said the judge, raising his chins and jowls from his cupped hand.

"Foreperson, Your Honor," repeated the first juror, her thin lips almost disappearing as they became even thinner and primmer.

"Oh," said Judge Williams. "Of course. Bailiff, please give the paper to the foreperson of the jury. Madam Foreperson, please pass it on to the other jurors, including the alternates, after you have read the message on it."

All eyes in the courtroom were riveted on Ms. Foreperson as she read the note, the muscles around her pursed lips twitching as if she had suddenly tasted something very, very sour. She shook her head as she handed the paper to the juror on her left.

Dar had noted earlier that Juror Number Two—an over-weight man wearing a madras sport jacket—had been on the verge of dozing off. Now the man sat with his arms folded above his ample belly, his eyes downcast. He was not quite snoring. Dar knew that dozing jurors was not an uncommon phenomenon in jury trials, especially on hot summer days. He had seen it many times himself, even while he was testifying in what amounted to murder trials.

Madam Foreperson elbowed Juror Number Two, whose head snapped up and eyes opened. Unaware that all eyes in the courtroom were on him, he turned to the buxom professional woman, took the piece of paper, and read it. Eyes widening, he read it again. Then he turned his head slowly back toward Madam Foreperson, gave the woman a wink and a nod, folded the piece of paper, and put it in his jacket pocket.

There was enough silence in the courtroom to carve into cubes and sell to schoolteachers by the pound. All heads swiveled back to the judge and the bailiff.

The bailiff started to walk back toward the jury box, paused, and looked to Judge Williams for direction. The judge started to speak, stopped, and rubbed his jowls. The plaintiff looked as if she were about to slide down out of sight in the witness box out of pure mortification.

Judge Williams said, "The court will take a ten-minute recess." He banged his gavel and disappeared in a flurry of robes as all the spectators stood, the geezers elbowing one another and wheezing with quiet laughter.

The jury filed out. Juror Number Two was still smirking and winking at Madam Foreperson, who looked back once over her shoulder at Number Two, rolled her eyes, and then disappeared from view, radiating chill into the air.

Back in Syd's basement interrogation-room office, Dar found Chief Investigator Olson hard at work. The secretary had stepped out. A portable fan and the open door alleviated the worst of the stuffiness, but fifty years of close encounters of the third kind between sweating felons and equally sweaty cop interrogators still left a hint of miasma in the little room.

"Thanks for waiting to see me," she said. "The DA and Dickweed showed me the morning papers. I see they've quit calling you the Road Rage Killer."

Dar poured himself a bit more cop coffee, and said, "Right. Now I'm the Mysterious Detective."

"Let's see how good a detective you are," Syd said, and gestured toward her map with the red, blue, green, and yellow thumbtacks. "Can you tell me what the legend is for my little tactical command center map here?"

Dar pulled his reading glasses out of his sport coat pocket and then peered over the top of them. "Red and blue are on roads—mostly freeways, not surface streets. So I'd guess...swoop-and-squats?"

Syd nodded, impressed. "Mostly swoop-and-squats. Can you tell the difference between the reds and blues?"

"Nope," he said. "There are a lot more reds than blues...Wait a minute, I remember this one on the I-5 here. It was a fatality accident. Ancient blue Volvo. Unemployed green-card immigrant driving. All the trappings of a swoop-and-squat, but the driver of the squat car died."

"All the red pins are swoop-and-squats with fatalities," said Syd.

Dar whistled softly. "So many? That doesn't make much sense. Swoop-and-squats are usually staged on surface streets, not freeways. Too dangerous on freeways—someone has to be alive to collect the money."

Syd nodded. "What about the green pins?" she said.

Dar studied the location of the more numerous greens. Two seemed to be out in San Diego Harbor. Another three were clustered together in an unlikely spot in the bare hills east of Del Mar. Others were scattered around the L.A. and San Diego metropolitan areas and much of the area in between. None were on roads.

"Construction-site accidents," said Dar. "The two in the bay looked at first like possible fraud cases because of the high coverage, but in each case they were long falls from scaffolds — both fatal. Nasty."

"Still fraudulent, though," said Syd.

Dar gave her a doubtful look. "I investigated the one at the aircraft carrier," he said. "The painter working for the civilian contractor had a history of fraudulent claims, but in this case he took a header sixty-five feet into a pile of steel pipes. His family didn't need the money that bad. The whole family was making a good living with slip-and-falls and swoop-and-squats."

Syd smiled and crossed her arms. "How about the yellow pins?"

"There's only one on the map," said Dar. "The others are all over here in the margins waiting their turn."

"And?"

"And the one on the map is above Lake Elsinore, about where The Lookout Restaurant is perched, so I'd guess yellow has something to do with me."

"Correct. Actually, the yellow pins will mark points where someone has tried to kill you."

Dar raised an eyebrow and looked at the margin of the map. Another dozen yellow pins were waiting.

"I need to visit Lawrence and Trudy's place," Syd said briskly, gathering up her huge shoulder bag and setting her personal computer in a carrying case. "I know roughly where they live out by Escondido, but I'd rather ride with you."

Dar shook his head. "I could get you out to Escondido, but I'm not coming back to the condo tonight. The media..."

"Oh, yes," said Syd with a smile. "I watched some of their stakeout on the seven A.M. local TV news. They still don't have a picture of you. It's driving them bug-fuck."

"Bugfuck?" repeated Dar. He rubbed his chin.

"How did you get out of there this morning without being mobbed?"

"The police who were on duty outside the warehouse kept them on the main street below," said Dar. "I just drove the Land Cruiser out the back way and through some alleys before coming down the hill."

"They probably have the tag number for your Toyota as well," said Syd.

It was Dar's turn to nod. "But I parked way and hell in the rear of the secure Hall of Justice lot," he said. "Right under the drunk-tank holding cell windows."

Syd made a face.

"Yeah, I know," said Dar. "I'll wash the truck tomorrow. But I don't think the media will see it there."

"All right," said Chief Investigator Olson, "but why can't you give me a ride out to the Stewarts' place?"

Dar sighed. "I can," he said, "but you'll

have to get back on your own. I'm headed up to my cabin in the hills after work."

"That's perfect," said Syd. "We'll stop by the Hyatt to pick up my stuff."

Dar frowned.

The chief investigator paused by the door to explain. "You still have San Diego cops tasked to protect you around the clock, but if you head for your cabin in the hills, we're out of their jurisdiction. We can't really ask some local county sheriff to use his manpower guarding you—"

"Look, I never said I wanted—" began Dar.

Syd held up her hand. "While I, on the other hand, will not only serve as a perfect bodyguard this long weekend, but will use the time properly going through your computerized and hard-copy case files to find the missing link here."

Dar looked at her for a long moment, seeing the two of them reflected in the mirrored window. He wondered who might be watching from behind the one-way glass.

"Do I have a choice?" he said at last.

"Of course you do," said the chief investigator, giving him the warmest smile he had seen so far. "You're a free citizen."

"Good—" began Dar.

"Of course, you're a free citizen facing a possible arraignment on vehicular manslaughter, and the court has ordered twenty-four-hour protective surveillance on you. So I guess you're free to decide whether you drive or let me drive," said Syd.

Lawrence and Trudy worked out of their home in a development not far from Escondido. Stewart Investigations, Inc., was a sprawling, two-level ranch house on a steep, ice-plant-covered hill above a county road that ran down to the development golf course. Neither Lawrence nor Trudy played golf. In truth, Lawrence and Trudy did very little that did not relate to their insurance investigation work or their one source of relaxation—auto racing. The house itself held more than forty-five hundred square feet of space, but most of the usable space was a clutter of offices upstairs and down for the man-and-wife team. The Stewarts' cathedral-ceilinged living room had been empty of furniture for the first three years Dar had known them.

He parked the Land Cruiser in front of a driveway filled with vehicles—Lawrence's old Isuzu Trooper, Trudy's leased Ford Contour, Lawrence's Ford Econoline surveillance van with its tinted windows, two race cars—one on a trailer and the other in the three-car garage, sitting next to a tarp-covered '67 Mustang covertible—and two Gold Wing motorcycles.

"These all theirs?" asked Syd as they walked up the drive through the pantheon of vehicles.

"Sure," said Dar. "They used to have a couple of later-model Mustangs, but sold them when they got the race cars."

"What kind of racing?"

"A special class using old Mazda RX-7s," said Dar. "Larry races in California, Arizona, Mexico…wherever they can get to in a weekend."

"Trudy always goes along?"

"Lawrence and Trudy do *everything* together," said Dar.

Dar rang a buzzer under an intercom. While they waited, Syd looked at the surrounding houses on the hill.

"No sidewalks," she said flatly.

Dar raised an eyebrow. "You new to California, Investigator?"

"Three years," said Syd. "But I still hate the idea of no sidewalks."

Dar gestured toward the seven vehicles in the driveway and open garage. "Why the hell would anyone in California need a sidewalk?"

"Come on in," said Trudy's voice over the intercom. "We're in the kitchen."

When Syd and Dar trekked through the acres of unused living room, scarcely used dining room, and overused work areas to the kitchen, Stewart Investigations was taking a coffee break. Lawrence was on a stool, hunched over the counter with his elbows on the Formica and his face red with concentration. Trudy was standing behind the counter but leaning toward her massive husband as if they were involved in a fierce but friendly contest of wills.

"Olds Rocket Eighty-eight," said Trudy in a bass growl.

"Toyota Rav Four," answered Lawrence in a mincing falsetto. He waved Dar and Syd toward two empty stools at the counter and gestured toward the coffeepot and clean mugs. As the two guests poured some coffee for themselves, Lawrence growled, "Pontiac Grand Prix."

"Mitsubishi Galant," said Trudy, now using the falsetto voice. "Mercury Cougar," she growled back, as if slamming a ball over the net.

Lawrence hesitated.

"Ford Contour," said Syd in a tone several octaves higher than her usual pleasant speaking voice.

"Ah, Jesus," said Dar.

"Shhh!" said Trudy. "You'll break the rhythm. Go ahead, Investigator Olson. Your serve."

"Ah, same letter," mused Syd. In a lumberjack's growl she said, "Dodge Charger!"

"Honda Civic," replied Lawrence in an exaggerated sissy voice. Then he roared, "Chevy Impala!"

"Infiniti!" said Trudy.

"Isuzu Impulse," minced Syd.

Trudy pointed. "Your point. Impulse is wimpier and more stupid than Infiniti. You can serve any letter."

"Ford Thunderbird," yelled Syd.

"Ford Taurus," cried Lawrence.

"Toyota Tercel," said Trudy triumphantly. She banged her coffee cup down and frowned at her husband. "Taurus means bull, Larry. A bull has balls. What's a Tercel, anyway? Some kind of bird? It means nothing."

"Lawrence," said Lawrence.

"Are you guys finished with the testosterone-estrogen game?" asked Dar.

"Nope," said Trudy. "It's forty-love. My serve." She paused only a second. "American Motors Eagle!"

"It's not produced anymore," said Dar.

Everyone ignored him. Obviously he did not understand the rules.

"Escort," lisped Lawrence.

"Hyundai Elantra!" said Trudy as if slapping down a trump card.

"Suzuki Esteem," said Syd.

Both Lawrence and Trudy nodded, giving Syd the point.

"What's wimpier than calling a car an 'Esteem'?" said Trudy. "Especially a piece of Suzuki junk. It's like naming a car, 'My Pride.' "

"When I was a teenager," said Dar, "I drove a big-finned 1960 Chrysler New Yorker that my girlfriend named 'Beatrice.' "

The other three looked at him as if he had passed wind.

"Where were we?" said Lawrence.

"Two points from match point," said Trudy. "Syd or me. I'll serve." She paused only a second. "Pontiac Firebird..."

"Ford Fiasco," snapped back Lawrence. "Nothing wimpier than a Fiasco."

"Ford Fiestas aren't being produced anymore," said Syd. "Now they're Festivas."

"Your point, your serve," said Trudy.

"Buick Roadmaster," growled Syd, drawing out the syllables in "master."

"Rav Four," said Lawrence.

"Foul," said Trudy. "You already used that one." She paused. "R's a tough one... Plymouth Reliant?"

"Too tough," said Lawrence.

"All I can think of is the Buick Reatta," said Syd. "And that's not sissy enough, even if it doesn't mean anything."

"RX-7 is sort of wimpy," said Trudy.

"Hey!" said Lawrence, sounding sincerely hurt. He raced rebuilt RX-7s.

"Why don't I serve?" suggested Dar. "Whoever wins this one, wins."

"Agreed," said the other three.

"Q45," said Dar.

"That's a new car," protested Trudy. "And there's nothing especially sexy about..."

"Q45," repeated Dar. "It's in play. *Go*."

There were several seconds of silence.

"VW Quantum," said Syd.

"Wow," said Trudy. "Winner."

"Not so fast," said Dar. "Alfa Romeo Quadrifoglio."

The others squinted at him suspiciously.

"It's real," said Lawrence at last. "I

worked a wreck of one on the 410 three years ago…"

"We *know* it's real," said Trudy. "We're just trying to decide if it's…"

"I win," said Dar.

"Who made you judge and jury?" said Lawrence pleasantly enough.

Dar smiled tightly. "I'm not judge and jury," he said. "I'm just the foreperson." He looked meaningfully at the boxes of files that were stacked in the other room. "Can we go to work now on finding out which case might have made the Russian mafia want to kill me?"

7

"G IS FOR WHIZ"

Three hours and eighty files later, Lawrence sat back in his chair and said, "I give up. What the hell are we looking for?"

"Fraudulent claims," said Syd, gesturing toward the stack of files they had separated under just that heading.

"That's sixty-some percent of what we deal with," said Trudy. "None of these in which Dar did the accident reconstruction seem important enough to warrant killing him."

The chief investigator nodded. Her eyes looked tired. Dar noticed that she wore rimless glasses when she read.

"Well," said Dar, "you can't say it's dull reading."

Syd nodded. "These accident victim reports are masterpieces, all right. Listen to this one—'The telephone pole was approaching fast. I was attempting to swerve out of its way when it struck my front end.' "

Trudy opened a file. "Here's one of my favorites—'I had been driving my car for forty years when I fell asleep at the wheel and had an accident.' "

Dar pulled an old file out. "This fellow's never heard of the Fifth Amendment—'The guy was all over the road. I had to swerve several times before I hit him.' "

Lawrence grunted and flipped through the file he had been skimming. "My claimant's been watching too many *X-Files* episodes—'An invisible car came out of nowhere, struck my vehicle, and vanished.' "

"I had an *X-File* one," said Syd, flipping through the thick blue folders. "Here—'The accident happened when the right front door of a car came around the corner without giving any signal.' "

"I hate it when that happens," said Dar.

"Notice how accident victims love passive voice in their depositions?" said Trudy. "Here's a typical one—'A pedestrian I did not see hit me, then went sliding under my car.' "

"But they're honest, in a stupid way," said Lawrence. "I remember taking this bozo's statement—'Coming home, I drove into the wrong house and collided with a tree I don't have.' "

Trudy was giggling as she read. " 'I pulled away from the side of the road, glanced at my mother-in-law in the other seat and headed over the embankment.' "

"I understand that one well enough," rumbled Lawrence.

Trudy quit giggling and gave him a look.

Syd suddenly laughed aloud. "Here's a possible case of overkill," she said, flipping to a statement transcript. " 'In an attempt to kill a fly, I drove into a telephone pole.' "

"We're getting silly, people," said Dar, glancing at his watch.

"We started silly," said Trudy. She looked at the stack of fraudulent claims. "Do we have anything that looks at all likely?"

"Two, I think," said Dar, pulling dossiers from the teetering pile. "Remember the rebar case on the I-5 in May?"

"What's that?" said Syd.

"Rebar is steel rods used to reinforce concrete," intoned Lawrence.

"I know what rebar is," said the investigator. "What's the case?"

"May twenty-third," said Dar, skimming through the file. "I-5 twenty-nine miles north of San Diego."

"Oh, God," said Lawrence. "You did the reconstruction video graphics for that, but I was one of the first on the scene. Jesus."

Syd waited.

"Asian guy, Vietnamese, just arrived in the States with his family—eight kids—three months earlier, working as a delivery driver for a florist, has one of those cab-forward Isuzu delivery vans with the engine under the seat, nothing in front of him except Plexiglas and a thin sheet of tin," said Lawrence, grimacing as he remembered. "He was tailgating an open truck owned by a little construction firm out of La Jolla—Burnette Construction, strictly a family business—Bill Burnette, the owner, driving a load of rebar."

"Sticking out behind the trailer bed?" asked Syd.

"By eight feet," said Lawrence. "It was red-flagged, but..." The insurance investigator took a breath. "The poor Vietnamese guy was tailgating, doing about fifty-five, when someone swerved in front of Burnette's truck and Burnette hit the brakes...hard."

"And the Vietnamese guy didn't," said Syd.

Dar shook his head. "No, he did, but the brakes didn't work. No fluid."

Syd exchanged glances with the others; this type of accident was rare.

"Bound bundles of rebar came through the windshield and front of the van and speared the delivery guy in four or five places," said Lawrence. "Dragged him right out through the shattered windshield. Burnette's truck hadn't stopped—was still doing thirty or so when the collision happened—and he told me he could see this poor son of a bitch hanging back there from the rebar…impaled in the face, throat, chest, left arm…"

"But still alive," said Dar.

Lawrence nodded. "For the time being. Burnette didn't know what to do, but he had the presence of mind not to hit the brakes again. That would have impaled the poor guy, Mr. Phong, even worse. So he pulled to the side of the road and gently slowed down with this poor devil dangling back there."

"That couldn't possibly be a swoop-and-squat," said Syd. "Not with the squatter *behind* the rebar truck. Plus there's no place for the squatter to squat and hide…"

"That's what we thought," said Trudy. "But when Dar did the reconstruction, it sure looked like a deliberate swoop. Very light traffic. A white pickup crossed two lanes, swooped in front of the Burnette vehicle, slammed on his brakes, and then accelerated away down an off ramp."

"Was he trying to get to the off ramp?" said Syd.

Trudy shook her head. "Ramp was on the right. The accident happened in the far left lane of five lanes. And the traffic was so light that there seemed to be no reason for the victim, Mr. Phong, to be tailgating the way he was. Several lanes were open. It *looks* like a swoop-and-squat set-up..."

"But the idea isn't to kill or permanently maim the 'victim' in a swoop-and-squat," Syd said. "They're supposed to be rear-ended in some sort of reinforced car and then claim whiplash or something, not be impaled from the front by rebar. Did Mr. Phong die?"

"Yeah," said Lawrence. "Three days later, without regaining consciousness."

"What was the settlement?" asked the chief investigator.

"Two point six million," said Trudy.

Lawrence sighed. "Burnette was running his construction company on a shoe-string and took the lightest coverage he could afford. The settlement drove him into bankruptcy."

Syd looked at the other file.

"This is also one of your red pins," said Dar. "The one on the I-5 that I mentioned. This is definitely a swoop-and-squat—the rear-car driver, Mr. Hernandez, had three disability and eight personal injury claims pending."

"But also a fatality," said Syd.

"Yeah," said Dar. "Everything went according to script up to the impact. Again, a pickup swooped in front of the squat car—a big old Buick—and hit its brakes. The target car, a new Cadillac, slammed into the rear of Hernandez's Buick just as planned. But then Hernandez's Buick exploded..."

"I thought that only happened in the movies," said Syd.

"Just about," said Dar. "But my investigation found remnants of a crude battery-driven spark igniter in the gas tank of Mr. Hernandez's Buick. It was rigged to ignite after any sharp contact with the rear bumper."

"Murder," said Syd.

Dar nodded. "But in each case, the lawyer—who was the same lawyer, by the way—had lawsuits against both the other driver and the car maker, so the evidence of brake tampering and sabotage of the

Hernandez car was dismissed in exchange for dropping the lawsuits against the manufacturers."

"I've been curious," said Syd, "about how they pick the target vehicle for these swoop-and-squats."

Trudy spoke. "Several factors. Expensive car, of course..."

"Especially one with a State Farm or other big insurance sticker on the bumper," said Lawrence.

"Usually older drivers," said Trudy. "Someone who doesn't react too quickly and will brake when they shouldn't."

"They don't want to hurt the people in the target vehicle, of course," said Dar. "The idea is for the accomplice in the squat vehicle to claim the disability—usually invisible injuries such as whiplash or lower back, although insurance companies are getting tougher about that."

"But the classic swoop-and-squat here—Hernandez—ended in the death of the driver," said Syd. "And the Phong accident doesn't fit the swoop-and-squat profile..."

"It's true," said Dar, shaking his head. "It

seems inconceivable that he would volunteer to collide with a load of overhanging
rebar."

"Unless it was his first time," said Syd.
"Unless he was set up. And Mr. Hernandez…"

"Found in the typical squat position,"
said Trudy. "Hunkered down under the
wheel. The trunk of the old Buick was
filled with sandbags and tires, typical re-
inforcement for a squat car to buffer the
impact. But it all burned—including Mr.
Hernandez—when the gas tank exploded."

"Settlement?"

"Six hundred thousand," said Lawrence.

"So now we come to the lawyer for both
cases, Mr. Jorgé Murphy Esposito," said
Syd. "We've known for a long time that
he's a pure ambulance chaser…"

Trudy laughed. "Esposito could dispatch
ambulances," she said. "He knows where
the accidents are going to happen before
they happen."

Syd nodded. "Dar, do you think Esposito's the one siccing the Russians on you?"

Dar sighed. "My gut instinct says no. Esposito's small time. He works with the usual underclass of fraud claimants. I just don't see him branching out and playing the game on the level high enough to justify using Russian mafia hitmen."

"But this is a lead," said Sydney. "Who are the other lawyers and doctors high on your list?"

"Our fraudulent-claims list?" asked Trudy.

"Yeah."

"Besides Esposito, there's Roget Velliers, Bobby James Tucker, Nicholas van Dervan, Abraham Willis—" began Trudy.

"Uh-uh," interrupted Lawrence. "Willis is dead."

Dar raised an eyebrow. "Since when? I testified in a case against his plaintiff just a month ago."

"Since last Thursday," said Lawrence. "The good counselor died in a single-car wreck up near Carmel."

"Well, live by the sword..." said Syd.

"Esposito's handling the family's lawsuit," said Lawrence.

Trudy grunted softly. "Professional courtesy."

Syd got up from the table and stretched. "Well, we'll cross-check Dar's files with these and try to see which of these ambulance chasers is most involved."

Trudy looked at the two of them. "Are you headed back to San Diego?"

Dar only shook his head.

Syd said, "We're hiding out from the press up at Dar's cabin for the weekend."

Lawrence did not exactly waggle his eyebrows, but the look he gave Dar might as well have been a leer and a wink. "Been a long time since you had anyone up there, isn't it, Darwin? Besides us, I mean."

"I've never had anyone up there besides you," said Dar, with a warning look. "It seems that I'm in protective custody."

There was a silence. Then Trudy said brightly, "Oh...before you go...Investigator Olson..."

"Syd," said Syd.

"Syd," continued Trudy. "Could you give us your professional opinion on a piece of surveillance tape?"

"Sure," said Syd.

"Aww, Trudy, no," said Lawrence. His face reddened behind his mustache. "Jeez…"

"We need an opinion," said Trudy.

"Aww, no," said Lawrence. He took his glasses off and wiped them with a handkerchief while his face grew redder and redder.

"It's just over an hour of tape," Trudy said to Syd, "but we'll fast-forward it. Dar, you've testified in a lot of these cases. I'd like your opinion as well."

Dar and Syd followed Trudy into the real living room where the 60-inch TV and the reclining La-Z-Boys were.

The half-inch VHS tape opened with a steady shot of a woman, early middle age, dressed in Lycra tights, gym shorts, and tennis shoes, walking out of a middle-class tract home and getting into a battered old Honda Accord. The camera zoomed in on the subject's face, but the woman was wearing dark glasses and a scarf over her hair, so it was difficult to get a clear image of her.

The video was in color with a digital read-out in the lower right corner of the screen giving the date, hour, minutes, and seconds.

"Shot from your surveillance van?" Syd asked Lawrence.

"Mmm," said Lawrence, who had not joined the group on the La-Z-Boy couch but was standing back toward the dining room, as if ready to flee.

Trudy cleared her throat. "The woman's name is Pamela Dibbs. She has three lawsuits pending—two of them relating to clients of ours, Jack-in-the-Box and WonderMart."

"Disability claims?" said Syd.

"Yes," said Trudy as the video showed the Accord driving away. There was a jump cut to the same Accord pulling into a parking space outside a large building. Lawrence had obviously known her destination and beaten her there in his Astrovan surveillance vehicle. The camera zoomed as Ms. Pamela Dibbs walked hurriedly toward the building.

"Three slip-and-falls," said Trudy. "She's claiming massive lower-back trauma that has left her housebound…essentially an invalid. She has affidavits from two doctors supporting this…Both the doctors work with Lawyer Esposito."

Syd nodded.

Suddenly the camera view shifted: no longer color, the rough black-and-white image wobbled as someone carried the camera down a corridor. The picture was relatively clear, but distorted—as if shot through an anamorphic lens.

The camera view panned right and all at once there was a reflection in a wall of mirrors: Lawrence—all 250 pounds of him—in a ragged sweatshirt, gym shorts, bare legs, knobby knees, and tattered sneakers. He was wearing a fanny pack, had a kerchief tied around his brow Rambo-style, and was sporting a pair of oversized, heavy-framed sunglasses. The reflection seemed startled and then Lawrence looked himself up and down in the mirror for a long moment before moving into the main exercise room.

"Shit," said Lawrence softly from behind the couch.

"Where's the camera?" asked Syd. "In the glasses?"

"Part of the glasses' frame," said Trudy. "Tiny little lens, hardly bigger than a rhinestone. The fiber-optic cable runs down to the recorder in his fanny pack."

"Where's the wire..." Syd began, and then said, "Oh." Lawrence's reflection was turning away from gazing at himself and now she could see the "sunglass cords" which hung down behind Lawrence's neck, disappearing under the collar of the sweatshirt.

They watched in real time as Lawrence joined the exercise group, standing one mat directly behind Ms. Dibbs. There was no sound, but one could imagine the music blaring its beat as the group began its warm-up exercises. Ms. Dibbs squatted, thrust, kicked, did jumping jacks, and ran in place quite nicely for a totally disabled person. She had taken her own sunglasses and scarf off and her face was quite clear in the mirror that faced the exercise group. The group leader was a woman in spandex tights, and the thong running between the muscled hills of her buttocks was also very visible in the mirror. Also visible—amidst all the women in black Lycra—was Lawrence hopping, squatting, huffing, and swinging his arms, always a beat or two behind Ms. Dibbs and the rest of the squadron. He was still wearing his sunglasses, of course.

"Are you asking my advice on this for legal reasons?" said Syd.

"Yes," said Trudy, holding the VCR remote in her right hand as if ready to pull it away if Lawrence lunged for it.

"Well, you've obviously got the goods on her," said Syd, "but you can't use it if this is a private recreation facility. It would be as illegal as videotaping her on a trampoline in her own backyard."

Trudy nodded. "It's a city exercise facility. Public property."

"And you cleared it with the manager there?"

"Yep."

"And the class is open to anyone in the community?"

Trudy looked up at the video where Ms.

Dibbs and the entire group of buffed-up young women had dropped into a quick squat, arms straight ahead of them. In the mirror, Lawrence tried to follow suit, almost lost his balance, pinwheeled his arms, and gained the squat just as the rest of the group hopped up and began more leg kicks. The video was in black and white, but Lawrence's face in the mirror was darkening, sweat stains beginning to appear through the thick sweatshirt cotton.

"I don't see any problem then," said Syd. "You can show this to the court and jury as long as it isn't edited."

"*That's* the problem," Trudy said, and began fast-forwarding through the tape.

Lawrence made a growling noise behind them.

After the set of exercises was over, Lawrence's point-of-view camera slogged slowly into the mirror-lined hallway and swooped down on a drinking fountain. The camera picked up his reflection as he wiped his mouth, removed the glasses for a second, showing his feet, and then set the camera lens back in place as he mopped his cheeks and forehead with the kerchief. He was pouring sweat.

"He should have left then," said Trudy in a monotone.

Lawrence growled, "It wouldn't have been polite. And I paid for the entire session. And I wanted to show Ms. Dibbs working out for the full hour."

"Well," said Trudy, "you did." She increased the fast-forward to high speed. The workout became a frenzied thrashing of Lycra-clad arms and legs, buttocks thrusting, thighs rippling—and several beats behind all this near-erotic sweaty female motion, the reflected image of the overweight, mustached man in sunglasses earnestly trying to keep up, breathing through his mouth now, his face so dark that the camera was showing the constant reddening without the benefit of color. Still in fast motion—three more breaks, three more trips to the drinking fountain. Then the fourth and final break before the end of the tape. The digital readout showed that the class had been exercising for forty-eight minutes.

The women broke ranks. Some ran in place during the break. Some chatted in groups. Ms. Dibbs was one of the runners. Lawrence, in subjective-camera, trudged out to the hallway again, there was a flash of reflection of him at the water fountain, sweatshirt now living up to its name, totally soaked through, face so dark that it looked like he was going to bust a blood vessel, and then the camera turned away from the drinking fountain and the exercise room, down the mirrored corridor, through a door marked MEN...

Syd started laughing.

"OK," yelled Lawrence from the dining room. "You can turn it off, Trude. They get the idea."

Trudy put it into fast-forward again. The camera seemed to rush at one of the urinals, looked down while gym shorts were tugged out of the way, then the view shifted to the tiles above the urinal, then down, then up again, then down, the final flips and tucking away, over to the sink, Lawrence's reflection in the mirror, still wearing the Jack Nicholson shades, the time-readout still flicking away in ghostly digital numbers, then back to the exercise room for the last few minutes of exercise. He followed Ms. Dibbs out to the parking lot. The claimant seemed invigorated by the workout and almost skipped to her Honda. The camera seemed to be lurching dangerously, once pausing by a fencepost where Lawrence's hand came into view, hanging on for support.

Syd was still laughing. "Nothing... nothing personal," she managed to say, raising her voice so Lawrence could hear in the kitchen, where he had retreated beyond the dining room.

"You see the problem," said Trudy.

Syd was rubbing her cheeks. "You can't edit video shown in a courtroom," she said, her voice shaking in its attempt to stay steady. "It's all or nothing."

"I goddamn *forgot*," yelled Lawrence from the kitchen.

"You can do it over," said Dar.

"We think Ms. Dibbs has made Larry," said Trudy.

"Lawrence," came the voice from the

kitchen. "And *you* can damn well do it over, Trudy."

Trudy shook her head. "I was the one who took Ms. Dibbs's statements. It looks like this is it."

"Well..." began Syd.

"I'd use it," said Dar. "Counting the van surveillance tape, it's almost an hour before we get to the...X-rated part. I don't think the jury or the claimant's attorneys will let you show that much. They'll want to shut it off as soon as possible."

"Yeah," agreed Syd. "Just put it in the record that there's another forty minutes of tape or whatever. I think you're safe."

"Easy for you guys to say," came Lawrence's voice from the kitchen.

Syd caught Dar's eye. "If we're going to get all the way up to Julian and your cabin by nightfall, we should get going."

Dar nodded. On his way out, passing through the kitchen, he patted Lawrence on the back. "Nothing to be ashamed of, amigo."

"What do you mean?" growled the big man.

"You washed your hands after," said Dar. "Just like our mommas taught us. The jury will be proud of you."

Lawrence said nothing but was staring daggers at Trudy now.

Dar and Syd climbed into the Land Cruiser and headed for the hills.

8

"H IS FOR PREPARATION"

Dar and Syd took Highway 78 from Escondido into the wooded mountains, stopping in the little town of Julian for dinner before going on to the cabin. Julian had once been a small mining town and now it was an even smaller tourist town, but the restaurant Dar chose served better than decent food in ample amounts for a decent price and had no large bar, so even on a Friday evening it was not filled with boisterous locals. The owner knew Dar and showed them to a table in a bay window of what had been the main parlor of an old Victorian home. The place served good wine. Syd knew the pros and cons of the vintages, she chose a bottle, and they shared an excellent merlot over conversation.

The conversation itself surprised Dar. Over the years he had become a master at subtly turning the focus on the other person; it was amazing, really, how easily people could be steered into talking about themselves for hours on end. But Chief Investigator Sydney Olson was different. She responded to his questions with a brief summary of her years with the FBI and an even briefer description of her failed marriage—"Kevin was also a special agent, but he hated fieldwork and that was all I wanted to do." Then she hit the ball back in his court.

"Why did the NASA review board fire you when you told them that some of the *Challenger* astronauts had survived the initial explosion?" she asked, holding her wineglass in both hands. Her nails, Dar noticed, were short and unpolished.

He gave her what Trudy had once called his "Clint East-wood smile." "They didn't fire me," he said. "They just replaced me quickly before I could put anything in writing. At any rate, I was just a junior member of the support staff for the real review board."

"All right, then," said Syd, "tell me how you *knew* that some of them had survived the explosion only to die after the fall."

Dar sighed. He saw no way out of some exposition. "Are you sure you want to talk about this over dinner?"

"Well," said Syd, "I suppose we could discuss poor Mr. Phong getting rebarred right out of the cab of his Isuzu van, but I'd rather hear about the *Challenger* investigation."

Dar did not comment on her use of "rebar" as a verb. He explained briefly about his doctoral work in physics.

"Shaped plasma events?" said Syd. "As in explosions?"

"Precisely as in explosions," agreed Dar. "They didn't really understand much about the dynamics of plasma wave fronts in those days because the analytical use of chaos mathematics—what they call 'complexity theory' today—was in its infancy."

"So you became an expert on chaos at the wave end of explosions?" said Syd.

"And other extremely high temperature events, yes," said Dar.

"Is there much demand for that sort of expertise in the job market?"

Dar sighed and set his wineglass down. "More than you can imagine. Shaped charges was the 'in' thing in armaments at the time. Ask the Iraqis in their Russian tanks after the American sabot round penetrated eight inches of armor and detonated in a shaped explosion."

"I don't suppose they're around to ask," said Syd.

"No."

"So you joined the National Transportation Safety Board," she said. "With your Ph.D. it sounds like you were overqualified."

"Unfortunately," said Dar, "there are more plasma events in commercial aviation than we like to think about. And it takes some training to work backward in deductive steps because the dynamics of the explosion itself have to be completely understood."

"Lockerbie," said Syd. "Or TWA Flight 800."

"Exactly," said Dar.

The waiter came by and cleared their plates. When their cups of coffee arrived, Syd said, "So that got you to the higher echelons of the NTSB and that put you on the staff of the *Challenger* Commission. So how did you know that they survived the explosion?"

"I didn't *know*," said Dar. "At first. It's just that I was more aware of how resilient the human body is in explosions. Most explosions are like leaps from tall buildings—it's not the fall that kills you..."

"It's the sudden stop at the end," supplied Syd.

Dar nodded. "The actual blast is not necessarily damaging to a human body that is restrained as tightly as the astronauts were in their couches. They're strapped in tighter than a NASCAR driver, and you see the horrific wrecks those guys walk away from."

Syd nodded. "So you think the poor teacher and some of the others survived that horrendous main fuel tank explosion?"

"No, not the teacher," said Dar, and even after all these years he felt the twinge of sadness. "She and another astronaut were on the lower deck, directly in the force of the blast. They probably died very quickly if not instantly."

"NASA made a point of saying that they all must have died without knowing what hit them," said Syd.

"Yeah. The whole country was in shock. That's what we all wanted to hear. But even in the first hours after the explosion, it was apparent from video and radar of the falling debris that the main crew cabin—the upper deck, so to speak—had stayed intact through the whole two-minute-and-forty-five-second fall to the water."

"An eternity," muttered Syd, her eyes becoming cloudy. "And you said that you *know*..."

"PEAPs," said Dar.

"Peeps?"

"Personal egress air packs. Essentially they're tiny little oxygen bottles that the astronauts use in case of sudden depressurization. They weren't wearing space suits, remember... The *Challenger* Commission made that recommendation after studying the tragedy. That's why John Glenn and all the others who've flown since have gone up in space suits, just like the early astronauts..."

"But these PEAPs...?" Syd's voice was very small and held none of the voyeuristic thrall that Dar had heard in so many people's tone when discussing fatal accidents.

"They recovered them from what was left of the main cabin," said Dar. "Actually, they recovered almost all of the shuttle. They rebuilt it in pieces on wood and wire frames just like we do airliners after the fact... but anyway, yes. Five of the PEAPs had been used... two minutes and forty-five seconds' worth. The exact time from the explosion until impact on the ocean."

Sydney closed her eyes for a second.

When she opened them, she said, "Couldn't that have been some sort of automatic thing…"

Dar shook his head. "The PEAPs had to be activated manually. In fact, the command pilot couldn't turn his own on without help. The astronaut behind him—the other woman aboard—would have had to loosen her harness straps and lean forward to turn his on from behind. And his had been used."

"My God," said Sydney.

They drank coffee in silence for a minute.

"Dar…" she began.

Dar could not remember if she had used his first name before, but he suddenly noticed it now. Her tone was different.

"Dar," said the chief investigator, "all this stuff about me coming to the cabin to protect you. All the eyebrow waggling back at Lawrence and Trudy's. You need to know that I'm not—"

"I know you're not," began Dar, a bit irritated.

Syd held up her hand. "Please, let me

finish. I'm telling you up front that I'm not looking for a romantic liaison and I'm certainly not looking for a roll in the hay. I like joking with you because you've got a sense of humor drier than the Borrego Desert, but I'm not going to play games."

"I know—" Dar began again, but again she silenced him with a raised palm.

"I'm almost through," Syd said very quietly. No one was at the nearby tables, and the waiter was far across the room. "Dickweed really did want to bring you up on vehicular manslaughter charges..."

"You're shitting me," said Dar. "Even after seeing the videotape?"

"*Because* of the tape," said the chief investigator. "It was the kind of case that even an asshole like Dickweed could win. Obvious road rage..."

"Road rage!" said Dar, angry now. "Those were Russian mafia hit men. They found their automatic weapons in the goddamn wreckage. And besides, this whole 'road rage' phenomenon is a load of crap, you know that, Olson. There's not a higher percentage of traffic-related assaults today than there was two decades ago—"

Syd used both palms now to calm him. "Yes, yes...I *know* that. Road rage has everything to do with how the news anchors enjoy the alliteration and almost nothing to do with facts. But Dickweed might still have brought charges just because road rage is a popular topic these days and it would have got him TV coverage..."

"Road rage," muttered Dar, sipping coffee so as not to say what he felt about the assistant district attorney and his political ambitions.

"Anyway," continued Syd, "I sold them all on using you as...well...as bait in uncovering this larger fraud ring that the state has been after. Dickweed and his boss saw that as an even bigger media plus than a road rage trial. But it meant that you either had to be kept under constant surveillance or protective custody..."

"Or be watched by you," said Dar.

"Yes," said Syd. She sat in silence for a

long moment. Then she said, "And I know about the Fort Collins crash."

Dar just looked at her. Part of him was not surprised—she had access to a hell of a lot of background dossiers, and his background would be important for her to check on in her ongoing case, but another part of him curled up in pain at the mention of something he never spoke about to anyone.

"I know it's none of my business," Syd said, her voice even softer than before, "but it said in the report that you were actually called to the scene of the crash. How could that be? How could they have done that?"

The muscles around Dar's mouth twitched an imitation of a smile. "They didn't know that...that my wife and baby were on that flight when it went down. Bar...my wife had planned to come back from Washington the next day, but her mother had recovered faster than anyone expected. She just wanted to get home a day earlier."

There was a silence, broken by loud

laughter from the bar. A young couple walked by on their way out. They were holding hands.

"You don't have to talk about it," said Syd.

"I know," said Dar. "And I haven't. Even to Larry and Trudy, although they know the basic facts of it. But I'm answering your question…"

Syd nodded.

"So that's it—my wife and the baby were supposed to arrive the next day…but they boarded this earlier flight—a 737 that went nose first into a park on the outskirts of Fort Collins."

"And you were called," said Syd.

"I was on the NTSB GO-team that staged out of Denver," said Dar, his voice without emotion. "We covered any crash in a six-state region. Fort Collins is only about seventy miles from Denver."

"But…" Syd began, and stopped. She looked down at her coffee cup.

Dar shook his head. "That was my job…looking at plane wrecks. Luckily, someone in the Denver office got a first look at the flight manifest and noticed my wife's name. They notified my team's supervisor only about half an hour after I got to the scene. But there wasn't much to see anyway. The 737 went in nose-first. The crater was almost twenty feet deep and sixty feet across. There was a lot of the usual crash detritus—shoes, always many shoes, a burned teddy bear here and there, a green purse—but most of the human remains had to be retrieved by archaeologists."

Syd looked up. "And it's one of the few accidents that the NTSB didn't solve...didn't find a clear cause for."

"One of four, counting TWA 800," said Dar softly. "Wind shear was suspected... and the FAA recommended changing certain control connections to the rudder of the Boeing 737s after that...but nothing seemed to explain such a sudden and complete loss of control. When they came to get me, I was actually interviewing a teenaged girl who lived in the apartment building right next to the park—a hundred feet shorter and the casualty list would have been doubled—and this girl said that when she looked out her fourth-floor window, she could see the faces of the people in the plane...upside down as the 737 augered in. The faces were quite clear because it was just after dark and the people had their reading lights on..."

"Stop, please," said Syd. "I'm so sorry. I'm so sorry I brought it up."

Dar was quiet for a moment. He felt as if he were returning from somewhere far away. He looked at the chief investigator and realized with a shock that she was crying. "It's all right," he said, stifling the impulse to pat her hand where it lay on the white tablecloth. "It's all right. It was a long time ago."

"Ten years isn't a long time," whispered Syd. "Not for something like that." She turned toward the window and wiped away the tears with two angry swipes of her hand.

"No," agreed Dar.

Syd looked back at him and her blue eyes seemed infinitely deep. "May I ask one thing?"

Dar nodded.

"You didn't resign from the NTSB and move out to California until almost two years after that crash," she said. "How could you...stay? Continue doing that work?"

"It was my job," said Dar. "I was good at it."

Sydney Olson smiled very slightly. "I've read your whole file, Dr. Minor. You're still the best accident reconstruction person in the business. So then why do you work primarily with Stewart Investigations? I know you're fairly well off and don't need a huge salary...but why Lawrence and Trudy?"

"I like them," Dar said. "Larry makes me laugh."

They arrived at Dar's cabin just after sunset, twilight hanging in the soft summer evening air like a muted tapestry. The cabin sat by itself up a half mile of gravel road, south and east of the town of Julian, on the very edge of the Cleveland National Forest. Its view looked down broad meadows and across great valleys of grass to the south. Above and behind the cabin, the ponderosa pines and Douglas fir grew thicker, ending in a rocky ridgetop.

Syd stared in admiration. "Wow," she said. "You say 'cabin' and I picture caulked logs and mice scurrying around."

Dar glanced at his trim stone-and-redwood structure with its long porch looking south. "Nope," he said. "It's only six years old. I bought the property when I first came out here; lived in the sheep wagon before this place."

"Sheep wagon?" said Syd.

Dar nodded. "You'll see."

"And I bet you built this all by yourself."

"Hardly," said Dar with a chuckle. "I'm incompetent with a hammer and saw. A local builder—seventy years old—named Burt McNamara did most of the work."

"My God," said Syd as she came around to the front of the building along the open porch, "a hot tub."

"It has a nice view. On a cold winter's night you can sit in the tub and see the few lights out on the Capitan Grande Indian Reservation way across the valley there."

Dar unlocked the front door and stood aside to let Syd enter first.

"I see why you don't have...ah...guests too often," said Syd softly.

The last of the evening light illuminated the large, single room. Dar had not partitioned the cabin except for the bathroom area, and only groupings of furniture and carpet delineated one area from another. Most of the walls were lined with bookshelves, but there were several huge French original posters—one advertising a fishing line and showing a woman catching a trout from a canoe, the art stylized in wonderful 1920s negative-space blacks and bold lines. The southeast corner held a large L-shaped desk under twelve-over-twelve paned windows. The view from that area was amazing. A huge fireplace took up much of the west wall, the windows on either side were soft with twilight, there was a scattering of comfortable leather chairs and couches near it, and the single bed, covered in a Hudson's Bay blanket, was just behind the long couch.

"I like to watch the fire from bed," said Dar.

"Uh-huh," said Syd.

Dar dropped his own bags. He picked two lanterns off hooks on the wall. "Come on, I'll get you set up in the sheep wagon."

Dar led her back out onto the porch in the fading twilight and about a hundred feet along a well-maintained trail. Japanese snow lanterns made of stone lined the path at twenty-foot intervals. After walking through a small stand of birch, they entered a grassy clearing, and the wagon came into sight.

The old Basque sheepherder's wagon had been completely renovated with ancient wood and glass. Now the wheeled structure had a small porch, a screen door, and a canvas awning on the south side. Near it, several Adirondack chairs had been set facing a view even more incredible than the cabin's.

Dar gestured and Syd walked up the four steps, opened the unlocked doors, and stepped into the small space.

"This may be the coziest room I've ever seen in my life," Syd said softly.

The sheep wagon was only eighteen feet long and seven feet wide, but the space was used with great ingenuity. There was a tiny bathroom to the right as one entered, a small sink under a window on the north side, a tiny eating booth on the south side, and the entire west end was comprised of a built-in bed under a hemisphere of old windowpanes. The barrel-vaulted ceiling was low, but it gleamed with slats of honey-colored old wood. Various pegs and hooks lined the walls, and Dar hung the lanterns on two of them. The high bed looked impossibly comfortable with a homemade patchwork quilt on it and several huge pillows at either end. Drawers were built into the wainscoting under the mattress area.

"There's no electricity," said Dar, "but the plumbing works...We ran a line down from the same cistern that serves the cabin. No shower or tub, I'm afraid...there just wasn't room, but there's no charge for using the big shower in the cabin."

"Did your Mr. McNamara build this as well?" asked Syd, sliding into the wooden booth and looking through the small panes at the last of the sunset. The tiny space gave the impression of being below decks in a very tiny but cozy boat.

Dar shook his head. "We...my wife and I had this built the summer before the crash. In a magazine—*Architectural Digest*—we read about an interior designer and an old rancher and builder up in Montana who were buying up old Basque sheep wagons and converting them into...well, this. They built the thing according to our plans and then disassembled it, shipped it to Colorado, and put it together again. I did the same thing when I moved it out here."

Syd looked up at him. "Did the three of you ever use it?"

Dar shook his head again. "We'd bought some property in the Rockies, not too far from Denver, but that was the winter that David was born, and then...well, we never got to spend time in it."

"But *you* did," said Syd. "Out here. Alone."

Dar nodded. "But I had to do more and more work on the weekends," he said. "Mostly on the computer. So I had the cabin built rather than electrify the sheep wagon."

"Good choice," said the chief investigator.

"French sheets and pillowcases in those drawers under the bed," said Dar. "Also clean towels. And no mice. I was up here last weekend and checked."

"I wouldn't care if there were mice," said Syd.

Dar opened a drawer, removed a box of kitchen matches, and lit the lanterns. Instantly the old wood everywhere and especially in the vaulted ceiling began to glow with a honeyed warmth.

"The little two-burner stove is propane," he said. "Like a camp stove, really. There's no fridge, so perishable things I keep in the cabin. You can leave the lanterns on when you leave—they're safe—but bring this to find your way back." He opened another drawer and pulled out a flashlight.

Dar went to the door. "You're welcome

to just settle in here or to come over to the cabin for some hot tea or something."

"We've still got a lot of files to go through," said Syd.

Dar made a face.

"You go on," said Syd. "I'm going to settle in—as you say—and just enjoy this perfect little place for a while before I come down."

Dar took some matches. "I'll light the snow lanterns so the path will be illuminated."

Syd just smiled.

She came down the trail to the cabin about an hour later. She had changed out of her professional-looking suit into jeans, a flannel shirt, and cross-trainer sneakers. Her nine-millimeter pistol was holstered to her belt.

It was full dark now and a mountain chill had set in. Dar had started a small fire in the huge fireplace and his old reel-to-reel tape player was playing classical music—he had not thought about the selection, merely flipped on the player as he usually did when alone in the cabin—but the music was an assortment of lovely pieces—the Adagietto fourth movement from Mahler's Fifth Symphony, the second movement from Brahms's Second Piano Concerto, the second movement from Beethoven's Seventh, the third and fourth movements from Mendelssohn's *Italian Symphony*, Kyoko Takezawa playing Mendelssohn's andante movement from the *Concerto for Violin and Orchestra, op. 64*, *Kyrie Eleisons* from both Beethoven's *Mass in Solemnis* and Mozart's *Requiem*, some Mitsuko Uchida and Horowitz piano solos (including Dar's favorite, the Scriabin Etude in C sharp minor, op. 2, no. 1 from the extraordinary *Horowitz in Moscow* album), Ying Huang singing opera arias with the London Symphony Orchestra, and lighter pieces with Heinz Holliger on oboe with orchestra.

At the last second, Dar was afraid that the chief investigator would think that he was trying to set a romantic mood, but he saw at once from her expression that she simply liked the music.

"Mozart," she said, listening to the amazing voices in the *Requiem*. She nodded and came over to join him by the fire, sitting in the other leather club chair across from his.

"Would you like some hot tea?" Dar had said. "Green, mint, Grey's breakfast, regular Lipton's…"

Syd's gaze had moved to the antique "hoosier" by the kitchen counter. "Is that a bottle of Macallan?" she said.

"It is indeed," said Dar. "Pure single-malt."

"It's almost full," she said.

"I don't like to drink alone."

"I'd love a whiskey," she said.

Dar went over to the counter, retrieved two crystal whiskey glasses from the cupboard, and poured.

"Ice?" he said.

"In good single-malt?" said the chief investigator. "You go near an ice cube and I'll draw down on you."

Dar nodded. The glasses of amber liquid glowed as he came back close to the fire. They savored the Scotch in silence for several comfortable minutes.

Dar was shocked to realize that he was taking great pleasure in this woman's company and that there was a slight but growing physical tension—awareness might be a better word—between the two of them. It shocked Dar, who had always known he was different from most men. The sight of a nude woman could arouse him, *did* arouse him still in his dreams. But beyond mere physical arousal, Dar linked true, deep desire with specificity. Even before he had met his wife, Barbara, he had never understood desiring a person not *known*, not *understood*, not...*central*.

And then he had loved *Barbara*. He had desired *Barbara*. It was Barbara's face and voice and red hair and small breasts and pink nipples and red pubic hair and pale, white skin that became and remained the source of his love, attention, and desire. In the past decade since her death, he had seemed to move further and further away from finding or being able to feel such specific desire toward any other person. But now Dar Minor found himself sipping Scotch and looking at Chief Investigator

Sydney Olson as she sat comfortably in the club chair, the red Indian blanket behind her head and the firelight soft on her. He noticed the weight of her breasts against the fabric of her shirt, and the brilliance of her eyes above the sparkling crystal of the Scotch glass, and...

"...reminds me of?" Syd was saying.

Dar shook his head—literally—to clear it. "I'm sorry," he said. "What did you say?"

Syd looked around the glowing room. Small halogen spots illuminated bookcases and works of art. The firelight was reflected in the many windowpanes. A single swing lamp put a circle of light on Dar's worktable at the far end of the long room.

"I said, do you know what all this reminds me of?"

"No," Dar said softly. Still feeling the tides of the sexual and emotional tension between them, he had the overwhelming feeling that Syd was about to make a personal comment that would bring them a step closer, would change both of their lives forever, whether he wanted it to or not. "What does all this remind you of?"

"It reminds me of one of those stupid action movies where a cop is put in charge of guarding the life of some witness, so they head far off to the woods, far from any backup. They set up camp in a house full of huge picture windows, to make it easy for a sniper," said Syd. "And then the cop is totally surprised when someone takes a shot at them. Did you ever see Kevin Costner and Whitney Houston in *The Bodyguard*?"

"No," said Dar.

Syd shook her head. "It was silly. The script was originally written for Steve McQueen and Diana Ross...that might have been better. At least McQueen *seemed* to be thinking when he was on screen."

Dar swallowed some Scotch and said nothing.

She paused for a second; she seemed far away. Then she shrugged. "Do you keep any weapons in the cabin?"

"You mean firearms?"

"Yes."

"No," said Dar, stating the literal truth, but lying just the same.

"I take it from your earlier comments that you frown on handguns."

"I think they're the bane and shame of America," said Dar. "Our worst sin since slavery."

Syd nodded. "But you aren't offended with me keeping my weapon handy?"

"You're an officer of the law," said Dar. "You're required to."

Syd nodded again. "But you have no shotguns, hunting rifles?"

Dar shook his head. "Not in the cabin. I have some old weapons stored away."

"You know what the best home-defense weapon is?" asked Syd. She took a drink of whiskey and held the glass in both hands.

"A pit bull?" ventured Dar.

"Nope. A pump-action shotgun. Doesn't matter what gauge."

"I guess it wouldn't require much target practice to hit someone with a shotgun," agreed Dar.

"More than that," said Syd. "The sound of a pump shotgun being racked in a dark house is absolutely unmistakable. You'd be amazed the deterrent effect it can have on burglars and ne'er-do-wells."

"Ne'er-do-wells," repeated Dar, savoring the word. "Well, if the *sound* of the shotgun being racked is the important thing, one wouldn't have to have shells for it, would one?"

Syd said nothing, but her expression showed her opinion of keeping weapons around with no ammunition.

"Actually," said Dar, "all I'd need would be a *tape recording* of a shotgun being racked, wouldn't I?"

Syd set her glass down and wandered over to Dar's main worktable. There were few loose papers there but several paperweights—a small piston head, a small carnivore's skull, a Disneyland paperweight with Goofy in a snowstorm, and a single, green shotgun shell.

Syd lifted the shell. "Four-ten gauge. Significance?"

Dar shrugged. "I used to have a Savage .410 over-and-under," he said quietly. "A gift from my father right before he died. It was an antique. I left it behind in storage in Colorado."

Syd turned the shell over and looked at the brass end. "This hasn't been fired, but the hammer's fallen on it. The firing pin missed the center."

"It happened the last time I tried to fire the gun," said Dar even more quietly. "The only time that weapon ever misfired."

Syd stood holding the shell and looking at Dar for a long moment before setting it down under the windowsill. "That shell is still dangerous, you know."

Dar raised his eyebrows.

"I know from your file that you were in the Marines...in Vietnam. You must have been very young."

"Not so young," said Dar. "I'd already graduated from college by the time I enlisted and was sent over there in 1974. Besides, there wasn't much for us to do that last year except listen to bits of the Watergate hearings on armed forces radio and go around the countryside picking up the M-16s and other weapons that the

ARVNs—the Army of the Republic of Viet Nam, our team—were dropping as they ran away from the North Vietnamese regulars."

"You graduated from college when you were eighteen," said Syd. "What were you...a prodigy?"

"An overachiever," said Dar.

"Why the Marines?" asked Syd.

"Would you believe it was out of sentiment?" asked Dar. "Because my father had been a Marine in the real war...World War II?"

"I believe that he was a Marine," said Syd, "but I don't believe that's the reason you enlisted in that service."

Correct, thought Dar. Aloud he said, "Actually, it was partially to get my service out of the way and get back to the States for graduate school, and partially out of sheer perversity."

"How so?" said Syd. She had finished her Scotch. Dar poured her another two fingers.

Dar hesitated and then realized that he was going to tell her the truth...sort of.

"As a kid, I was obsessed with the Greeks," said Dar. "The obsession lasted through college, even while I was pursuing a degree in physics. All of the liberal arts majors were studying ancient Athens—you know, sculpture, democracy, Socrates—while I was always obsessed with Sparta."

Syd looked quizzical. "War?"

Dar shook his head. "Not war, although that's all the Spartans are remembered for. The Spartans were the only society I knew of that made a science out of the study of fear—they called it *phobologia*. Their training—which began at a young age—was all geared at recognizing fear, *phobos*, and defeating it. They even taught of parts of the body that were *phobosynakteres*—places where fear accumulated—and trained their young men, their warriors, to be able to put their minds and bodies in a state of *aphobia*."

"Fearlessness," translated Syd.

Dar frowned. "Yes and no," he said. "There are different forms of fearlessness. A berserker warrior or a Japanese samurai caught up in mindless rage, or, for that matter, a Palestinian terrorist on a bus with a bomb, they're all *fearless*—that is, they don't fear their own deaths. But the Spartans wanted something more."

"What could be better for a warrior than fearlessness?" asked Syd.

"The Greeks, the Spartans, called such fearlessness brought on by rage or anger *katalepsis*," said Dar. "Literally, being possessed by a daemon—a loss of control by the mind. They spurned that completely. Their hoped-for *aphobia* was a completely...well, controlled, *minded* thing—a refusal to become absorbed and possessed, even in the midst of battle."

"And did you learn *aphobia* in the Marines...in Vietnam?" said Syd.

"Nope. I was scared shitless every second I was in Vietnam."

"Did you see much action there?" asked Syd, her eyes intent. "Your Marine Corps files are still classified. That must mean something."

"It doesn't mean anything," he lied. "For example, if I was a clerk typist and typed a lot of classified material, you wouldn't be able to get access to my files."

"Were you a clerk typist?"

Dar held his Scotch glass in both hands. "Not all of the time."

"So you saw combat?"

"Enough to know that I never wanted to see any again," said Dar truthfully.

"But you're comfortable around weapons," said Syd, getting to the point.

Dar made a face and sipped his whiskey.

"What kind of weapon were you issued in the Marines?" asked Syd.

"Some sort of rifle," said Dar. He did not enjoy discussing firearms.

"Then an M-sixteen," said Syd.

"Which all have a tendency to jam if not kept perfectly clean," said Dar, a bit disingenuously. He had not been issued an M-16. His spotter had carried an accurized M-14—an older weapon, but one that shared the same 7.62 millimeter ammunition as the bolt-action Remington 700 M40 that Dar had trained with. And train he had—120 rounds a day, six days a week, until he was able to hit a mansized moving target at five hundred yards and a stationary one at one thousand.

He finished his Scotch. "If you're trying to palm a handgun off on me, forget it, Chief Investigator. I hate the goddamn things."

"Even when the Russian mafia's trying to kill you?"

"They *tried* to kill me," corrected Dar. "And I still think it may have been a case of mistaken identity."

Syd nodded. "But you've handled weapons," she persisted. "You were taught what to do if a shell misfired…"

Dar looked up at her. "Aim your weapon at a safe, neutral target and wait. It may still fire without warning."

Syd pointed to the .410 shell. "Should we throw that away?"

"No," said Dar.

They each had a final glass of Scotch and watched the fire. The bit of smoke that stayed in the room was aromatic, mixing with the smoky peat taste of the whiskey.

The tension of the earlier conversation

had almost disappeared. They were talking shop.

"Did you hear about the directive from the last political appointee to head the National Highway Traffic Safety Agency?" asked Syd.

Dar chuckled. "Absolutely. The word accident is never to be used in any official reports, correspondence, and/or memos."

"Doesn't that seem a little odd?"

"Not at all," said Dar. A log broke and crumbled into embers and he glanced at it for a second before looking back at his guest. Syd's face appeared younger and softer in the firelight, her eyes as alive and intelligent as always. "You have to follow their chain of logic," he said. "All accidents are avoidable. Therefore they shouldn't happen. Therefore the agency can't use the word accident—they don't exist. They have to circumlocute and say crash or incident or whatever."

"Do you agree that all accidents are avoidable?" asked Syd.

Dar laughed heartily. "Anyone who's ever investigated an accident…whether it's the space shuttle or some poor schmuck who runs a yellow light and gets broadsided...knows that they're not only *not* avoidable, they're inevitable."

"How so?" said Syd.

Dar looked at her. "They *happened*. The probability of the series of events that led up to the accident may each be a thousand to one, or a million to one, but once those events occur in the right sequence, the accident is one hundred percent inevitable."

Syd nodded but did not look convinced.

"All right," said Dar, "take the *Challenger* accident. NASA had become the careless driver who runs yellow lights. You get away with it once—five times—twenty times— and pretty soon you assume it's a natural and safe behavior. But if you keep driving, the odds of being hit by some other sono-fabitch with the same intersection philoso-phy become almost one hundred percent."

"How was NASA taking extra risks?"

Dar shrugged. "The Commission docu-mented it pretty well. They knew about the O-ring problem—even the Crit-One severity of it—but didn't fix it. They knew

that cold weather made the O-ring problem much worse, but launched anyway.
They violated at least twenty of their own
no-go guidelines because that teacher was
on board, and they were feeling political
pressure to get her launched into orbit so
President Reagan could mention it in his
State of the Union Address that evening.
The odds caught up to them."

"You believe in odds, then?" said Syd.
"Do you believe in anything else?"

Dar looked at her quizzically. "Are you
asking me a philosophical question, Chief
Investigator?"

"I'm just curious," said Syd, swallowing
the last of her whiskey. "You see so many
accidents, so much carnage. I wonder what
philosophical framework you apply to it."

Dar thought a moment. "The Stoics, I
guess," he said. "Epictetus. Marcus Aurelius and his ilk." He chuckled. "The
one time I ever felt political enough to
drive to Washington and throw a brick at
the White House was when Bill Clinton
was asked what the most important book
was that he'd read recently—and he said

Marcus Aurelius's *Meditations*." He chuckled again. "That love-handled mass of appetites... quoting Marcus Aurelius."

"But what do *you* believe?" pressed Syd. "Other than a Stoic point of view." She paused a moment and recited quietly, "'To the rational creature, only the irrational is unbearable; the rational he can always bear. Blows are not by nature intolerable.'"

Dar stared at her. "You can quote Epictetus."

"So would you say that's your philosophy?" repeated Syd.

Dar set his empty glass down and steepled his fingers, tapping his lower lip. The dying fire crumbled again and the embers glowed in their final brightness. "Larry's older brother, a writer who lived in Montana until his marriage broke up, came to visit several years ago; I got to know him a bit. Later I saw him interviewed on TV and he was asked about *his* philosophy; his novel was about the Catholic Church, and the interviewer kept pressing him on his own beliefs."

Syd waited.

"Larry's brother—Dale's his name— was going through a rough patch then. In response to the question, he quoted John Updike. The quote went something like—'I am neither musical nor religious; each time I set my fingers down it is without confidence of hearing a chord.' "

"That's sad," said Syd at last.

Dar smiled. "It was Larry's brother quoting another writer—I didn't say it's what *I* believe. I subscribe to Occam's Razor."

"William of Occam," said Syd. "What…fifteenth century?"

"Fourteenth," said Dar.

"Maxim," continued Syd. "The assumptions introduced to explain a thing must not be multiplied beyond necessity."

"Or," said Dar, "all other things being equal, the simplest answer is usually the right one."

"Rules out alien abduction," laughed Syd.

"Area Fifty-one, kaput," said Dar.

"Kennedy conspiracy shit…adios," said Syd, her smile very wide.

"Oliver Stone, bye-bye," agreed Dar.

Syd paused. "Did you know you're famous for Darwin's Blade?"

"For what?" said Dar, blinking in surprise.

"Some statement you made a few years ago—I think it was at the meeting of the National Association of Insurance Investigators."

"Oh, Christ," said Dar, putting his hand over his eyes.

"You had a corollary to Occam's Razor," persisted Syd. "I think it went—'All other things being equal, the simplest solution is usually stupidity.' "

"Which is stupidly obvious," muttered Dar.

Syd nodded slowly. "No, I know what you were saying. It's like those guys in the pickup trying to crash that rock concert…"

Dar suddenly looked over at the box of files and stacks of Zip drives and floppy disks that still awaited them. "Maybe we've been looking for the wrong thing in our files," he said.

Syd cocked her head.

"Maybe it's not my investigation of

stupid accidents—even fatal ones—that drew someone's attention to me," he said. "Maybe it's murder."

"Have you solved a murder recently?" said Syd. "Other than the Phong swoop-and-squat, I mean."

Dar nodded.

"And are you going to share it?" said Syd.

Dar glanced at his watch. "Yeah. Tomorrow."

"You bastard," said Chief Investigator Olson, but she said it with a smile. "Thanks for the Scotch."

Dar walked her to the door.

Syd paused. Dar had the sudden, wild thought that she was going to kiss him.

"Sleeping up in my wonderful sheep wagon," she said, "how will I know if the bad guys have come and you're in deep shit?"

Dar reached under a heavy coat on a wall hook and pulled down a bright orange whistle on a string. "It's for hiking, in case you get lost in the woods. You can hear this damned whistle two miles away."

"Like a rape whistle," said Syd.

"Yeah."

"Well, if the murderers show up tonight, just whistle." She paused and Dar could see a glint of mischief in her blue eyes. "You know how to whistle, don't you, Steve?"

Dar grinned. The nineteen-year-old Lauren Bacall had said the line to Humphrey Bogart in *To Have and Have Not*. He loved that movie.

"Yeah," he said. "Just put my lips together and blow."

Syd nodded and went up the path with her flashlight, blowing out each lantern as she passed.

Dar watched until she was out of sight.

9

"I IS FOR WITNESS"

Syd came knocking early on Saturday morning, but Dar was already up, showered, shaved, and with coffee and breakfast ready. Syd ate bacon and eggs happily and refilled her coffee cup twice.

Before starting work, Dar took her on a long walking tour of the property: the ravine to the east with its abandoned gold mine, the stream that fed into the canyon, the small waterfall up the hill bridged by a fallen tree that looked too slick and mossy to cross, the rock slabs and boulders along the high ridge to the north, the stands of birch trees and acres of thick pine on the hillside just above the cabin, and the endless fields of grass in the valley below. All during the walk, Dar felt the same pleasure that had shocked him so much the night before—the strange *awareness* of Syd's physical self, the warmth of her smile, the glow that her tone of voice and laughter gave him.

Cut it out, Darwin, he warned himself.

"I know this is a forbidden question between men and women anymore," said Syd, stopping and looking straight at him, "but what are you thinking about, Dar? I can hear the gears meshing from two feet away."

She *was* only two feet away. When Dar stopped, he almost surrendered to the urge to put his arms around her, draw her closer, set his face against the curve of her neck just beneath her ear, just where her hair curled onto her neck, just to breathe in her fragrance.

"Billy Jim Langley," he said at last, taking half a step back.

Syd cocked her head.

Dar pointed to the south. "An accident I worked a year or so ago way back in the national forest there. Want to hear it? Want to solve it?"

"Sure."

Dar cleared his throat. "OK—I was called out to the scene of a suspected homicide about five miles back in the woods there—"

"This isn't the murder you promised me last night, is it?"

Dar shook his head. "Anyway, a Mr. Billy James Langley, one of Larry and Trudy's CalState insureds, was reported missing a day after he should have returned from a fishing trip. The sheriff drove back toward Billy Jim's favorite fishing hole and found his pickup—a 'seventy-eight Ford 250—upside down in a creek. Billy Jim was inside. Drowned. It looked as if he had run off a little bridge in the darkness the night before and not been able to get out of the cab of the pickup in time. The coroner confirmed the time."

"Where's the suspected homicide?" she asked.

"Well, when the coroner removed Billy Jim's body," said Dar, "he pronounced the cause of death as drowning. But it seems as if Billy Jim had also been shot with a 22-caliber bullet..."

"Where?" said Syd.

"While driving his truck," said Dar.

"No, I mean *where* on his body?"

Dar hesitated. "Once. In the...ah... groin area."

"Testicles?" said Syd.

"One of them."

"Left or right testicle?" said Syd.

"Do you think it matters?" said Dar.

"Doesn't it?"

"Well, yes, but..."

"Left or right?" said Syd.

"Right," said Dar. "Can I get on with the story?"

They walked down the hill together.

"OK," said Syd, "we have a Mr. Billy James Langley coming back from a fishing trip in the dark. Suddenly he gets shot in the right ball and—not surprisingly—is startled enough to drive his pickup into the creek and then drowns. Let me guess: no .22 rifle or pistol in the pickup?"

"Right," said Dar.

"Entrance or exit holes in the truck?"

said Syd. "It'd have to be a pretty flimsy pickup to let a .22 pass through, and Ford 250s aren't flimsy."

"No entrance or exit holes," said Dar. "Except in Billy Jim."

"Windows rolled up?"

"Yeah. It was raining hard the night Billy Jim was driving out from his favorite fishing hole."

"After dark, right?" said Syd.

"Right. About eleven P.M."

"I've got it," said Syd.

Dar stopped walking. "Really?" It had taken him two hours at the scene to figure it out.

"Really," said Syd. "Billy Jim didn't have a .22 rifle or pistol along, but I bet he had a box of cartridges in the cab, right?"

"In the glove box," said Dar.

"And I bet Billy Jim's headlights went off on the way out."

Dar sighed. "Yeah—my guess was about a mile and a half short of the bridge."

Syd nodded. "About how long it would take for the .22 cartridge to heat up and discharge," said Syd. "I know those Ford pickups. The fuse box for the lights is right under the panel in front of the steering wheel. Your Billy Jim is driving along, the headlights go out, he can't keep driving in the rain but he wants to get home, so he pokes around, figures the fuse has blown...hunts around for something in the cab the right size to replace the fuse...A .22 cartridge fits perfectly...He drives on, not thinking about the cartridge heating up. And then it fires..."

"Well, I guess it wasn't much of a mystery after all," said Dar.

Syd shrugged. "Hey, I'm starved. Can we have lunch before we tackle your real mystery?"

They made roast beef sandwiches for lunch, grabbed beers, and took them out onto the porch. The day was getting hot and they had long since doffed their denim jackets. Syd wore an oversized T-shirt with the tail out, to cover the holster on her hip. Dar wore a faded old black T-shirt with equally faded blue jeans and running shoes. The cabin itself was shaded by tall ponderosa pine and small birch, but the valley opening before them was bright with summer grass and willows, all seeming to ripple in the wind and heat haze. They sat on the edge of the high porch and dangled their legs.

Syd asked, "Doesn't all the death, pain, suffering you witness...investigate... weigh you down after a while?"

If she had asked Dar that question twenty-four hours earlier, he probably would have answered *I imagine it's a little like being a doctor. After a bit you become... not callous, that's not the word...but you have a perspective for it all. It's your job, right?* And he would have believed it. But now he was not so sure. Perhaps something *had* changed him over the past decade or more. All that he knew at this instant was that—contrary to all intentions and expectations—he would like to kiss Chief Investigator Sydney Olson on her full lips, press her back against the redwood deck, feel the softness of her breasts against him...

"I don't know," he managed to say, chew-

ing on his sandwich. He had forgotten her
question.

The file was in a regular manila folder,
was stamped *Closed*, and was at least
three inches thick with documents. Dar
set two wheeled chairs at his desk near
the large CAD computers. Syd sat to his
right as he laid out the documents in
front of her.

"You see the date of the accident," he
said.

"Seven weeks ago." Syd glanced down at
the LAPD Traffic Collision Report. "East
L.A....a little far afield, weren't you?"

"Not really," said Dar. "Some of these
cases take me as far north as your neck
of the woods...Sacramento and San Francisco...and even out of state."

"Did the LAPD Traffic Investigation
Unit call you in freelance on this one? I
know both Sergeant Rote of the TIU and
Detective Bob Ventura, whose name is on
the investigation report here."

Dar shook his head. "Lawrence was in
Arizona working a case, so Trudy asked me

to follow up on this. The client was the van rental company."

Syd looked at the initial collision report. "A GMC Vandura...red. Small moving van?"

"Yeah. Read the reporting officer's statement."

Syd read it aloud:

"Collision location, 1200 Marlboro Ave. (N. Frontage Road).

"Origin: at about 0245 hrs., May 19, I was transporting a prisoner to the East Los Angeles Women's Detention Facility when I heard a report of a fatal accident in the area of Marlboro Ave. and Fountain Blvd. I asked the dispatcher if she could find a unit that could meet me at E. 109th St. and I–5 so as to transport my prisoner the rest of the way to the detention facility, so I could in turn respond to the accident. Officer Jones #2485 responded immediately and took over the transport. I arrived at the scene at about 0300 hours. When I arrived the scene had been secured by patrol units. Sgt. McKay, #2662 (traffic supervisor), Officer Berry #3501 and Officer Clancey #4423 were already on scene. The 1200 block of Marlboro was blocked off to all through traffic from Fountain Blvd. to Gramercy St.

"Street description: 1200 Marlboro Ave. (N. Frontage Road) is a west bound one-way street. Fountain Blvd. to the east is a north and south bound street. Gramercy St., to the west, is also a north and south bound street. 1200 Marlboro Ave. (N. Frontage Road) has a .098 w/e grade, uphill. The closest lighting on the street was provided by off street lights and intersection lights. The un-posted speed limit is 25 mph for that stretch of roadway.

"Weather conditions: at the time of the accident it was cloudy and overcast. It was raining and the temperature was cool and slightly windy. It was night time and the moon was not shining through the cloud cover.

"Vehicle identification: the GMC Vandura (v-2) displayed large U-Rental truck decals on all 4 sides. A check of the vehicle's license plate revealed there was no record to be found.

"Driver identification: Miss Gennie Smiley was identified as the driver of the vehicle per her California driver's license, her own statement, and Donald M. Borden's statement.

"Vehicle damage: there was slight damage to the front grill of the GMC Vandura. The grill was bent inward approximately three inches at its furthest incursion and there were fibers from the victim's sweater embedded in the grill.

"Injuries: Richard Kodiak suffered fatal massive head trauma. Peterson #333 and Royles #979 (Samson's paramedic unit #272) responded to the scene. Kodiak was pronounced dead at the scene by Dr. Cavenaugh of Eastern Mercy Hospital via the radio..."

Syd quit reading and flipped through the next few pages. "All right," she said at last. "We have this thirty-one-year-old male, Richard Kodiak, dead of head injuries. He and his roommate, Donald Borden, were in the process of moving from East L.A. to San Francisco when a female friend, Gennie Smiley, seems to have hit Mr. Kodiak straight on with the van and then, somehow, managed also to run over him with the van's right front wheel." She flipped a dozen more pages. "Mr. Borden and Ms. Smiley sued the truck rental agency, stating that the brakes were inadequate and the headlights deficient—"

"Hence my involvement," said Dar.

"—and they also sued the owners of the apartment building for not providing adequate lighting." She flipped back twenty or thirty pages. "Ah...here it is in her statement...Ms. Smiley said that bad exterior lighting and poor rental truck headlights prevented her from seeing Kodiak when he stepped out in front of the van. They wanted six hundred thousand dollars from the van rental company."

"And another four hundred thousand from the apartment building owner," said Dar.

"An even million," mused Syd. "At least they knew what their friend was worth."

Dar rubbed his chin. "Mr. Borden and Mr. Kodiak had lived at that same address for two years and were universally known as Dickie and Donnie to their neighbors, shop owners, local restaurateurs..."

"Gay?" said Syd.

Dar nodded.

"Then who was Gennie?"

"It seems that Mr. Borden…Donnie… swings both ways. Gennie Smiley was his secret girlfriend. Dickie discovered them together…there was a row that lasted three days, according to the neighbors… and then Dickie and Donnie patched things up by agreeing to move to San Francisco."

"*Sans* Gennie," said Syd.

"*Sans* Gennie indeed," said Dar. "But as a gesture of goodwill, she helped them pack up the van in preparation for moving."

"At two forty-five A.M. on a rainy morning?" said Syd.

Dar shrugged. "Dickie and Donnie were two months in arrears on their rent. It seems they were skipping." He turned on one of the twenty-one-inch CAD monitors and tapped out a code. "OK, here are some of the accident-scene photos as recorded by Sergeant McKay of the Traffic Investigations Unit." An electronic version of the black-and-white photo appeared on the large screen. And another. And another.

"Uh-oh," said Syd.

"Uh-oh," agreed Dar.

One photo showed Mr. Kodiak's body lying in the middle of the street about thirty feet west of the main doors of the apartment building. The body was lying facedown to the east—head toward the van—and there were visible patches of blood and brain matter spilled in both directions. Another photo showed broken glass, a single shoe, shoe scuff marks, and body scuff marks directly in front of the apartment building's main doorway. Another photograph showed continuous, nonstriated skid marks running back almost to the turn from Fountain Boulevard some 165 feet east of the impact site. In all of the photos, the van was backed east of the point of impact, its own skid marks running at least thirty feet in front of it.

"Gennie backed up when she heard a noise and thought she may have hit something," said Dar.

"Uh-huh," said Syd.

"Donnie was the only witness to Dickie's death," said Dar, pointing to the thick sheaf of statements. "He said that the two of them had been arguing. When Gennie arrived, they asked her to drive around the block and come back..."

"Why?" said Syd.

"Donnie said that they didn't want to argue in front of her," said Dar. "So she came around the block, traveling about thirty miles per hour, according to her estimate. She didn't see Dickie, who had stepped off the curb, until it was too late to stop." Dar ran the photos across the computer screen again and then froze on the widest shot. He turned on the second monitor and tapped up a program. A three-dimensional view of the same scene appeared, but this one was computer-animated.

"You do three-D accident reconstruction videos," said Syd. "I didn't see the CAD monitors in your loft."

"They're there," said Dar. "Tucked away in a corner behind some bookcases. Preparing these provides a big share of my income."

Syd nodded.

"So, Chief Investigator," said Dar, "do

you see some irregularities in this accident?"

Syd looked at the dossier, at the photograph on the screen, and then at the 3-D image that showed essentially the same picture as the photograph. "Something's wrong here."

"Correct," said Dar. "First I investigated the lighting under similar conditions with a specialized light meter."

"At two-forty-five A.M. on a cloudy, rainy night," said Syd.

Dar raised his eyebrows. "Of course." He tapped some keys.

Suddenly numbers appeared on the 3-D image of the street scene. Dar moved the mouse and rotated their viewpoint until they were looking straight down at the street, east to west, with the van near the bottom of the screen, the body centered, and the rest of the block visible. Areas on both sides had small rectangles of data listed as FC.

"Foot-candles of light," said Syd.

Dar nodded. "Despite Donnie and Gennie's claims, it was fairly well lighted for such a poor neighborhood. You can see that at both intersections, there are large pools of light covering most of the street at three foot-candles. The lighting at the front steps of the building puts out about one and a half foot-candles, and even in the middle of the street beyond where Dickie was hit, the lowest reading was one foot-candle."

"She should have seen the victim even if the van's lights weren't working," said Syd.

Dar touched the screen with a stylus and a red line appeared, running most of the way back to the intersection with Fountain Boulevard from whence the van had come. "Gennie came around through rather bright lighting—three foot-candles—and moved through this long area of two foot-candles of light until just before the impact. The van headlights were both intact and working. In fact, she had the brights on."

Dar tapped keys and the visual on the screen disappeared, to be replaced by a real-time animation. Two men, three-dimensional but featureless, emerged from the front door of the apartment building. Suddenly the viewpoint switched to an aerial shot. The van accelerated around the corner from Fountain Boulevard and continued to accelerate. One of the figures stepped out into the street and faced the oncoming van. The van slammed on its brakes and slid most of the distance from the intersection to the impact site—finally hitting the man head-on and continuing to skid for another thirty feet or so. The featureless victim—Dickie—flew through the air and landed on his back in the roadway, head away from the van.

Dar tapped keys and the earlier aerial animated view was superimposed over this one. "This is the actual position of the van and body at the scene." Suddenly the van was at least forty feet back up the street to the east and the body had also moved east—at least twenty feet from its actual point of rest, its head now pivoted around toward the van.

"Quite a discrepancy," said Syd.

"It gets better," said Dar. He pulled a six-page typed statement out of the dossier and let Syd glance over it. "Officer Berry, number 3501, took this statement from the first witness to drive down the street…a Mr. James William Riback."

Syd's eyes flicked back and forth down the pages. "Riback says that he saw a van pull away from the scene, almost cut him off, and then he saw Dickie—Mr. Kodiak—lying on his back in the street. Riback stopped his Taurus, got out, and asked Richard Kodiak if he was alive. He reports that Kodiak said, 'Yes, go call an ambulance.' Ribeck left his car in the street and ran to a friend's apartment around the corner—3535 Gramercy Street—awoke his friend, told her to call 911, grabbed a blanket, and rushed back to the scene… where he found Mr. Kodiak lying in what Ribeck thought was a different location, certainly turned in a different direction, in much worse shape and unconscious. The paramedics arrived seven minutes later and Kodiak was pronounced dead. The van was parked where it is in the police photos." Syd looked up at Dar. "The bitch drove around the block and ran over Dickie Kodiak again, didn't she? But how do you prove it?"

"The details are pretty boring," said Dar.

"Details don't bore me, Dr. Minor," said the chief investigator coolly. "They're the core of my job, too, remember."

Dar nodded. "OK, first I'll run through the data and equations and then show you the forensic animation that results from them," he said. "I prefer metric units in this sort of work, though I usually translate to English units of measurement for demonstrations."

Dar typed and the street scene appeared again without a van, with only the two men emerging from the apartment building and one of them stepping into the street. The viewpoint swooped down again as if the viewer were looking from a van turning west onto Marlboro Avenue from Fountain Boulevard. The figure far down the street was clearly visible.

"Nighttime visibility studies show that even on a dark country road, even with the van's dim lights on, the pedestrian—in dark clothing—would be visible for about one hundred seventy-five feet, even if the driver had poor to mediocre eyesight. It's one hundred and sixty-nine feet from the Fountain Boulevard intersection to the point of impact with Mr. Kodiak."

"She saw him as soon as she came around the corner," mused Syd.

"Had to," said Dar. "Whether he was still on the curb or had stepped out. Her high beams would have picked him out at more than three hundred forty-three feet away. Hell, if she'd had no headlights on at all, she could have seen him from one hundred fifty feet away because of the streetlights and spill light from the apartment building main lobby."

"But she accelerated," said Syd.

"She sure did," said Dar. "The front tires of the van left skid marks for a total distance of one hundred thirty-two feet. That is, she kept skidding for twenty-nine feet beyond the point of impact where Mr. Kodiak left his right shoe and scuff marks from his left shoe."

"She says she ran over him at that point," said Syd.

"Impossible," said Dar. "Once we have the skid marks, everything becomes a matter of simple ballistics. Velocities and distances traveled—for the van, the man, and the body—can be figured easily. Shall we skip the equations?"

"No," said Syd. "I meant it when I said that I liked details."

Dar sighed. "All right. Both the LAPD Accident Investigations Unit and I conducted separate skid tests on this street with vehicles equipped with bumper guns—"

"Pavement spotters," said Syd.

"Right. The test vehicles' speeds were determined by radar. The test skids yielded a consistent value for a drag factor, f, to be 0.79. From that we can find the initial velocity of the pedestrian at the contact point...Remember, all testimony says that Mr. Kodiak was struck while standing still and facing the van. His velocity can never be greater than the van's. So we use this equation—

$$v_i = \sqrt{v_e^2 - 2ad}$$

The values are simple. The van skidded to a full stop, so its velocity can be given as $ve = 0$. The value for acceleration, a, is given by $a = fg$. As I explained, we determined the drag factor, $f = 0.79$. The figure for g, the pull of gravity, $= 32.2$ feet per second in U.S. measurement."

"Or 9.81 meters per second," Syd said quietly.

Dar blinked at her. "*You* think in metric equivalents," he said. "Shall I skip the rest of these equations and go to the animation? You're probably ahead of me."

Syd shook her head. "Details. Show me."

"OK," said Dar. "Because the van was decelerating, a has to be a negative number. Gennie's van skidded a total of one hundred thirty-two feet. Therefore, we just substitute back into the equation for initial velocity—

$$v_i = \sqrt{0^2 - 2(-0.79)(32.2)(132)}$$
$$v_i = 82\,\text{ft/sec} = 55.7\,\text{mi/hr}$$

The van's velocity when there are twenty-nine feet left to skid can be done in the same way. The only value that changes is the value for distance, *d*. So that equation would read—

$$v_i = \sqrt{v_e^2 - 2ad}$$
$$v_i = \sqrt{0^2 - 2(20.79)(32.2)(29)}$$
$$v_i = 38.4\,\text{ft/sec} = 26\,\text{mi/hr}$$

That was the van's speed at impact. And that would become Mr. Kodiak's speed as he became airborne at impact. This equation works with tall-fronted vans, by the way, but won't work with most smaller cars."

Syd nodded. "The vertical grille of a truck or tall van produces a flat-on impact, near the pedestrian's center of mass," she said. "A regular sedan or a smaller car would hit below that center of mass and throw the victim onto the hood or over the roof of the car."

"Yep," said Dar. "Or cut him in half." He looked back at the equations on the screen. "So because Ms. Gennie was driving this rental van and got Dickie front on with the grille, the math is simple. We just have to know the typical values for pedestrian drag factors over various surfaces."

He tapped a key. The screen read—

SURFACE	RANGE
Grass	.45–.70
Asphalt	.45–.60
Concrete	.40–.65

"And Marlboro Avenue?" said Syd.

"Asphalt." Dar typed in the pedestrian drag factor, f, as 0.45.

"The value for this particular pedestrian's center of mass height, h, was—2.2 feet," said Dar. "And the measured distance between the initial contact point of impact—confirmed by the shoe he left behind and the scuff marks from the other shoe—to his final position as determined by blood and body scuff marks was seventy-two feet. So we substitute those values into the above equation—

$$d_f = 2fh - 2h\sqrt{f^2 - fd/h}$$

$$d_f =$$
$$2(.45)(-2.2) - 2(-2.2)\sqrt{(.45)^2 - (.45)(72)/(-2.2)}$$
$$d_f = 15\,ft$$

"So the velocity at the beginning of Mr. Kodiak's fall—that is, his separation from the braking van—calculates out as—

$$v = d_f\sqrt{-g/2h}$$
$$v = 15\sqrt{-32.2/2(-2.2)}$$
$$v = 40.6\,ft/sec = 27.6\,mi/hr$$

Which is consistent with the earlier skid analysis," said Dar.

"So she actually hit him doing about twenty-seven miles per hour, braking from a top speed of almost fifty-six miles per hour," said Syd.

"Fifty-five point seven," agreed Dar.

"And he flew backwards seventy-two feet from the point of impact, coming to rest on his back with his head farthest from the van," continued the chief investigator.

"As ninety-nine-plus percent of pedestrians hit straight on by such a van would," said Dar. "That's why Larry and I knew that foul play was involved as soon as we saw the officer's photographs." He tapped at keys until the equations disappeared from the screen and the original animated street scene returned. Another tap got rid of all the numerical values of lighting, curb height, skid length, and so forth.

Two male figures stepped out of the building. The van screeched around the corner from Fountain Boulevard and began accelerating madly down Marlboro Avenue. One of the men pushed the other man, who stumbled into the street, almost fell, and then righted himself just as the skidding van slammed into him. The body flew a long distance, landed on its back, and skidded farther, finally coming to a stop. The van pulled away and accelerated around the corner of the next intersection, cutting off a Ford Taurus that stopped. A man got out, knelt by the victim, and then ran west, disappearing around the corner to go to his friend's apartment to call 911.

"We found blood, hair, and brain matter on the right wheel, the hub of the right wheel, the front transaxle, the shocks, and on part of the catalytic converter of the van," said Dar tonelessly.

In the animation, the van comes around the corner from Fountain Boulevard again, slows as it approaches the supine figure in the highway, then drives over it and backs up, dragging the body almost half the distance it had been thrown from the initial impact. Finally the body scrapes free, head pointed to the east, toward the van, as the rented vehicle continues to back up onto its own skid marks and finally comes to a stop.

"She had to finish the job," said Syd.

Dar nodded.

"What did the jury have to say when they saw this animation?" asked the chief investigator.

Dar smiled. "No jury. No trial. I showed this to Detective Ventura as well as to the Accident Investigations people, but no one was interested. By this time, Donald and Gennie had dropped their lawsuit against the owner of the apartment building—I think it was because I confronted them with the light-meter readings—and settled with the van rental people for fifteen thousand dollars."

Syd shifted in her chair and stared at Dar. "You have absolute proof that these two killed Richard Kodiak and the LAPD dropped it."

"They said it was just another fag killing, 'another garden-variety *homo*cide,' to quote the venerable Detective Ventura," said Dar.

"I always thought that Ventura was an ass," said Syd. "Now I know."

Dar nodded, chewed his lip, and looked at the animation repeating itself on the screen. The human figure was hit, hurled, the van drove away, returned, drove over it again—dragging it back toward the front vestibule of the building, crushing the skull. The animation began again with two male figures, featureless, emerging from the well-lighted lobby...

"Lawrence's clients...the rental people...were happy to settle for the fifteen grand," he began.

"Wait a minute," said Syd. "Wait a minute." She went over to her big leather tote bag and pulled a top-of-the-line Apple PowerBook from it.

As she set the computer up on the table next to Dar's PC equipment, he looked at her dubiously, the way a Lutheran would have regarded a Catholic in the seventeenth century. Apple people and PC people rarely mix well.

Syd brought her computer to life. "Gennie Smiley," she repeated. "Donald Borden. Richard Kodiak. These names ring a bell..."

Columns of data flowed down her portable screen. She hurriedly typed in a search command. "Ahh," she said, typed again, watched data whirl by and stop again. "Ahah!" she said.

"I like 'Ahah!' " said Dar. "What?"

"Did you and Lawrence check into the backgrounds of these three...lovers?" asked Syd.

"Sure we did," said Dar. "As much as we could without treading on Detective Ventura's toes. It was his case. We found

that the victim—Mr. Richard Kodiak—had three addresses in addition to
the Rancho la Bonita residence given on
his driver's license: all in California—one
in East L.A., one in Encinitas, and one
in Poway. Tracing his social security number, we found his listed employment as
CALSURMED with no address. In old
telephone listings, Trudy found a California Sure-Med listed in Poway, but the
business is no longer in existence and all
information regarding it has been purged
from city records. Then we checked with
the Poway post office and found that the
Poway address was the same as that listed
for the CALSURMED business—box
number 616840. We suggested to the Accident Investigation team and Detective
Ventura that they check with the Los Angeles and San Diego counties' Fictitious
Business Filings under both the subject's
name and the CALSURMED and California Sure-Med listings. They never followed up."

Syd was grinning at her computer screen.
"You know those red pins on my map?"

"The fatal swoop-and-squats?" said Dar. "Yeah?"

"California Sure-Med was the health provider for six of the victims. A certain Dr. Richard Karnak was instrumental in testifying in the liability cases."

"You think Richard Karnak equals Dickie Kodiak?"

"I don't have to guess," said Syd. "Do you have a photo of the victim? When he was alive, I mean?"

Dar fumbled through the file and came up with a small passport photo labeled KO-DIAK, RICHARD R. Syd had tapped keys, and a high-resolution black-and-white photo filled a third of her PowerBook's screen. It was the same photograph.

"And Donald Borden?" said Dar.

"Alias Daryl Borges, alias Don Blake," said Syd, calling up a photograph and data column on the other man. "Eight priors—five for fraud, three for assault and battery." She looked at Dar and her eyes were bright. "Mr. Borges was a member of an East L.A. gang until he was twenty-eight, but now he works for an attorney...a certain Jorgé Murphy Esposito."

"Shit," Dar said delightedly. "And Gennie Smiley. That has to be fake."

"Nope," said Syd, looking at another column of data. "But it wasn't her current legal name, either. She was married seven years ago."

"Gennie Borges?" guessed Dar.

"*Sí,*" said Syd, and her grin grew broader. "But Smiley was an earlier married name...married briefly to a Mr. Ken Smiley who died in a car accident seven years ago. Can you guess her maiden name?"

Dar looked at Syd for a quiet minute.

"Gennie Esposito," said Syd at last. "Sister to the ubiquitous attorney."

Dar looked back at his screen where the van continued hitting the pedestrian, accelerating away out of sight into the night, and then returning to run over the poor man again...and again.

"They know I know this," muttered Dar. "But for some reason they felt threatened by me."

"It *is* murder," said Syd.

Dar shook his head. "The LAPD had already passed on the whole matter… the rental people settled…Donnie and Gennie moved to San Francisco. No one was interested. It has to be something else."

"Whatever else it is," said Syd, "it points directly at our Attorney Esposito. But there's something even more interesting here." She tapped at her computer keys.

Dar caught a glimpse of the Power-Book's screen as the FBI symbol appeared, an asterisk password was typed, and directories, data, and photographs began flashing by.

"You can access the FBI data banks?" said Dar, surprised. Even ex–special agents did not reserve that privilege.

"I'm officially working with the National Insurance Crime Bureau," said Syd. "You know, Jeanette from Dickweed's meeting—her group. It merged with the Insurance Crime Prevention Institute in 1992, and to show its support, the FBI gives the NICB full access to its computer files."

"That must come in handy," said Dar.

"Right now it does," said Syd, pointing to the photograph and fingerprint ID of the late Dickie Kodiak, a.k.a. Dr. Richard Karnak, original legal name—Richard Trace.

"Richard Trace?" said Dar.

"Son of Dallas Trace," said Syd, tapping more keys and looking at more data.

Dar blinked twice. "Dallas Trace? The big-time, good-old-boy lawyer? The guy in the buckskin vest and bolo tie and long hair who has that stupid legal show on CNN?"

"The same," said Syd. "Next to Johnnie Cochran, America's best-known and most-loved defense attorney."

"Bullshit," said Dar. "Dallas Trace is an arrogant twit. He wins trials with the same tricks that Cochran used in the O.J. trial. And he has a book out—*How to Convince Anyone of Almost Anything*—but he couldn't convince me to read it in a thousand years."

"Nonetheless," said Syd, "it was his son Richard who was run over and killed—murdered—in your Kodiak-Borden-Smiley van accident."

"We need to get started on this," said Dar.

"We just *did* get started," said Syd. "The murder attempt on you and my investigation into the fraud-business gang wars are now on the same track. Monday we'll move ahead on it."

"Monday?" said Dar, shocked. "But it's only *Saturday* afternoon."

"And I haven't had a goddamned weekend off in seven months," snapped Syd, her eyes fierce. *"I want one more day off and one more night to sleep in the sheep wagon before this goes any further."*

Dar held both palms up. "It's been a long time since I've had even a Sunday off."

"Agreed then?" she said.

"Agreed," Dar said, and held out his hand to shake hers.

She reached up, pulled his face closer to hers, and kissed him firmly, slowly, surely, on the lips. Then she went to the door.

"I'm going to take a nap, but when I come back this evening, I expect steaks to be grilling."

Dar watched her leave, considered following her, considered kicking himself in the ass, and then drove into town to buy the steaks and some more beer.

10

"J IS FOR JORGÉ"

Dar pulled the lap belt tight and then tugged the shoulder straps snug as he settled into the L-33 Solo and moved the rudder pedals back and forth to make sure he was comfortable. Ken taxied the towplane forward a bit while his brother, Steve, stood watching the two-hundred-foot-long tow rope lose slack. Ken stopped for a moment. Steve looked over at Dar in the bubble cockpit of the L-33 and made a circular motion with his fist and thumb up, meaning "check controls." Dar had checked them, and gave the thumbs-up signal for ready to go.

Steve caught his brother's eye in the towplane and swung his right hand low across his body from left to right. Ken pulled the tow rope taut and glanced back from the single-seater Cessna. Steve looked over at Dar again, who nodded, his right hand comfortably loose on the stick, his left hand on his knee but ready to grab the tow-hook release knob at the first sign of trouble. The towplane began its roll-out and the sailplane jerked slightly and began to bump along behind it off the grass and then down the asphalt runway.

Dar went back through his A-B-C-C-C-D checklist again as he rolled toward take-off speed: Altimeter, Belts, Controls, Canopy, Cable, Direction. Everything all right. He shifted slightly to get more comfortable. Besides his lap belt and shoulder straps, he was strapped into a model 305 Strong Para-Cushion Chair parachute— the integrated seat pad putting something between his butt and the metal seat, and the inflatable air bladders along the back of the chute giving him much better back support than the upright strip of metal offered by the plane's seat. Most sailplane pilots of Dar's acquaintance disdained parachutes, but two of those he'd known had died for the lack of them: one in a totally foolish midair collision above Mount Palomar a few miles to the north, and the other in a highly improbable accident doing loops in his high-performance glider when the left wing simply detached.

Dar liked both the physical comfort of the integrated chute seat under him and the mental comfort of having the chute aboard.

The sailplane left the ground before the towplane, of course, and Dar held it a firm six feet above the runway until Ken got the Cessna airborne in a few hundred feet, and then Dar expertly put the L-33 in the normal "high tow" position, staying just about level with Ken's little Cessna and just above the towplane's wake. Officially, Dar was using a standard mountain-country technique of keeping his glider aligned properly with the towplane—that is, keeping the towplane at a fixed position on his windshield just above the sailplane's simple instrument console—but in truth he was using the skilled pilot's trick of just placing himself where he wanted to be in relationship to the towplane and staying there. This skill required a certain amount of precognition and telepathy, but after being aero-towed by Ken several hundred times, both those elements were there.

It was a beautiful morning with unlimited visibility, a gentle three-knot wind out of the west, and lovely thermals building in the foothills and mountains around the valley airstrip. But when they had gained a thousand feet of altitude, Dar could see a storm front far to the west. It would be moving in over the coast soon and would spoil the day's soaring within a few hours.

They climbed at a steady rate as the towplane turned north and then west, then continued climbing as the Cessna turned them back onto a northeasterly course, toward Mount Palomar and into the wind. At the prearranged altitude of two thousand feet, Dar let the tension on the towline grow taut so that Ken could feel the imminent release. Then Dar pulled the release knob twice, saw and felt the towrope go free, and banked into a right climbing turn as Ken dropped the Cessna into a steep left descent.

Then the L-33 was on its own, lifting into the thermals rising from the foothills and steep ridges north of the airfield, and Dar settled back to enjoy silence broken only by the lulling and informative rush of air over the metal wings and fuselage.

Dar had awakened early that Sunday morning, prepared coffee, set out bagels, cereal, and a note for Syd, and was prepared to leave for the Warner Springs gliderport when Syd herself showed up at the door, dressed again in jeans with a red cotton shirt this day and a light khaki vest with many pockets. Her holster and pistol were on her belt under the vest.

"I was out for a walk," she said. "Are you skipping out on me?"

"Yep," Dar said, and explained.

"I'd love to go along."

Dar hesitated. "It's boring just standing around the field waiting," he said. "You'd have a better time hanging around here and reading the Sunday paper...I can drive down to the junction and get it. They have a paper dispenser near the row of mailboxes."

"Won't you let me fly with you?" she asked.

"No," said Dar, hearing more harshness in the syllable than he had meant. "I mean, my sailplane is a one-seater."

"I'd still like to go watch," said Syd. "And remember, I'm not really your guest this weekend, I'm your bodyguard."

So they rinsed a Thermos with hot water and filled it with coffee, put some bagels in a bag, drove back through the little town of Julian on Highway 78 and then turned north and west through canyons on Highway 79 before coming out into the broad valley at Warner Springs.

Syd was surprised at how small his sailplane was. "It's not much more than a pod, a boom, wings, and a tail," she said as he unlashed the tie-down cords.

"You don't need much else for a sailplane," he said.

"I thought they were called gliders," said Syd.

"That too."

She steadied one wing while he lifted the tail boom, and together they pushed the red-and-white sailplane out from the tie-down area onto the grassy berm of the airstrip. Ken, flying his Cessna towplane, was making frequent touchdowns, tying onto other gliders, and towing them skyward.

"It's light," said Syd, moving the wing easily up and down. "But it's made of metal. I thought gliders were canvas over wood or something, like the old biplanes."

"This is an L-33 Solo," said Dar, "designed by Marian Meciar and manufactured at the LET factory in the Czech Republic. It's almost all aluminum alloy except for the fabric on the rudder part of the tail. It weighs only four hundred and seventy-eight pounds empty."

"Do the Czechs make good gliders… sailplanes?" asked Syd as Dar opened the cockpit and dropped the seat-cushion-parachute in place.

"With this one they sure did," said Dar.

"I had to sand down some original paint ridges that were creating a high drag knee in the polar at about fifty-nine kts, and this model does have a tendency to stall without any prestall warning buffet, but for someone with enough experience it's a nice craft."

"How long have you been flying sailplanes?"

"About eleven years," said Dar. "I began along the Front Range of Colorado and then bought this plane used when I moved out here."

Syd opened her mouth to speak, hesitated the briefest of seconds, and said, "How much does a plane like this cost…if you don't mind my asking?"

Dar smiled at her. "It was a good value at $25,000. But that's not what you were going to ask. What?"

Syd looked at him a second. "I know you don't fly commercially. I thought that you hated flying."

Dar had started his walk-around preflight inspection. "Uh-uh," he said, not looking at the chief investigator. "I love flying.

Let's just say that I don't like being a passenger in the air."

Now Dar turned back into the wind and climbed over the foothills below Mount Palomar. To his east he had seen Beauty Peak standing alone—its summit at about his altitude of fifty-five hundred feet—and Toro Peak farther to the southeast, its lone cone several thousand feet higher. But it was the thermals from these lovely ridges and foothills that Dar was seeking.

The L-33, as with most sailplanes, had very little in the way of instrumentation and controls. Dar had the stick, tubular rudder pedals, a short handle for the spoiler and air brake controls, another handle to lower and lock the undercarriage, the large knob for tow rope release, and a small instrument panel with his altimeter, variometer, and airspeed indicator. The little sailplane had no radios or electronic navigation devices. Actually, the instrument that Dar used most commonly was the "yaw string"—a bit of colored string attached to the fuselage directly in front of the cockpit. That and familiarity with the sound of the wind over the wing and fuselage let him know his airspeed better than the instruments. Dar knew from experience that the ASI pitot on the fuselage nose that fed wind speed/velocity data to the airspeed indicator was fairly reliable, but that the two ASI static ports on the aft fuselage sides were not flush, so they registered airspeeds about 6 percent above what they actually were. As long as he knew this bias, he was safe enough. Mental arithmetic had never been a problem for Dar. Besides, the yaw string never lied to him.

Moving his head constantly to keep track of other gliders and powered aircraft—only a few were visible far to the east—Dar sought out the thermals rising from east-facing foothill slopes, bare patches of rock, and even from the tile roofs of the clusters of homes below. Two thousand feet above him and closer to Mount Palomar, a large hawk circled lazily in its own massive thermal. A few clouds were floating on the east side of the mountains now, and Dar could see a foehn wall of heavy clouds piled on the western slope of Palomar, with some spilling over the summit. Farther west he could see tall, black nimbo and stratocumulus building as the storm came in across the coast. This did not worry him. His plan was to continue his elementary 270-degree looping climbs through the foothill thermals until he had at least a safe eight thousand feet of air beneath him, and then tackle the lift and sink areas on the leeward side of the big peaks. This was known as "wave soaring" and took a bit more experience and skill to do right than simple thermal soaring.

Dar worked the ridges, finding the stronger thermals on the sun-soaked slabs, climbing, and then swooping back to the east in places to come on the downwind side of the slope to use the venturi effect to lift and soar through the notches between lower peaks, then circling back for more thermal lift. Finding these anabatic lift points and east-slope thermals meant working within a hundred or two hundred feet of the steep slopes—sometimes much closer. The tall Douglas fir and ponderosa pine on those slopes seemed very near each time Dar lazily banked the L-33 to the right and up, the variometer showing the climb in feet per minute. Dar glanced back over his left shoulder as he crossed one of these ridges and saw three deer running silently along the ridgetop. The only sound in his universe was the soft lull of the wind over the canopy and aluminum fuselage. The morning sun was getting very hot and he slid open the small panels on the left and right of the Plexiglas, *feeling* the warm winds that were lifting him as well as sensing the slight drop in performance as the airflow over the canopy was disturbed.

Now Dar was clearing the last of the steep ridges before the serious mountains, necessarily coming at them from the downwind side so approaching with plenty of speed and extra altitude, always ready to bank hard and turn and run if the curl-over downdrafts were too heavy to handle. But each time he cleared the ridge—sometimes only thirty or forty feet above the ridge of rock or pinnacles of pines—and then gained lift for the next one. Finally he was west of the line of ridges and some six thousand feet above a valley floor, approaching the slopes of Palomar, crabbing the L-33 sideways into the strengthening winds, and planning his wave-lift approach. The obliging presence of some "lennies"—flying-saucer-shaped lenticular clouds which rose above the rotor effect in the trough of the wave beyond the leeward foehn gap—showed him the crests of the lift-area waves by stacking lenticulars like so many dishes on a shelf.

Dar glanced over his shoulder before beginning a 270-turn to gain a bit more altitude and was shocked to see another high-performance sailplane approaching from above and to his right. Sailplanes did not like to fly in formation—midair collisions were the most serious things glider pilots could face—and for this one to be so close when there was so much good empty sky today was unusual. If not actually impolite.

The blue-and-white glider came closer and Dar immediately identified it as

Steve's Twin Astir—a nice, high-performance, two-seater glider in which the airport owner gave rides and instruction. Then Dar recognized Syd in the front seat.

For a second, his response was irritation, but then he relaxed, loosening his hand on the stick. It was a beautiful day. If Syd wanted to go soaring, why not?

But Steve's Twin Astir was coming closer, rocking its wings as it came. The wing rocking was a signal during aero-tow to *release now!* but Dar had no idea what Steve was trying to say as the two sailplanes came abreast of each other, wingtips about thirty feet apart, both of them rising quickly on the next lift wave coming off Palomar.

Syd was gesturing. She held up her cell phone, pantomimed talking into it, and pointed back toward the Warner Springs valley.

Dar nodded. Steve peeled away first, gaining altitude over the foothills but making a beeline for the airfield. Dar followed a few hundred meters behind. Coming out of the hills over the wide valley, he followed the Twin Astir into the usual entry-leg point south of the Warner Springs airport, dropped farther back as the two aircraft entered the eastern downwind leg at about seven hundred feet above the ground, made the base-leg turn north at about four hundred feet of altitude, watched the Twin Astir touch down smoothly on the grass to the right of the asphalt strip, and set his aiming point for flare-out about 150 feet behind that.

The wind was gusting now, but Dar came in smoothly, keeping his airspeed steady during the final approach while watching the yaw string flutter and estimating his minimum stalling speed plus 50 percent plus half of the estimated wind velocity, now at about twelve knots.

Steve had used a rather steep angle of descent and now so did Dar, using his spoilers and flaps to keep himself on the proper glide path, finally smoothing out the glide perfectly parallel to the ground at an altitude of exactly one foot, feeling the slight crosswind at the last second and ruddering around to perfectly align the nose of the L-33, and then touching down so gently with the nosewheel that he could hardly feel the contact. Dar focused his attention on the rudder, keeping the Czech-built aircraft moving smoothly across the short-cropped grass and finally braking to a stop less than six feet from the left wing of Steve's Twin Astir.

Dar popped the canopy and was out of his parachute harness and shoulder straps in a few seconds. Syd was already jogging toward him.

"Dickweed called," she said before Dar could speak. "Jorgé Murphy Esposito is dead. If we hurry, we can get to the scene before everyone mucks it up."

It was raining hard when they arrived at the construction site in south San Diego. They had decided to get their luggage, documents, and videotapes, so it had taken extra time to go back to the cabin, load up, lock up, and then get back to the city. By the time they arrived, Esposito's body had been taken away, and there was yellow police tape around the accident site, but the place was still milling with uniformed police and others.

Captain Frank Hernandez, who had been at Wednesday's meeting in Dickweed's office, was the ranking plainclothes officer on the scene. Hernandez was short but solid—a light heavyweight without the altitude but with all the attitude, his face all angles and planes—and he wasted neither his words nor his time on fools. Dar had heard from Lawrence and others that Hernandez was an honest cop and an excellent detective.

"What are you two doing here?" asked the captain as Dar followed Syd through the pouring rain to the collapsed scissors lift which was wrapped about with yellow tape.

"The DA's office called," said Syd. "Esposito was a potential witness in our investigation."

Hernandez grunted and smiled slightly at the word *witness*. "I could see why you would have an interest in Mr. Esposito, Chief Investigator," he said. "He was definitely one of the area's top cappers."

Syd nodded and looked at the scissors lift. If the heavy platform had fallen from its highest point, it would have been about a thirty-five-foot drop. Now the platform itself was held up by jacks on each side. While the ground around the area was a sea of mud, it was dry under the scissors lift platform except for sprays of blood, brains, and a darker liquid. Flecks and spatters of brain matter were also visible on the cinderblock wall at the far side of the scissors lift.

"Are you here because it's being considered a homicide?" Syd asked Hernandez.

The detective shrugged. "We have an eyewitness who says otherwise." He nodded toward where a construction foreman holding a clipboard was talking to a uniformed officer. "There were only a few workers on the site today," continued Hernandez. "Vargas—that's the foreman there—he didn't see Attorney Esposito show up, but noticed him talking to someone by the scissors lift."

"Did he recognize the other man?" asked Syd.

Hernandez nodded again. "Paulie Satchel.

Used to work this site but has been laid up due to a fall. Paulie's suing the company..."

"Let me take a wild guess," said Syd. "Esposito was his attorney."

Hernandez's dark eyes showed no amusement as he smiled.

"So is this Satchel a suspect?" asked Syd.

"No." Hernandez sounded certain. "We're looking for him to interview him, but only as a witness. The foreman... Vargas...saw Satchel leaving just as it started raining. Esposito stepped under the scissors lift to get out of the rain. The lift was up at the third-floor level there. Esposito was all by himself the last time Vargas saw him there. Then the lift suddenly gave way, it looks like Esposito jumped the wrong way—toward the wall—and his head was caught in the scissors."

Syd looked at the spray of gray matter on the dry cinder-block wall and said, "Did Vargas actually see the accident?"

"No," said Hernandez, "but he turned his head as soon as he heard the sound it made. He didn't see anyone else around."

"How does a scissors lift just collapse?" asked Dar. He was snapping images with his digital camera.

Hernandez looked the insurance investigator up and down a long moment, as if sizing him up, and said, "Vargas thinks that Esposito was fucking around with that oversized bolt and screw there on the closest column. That's where they fill and drain the hydraulic reservoirs. When the screw came out, the hydraulics lost pressure almost at once and the lift came down just as fast."

"Why would Esposito do that?" said Syd.

Hernandez mopped his wet, black hair off his forehead. "Esposito was a fuckup," he said simply.

Dar came close to the lift, did not step under it, but crouched to look at the dry area underneath. "There are more footsteps here than Mr. Esposito's."

"Yeah," said Hernandez. "The paramedics who extricated him. And the ME who declared him deceased. Only Esposito's footprints were under there when the uniforms and I arrived."

"How could you tell?" said Dar.

Hernandez sighed. "You see any of the construction guys wearing Florsheims with a reinforced heel?"

Syd crouched next to Dar and reached into the taped-off zone, dipping two fingers into some of the dark fluid on the ground and raising the fingers to her face. "So this longer, narrow spray is hydraulic fluid..."

"Yeah," said Captain Hernandez. "And the rest is Esposito."

"But you're keeping the case open," said Syd. "Considering foul play."

"We're going to talk to Paulie Satchel," said Hernandez. "Do formal interviews with some of the other guys who were on site at the time. Somebody like Jorgé Esposito makes a lot of enemies and has a lot of rivals. But right now it looks like it'll be logged as an accident."

"What about Vargas?" said Dar.

Hernandez frowned. "The foreman? He's been with the company for eighteen years. Doesn't even have a parking ticket on his record."

"Mr. Esposito was suing the company," Syd said quietly.

The detective shook his head. "Vargas was on the phone in the main shack over there when the lift came down. He was talking to one of the architects. We can check the phone records and interview the architect. But Vargas is clean. I feel it."

"Instinct?" asked Dar, curious, as always, about how cops deduced things. He almost believed in their sixth sense.

Hernandez squinted at Dar as if he'd read sarcasm in the remark. He said nothing.

Syd broke the silence. "Where did the ME send the body?"

"City morgue," said Hernandez, still looking at Dar with cold, dark eyes. Finally he moved his gaze to Syd. "You thinking of going there?"

"I might."

Hernandez shrugged. "Esposito wasn't a pretty sight when we got here…I doubt if he's any prettier in the morgue. But hey…it's your Sunday."

*   *   *

Dar had noticed in recent years that in the movies, morgues were always filled with naked, beautiful young female bodies and the medical examiners tended to be written and played as fat, insensitive pigs. But the ME of San Diego County, Dr. Abraham Epstein, was a small, meticulously dressed and tailored man in his early sixties, who spoke so softly and seriously that one was reminded of a funeral director, but with more sincerity. Nor did Dar and Syd have to walk past bodies to see Esposito's corpse. The procedure now was to sit in a small, comfortable room while a video of the deceased was shown on a high-resolution thirty-two-inch TV monitor.

As soon as Esposito's face appeared, Dar cringed. He could feel Syd recoiling next to him.

"In medical terminology," Dr. Epstein said quietly, "this is called the Face of Frozen Horror. An antiquated term, but still quite appropriate."

"Dear God," said Syd. "I've seen many dead bodies, many resulting from violent death, but never…"

"An expression such as this," finished the medical examiner. "Yes, very rare. Usually the phenomenon of death, even violent death, eliminates most or all expression from the face—at least until rigor mortis sets in. But this occurs in rare cases involving massive and almost instantaneous trauma to the brain—such as one might find on a battlefield—"

"Or in the closing struts of a scissors lift," said Dar.

"Yes," said Dr. Epstein. "And as you can see, the top of the skull was not only cut open and peeled back—'capped' is what convicts call it, as if in an autopsy—but the skull itself was squeezed quite violently. Much of the brain matter was expelled, and that which remained lost contact with the deceased's central nervous system in less time than it takes for the nerve impulses to travel to the body."

They sat in silence for a moment—silence broken only by the soft sound of Dar tapping in numbers on his pocket calculator—and Jorgé Murphy Esposito's expression stared at them from the monitor. His eyes were rolled upward as if watching a guillotine descending, his mouth opened impossibly wide in a scream that would never end, the muscles of his face and neck distorted almost to the point of cartoon absurdity—all under the peeled-back skull, the remaining bit of bone and hair looking like a cheap toupee that had blown half off.

"Dr. Epstein," said Dar, "my calculations suggest that if the platform were at its maximum height...which is what the construction foreman and the few other workers on the job today said in interviews...a loss of hydraulic fluid would mean that the platform would reach near-terminal velocity almost immediately. The platform would have struck Mr. Esposito in less than two seconds."

Dr. Epstein nodded slowly. "This is consistent with the studies done on the so-called Face of Frozen Horror. The brain must be...disconnected...from the nervous system in one point eight seconds or less for the facial expression to remain fixed in such a manner."

Dar looked at Syd. "And how far do you think Esposito's body was from the column where the screw was opened to spill the hydraulic fluid?"

"The platform is twelve and a half feet wide," said Syd. "Esposito was on the side opposite the column with the released screw, and his head was protruding from the scissors' struts by several inches, as if he were trying to throw himself out through the closing X of metal."

"Do you think he could have turned that bolt, removed that long screw, and jumped across that space in less than two seconds?" asked Dar.

"No," said Syd. "And if, as his expression suggests, Esposito *saw* the platform falling, his instinct—anyone's instinct—would have been to jump forward, out from under it. Not run deeper under and try to escape near the wall."

Dar put his calculator away.

"There is something else," said Dr. Epstein. He led them into a medical work and storage area between the waiting room and the actual morgue lockers. There were various bags on shelves, most labeled with the international symbol for toxic bio-waste. Epstein pulled a box from a drawer, pulled on disposable surgical gloves of the type used by paramedics since the AIDS epidemic began, and handed a pair to both Dar and Syd. He lifted down one of the clear bags. The tag on it said ESPOSITO, M. JORGÉ and had the current date and case number on it.

"This has all been photographed and videographed by the police, of course," said Dr. Epstein, "but you should see the actual thing." He opened the bag and laid Esposito's clothes out on a stainless steel table with blood gutters.

The pinstripe suit had been a cheap one, Dar could see, and the blood and brain matter on it did not make it look any more attractive. The white shirt was almost completely red. Esposito had been wearing a bold, yellow tie, now stained mostly crimson.

The medical examiner lifted the sleeves of the suit jacket and then the sleeves of the shirt. "You see," he said.

Syd nodded immediately. "Blood... human tissue... but no hydraulic fluid."

"Exactly," said Dr. Epstein, in his modulated, mournful tones. "Nor was there any hydraulic fluid on the body's hands, face, or upper body. But here..."

He lifted the trouser legs. Dar put his gloved hand on them to turn them better into the overhead light. The right trouser leg was black and oily from hydraulic fluid. Epstein removed worn, black Florsheim shoes with a reinforced heel from the bottom of the bag. Both shoes had blood on them, but only one, the right one, had been soaked in hydraulic liquid. And even the sole of the shoe stank of the fluid.

"The spray trail we saw must have spurted out of the pipe about eight feet," said Syd. "For some reason, Esposito was under the lift—probably near the middle of the area or closer to the wall—and couldn't run for the opening. He turned and jumped for the gap between the cross struts just as the scissors closed. The hydraulic fluid caught just his pant legs and his right shoe as he jumped."

"What could keep someone from running the shortest distance to safety with two tons of platform dropping toward him?" asked Dar.

"Or *who?*" added Syd.

Dr. Epstein put the clothing back in the evidence bag. He peeled off his now bloody gloves, dropped them in the toxic bio-waste bin, and scrubbed his hands at the sink. Syd and Dar followed suit.

In the waiting room again, the monitor now mercifully blank, they both thanked the medical examiner.

Dr. Epstein smiled, but his eyes remained sad. "I know about Attorney Esposito," he said so quietly that Dar had to lean closer to hear him. "Ambulance chaser. Almost certainly an accident capper. But it was a terrible death. And... even though Detective Hernandez and others do not seem interested...it must be reported as a wrongful death."

"A wrongful death," agreed Syd.

"Murder," said Dar.

The two went out into the heavy rain.

11

"K IS FOR STRIKE OUT"

It was nearly noon when Sydney Olson's Ford Taurus turned off the Avenue of the Stars in Century City and rolled down the steep ramp toward the underground parking garage.

"So are you going to tell me now what all this is about?" asked Dar, sipping the last of his 7-Eleven coffee and trying not to spill it as Syd took the ticket and drove quickly down the curving concrete ramp that seemed to be leading them to the parking lot for Hell.

"Not quite yet," said Syd. She noticed an empty slot next to a scarred concrete pillar and swung the Taurus in expertly.

Dar grunted.

Dar hated rising early, and he hated driving into L.A. during Monday rush-hour traffic even more. This morning he had done both. Syd had picked him up at seven-thirty for this lunch-hour meeting with... Dar had no idea with whom. The traffic had been as bad as he had ever seen it, but Syd had driven calmly, resting her thin wrist on the steering wheel and becoming lost in thought when the miles of packed vehicles came to a total stop. They had spoken little during the long commute.

At least the press was gone. There had been no TV vultures skulking outside Dar's warehouse condo when he had returned on Sunday evening, and none this morning. Last week's "road rage killing" was evidently old news and all the Insta-Cams and satellite trucks were off covering this week's top story—a sex scandal involving someone high up in the mayor's office and a well-known lobbyist. The fact that both the principals were attractive women did not make the press's appetite any less voracious.

In the elevator from the basement parking garage, Syd said, "You sure you've got the video?" Dar hefted his old briefcase.

They passed the floor where Robert Shapiro had leased his office space during the O. J. trial. Dallas Trace's office suite was on the penthouse floor.

Dar was surprised by how spacious and busy the suite was. Once beyond the foyer, receptionist, and plainclothes security guard, they passed through a large area bustling with at least a dozen secretaries. Dar could see five smaller offices, undoubtedly staffed by Trace's young legal associates, before they reached the main man's corner office. The door was open and Dallas Trace looked up, grinned, and leaped out of his leather executive chair, gesturing them in and grinning as if they were old friends.

Again, Dar was surprised by the sumptuousness of the office. He could see the hills to the north—and because yesterday's storm had blown away most of the smog for the time being, Dar knew that if he looked out the west window wall, he could make out Bundy Drive in Brentwood, about three miles west, where Nicole Brown Simpson and Ronald Goldman had been murdered years before by someone cleverly disguised in the DNA of O. J. Simpson.

Dar was surprised by the size of the staff and the elegance of the office because most defense attorneys of his acquaintance—even the very successful and somewhat famous ones—tended to run a lean, mean business operation, often paying office expenses, including their lone secretaries and one or two young legal associates, with their own personal checks each week. It was—as legal writer Jeffrey Toobin once said—the famous criminal attorney's dilemma: successful though one may be, repeat business is rare.

Dallas Trace showed no signs of financial anxiety. The man was taller and thinner than he looked on television—at least six three, Dar thought—with a chiseled and manly face, a Marlboro Man face. His smile was easy and emphasized the laugh lines around his eyes and the muscles around his thin-lipped mouth. Trace wore his long, gray hair tied back with a leather thong. His eyebrows were deep black, which emphasized his light gray eyes and made them all the more startling and photogenic in the tanned, lined face. Trace was wearing his trademark denim shirt and bolo tie—although Dar noticed that the shirt was blue silk rather than actual denim—and a leather western vest. This one looked as if it had been tanned from the hide of a stegosaurus—an old stegosaurus—and probably cost several thousand dollars. The bolo was held in place by the *de rigueur* jade-and-silver piece of jewelry, and there was a small diamond in the cowboy attorney's left ear. Dar always realized how old he was when he reacted negatively to jewelry on men: sometimes, alone on a summer night, he would yell at his TV when a ballplayer was thrown out at first—"You would've made it, you jerk, if you weren't carrying ten pounds of gold chain!" Dar recognized it as age, intolerance, and possibly the onset of Alzheimer's in him, but he did not change his opinion. Dallas Trace wore six rings. His suede Lucchese cowboy boots looked as if they were as soft as butter.

Trace shook Sydney's hand first and then Dar's. As Dar had expected, the big attorney, although slim, was a bone-crusher.

"Investigator Olson, Dr. Minor, take a seat, take a seat." Trace moved back around to his huge leather chair with real speed. Dar guessed that the man was in his early sixties, but he was buff as a twenty-five-year-old athlete. Dar had seen Dallas Trace's twenty-five-year-old wife on TV, and guessed he had good reason to stay in shape.

Dar glanced around the office. Dallas Trace's desk was at the nexus of the two window walls, the attorney's back to the view as if he did not have time for such things. But other walls and shelves and bookcases were covered with photographs of Trace with celebrities and power brokers, including the last four U.S. presidents.

Trace lounged back in his luxurious chair, steepled his fingers, propped his butter-soft Luccheses on the edge of his desk, and asked in his familiar gravelly tenor, "To what do I owe the honor of this visit, Chief Investigator? Doctor?"

"You may have heard about the attempt on Dr. Minor's life last week," said Syd.

Trace smiled, picked up a pencil, and tapped at his perfectly white teeth. "Ah, yes, the famous Road Rage Killer. Are you seeking counsel, perhaps, Dr. Minor?"

"No," said Dar.

"There have been no charges filed," said Syd. "There probably won't be. The two men who opened fire on Dr. Minor were Russian mafia hit men."

Even though this had been reported on the television news ad nauseum, Dallas Trace managed to look surprised and raised one dark eyebrow. "So if you're not here about representation..." He let the question hang.

"When I called for the appointment, counselor, you seemed to know who we each were," said Syd.

Dallas Trace's smile expanded and he tossed the pencil expertly back into its leather cup holder. "Of course, I do, Chief

Investigator Olson. I've taken great interest in the state's attorney's efforts to rein in insurance fraud and its teamwork with the FBI and the NICB. Your investigative work in California the past year or so has been excellent, Ms. Olson."

"Thank you," said Syd.

"And everyone interested in expert accident reconstruction knows about Dr. Darwin Minor," continued the attorney.

Dar said nothing. Beyond Trace's silhouette in the tall chair, traffic moved through Hollywood, Beverly Hills, and Brentwood. Beyond, Dar could see the dark smudge of the sea.

"Dr. Minor has a videotape that you should see, Mr. Trace," said Syd. "Do you have media equipment handy?"

Trace tapped a button on the speakerphone console. A minute later, a young man wheeled in a cart carrying a thirty-six-inch monitor and a stack of VCR and DVD players of every religious denomination. "Is there anything I should know, Ms. Olson, Dr. Minor, before I play this tape? Anything incriminating or which would put us in a lawyer-client relationship?" said Trace, the amusement now absent from his gravelly rasp.

"No," said Syd.

Dallas Trace popped the tape in, closed the office door, returned to his chair, and activated the half-inch VCR with a credit-card-size remote. They watched the video in silence. Actually, Dar noticed, he and Dallas Trace were watching the video; Syd was watching Dallas Trace.

The video showed only the three-dimensional computer animation of the accident: two men coming out of a building, one pushing the other in front of a skidding van, the van circling around to hit him again. Trace remained completely impassive during the presentation.

"Do you recognize the accident depicted in this visual reenactment, counselor?" said Syd.

"Of course I do," said Dallas Trace. "It's a mixed-up computer representation of the accident that killed my son."

"Your son, Richard Kodiak," said Syd.

Trace's cool, gray gaze stayed on the

chief investigator for a moment before he replied. "Yes."

"Counselor, can you tell me why your son had a different last name than yourself?" Syd's voice was low, conversational.

"Am I being interrogated, Chief Investigator?"

"Of course not, sir."

"Good," said Trace, leaning back in his chair again and propping his boots on the edge of the desk. "For a minute I was afraid I might need my lawyer present."

Syd waited.

"My son, Richard, chose to take his stepfather's name...Kodiak," said Trace eventually. "Richard is...was...my child by my first wife, Elaine. We were divorced in 1981 and she has since remarried."

Syd nodded and continued to wait.

Dallas Trace quirked his lips into a curve that was equal parts sadness and smile. "It is no secret, Ms. Olson, that my son and I had a serious falling out some years ago. He legally took his stepfather's name—I can only surmise—at least in part to hurt me."

"Was that falling out related to your son's…ah…lifestyle?" said Syd.

Trace's smile became thinner. "That, of course, is none of your business, Investigator Olson. But in the spirit of good-will, I'll answer the question—as invasive and presumptuous as it is. The answer is no. Richard's discovery of his sexual orientation had nothing to do with our disagreement. If you know anything about me, Ms. Olson, you must know of my support for gay and lesbian rights. Richard is…was… a headstrong youth. Perhaps you could say that there was only room for one bull in the family herd."

Syd nodded again. "What is your reaction to this video, Mr. Trace?"

"I would have been outraged by it," Trace said easily, "except for the fact, of course, that I've seen it before. Several times."

Dar had to blink at this news.

"You have?" said Syd. "May I ask where?"

"Detective Ventura showed it to me during the course of the investigation of the accident," said Trace.

"Lieutenant Robert Ventura," said Syd, "of the Los Angeles Police Department's homicide unit."

"That's correct," said Trace. "But both Lieutenant Ventura and Captain Fairchild assured me...*assured* me, Ms. Olson... that this...video 'reenactment' was based on faulty data and completely unreliable."

Dar cleared his throat. "Mr. Trace, you seem confident that the video is not showing you the murder of your son. May I ask why you're so confident?"

Dallas Trace fixed Dar with his cold stare. "Of course, Dr. Minor. First of all, I respect the professionalism of the detectives in question—"

"Ventura and Fairchild of LAPD homicide," interrupted Syd.

Trace's gaze never left Dar. "Yes, Detectives Ventura and Fairchild. They spent hundreds of hours on the case and ruled out foul play."

"Did you speak to anyone in the LAPD Traffic Investigation Unit?" asked Dar. "Sergeant Rote, perhaps? Or Captain Kapshaw?"

The attorney shrugged. "I spoke to many people involved, Dr. Minor. I probably spoke to those men. Certainly I spoke with Officer Lentile—who wrote the accident report—as well as with Officer Clancey, Officer Berry, Sergeant McKay, and the others who were there that night." The strong muscles around Trace's thin lips quirked upward again, but the resulting smile did not reach his eyes. "I am not without my own slight abilities of interrogation and cross-examination."

"Undoubtedly," said Syd, drawing the attorney's gaze back to her, "but did you speak to the claimants—the other two people directly involved in the accident— Mr. Borden and Ms. Smiley?"

Trace shook his head. "I read their depositions. I had no interest in speaking with them."

"They were reported to have moved to San Francisco," said Syd, "but the San Francisco police cannot locate them at the present time."

Trace said nothing. Without actually glancing at his watch, he made it obvious that they were wasting his expensive time. Dar could only look at Syd. When had she tracked down this information?

"Did you know that your son had an alias, Mr. Trace? That he had identity papers under the name of Dr. Richard Karnak and worked at a medical clinic called California Sure-Med?"

"Yes," said Trace, "I became aware of that."

"Was your son a doctor, Mr. Trace?"

"No," said the attorney. His voice seemed to hold no tension or defensive tone. "My son was a perpetual student… He was in his thirties and still attending graduate classes, never finishing any. He spent one year in medical school."

"How did you become aware of your son's alias and involvement with the Sure-Med clinic, Mr. Trace?" said Syd. "Through Detectives Ventura or Fairchild?"

Trace shook his head slowly. "Nope. I hired my own private investigator."

"And you're aware that the California Sure-Med clinic was an injury mill—a source for fraudulent insurance claims—and that your son had violated state and federal laws by posing as a doctor and sending in false injury reports," Syd said.

"I am aware of that now, Investigator Olson," Trace said, voice flat. "Do you intend to indict my son?"

Syd did not break away from the lawyer's eagle gaze.

Trace sighed and dropped his feet to the floor. He ran his hands over his combed-back gray hair and adjusted the leather thong holding his ponytail in place. "Investigator, I'm afraid I'm ahead of you here. What the police didn't turn up, my private investigator did. I discovered and acknowledge now, on the record, that my son was part of—what did you call it?—an injury mill. A fraudulent-claims network run by what the fraud business calls a 'capper'?"

"Yes."

"A capper named Jorgé Murphy Esposito." Dallas Trace said the last three words as if they tasted of pure bile.

"Who died this weekend," said Syd.

"Yes," said Dallas Trace. He smiled. "Would you like to hear my alibi for the time of the accident, Investigator?"

"No, thank you, Mr. Trace," said Syd. "I know that you were at a charity auction in Beverly Hills on Sunday afternoon. You bought a Picasso drawing for sixty-four thousand two hundred and eighty dollars."

Trace's smile eroded. "Jesus Christ, woman," he said, "you actually *do* suspect me in all this petty shit?"

Syd shook her head. "I really am trying to gather information about one of the most profitable injury mills in Southern California," she said. "Your son, who was involved in it, died under mysterious circumstances—"

"I disagree," Trace said sharply. "My son died in an accident while skipping out on his rent with his friends, two petty thieves, one of whom could not drive a van worth shit. A senseless ending to a largely useless life."

"Dr. Minor's video reconstruction of the event—" began Syd.

The lawyer turned his gaze back to Dar,

without a hint of a smile. "Dr. Minor, a few years ago I went to see this popular movie about a great big ship that sank almost ninety years ago…"

"*Titanic,*" Dar said.

"Yes, sir," continued the lawyer, his West Texas accent becoming more pronounced. "And in that movie, I saw with my own two eyes that big ship sinking—standin' on end, breakin' in two—people fallin' like frogs out of a bucket. But you know somethin', Dr. Minor?"

Dar waited.

"None of it was true. It was *special effects.* It was *digital.*" Dallas Trace spat the words out.

Dar said nothing.

"If I had you on the witness stand, *Doctor* Minor, you on the stand and your precious video in the machine playin' right in front of the jury, it would take me thirty seconds…shit, no, twenty seconds…to show them how in this digital-computer-special-effects age we live in, we can trust *nothing* on tape anymore."

"Esposito is dead," interrupted Syd.

"Donald Borden and Gennie Smiley—actually the former Gennie Esposito, as I'm sure your PI informed you—are missing. And you still don't find that suspicious?"

He swiveled his raptor gaze toward her. "I find *everything* suspicious about it, Ms. Olson. I was suspicious of everything Richard did...every friend he had...every mess he wanted me to bail him out of. Well, finally he got into a mess that no one could bail him out of. I'm convinced it was an accident, Ms. Olson...but I'm also convinced it just doesn't matter a good goddamn. If he hadn't died that night on Marlboro Avenue, he'd probably be in jail now. My son was a poor, confused, weak, and manipulative little shit bird, Ms. Olson, and it doesn't surprise me one steer turd of an iota that he ended up with bottom-dweller losers like Jorgé Esposito and Donald Borden and Gennie former-Mrs.-Esposito Smiley."

"And their disappearance?" said Syd.

Dallas Trace laughed, and for the first time it sounded sincere. "These people perfect turning their whole lives into a disappearing act, Ms. Olson. You know that. It's what they do. It's what my son did. And now he's gone for good and nothing I can do, or you can find out, will bring him back."

Dallas Trace jumped to his feet—he moved very fast for a man in his sixties, Dar noticed again—pulled the tape from the machine, gave it to Syd, and opened the office door.

"And now, if there's nothing else I can help you both with today...."

Dar and Syd got to their feet and moved to the door.

"There is one other thing I was curious about," said Syd. "Your contribution to the Helpers of the Helpless."

The dark eyebrows became almost vertical exclamation points. "What? If you don't mind my bluntness, Ms. Olson, what in the sacred halls of fuckdom does that have to do with anything?"

"You contributed a large amount to that charity last year," said Syd. "How much was it?"

"I have no idea," said Trace. "You'd have to ask my accountant."

"A quarter of a million dollars, I believe," said Syd.

"Then I'm sure you're correct," said Trace, opening the door wider. "You're a good investigator, Ms. Olson. But if you have that figure, you must also know that Mrs. Trace and I are active in—and contribute to—more than two dozen charities. The...what do they call themselves again?"

"The Helpers of the Helpless," said Syd.

"The Helpers of the Helpless serve the Hispanic community," said Trace. "It may also surprise you to know that I do quite a bit of *pro bono* work for the Hispanic community in this state...especially the poor immigrants who are constantly being persecuted...and not infrequently persecuted by the state's attorney's office."

"I am aware of the wide range of charities which you and Mrs. Trace support," said Syd. "You're a generous man, Counselor Trace. And you have been more than generous with your time. Thank you." She held out her hand.

Trace hesitated in surprise, and then shook both Dar's hand and hers.

Once in the basement parking garage, Dar said, "Interesting. Now where?"

"One more stop," said Syd.

It had been a long while since Dar had been to L.A.'s County Medical Center. It was the largest hospital in Los Angeles County and still growing—at least two new additions were being noisily built as Syd found them a parking space on the sixth upper level.

The hospital smelled like all hospitals smell, had the same miserable lighting—that fluorescent glow, like decaying vegetation, that seems to illuminate all the blood under the skin—and the same background noises of coughs, weak voices, laughing nurses, phones ringing, doctors being paged, and rubber soles on linoleum. Dar hated hospitals.

Syd led them through the halls as if giving him a tour, using her chief investigator

ID to gain access to the emergency room, the intensive care center, the birthing ward, the patient rooms, and even the scrub room outside of surgery.

Dar figured it out quickly enough. In addition to the doctors, nurses, interns, orderlies, candy stripers, custodians, administrators, patients, and visitors, there was one other conspicuous presence—men and women wearing white jackets adorned with colorful patches. The patches included a red cross, the medical caduceus in gold on a royal blue background, a round shoulder patch showing an eagle with an olive branch—the patch looking like something one of the NASA Apollo astronauts might have worn—and an American flag. But most prominent—on the left breast of each jacket—was a blue square with a large, red capital H centered in it. Inside the upper bars of the H was a smaller gold cross. To Dar, it looked as if someone had kicked a crucifix for a perfect field goal.

They were in one of the waiting areas for the emergency room when Dar made the connection. They had seen personnel with these H jackets pushing carts loaded with magazines, fruit juice, and teddy bears; they had seen two H-jacketed women holding, hugging, and reassuring a wildly weeping Hispanic woman in one of the hospital chapels; there had been H people in intensive care, whispering—in Spanish, Dar remembered—to some of the most serious cases, and here in the emergency room waiting area, a young Hispanic woman in an H jacket was reassuring an entire family. Dar overheard enough to understand that the family was Mexican, immigrants without green cards. Their daughter, who looked to be about eight, had broken her arm. The arm had been set, but the mother was hysterical, the father was literally wringing his hands, the baby was crying, and the girl's younger brother was on the verge of tears. Dar overheard enough to understand that their fear was that they would be deported now that they had been forced to come to the hospital, but the woman in the H jacket was assuring them in perfect, rapid-fire Spanish that no such thing would happen—that it was against the law, that there would be no report, that they could go home without fear—and that in the morning they could call the Helpers' Hotline and receive further instructions and help that would keep them healthy and happy and in the country.

"Helpers of the Helpless," said Dar quietly as they headed out to the parking garage.

"Yes," said Syd. "I counted thirty-six in our little tour."

"So?"

"So there are thousands…*thousands*…of volunteers for Helpers of the Helpless working in L.A. County. They're in every hospital. It's even chic for movie stars and Rodeo Drive shopper-matrons to volunteer their time, *if* their Spanish is good enough. They've even begun expanding to serve Vietnamese, Cambodian, Chinese, you name it."

"So?"

"So it started as a small Catholic charity," said Syd, "and now it's grown into a huge, nonprofit machine. The Church found a small-time Hispanic lawyer to head it all up, and now it really has nothing to do with the Catholic Church. You'll find Helpers in all the San Diego hospitals and medical centers, in Sacramento, all over the Bay Area, and—in the last year or so—in Phoenix, Flagstaff, Las Vegas, Portland, Eugene, Seattle—even as far away as Billings, Montana. In another year it will be nationwide."

"So?"

"They're part of it, Dar. They're part of this huge capping syndicate that's creating injury mills. They recruit immigrants from everywhere—showing them how to make money on the slip-and-falls and the swoop-and-squats, on industrial accidents and fender benders."

"So?" said Dar again as they got in the hot car, put the air conditioner on, and headed for the freeway. "Nothing new about that. Ever since the big insurance companies grew up and litigation became a business, it's the fastest way for immigrants to get rich in America. Before the

Mexicans and Asians, it was the Irish and the Germans and the rest. Nothing new."

"The scale is what's new," said Syd. "We're not talking about fly-by-night clinics and a few dozen cows and bulls being run by a capper or two, Dar. We're talking RICO here. We're talking organized crime on the scale of the Colombian drug dealers and their American connections." She nodded toward the medical center as they pulled out into traffic. "Doctors and surgeons—*legitimate* doctors and surgeons—are referring patients to the Helpers for... well, help. The goddamn Mexican *consulate* makes referrals."

"So, it makes it easy to recruit more swoop-and-squatters," said Dar, looking out at the jumble of closely cramped, oversized houses along the freeway. "Big deal."

"A several-hundred-billion-dollar-a-year big deal," said Sydney. "And I'm going to find out just who's behind it. Who's organizing this monstrosity."

Dar looked at Syd and only then realized how angry he was. It had all been a lark up to now—letting her be his "bodyguard," letting her stake him out like the goat in *Jurassic Park*, showing her his amusing little accidents and tagging along with her in turn, playing Watson to her Sherlock Holmes.

"You think Dallas Trace is behind this?" he said. "Probably the most famous lawyer in America? Mr. CNN answer man? That posturing, West Texas–from–Newark asshole with his silk work shirts and dork knob? You really think someone that famous is the Don Corleone of Southern Cal capping?"

Syd chewed her lip. "I don't know. I don't *know*, Dar. Nothing connects. But all the loose strings seem to point in his direction somehow."

"You think Dallas Trace ordered his own son to be killed?"

"No, but—"

"You think he killed Esposito, Donald Borden, and the girl, Gennie Smiley?"

"I don't know. If—"

"You think he's the head of the Five Families, Chief Investigator? Squeezing it in between his law practice, his book writing, his weekly CNN show, his public appearances, his stints on *Nightline* and *Good Morning America*, his charity work, and his nights with that beautiful new child-bride?"

"Don't get angry," Syd said.

"Why the hell not? You *knew* he'd seen my accident reconstruction video before."

"Yes."

"So you dragged me in there just so you could watch *him* and he could see *me*. On the off chance that he's the Big Man, you had him take a good look at me, so he would know for sure who to send his hit men after next time."

"It's not like that, Dar..."

"Bullshit," said Dar.

They drove in silence for some time.

"If this conspiracy is as big as I believe it is—" began Syd.

Dar cut her off. "I don't *believe* in conspiracies."

Syd glanced at him.

"I believe in evil institutions," said Dar, trying to control his anger but unable to keep his words light. "I believe in La Cosa Nostra and shitty car makers and evil people like tobacco merchants and those shitheads who give away baby formula to Third World mothers so they'll keep on buying their baby formula even while the babies die of diarrhea from the filthy water..." Dar stopped and took a breath. "But conspiracies...no. Plots are like churches or other multicelled organizations—the bigger they get, the dumber they are. The law of inverse IQ."

"If there are no conspiracies, what do you believe in, Dar?"

"What does it matter?"

"I'm just curious." Syd's voice was flat and emotionless now as well.

"Well, let's see," said Dar, looking out at the traffic mess ahead of them, the solid wedge of automobiles and trucks moving at ten miles per hour. "I believe in entropy. I believe in the unbounded limits of human perversity and stupidity. I believe in the occasional combination of those three elements to create a Friday in Dallas, Texas, with some asshole named Lee Harvey Oswald who learned to shoot well in the Marines getting a clear field of fire for six seconds…"

Dar stopped speaking. *What the hell am I talking about?* Had it been Dallas Trace's arrogance or the death stench of the hospital that had set him off? Maybe he was just going crazy.

After several minutes of silence, Syd said, "And you don't believe in crusades, either."

He looked at her. At that moment she was a total stranger to him—certainly not the woman whose company and repartee he had enjoyed so much over the past several days…

"Crusades always end up sacrificing innocents. Like the original Crusades to free the Holy Land," said Dar harshly. "Sooner or later it's a fucking Children's Crusade, and kids are on the front line."

Syd frowned. "What are you so angry about, Dar? Vietnam? Or your work with the NTSB? The *Challenger*? What are we—"

"Never mind," said Dar. He was suddenly very tired. "The grunts in Vietnam had a saying for everything, you know."

Syd watched the traffic.

"No matter what happened," said Dar, "the infantrymen would learn to say, 'Fuck it. It don't matter. Move on.' "

The traffic stopped. The Taurus stopped. Syd looked at him and there was something more than anger in her eyes.

"You can't base your philosophy on that. You can't live like that."

Dar returned her stare, and only when she looked away did he realize how angry his gaze must have been. "Wrong," he said. "It's the *only* philosophy that lets you live."

They drove into San Diego in absolute silence. When they were near Syd's hotel, she said, "I'll take you up the hill to your condo."

Dar shook his head. "I'll walk to the Justice Center from here. They're releasing my NSX from impoundment this afternoon and I'm meeting the body-shop guy there."

Syd stopped the car and nodded. She

watched him as he got out and stood on the curb. "You're not going to help me any further with this investigation, are you?" she said at last.

"No," said Dar.

Syd nodded.

"Thanks for..." began Dar. "Thanks for everything."

He walked away and did not look back.

12

"L IS FOR LONG SHOT"

Tuesday was a big day for guns, culminating in a high-velocity rifle bullet aimed directly at Darwin Minor's heart.

The day started dismally with more heat, more rain clouds threatening—unusual for Southern California for this time of year, of course, but almost *all* of Southern California's weather was unusual at almost any time of year. Dar started his own day in a foul mood. His anger from the previous day bothered him. The fact that he would not see Sydney Olson again bothered him. The fact that this bothered him, bothered him the most.

The repairs to the NSX were going to cost a fortune. When Harry Meadows, his body-shop friend—and one of the few people in the state who could do decent bodywork on the Acura's aluminum skin—met him at the Justice Center on Monday evening, all he could do was shake his head. The final estimate on repairs had made Dar take a full step backward.

"Jesus," Dar had said, "I could buy a new Subaru for that."

Harry had nodded slowly and mournfully. "True, true," he said. "But then you'd have a fucking Subaru rather than an NSX."

Dar could not argue with the logic of that. Harry had taken the bullet-scarred NSX away on a trailer, swearing that he would take as good care of the car as he would of his own mother. Dar happened to know that Harry's aged mother lived in poverty in an un-air-conditioned trailer sixty-five miles out in the desert where he visited her precisely twice a year.

On Tuesday morning Lawrence called. There were several new cases that needed photographing. Lawrence did not know which ones would require reconstruction work—it depended upon which went to litigation and jury trials—but he thought that he and Dar should visit each site.

"Sure," said Dar. "Why the hell not? I'm only about a month behind in my paperwork as it is."

As Lawrence drove, he must have sensed something was wrong with Dar. There is a certain bond between men that goes deeper than verbal communication. Men who have known each other for years and worked together—occasionally on dangerous projects—begin to gain a sixth sense about their friends' thoughts and emotions. This allows them to communicate on a level deeper than women could ever understand. Lawrence and Dar had just picked up coffee and donuts at a Dunkin' Donuts in north San Diego when Lawrence said, "Something wrong, Dar?"

"No," said Dar.

Nothing more was said.

The first accident site was halfway to San Jose. Lawrence parked the Trooper in the crowded parking lot of a low-rent condo

complex and they walked over to the inevitable yellow-taped-crime-scene rectan-
gle around a 1994 red Honda Prelude. The
accident had occurred in the middle of the
night, but there were still two uniformed
officers there as well as a few gawkers—
mostly gang-banger-aged kids in droopy
shorts and three-hundred-dollar athletic
shoes. Lawrence identified both himself
and Dar to the nearest police officer, politely asked permission for Dar to take pictures, and then got a statement from the
officer.

As Dar shot images, the young patrolman
tried to explain, pointing happily to the
various pieces of evidence—the broken
windows on the car, the cracked windshield, dents in the hood of the Prelude,
slimy gray matter on and around the front
of the car, as well as blood on the shattered
windshield, the hood, the fenders, the
front bumper, and pooled in a wide, dark
stain on the asphalt. Obviously it had not
rained very hard here during the night or
morning.

"Well, this guy, Barry, he's mad at his girlfriend—Sheila something—she lives up-stairs in 2306, she's down at the station now making out a statement," said the cop. "Anyway, Barry's a biker, big fucker with a beard, and Sheila gets tired of him and starts seeing other guys. Well, at least one other guy. Barry, he doesn't like that. So he comes by here, we figure about two-thirty A.M., the reports of a disturbance come in about two forty-eight, and the first report of shots fired came in to 911 at three-oh-two A.M. At first Barry is just, you know, scream-ing up at Sheila's window, shouting obscen-ities at her, her shouting obscenities back, you know. The main entrance, it's got an automatic lock so you gotta buzz to get in and go up, only Sheila doesn't buzz him in.

"This really pisses Barry off. So he goes back to his truck—that's it, the Ford van parked over there—and comes back with a loaded shotgun, double barrel. He starts using the butt of the shotgun to bash in the side windows of Sheila's Prelude there. Sheila starts shitting bricks and screaming louder. The neighbors call the police, but before a black-and-white can answer, Barry

gets it in his mind to get up on the hood—
he must've weighed about two sixty, you
see how he dented the shit out of it just
standing on it—and he begins bashing in
the windshield with the butt of the shotgun. We figure, to get a better grip or
something, he somehow got a finger inside
the trigger guard..."

"And shot himself in the belly?" said
Lawrence.

"Both barrels. Blew his guts all over the
hood, headlights, front bumper—"

"He was still alive in intensive care when
I got the call this morning," interrupted
Lawrence. "Do you have an update?"

The cop shrugged. "When the detectives came to take the girl downtown, word
was that the medics had pulled the plug
on Barry. Sheila's comment was 'Good rid-
dance.'"

"Love," said Lawrence.

"It's a many-splendored thing," agreed
the uniformed officer.

They stopped for three obvious slip-and-
fall scams—two at supermarkets and one

at a Holiday Inn where the claimant was famous for slip-and-falls near ice machines that leaked—and a slow-motion parking-lot swoop-and-squat where five family members were all claiming whiplash. The last accident scene was in San Jose itself. On the way, Lawrence and Dar stopped for lunch. Actually, they just went through a Burger Biggy drive-through and ate their Biggies and slurped their Biggy milk shakes while Lawrence drove.

"So how did Barry's shotgun *sepaku* relate to any of your insurance carriers?" Dar asked between sips.

"First thing Sheila did this morning was file a claim on the Prelude," said the big insurance adjuster. "She says that it's to-taled—that State Farm owes her a brand-new car."

"I didn't see that much damage," said Dar. "Some broken glass. The dents in the hood. Nothing else that a car wash won't take care of."

Lawrence shook his head. "She claims that she would be too traumatized to ever drive the Prelude again. She wants full payment...enough to buy a brand-new SUV. She's had her eye on a Navigator."

"She told the insurance people all this this morning before going to the cops to give her statement?"

"Sort of," said Lawrence. "She called her insurance agent at four A.M."

The last accident site was also in a run-down condo complex, this one right in San Jose. There were uniformed officers on the stairway and an obviously bored plain-clothes detective on the third floor. There was also the smell of death.

"Jesus," said Lawrence, pulling a clean, red bandana out of his hip pocket and holding it over his nose and mouth. "How long has this guy been dead?"

"Just since last night," said Lieutenant Rich of the San Jose PD. "Everyone heard the gunshot about midnight, but no one reported it. The apartment's not air-conditioned, so things have been getting ripe since about ten A.M."

"You mean the body's still *in there?*" Lawrence asked incredulously.

Lieutenant Rich shrugged. "The ME was here this morning when the body was discovered. The cause of death has been established. We've been waiting for the meat wagon all day, but the county coroner has jurisdiction on this and his vehicle's been busy all day. Real mess on the freeways this morning."

"Shit," said Lawrence. He gave Dar a look and then turned back to the lieutenant. "Well, we have to go in and take photos. I have to do a scene sketch."

"Why?" said the detective. "What the hell has the insurance got to do with it at this point?"

"There's already threatened litigation by the deceased's sister," said Lawrence.

"Against who?" said Officer Rich. "Do you know how this guy died?"

"Suicide, isn't it?" said Lawrence. "The lawsuit is against the deceased's—Mr. Hatton's—psychiatrist. His sister says that Mr. Hatton was depressed and paranoid and that the psychiatrist didn't do enough to prevent this tragedy."

The detective chuckled. "I don't think

that's gonna fly. I'd have to testify in court that the psychiatrist did everything she could to keep this poor nut happy. Come on in, I'll show you. You can take your photos, but I don't think you'll want to hang around long enough to do too careful a scene diagram."

Dar followed the plainclothes officer and Lawrence into the small, overheated apartment. Someone had opened the only window that would open, but that was in the kitchen and the body was in the bedroom.

"Jesus Christ," said Lawrence, standing next to the bloodsoaked bed and pillows, looking at the crimson spatters on the headboard and wall. "The .38's still in the poor bastard's hand. The ME says that this isn't suicide?"

Lieutenant Rich, who was trying to hold his nose and look dignified at the same time, nodded. "We have testimony from the shrink that Mr. Hatton was definitely depressed and paranoid, also schizophrenic. The psychiatrist was aware that the late Mr. H. always slept with the .38 Smith and Wesson on his nightstand next to his bed. He was afraid the UN was planning an invasion of the United States... you know, black helicopters, bar codes on road signs to show the African troops where to go to get the gun owners...the usual shit. Anyway, the shrink—she's a woman, by the way, and quite a looker—says that the short-term goal of her therapy was to have Mr. Hatton bring in the pistol for safekeeping."

"Guess that goal won't be reached," said Lawrence through his bandana.

"The shrink says that Hatton was extremely paranoid, but in no way suicidal," said the detective. "She's willing to testify to that. But the poor schmuck was on about five types of meds, including Doxepin and Flurazepam to sleep. Knocks him right out. According to the doctor, Hatton always tried to get to sleep by ten-thirty P.M."

"So what happened?" said Lawrence as Dar shot some regular thirty-five-millimeter stills with high-speed film.

"Hatton's sister called him at three minutes before midnight," said Lieutenant

Rich. "She says that she usually doesn't call him that late, but that she'd had a terrible dream…a premonition of his death."

"So?" said Lawrence.

"Hatton didn't answer the phone. His sister knew that he was taking sleeping pills, so she waited until nine this morning to start calling again. Eventually she called the cops."

"I don't get it," said Lawrence.

Dar crouched by the body, studied the angle of the arm and the turn of the wrist that rigor mortis had sculpted in place, studied the wound high on the dead man's temple, and then moved around the bed to sniff at the pillow on the empty side. "I do," said Dar.

Lawrence looked at Dar, at the body, back at Lieutenant Rich, and then at the body again. "Aw, no. You're shitting me."

"That's the ME's analysis," said the detective.

Lawrence shook his head. "You mean—he was all doped up with sleeping pills, his sister calls because she has a dream that he's died, and this guy thinks he's answering the phone but actually picks up the .38 on the nightstand and blows his brains out? There's no way anyone could prove that."

"There was a witness," said Lieutenant Rich.

Lawrence looked at the empty but mussed side of the bed. "Oh," he said, getting the picture... or at least part of it.

"Georgio of Beverly Hills," said Dar.

Lawrence turned slowly to look at his friend. "Are you telling me that you can look at the imprint on the other side of the bed and sniff around—amidst all this stench—and tell me the name of the guy from Beverly Hills that Mr. Hatton was sleeping with?"

The police detective laughed, then covered his mouth and nose again.

Dar shook his head. "The perfume. Georgio of Beverly Hills." Dar turned to the plainclothes officer. "Let me take a wild guess. Whoever was in bed with Mr. Hatton at the time of the accident didn't come forward last night—either because she's married or the situation would be embarrassing in some other way—but she's given you a statement since then. Whoever she was, you found her this morning…and probably not by checking all of the women in Southern California who wear Georgio."

Detective Rich nodded. "Two minutes after the patrol car pulled up this morning, she broke down and started sobbing, told us all about it."

"What are you two talking about?" said Lawrence.

"The psychiatrist," said Dar.

Lawrence looked back at the body. "Mr. Hatton was boffing his shrink?"

"Not at the time of the accident," said Lieutenant Rich. "They'd finished their boffing for the night, Mr. Hatton had taken his Flurazepam and Doxepin, and they were both asleep. The psychiatrist…I'll keep her name out of it for right now, but my guess is that you'll be hearing it on the eleven-o'clock news a lot in the days to come…she heard the phone ring at midnight, heard Hatton fumble around and say, 'Hello?'—just as the gun went off."

"She obviously decided that discretion

was the better part of valor on her part," said Dar.

"Yeah," said the detective. "She got her ass out of here before the blood quit sprayin'. Unfortunately—for the shrink—the snoopy live-in manager saw her drive off in her Porsche about five minutes after midnight."

"Does Mrs. Hatton's sister know about this yet?" asked Lawrence.

"Not yet," said the detective.

Dar exchanged glances with Lawrence. "That should make the lawsuit even more interesting."

The detective led the way back out into the hallway. Lawrence and Dar followed readily enough. They stood on the balcony to let the breeze blow some of the smell off their clothes.

"It's like the old story of how Helen Keller burned her ear," said Lieutenant Rich.

"How's that?" said Lawrence, making notes and fast sketches in his notebook.

"By answering the iron," Lieutenant Rich said, and began laughing almost hysterically.

Lawrence and Dar did not speak for some time after leaving San Jose. Finally Lawrence muttered, "To protect and serve. Ha!"

At the end of the drive back to San Diego, Dar suddenly said, "Larry, remember when Princess Diana was killed a few years ago?"

"Lawrence," said Lawrence. "Sure I remember."

"What did we talk about...more or less?"

The burly insurance adjuster sighed. "Let's see...the first reports were that the Mercedes that Princess Di and her boyfriend were in had been going a hundred and twenty miles per hour. We knew that was incorrect right from the beginning. We used the TV's freeze-frame to get some stills of the news report, remember? Then we videotaped the later scene reports and studied the stills from them."

"And we talked about how the impact incursion wasn't consistent," said Dar.

"Right. The Mercedes hit that pillar

pretty much dead on, so we know that the front-end incursion wasn't significant enough to show that the car had been going anywhere near a hundred and twenty miles per hour. Also, the TV networks kept reporting that the car had obviously rolled over, but when we looked at the raw video we knew that wasn't so."

"You and Trudy identified the missing roof as the emergency workers' efforts to cut the victims free, right?" said Dar.

"Sure. So did you. And the dents visible in the roof didn't come from a rollover. They came from the rear passengers' heads hitting the inside of the roof after the initial impact."

"And what did we judge the real speed of impact to be, according to the video, the passengers' injuries, and the other scene reports?"

"I said...let's see...I said sixty-three miles per hour. Trudy said sixty-seven. I think you had the low number, sixty-two."

"And when the final report came out, you were right," mused Dar.

Lawrence went on. "None of the reporters seemed to want to mention it, but we all knew that Princess Diana would have almost certainly survived the crash if she'd been wearing her seat belt and shoulder harness. And they'd all be alive if the accident had happened in the United States..."

"Because?" said Dar.

"Because it's both federal and state regulations that pillars in an underpass have to be protected by guardrails," said Lawrence. "You know that; you mentioned it the night of the accident. You even worked out the kinetic-impact-velocity-diminution equations on our computer—showing that if it had been a guardrail rather than a concrete pillar, the Mercedes would have gone ricocheting back and forth through that tunnel, wall to guardrail and back again, dissipating energy as it went. If the occupants other than the bodyguard had been buckled in..."

"But they weren't," said Dar quietly.

"Uh-uh. Trudy calls that the taxi-limousine syndrome," said Lawrence. "People who would never drive or ride in their own automobiles without a seat belt don't even think about buckling up in a limo or taxi. For some reason, you feel invulnerable when a hired driver is behind the wheel."

"Trudy even remembered video of Princess Diana buckling up when driving her own car," said Dar. "What else did we discuss?"

Lawrence scratched his chin. "I'm assuming you'll get to your point here sometime. Let's see. We all agreed that the paparazzi didn't have anything to do with the accident. First, the Mercedes could have easily outrun those little paparazzi motorcycles. Secondly, it could have driven over them without feeling a bump. But we all suspected that a second vehicle was involved...a second automobile, that is. That the driver swerved down into the tunnel and then lost control trying to miss another car."

"Which turned out to be the case," said Dar.

"Yeah. And we were sure they'd discover that the driver had been legally drunk."

Dar nodded. "Why did we assume that?"

"He was French," said Lawrence. Lawrence did not travel to parts of the world where all the people did not speak English. He also did not like the French just on general principles.

"Why else?" said Dar.

"Oh, I think it was Trudy who made the point that the swerve to the left after entering the tunnel—the swerve that sent them directly into the pillar—almost certainly had to be an evasive maneuver and that any competent driver—or sober driver—could have made it at sixty-five miles per hour without losing control of that make of Mercedes. After all, the car was trying to help the driver keep control."

"So the three of us were right about all of the particulars of the accident, even down to the hypothetical extra car involved," said Dar. "But do you remember any other reaction on our part?"

"Oh, I remember keeping a watch on the Net and the professional journals for a while," said Lawrence. "The facts came trickling in that way—through comments by other insurance investigators—long before the networks or news services figured it out."

"Do you remember us crying?" said Dar.

Lawrence took his eyes off the traffic and looked at Dar for what seemed like a long time. Then he looked back at the road. "Are you shitting me?"

"No, I'm trying to remember our emotional reaction."

"Everybody else in the world went apeshit," said Lawrence in obvious disgust. "Remember the TV views of the long lines of sobbing people—grownups—outside the British consulate in L.A.? There were church services up the wazoo and more blubbering on television idiot-on-the-street interviews than I've seen since Kennedy was shot. More than Kennedy. It was like everyone's favorite aunt, wife, mother, sister, and girlfriend had died. It was crazy. It was absolutely nuts."

"Yes," said Dar, "but how did the three of us react?"

Lawrence shrugged again. "I guess Trudy and I were sorry the lady was dead.

It's sad when any young person dies. But Christ, Dar, it wasn't *personal*. I mean, we didn't know the woman. Besides, there was a certain irritation at their carelessness—hers and the boyfriend, Dodi—at letting a drunk drive, at playing games driving that fast just to get rid of a few fucking photographers, and for thinking that they were so above the laws of physics that they didn't need their belts on."

"Yes," Dar said, and was quiet a moment. "Do you remember when the conspiracy theories began about her death?"

Lawrence laughed. "Yeah…about ten minutes after the first news reports were aired. I remember after you did the kinetic equations, we went onto the Internet to find some more facts and already people were yapping about how the CIA killed them or the British secret service or the Israelis. Morons."

"Yes," said Dar. "But our reaction was just one of…what?"

Lawrence frowned at Dar again. "Professional interest," he said. "Is there a problem with that? It was an interesting accident and the media got the details all wrong, as they usually do. It was fun figuring out what really happened. We were right…right down to the phantom car, the alcohol, and the speed of impact. We didn't get involved with the orgy of mourning going on everywhere because that was media-hype celebrity-cult bullshit. If I want to weep for the dead, I'll visit the graveyard in Illinois where my parents are buried. Is there a problem with any of that, Dar? Did we react wrong? Is that what you're saying?"

Dar shook his head. "No," he said. And a moment later, he said it again. "No, we didn't react wrong at all."

Back at his condo loft that evening, Dar could not concentrate. None of the accidents he and Lawrence had investigated that day would take much reconstruction. The gunshot accidents had been a little out of the ordinary, but not that much. Three weeks earlier, Dar and Lawrence had investigated a claim in which an inner-city teenager had shoved a loaded revolver into his waistband and blown off most of his genitals. The family was suing the school district, even though the ninth-grader had skipped school that day. The mother and live-in boyfriend were arguing in the $2 million claim that the school was responsible for making sure the sixteen-year-old was in school.

Dar had twenty other projects he could work on, but he found himself wandering the apartment, pulling books off the shelves and putting them back, checking his e-mail and updating his chess games. Of the twenty-three games he had going, only two required any real concentration. A mathematics student in Chapel Hill, North Carolina, and a mathematician/financial planner in Moscow—financial planner in Moscow!—were giving him real problems. His Moscow friend, Dmitry, had beaten him twice and played him to a stalemate once. Dar looked at the e-mail, went to the physical chess board he kept set up for that game, moved Dmitry's white knight, and frowned at the result. This would take some thought.

Dar was surprised when Sydney called.

"Hey, I was hoping to catch you home. Would you mind some company?"

Dar hesitated only a fraction of a second. "No...I mean, sure. Where are you?"

"In the hall outside your apartment," said Syd. "Your police protection didn't even notice us when we came in the back way...carrying a suspicious package."

"Us?" said Dar.

"I brought a friend," said Syd. "Shall I knock?"

"Why don't I just open the door," said Dar.

Syd was indeed carrying a suspicious package. Dar guessed that it was a rifle or shotgun wrapped in canvas. Her friend was a strikingly handsome Latino a few years younger than Syd or Dar. The man was only of medium height, but he had the muscular presence of a long-ball hitter. His wavy black hair was brushed straight back, he looked lean and comfortable in khaki pants, a khaki wind-breaker, and a gray polo shirt, and although he wore cowboy boots, the effect was natural—as if he belonged in them—exactly the opposite of the costume effect that Dallas Trace's boots had created. He introduced himself as Tom Santana and his handshake was also the opposite of Dallas Trace's: where Trace had attempted to impress with his bonecrushing intensity, Santana was obviously a very powerful man with the restraint of a gentleman.

"I've heard of you, Dr. Minor," said Tom. "Your reconstruction work is much admired. I'm surprised we haven't met before."

"Dar," said Dar. "And I don't get out much. But I do know the name Tom Santana...You started out with the CHP Staged Collision Unit and shifted over to the Fraud Division in 'ninety-two...working undercover. You were the one who blew open the Cambodian and Vietnamese capper gangs in 'ninety-five and put those two attorneys in jail."

Santana grinned. He had the smile of a movie star but none of the self-consciousness. "And before that, the Hungarians who literally wrote the book on capping in

California," he said with a laugh. "As long as the Hungarians and the Vietnamese and the Cambodians stayed within their own ethnic group, we couldn't get to them. But once they started recruiting Mexicans as *el toros y la vacas*—then I could go undercover."

"But you're not undercover anymore," said Dar.

Tom shook his head. "Too well known for that now. Last couple of years I've been heading up FIST... The last year, I've been working on and off with Syd here."

Dar knew that FIST was a Fraud Division acronymic cuteness standing for Fraud Intelligence Specialist Team. And the way this man and Syd acted around each other... just stood so easily together... sat so comfortably on his leather couch next to one another, not too close, not too far apart... Dar did not know what the hell it meant, but he was irritated at himself for feeling some pang about it. How long had he known Chief Investigator Olson anyway? Five days? Did he expect her not to have a life before that? *Before what?*

"Drink?" said Dar, walking to the antique dry sink he used as a bar.

Both shook their heads. "We're still on duty," said Tom.

Dar nodded and poured himself a bit of single-malt Scotch, then sat in the Eames chair across from them. The last of the evening sunlight came through the tall windows and fell across them in slowly moving trapezoids of gold light. Dar sipped his Scotch, looked at the canvas-wrapped package, and said, "Is that for me?"

"Yes," said Syd. "And don't say no until you hear us out."

"No," said Dar.

"Goddamn it," Syd said. "You are one stubborn man, Dar Minor."

Dar sipped Scotch and waited.

"Will you hear us out at least?" asked Syd.

"Sure."

The chief investigator sighed and said, "I'm going to get a drink, on duty or not…

No, don't get up, Dar. I know where the Scotch is. Go ahead, Tom."

Tom Santana used his hands for emphasis when he spoke. "Syd tells me that you feel like you were being used, Dr. Minor…"

"Dar."

"Dar," continued Tom, "and in a way, you were. We both apologize for that. But when the Russians made their move against you, it was the biggest break we've had in the Alliance case."

Syd came back to the couch with her glass of Scotch and settled back into the cushions. "We've been watching about a dozen top lawyers around the country…I mean *top* lawyers, famous men…about half of them here in California, the rest in places like Phoenix, Miami, Boston, New York."

"Including Dallas Trace," said Dar.

"We think so," said Tom.

Dar took a drink of single-malt again before speaking. The light made the amber whiskey glow in its glass. "Why would these lawyers—presumably if they're at or near Trace's level of success—take such a risk when they already make millions of dollars legitimately?"

Tom's hands stabbed out like an infielder getting ready to handle a hot grounder. "At first we couldn't believe it either. Some of it may be personal...like Esposito's involvement in the death of Dallas Trace's son, Richard...but most is just business. You know how many billions are hauled in every year through injury mills and fraudulent claims. This...Alliance...of big-time lawyers appears to be taking out the middlemen."

"Literally taking them out?" said Dar. "As in murdering them?"

"Sometimes," said Syd. She looked tired. The last of the evening light on her face showed wrinkles that Dar had not noticed before. "Gennie Smiley and Donald Borden, for instance...We haven't found them in San Francisco or Oakland. We haven't found them anywhere."

Dar nodded. "You might try the bay itself." He glared at Syd without meaning to. "So when the Russians took their shots at me, you got me into this because you hoped I'd trip Dallas Trace's hand somehow? Why? Because you knew that I'd made the videotape reconstructions?"

Syd leaned forward quickly, a look of concern or pain on her face. "No, Dar, I swear. I knew that Dallas Trace had seen evidence that his son had been killed—we interviewed Detectives Fairchild and Ventura because it was strange that the homicide unit had taken over the investigation from the accident unit—but I swear, I promise you that I didn't know that you'd done that reconstruction tape until you showed it to me at the cabin." Tom remained silent, looking from one to the other of them as if trying to understand the tension that suddenly filled the room.

"So why did you bring me along to face Dallas Trace?" asked Dar after a moment.

Syd set her Scotch down on the rough-planked coffee table. "Because the tape was so *good*," she said. "No rational man could look at that and not believe that his son had been murdered. I was willing to give Dallas Trace the benefit of the doubt until yesterday. But once he looked at that reconstruction video and then threw us out, I *knew* he was into all this up to his neck."

Dar sighed. "So what the hell do you want me to do?"

"Help us," said Tom Santana. "Keep working with Syd. Use your reconstruction skills to get to the bottom of this Alliance conspiracy."

Dar did not respond.

Syd turned to Tom Santana. "Dar doesn't believe in conspiracies."

"I didn't say that," snapped Dar. "I said I don't believe in *successful* conspiracies. After a while, they collapse from their own weight of ignorance or because the people involved are too stupid to keep their mouths shut. That Helpers of the Helpless crap…"

"It's not crap," Tom said. "Things are changing. Things are getting deadly. Instead of swoop-and-squats on surface streets, you're seeing these fatalities on the freeways…"

"And at the construction sites," said Syd. "People are getting recruited for the usual stuff—fender benders, whiplash claims," said Tom. "But they're dying instead, and guys like Esposito and Dallas Trace are making more money off of them than ever before."

"Esposito's not making any more money for anyone," muttered Dar.

Syd leaned forward, her hands clasped. "Will you join us, Dar? Will you help us on this project?"

Dar looked at the two of them sitting there on his couch, so comfortable with one another. "No," he said.

"But—" began Tom.

"If he says no, he means no," interrupted Syd. She pulled a semiautomatic pistol from her belt under her loose vest. It looked like her own nine-millimeter pistol, but chambered for a heavier round. "Are you familiar with one of these, Dar?"

"A handgun?" said Dar. "I saw one in a dead man's hand this afternoon."

Syd ignored his sarcasm. "This kind of Sig Pro, I mean."

Dar looked down at the small semiautomatic with obvious distaste.

"I know you've seen Sig-Sauers," said Syd. "This is the new SIGARMS polymer design. Very small, very light." She set the pistol on the table. "Go ahead...heft it, try it."

"I'll take your word for it," said Dar.

"Look, Dar," Syd began, and stopped as if fighting to keep her voice under control. "We didn't get you into this. When those LAPD detectives—and we think they're both on the take—showed Trace the video reconstruction you'd given the accident unit, well...that's when the Russians were sent after you."

"We're certain the Alliance has brought in some top Russian mafia figures to enforce their takeover of major fraud," said Tom Santana softly, slowly. "We have evidence that Dallas Trace himself has hired an ex-KGB agent as his primary enforcer—a member of the *Organizatsiya*, Russia's organized-crime syndicate. This enforcer is bringing in more Russian mafia as the need arises."

"And you think this little polymer Sig Pro is going to make a difference?"

"It could make all the difference," said Syd, her voice angry now. "You saw how easily Tom and I got into your condo building. There's a single San Diego PD unmarked car parked across the street, but those guys are on overtime and they're probably both half asleep by now." She dropped the magazine out of the pistol and set it aside, racking the semiautomatic to show that there was no bullet in the chamber. "This is my personal weapon, Dar. This type of Sig Pro fires .40-caliber Smith and Wesson ammo and it's about the most accurate semiauto on the market. The U.S. Secret Service likes these weapons...the Sig Pro comes up well on target and puts the rounds right where they're pointed."

"At another human being," said Dar.

Syd ignored him. She took the canvas off the long package. "The pistol would be for personal protection when you're out alone," she went on. "I've got a permit in the works for you, but you won't be arrested for carrying it no matter what. And for the apartment and the cabin..."

"A shotgun," said Dar.

"I know you were in the Marines," said Syd. "I know you were trained in the use of weapons…"

"More than a quarter of a century ago," said Dar.

"It's like riding a bike," said Tom Santana, no sarcasm in his words.

"You had a .410 Savage over-and-under at some point," said Syd. "You probably recognize this shotgun. It's a classic."

"A Remington Model 870 pump-action twelve-gauge," said Dar flatly. "Yeah, I've seen them."

Syd reached into her big bag and then set two boxes of cartridges on the coffee table. Dar could see that one box held Smith & Wesson .40-caliber bullets, the other a yellow box of 00 buckshot shells.

The chief investigator nodded toward Dar's front door. "Somebody you don't like comes through that door, Dar, a single pull on this trigger releases nine .33-caliber lead pellets at muzzle velocities ranging from eleven hundred to thirteen hundred feet per second. That means as much lead in the air as eight rounds from a nine-millimeter semiautomatic."

"Close-range firepower," said Tom Santana, "with quick-velocity drop-off and less risk of overpenetration than most firearms. It's why police prefer them for close-in situations. And under...say, twenty-five yards...it's almost impossible to miss."

Dar said nothing. The three sat in silence for several minutes. The sunlight had gone.

"Dar," said Syd at last, leaning over the table to touch his knee, "if you're not going to work with us, or let me be around you, then you need some extra protection."

Dar shook his head. "No on the pistol. That's final. I'll keep the shotgun under the bed."

Chief Investigator Olson and Inspector Santana looked at one another. Then Syd took the Sig Pro and its ammunition and put them away in her bag. "Thank you for keeping the shotgun at least, Dar. The magazine holds five shells, and the pump-action—"

"I've fired a Remington 870 before," interrupted Dar. "It's like riding a bike." He stood. "Anything else?"

Both Syd and Tom shook his hand at the door, but neither said anything until Tom handed Dar his card. "I can be reached at the last number at any time, day or night," said the FIST investigator.

Dar slid the card in his jeans pocket, but said, "I've already got Syd's card somewhere."

For an hour after they left, Dar just paced the apartment, not even turning on the lights. He slid the shotgun and the shells under his bed and came back out into the main living area, restless. He poured another glass of Scotch and stared out at the lights of the city below and at the slow movement of boats in the bay. Aircraft landed and took off from Lindbergh Field, suggesting a purposefulness and energy that Dar did not share.

Finishing his drink, he went into his bedroom cubicle again. In the bathroom he turned on the shower and stood under the hot spray for several minutes, letting the water pound some of the whiskey fuzziness out of his head.

He came out into the dark bedroom carrying the towel and drying his short hair. He turned on a light. The bedroom was merely an enclosure created by built-in bookcases, but his closet was fully enclosed and its door had come with a full-length mirror that he had meant to take down. Now he blinked at his own reflection.

Is there anything sadder-looking than a naked middle-aged man? thought Dar. He started toward the closet door, as much to get the mirror out of view by opening the door as to find his pajamas, when the first shot was fired. The mirror shattered. Broken glass cut Dar's face and chest. He stumbled backward, knocking the lamp off the low dresser.

The second shot was fired into darkness.

13

"M IS FOR MIST"

There were so many cops in Dar's apartment that it looked like a donut shop during graveyard watch.

A ballistics team worked on re-creating the precise angle of the two bullets from where they shattered the high windows on the north side to their point of impact. Sheets and painter's canvas had been hastily nailed up over the other windows. There were half a dozen uniformed officers in the room and more plainclothes people. Special Agent Jim Warren was there representing the FBI, with his assistant, a short, intense woman. Captain Hernandez from the San Diego Police Department was there with six or eight of his usual entourage, as was Captain Tom Sutton of the CHP. Syd Olson and Tom Santana were also there, sitting on the leather couch and staring at the rifle on the coffee table.

"I've never seen a rifle like that before," said one of the CHP officers. The man was sipping coffee from one of Dar's white mugs.

"It's a civilian version of one of the sniper rifles your SWAT team would use," said Syd.

"Have we run down the make?" asked Captain Hernandez.

"I recognize it," said Tom Santana. "It debuted at an NRA show in Seattle a few years ago. It's a Tikka 595 Sporter with a Weaver T32 scope."

"How far away was the rooftop?" asked Captain Sutton.

"Almost seven hundred yards to the north of here," said Syd. "I actually saw the first muzzle flash and was on my way before the second shot was fired." She nodded toward two uniformed officers sipping soft drinks in the kitchen area. "I was staked out on the hill above the condo, so

I radioed the unmarked car out front to check on Dr. Minor while I went in pursuit of the assailant."

"But you didn't know about the fire escape," said Special Agent Warren.

"No," said Syd. "I went up the main stairs and onto the roof as fast as I could. I saw the suspect on the second level of the fire escape and still descending. I fired two shots, but missed."

"One of them was a warning shot, presumably," said Captain Hernandez dryly.

"The shots made the assailant drop the heavy rifle into the dumpster below the fire escape," said Tom Santana. "But then he reached his car and got away before Investigator Olson could get down the fire escape."

"No make on the car, Syd?" asked Captain Hernandez.

"I couldn't see any plate numbers. It was American-made. Compact. And it was long gone by the time I was down the fire escape."

"You missed from three flights above the assassin," said the CHP's Captain Sutton, "but the marksman put two bullets right on the mark from seven hundred yards... in a light drizzle? Incredible."

"Not so remarkable," said Syd. "The shooter had been up there for some time, waiting for Dr. Minor to turn on a light. He'd even dragged up two sandbags to create an optimal shooting position. You notice that the cheekpiece on the hardwood stock of these military-style sniper rifles is adjustable... Our man had time to adjust the locking screws so that the cheekpiece was raised just the perfect height for his angle shot."

"No fingerprints," said one of the forensics people.

Syd and the others gave the man a tired look. "Of course not," said Captain Hernandez. "We're dealing with a professional here."

One of the ballistics men came over to the rifle. "Remarkable shooting from six hundred and eighty yards. We've calculated that the first was a perfect heart shot. We dug the slug out of the rear wall of the closet. The shooter was using Winchester .748 forty-five-gram hand-loads—"

"We know that," said Syd. "There were still three cartridges in the five-capacity chamber when we recovered the weapon. No brass at the shooting site."

"Bolt action," continued the forensics man, undeterred. "He pocketed the brass from the first two shots, but he still got off the second shot in less than two seconds. And it would have passed right through Dr. Minor's skull on the floor if Dr. Minor had fallen where the shooter rightly expected him to be. Also—"

"Would you all please quit referring to Dr. Minor in the third person?" said Dar irritably. "I'm right here." He was sitting in his Eames chair, wearing a green bathrobe that didn't cover all the dressings the paramedics had put on his chest and neck for glass cuts.

"You wouldn't be there," said Syd, "if the shooter hadn't sighted in on your mirror reflection rather than you."

"Lucky me," said Dar.

"Damned right, lucky you," agreed Syd,

sounding angry. "If it hadn't been for that very light drizzle, the slight fog that came in from the ocean this evening, a slight mist, this scope would have told the shooter he was looking at your reflection in the mirror rather than a flesh-and-blood target. Even from almost half a mile away, this guy put a bullet right through your heart."

"In the mirror," said Dar. "Seven years' bad luck." He sipped hot tea and paused to look at his hand as he held the cup. It was shaking very slightly. Interesting. "And why were you staked out there anyway, Investigator Olson?"

Syd's eyes narrowed. "Just because you weren't going to help us catch these bastards didn't mean that I was leaving you unprotected."

"Not much protection involved, was there?" said Dar. "The fellow got two shots off... By the way, are you sure it was a man?"

"Ran like a man," said Syd. "Dressed in a windbreaker and ball cap. Average height. Average to slim build. Never saw his face and it was too dark to tell his race or nationality."

Captain Hernandez was straddling a kitchen chair pulled into the circle around the coffee table. He put his chin on his forearm and said, "Is it standard procedure, Investigator Olson, for law enforcement officers from the state's attorney's office to go after shooters single-handedly... not wait for backup?"

Syd smiled at him. "No, Captain, it certainly isn't. But Tom was my backup and he and I were going to take turns on shifts for a few nights. I'm sure that my superiors in Sacramento will remind me of proper procedure."

"Good," said Hernandez. "So where does that leave the investigation?"

Jim Warren of the FBI crouched next to the coffee table. "Well, we don't have prints, we don't have a description of the shooter or tag numbers on his car, but we've got his weapon. The Weaver scope isn't that unusual, but there can't be many of these Tikka 595s sold. And even though an initial dusting didn't turn up any prints

on the three cartridges still in the magazine, perhaps the FBI lab will find something. They usually do. And we'll back-
track on the hand-loaded Winchester .748
MatchKing 8THPs…It's not your usual
deer-hunting ammo."

There was more talk. Dar finished his
tea and found himself half dozing, feeling
the pain from the cuts and an ache from
the tetanus shot but mostly feeling sleepy.
Lawrence and Trudy called about 2:00
A.M.—they were plugged into a serious
network—and it was everything Dar
could do to keep them both from coming
over, too.

It was dawn by the time the last of the
uniforms and CHP people left. There
were two San Diego PD unmarked cars on
sentry duty now, a CHP cruiser on regular patrol, and Dar could just barely make
out the uniformed officer with a rifle on
the roof of the shooter's building—an old
warehouse two blocks north. Dar didn't
think the assassin was coming back today.

Finally only Tom Santana and Syd Olson
were left; both looked very tired.

"Dar," said Syd, setting her hand on his knee.

Dar snapped awake. He suddenly was very aware of the pressure of Sydney Olson's hand, the presence of the other man, and the fact that he had only had time to pull on his bathrobe by the time the mob arrived. "What?"

"Does this change anything?"

"Getting shot at always changes things," said Dar. "If it keeps up, I may become religious."

"Goddammit, stop playing games. Will you consider helping us directly now? It will be the only way we can insure your safety and put these arrogant bastards away."

"All of them?" said Dar. "You think you can catch all of them? Tom, how many cappers and bulls and cows and clinic workers and attorneys were there in that Vietnamese operation you broke up some years ago?"

"About forty-eight people," said Tom Santana.

"And how many did you get indictments on?"

"Seven."

"And how many did you send away?"

"Five...but that includes both attorneys, the only legitimate doctor in the bunch, and the head capper."

"And they were out in...what? Two years? Three?"

"Yeah," said Tom, "but the attorneys aren't practicing anywhere, the doctor moved to Mexico, and the capper is still on parole. They're not staging accidents any longer."

"No," said Dar. "Now it's the Alliance and the *Organizatsiya*. The game never changes...just the faces."

Santana shrugged and walked to the door.

"Don't forget to put the police bar in place," Syd said, and turned to follow Tom Santana to the elevator.

Dar took her by the wrist. "Syd...thank you."

"For what?" she said, looking deep into his eyes. "For what?" She left without waiting for an answer.

It was strangely dark in the condo, even

after sunrise, because of the canvas over the tall windows. Dar made a mental note to have some blinds installed as soon as he could. He went back to the bedroom, shrugged off his bathrobe, and crawled under the comforter. He thought he would be asleep in seconds, but he lay there for some time, watching the filtered sunlight move across the high ceiling.

Eventually Dar slept. He did not dream.

14

"N IS FOR LOS NIÑOS"

Wednesday was a lost day. Dar slept only a few hours—sleeping during the daylight made him feel creepy. When he got up, he found someone in the yellow pages who could install window blinds in a hurry and waited for them to come, puttering around the apartment. He was not afraid to go outside—he did not think he was afraid—but he also wasn't ready to unless he had a reason.

Lawrence came over about noon with a hot lunch for them to share and made sure that Dar was hiding no horrific bullet holes. Lawrence said that he was working "in town," which meant San Diego proper and usually meant testifying at the Justice Center. He said he'd be in town until late, and asked if he could crash on Dar's sofa. Dar was suspicious—he suspected that his insurance adjuster friend was looking out for him—but Dar could hardly say no.

When Lawrence left and the venetian blind installers were finished, Dar finished his old case files, e-mailed his chess moves to all of his opponents except Dmitry in Moscow, and found himself in the bedroom, going to one knee and pulling the Remington 870 and the box of shells out from under the bed. He fed five of the clunky shotgun shells into the bottom of the receiver and then balanced the weapon on his knees. The embossed lettering on the left side of the chamber above and in front of the trigger guard read *Remington 870 EXPRESS MAGNUM*, designating a shotgun made after 1955, when Remington modified the 870 to accept modern 3-inch magnum shotshells as well as the older, 2¾-inch twelve-gauge shells. Dar touched the release catch for the sliding pump—a tiny latch on the left forward portion of the trigger guard—pumped the action once, chambering a shell, and then pressed the cross-bolt safety button at the rear of the trigger guard. The blue-steel touch of the weapon and the smell of gun oil coming from it reminded Dar of his childhood—of hunting ducks and pheasants with his father and his uncles in southern Illinois—of crisp autumn mornings, brittle cornstalks, and well-behaved bird dogs trotting behind them.

Dar put the weapon back under the bed and closed his eyes. Flashes of images were haunting him—not recent images, not of the mirror shattering, but images of shoes scattered across grass, shoes of every sort, men's polished wing tips, children's Keds, a woman's sandals. After every air crash, the first thing the investigators noticed—even before the stink of aviation fuel, the torn and burned metal, or the bits of bodies—was the hundreds of shoes seemingly tossed at random around the site. It always said something to Dar about the terrible kinetic energies being unleashed in a crash that shoes—even those laced tightly—almost never stayed with the body. It seemed a final indignity somehow. Dar remembered the shoes in the Richard Kodiak a.k.a Richard Trace investigation. The young man had been completely knocked out of his right loafer, but the shoe was in the wrong place—Gennie Smiley had backed the van up too far the second time she ran over him. *The boy's a little light in his loafers*. Dar could hear Dallas Trace saying that to some of his country-club friends.

As night fell, Dar wandered to the bookcases and pulled down a well-thumbed copy of the Stoics. He started with Epictetus but skipped ahead to Marcus Aurelius—Book XII of the *Meditations*. Dar had read and reread the passages so often in the last decade that some of the lines had taken on the singsong familiarity of a mantra:

The things are three of which thou art composed, a little body, a little breath (life), intelligence. Of these the first two are thine, so far as it is thy duty to take care of them: but the third alone is properly thine. Therefore if thou shalt separate from thyself, that is, from thy understanding, whatever others do or say, and whatever thou hast done or said thyself, and whatever future things trouble thee because they may happen, and whatever in the body which envelops thee or in the breath (life), which is by nature associated with the body, is attached to thee independent of thy will, and whatever the external circumfluent vortex whirls round, so that the intellectual power exempt for the things of fate can live pure and free by itself, doing what is just and accepting what happens and saying the truth: if thou wilt, separate, I say, from this ruling faculty the things which are attached to it by the impressions of the sense, and the things of time to come and of time that is past, and wilt make thyself like Empedocles' sphere

**All round, and in its joyous
rest reposing:**
and if thou shalt strive to live only what is really thy life, that is the present—

then thou wilt be able to pass that portion of life which remains for thee up to
the time of thy death, free from pertur-
bations, nobly, and obedient to thy own
daemon (to the god that is within thee).

Dar closed the book. Those lines—so
many lines like those—had comforted
him after Barbara and little David had died
in the Colorado crash, after his own brief
descent into madness and suicide attempt.
He remembered the sound of the firing
pin striking hollowly on that .410 shell that
did not fire, did not fire. It had been the
only time his father's .410 had ever misfired; the hollow sound of that misfire
woke him often but was counterbalanced
by the sensible reply of the Stoics.

Not this night.

Dar made sure the blinds were closed
and the police bar was in place, but tired
as he was, he could not sleep. He did not
believe in sleeping pills—he had seen too
many accidents not that dissimilar from
poor Mr. Hatton who answered his own .38
when the phone rang—but he knew the

soporific potential of reading Immanuel Kant, and this he did until he was on the verge of sleep.

There was a knock at the door. Dar considered pulling the shotgun out from under the bed, but the knock had been the familiar shave-and-a-haircut. It was Lawrence, wrinkled, rumpled, and sweaty after a long day testifying. Dar went back to his Kant while Larry showered and came out in the extra, oversized bathrobe Dar kept for just these visits.

While Lawrence was straightening his stuff and fluffing his pillow on the couch, Dar was eyeing the shoulder holster and .32 Colt revolver that his friend had nonchalantly draped over a chair.

"You and Trudy going into L.A. for dinner tomorrow?" asked Dar.

"What do you mean?" said Lawrence from the couch. He was comfortable in his bathrobe, a Hudson's Bay blanket over him, reading a *Car & Driver* magazine.

"You usually only pack heat when you guys are going into the city." Dar knew that his friend had a permit to carry a concealed weapon because of all the threats the adjuster had received from car thieves and fraud artists, who were behind bars thanks to Lawrence's testimony.

Lawrence grunted. "Coming to see you is enough reason to carry," he said. "It's like hanging around Charles de Gaulle in *The Day of the Jackal*."

"Only in the original," said Dar. "In the remake it's the head of the FBI who's being stalked. And not by Edward Fox but by Bruce Willis."

"They always screw up remakes," said Lawrence, putting down his magazine and snapping off the light at the head of the couch.

"Don't they," agreed Dar. He went to check that the door was locked and the police bar in place. He glanced at the ugly but closed blinds on all of his tall windows.

"Good night, Larry."

Dar waited for the correction in the name, but Lawrence was already snoring softly. Dar went into his bedroom and was asleep within minutes.

*   *   *

Dar awoke on Thursday morning to the sound of the phone ringing. He grabbed the phone. Nothing. His bedside phone only gave him a dial tone. He jumped up and grabbed his cell phone from the dresser. It wasn't even powered up. Dragging on a robe, he walked to his fax machine. Nothing there.

The phone rang again.

It was Lawrence's cell phone. Dar had forgotten that his friend was sleeping on the couch, but now he sat on one of the high stools at the counter while Lawrence answered his Flip Phone and exchanged some fast but groggy sentences—obviously with Trudy, unless the totally faithful Lawrence had suddenly found someone else to call "Honey Bunch."

Dar put the coffee on as Lawrence sat up on the couch, moaned, growled, tried to clear his throat, rubbed his eyes, rubbed his cheeks and jowls, growled again, and went through a series of throat-clearing exercises that sounded like a 240-pound cat being strangled.

How the hell does Trudy put up with that ev-

ery morning? thought Dar, not for the first time. He said, "Coffee'll be ready in a minute. Do you want any toast or bacon? Or just cereal?"

Lawrence put on his glasses, and grinned across the wide space at Dar. "Shut the coffee off. We'll grab some coffee and a Toad McMuffin on the way. We've got a case already and you're going to love it."

Dar glanced at his watch. It was already eight-thirty, but strangely dark in the condo with all of the blinds closed. "I've got a lot of work to catch up—" he began.

Lawrence was shaking his head. "Nope. This is just a few miles out... halfway to my place... and you'd hate yourself if you missed it."

"Mmmm," said Dar.

"Attempted nunicide by a chicken cannon," said Lawrence.

"Pardon me?" Dar shut off the coffee maker.

"Attempted nunicide by a chicken cannon," repeated Lawrence as he flip-flopped into Dar's bathroom to use the facilities and take a shower before Dar did.

Dar sighed. He found the rod that opened the venetian blinds and then the cord that tugged them up. It was a beautiful, sunny San Diego summer day. Every detail on the aircraft carrier permanently berthed across the bay stood out in the crisp light. The sound of traffic was a reassuring hum. A plane roared in to Lindbergh Field, some of the passengers staring up at the overtowering buildings in pure terror while the old hands kept reading their morning papers. Dar could almost read the headlines through the starboard windows as the DC-9 passed by.

"Nunicide by chicken cannon," he muttered. "Christ."

They argued in the condo warehouse parking garage about who would drive. Lawrence hated ever being a passenger. Dar was tired of being one. Lawrence admitted that he had to come back into the city for more testimony. Dar pointed out the logic of leaving his Trooper in the parking area and taking the Cruiser. Lawrence sulked, finally saying that they should both drive. Dar headed for the elevator.

"Where are you going?" shouted Lawrence.

"Back to bed," said Dar. "I don't need this nonsense before breakfast."

Dar drove. The unmarked San Diego police car that had been parked across the street followed them to the city line and then turned back.

It was a short distance, halfway to Escondido. Lawrence gave the address of a Saturn dealership just off the freeway. Dar knew the place.

Lawrence and Dar had shared their contempt for Saturns in the past. Both knew that they were decent value automobiles, but the image that Saturn created in their advertising of a typical Saturn owner made car lovers like Lawrence and Darwin want to throw up. "It's Jennifer's first car," says the sales manager. All of the other salespeople applaud while Jennifer stands and blushes, car keys in her hand.

"Saturns were invented for people who are afraid to buy cars," Trudy had once said. Lawrence and Trudy bought or traded for a new car about once every five months. They loved the process. "Just like Volvos are for people who hate automobiles and need to tell the world," Lawrence had added. "College professors, professional tree huggers, liberal Democrats...they have to drive, but they're letting us know that in their hearts they'd prefer walking or biking."

"Maybe they buy Volvos for safety," Dar had said, knowing it would provoke the two adjusters.

"Hah!" Trudy had cried. "A car has to be able to go *fast* before safety becomes much of an issue. Volvo drivers would own Sherman tanks if the government allowed them on the highway."

"And remember that touching Saturn commercial a few years ago where all the Tennessee Saturn workers got up at three A.M. to watch the first Saturns being unloaded in Japan?" said Lawrence derisively. "All those happy Anglo, black, and Hispanic faces watching the live TV feed...such pride in America. What they didn't show is ninety-nine percent of those cars being reloaded on vehicle containers a year later when the Japanese spurned the Saturns."

"The Japanese like Jeeps," said Trudy.

Dar nodded. That was true enough. "And huge old Cadillacs," he said.

"Just the *Yakuza*," Lawrence had amended.

Halfway to the Saturn dealership, Lawrence said, "So do you know what a chicken cannon is?"

"Of course," said Dar, driving with one hand and sipping his McDonald's coffee with the other. A typeset warning on the coffee cup said essentially that the beverage was hot and could cause injury if dumped on one's genitals. Dar had always been of the opinion that anyone too stupid to realize that wouldn't know how to read or drink from a cup anyway. "Of course I know what a chicken cannon is."

Lawrence looked crestfallen. "You do? Really?"

"Sure," said Dar. "I used to be with the

National Transportation Safety Board, remember? The chicken cannon is the nickname for a gadget the FAA invented to test cockpit windshields against birdstrikes. Actually the cannon is just so much medium-bore oil pipe rigged up to a fancy air compressor. They fire birds into the cockpit composite-glass at speeds of up to six hundred miles per hour—but usually slower than that. They use dead chickens because a chicken represents a large to midsize bird in mass, a little heavier than a seagull but smaller than a flamingo or hawk."

"Oh," said Lawrence. "Right. Damn."

"So how do Saturns and chicken cannon coincide?" said Dar as they took the exit to the dealership.

Lawrence sighed, obviously disappointed that Dar knew the punch line. "Well, Saturn is promoting this new so-called shatterproof windshield glass—actually it just has about thirty percent more plastic composite than the usual safety glass—and the owner of this dealership decided to borrow a chicken cannon from the Los Angeles FAA headquarters to demonstrate."

"I didn't know the FAA was in the business of loaning its chicken cannons out," said Dar.

"It's not, usually," said Lawrence. "But the L.A. FAA guy is the Saturn dealer's brother-in-law."

"Oh," said Dar. "Well, I hope they didn't fire a dead chicken into even that new Saturn window at six hundred miles per hour."

Lawrence shook his head and sipped his own coffee. "Naw. Just a little over two hundred miles per hour. But it was still supposed to be hot stuff. They were shooting one of Up Front Sam the Saturn Man's commercials this morning and they used the chicken cannon and Sister Martha."

"Oh, shit," said Dar. Sister Martha had been a nun before leaving the convent to peddle Saturns full-time. She starred in most of Up Front Sam's Saturn commercials. Sister Martha was about five feet tall, sixty-one years old, and looked like an apple doll with rosy cheeks and vaguely blue hair. Her favorite sales practice had been jumping up and down on a removed plastic door of a Saturn sedan, to show how they wouldn't bend or ding. That was before Saturn went back to steel doors because in accidents, the plastic tended to burn like the smelly petroleum product it was. Now Sister Martha just kicked tires and looked lovable while advertising non-negotiably priced sedans and coupes to the haggle-challenged. Trudy had once commented while watching a Sister Martha from Up Front Sam's commercial, "Butter wouldn't melt in that old broad's mouth."

The salespeople were running around in agitated circles. The commercial video crew members were equally nonplussed, arguing with each other over portable radios even though they were standing only twenty feet apart. The commercial director appeared to be about nineteen years old and wore a ball cap, a ponytail, an attempt at a goatee, and a pale, shocked expression.

The chicken cannon was relatively imposing: a thirty-foot barrel mounted on a tractor-trailer platform that could be raised on a hydraulic scissors hoist—Dar immediately thought of poor Counselor Esposito—with a jury-rigged breech mechanism that looked like an air lock for a chicken-sized space shuttle. The compressor was still humming away, the cannon aimed at a brand-new Saturn coupe sitting about fifteen meters from the muzzle.

Dar walked through the milling, babbling crowds and took a look at the coupe. The chicken had passed through the windshield like a bullet, taken off the head restraint on the top of the driver's seat, punched a chicken-sized hole in the rear window of the coupe, and embedded itself in the cement-block wall of the dealership about fifty feet away.

The dealer, Up Front Sam, a skinny liberal-arts major gone bad but still given to wearing nubbly Harris tweed jackets— even on this broiling summer day—had no clue as to who Lawrence and Dar were, but he was babbling away at them as if confessing to his parish priest. "We had no idea...I had no idea...My brother-in-law's FAA experts.... *experts*...said that the windshield would be fine in impacts up to two hundred and fifty miles per hour...The dial was set at two hundred... I'm sure of that...Sister Martha was in the driver's seat...we were ready to roll tape...then the director suggested one test run...I didn't want to waste the time and money, they charge by the second, you know...but Sister Martha insisted, so she got out of the car...We figured it would just take a few minutes to clean up the mess on the windshield and then we could shoot for real..."

"Where's Sister Martha?" interrupted Lawrence.

"In her sales cubicle," said the dealer, close to tears. "The paramedics are giving her oxygen."

Lawrence led the way into the showroom, sniffing appreciatively at the new-car-temple incense of new-car smell. Dar thought they'd be lucky to be on their way before Larry bought a new car just for the hell of it.

Sister Martha, in full nun uniform, had finished her intake of oxygen but was sobbing uncontrollably. Two female paramedics, Martha's family, and a herd of curious bystanders stood around trying to comfort her.

"It w-w-w-w-w-was the ha-ha-ha-bit," she said. "I've never w-w-w-worn it on any of these com-com-commercials b-b-b-before, never. It's the L-L-L-Lord's way of telling me that I c-c-crossed the line this time."

"She's all right," said Lawrence. He and Dar went back outside to inspect the tail end of the chicken still visible in the impact crater in the wall. They headed for Dar's Land Cruiser.

"Whose insurance brought you out here?" asked Dar as they passed the video crew.

"None. No involvement at all," Lawrence said. "Trudy just heard it on the police scanner and I thought it might brighten your day."

Suddenly Up Front Sam was beside them again. Evidently someone had told him that they were accident investigators. "I talked to my brother-in-law," he said. "The engineers insist that if the specifications for the windshield were accurate, the chicken should have just bounced off." He looked back at the hole in the windshield. "Mother of God, what did we do wrong? Did Saturn lie to us?"

"No," said Lawrence. "That windshield could probably take an ostrich strike at two hundred miles per hour."

"Then what...how did we...why... how in God's name..." said the dealer.

Dar decided to be succinct.

"Next time," he said, "defrost the chicken."

They were two thirds of the way back to San Diego when Dar saw the huge traffic tie-up ahead of them. Emergency lights were flashing. All but one lane was closed heading into the city. Cars were backing up to the last exit ramp or illegally crossing the median to head back north to avoid the tie-up. Dar drove the Land Cruiser onto the breakdown lane and then far out onto the grassy shoulder to get as close to the mess as possible.

A CHP officer angrily flagged them down fifty yards from the actual scene. Dar saw at least three ambulances, a fire truck, and half a dozen CHP vehicles around the jackknifed trailer truck and the heap of automobiles in the right lane. He and Lawrence showed their credentials— Larry had legitimate press-photographer credentials as well as his insurance investi- gator's ID and an honorary membership in the CHP.

Even with all of the vehicles blocking the scene, Dar could see what had hap- pened. The truck was a car-carrier hauling new Mercedeses—E 500s from the look of those still on the bottom layer of the car- rier and those in the heap on the highway. There were striated skid marks across all three lanes of traffic. The hood and wind- shield of an old Pontiac Firebird were just visible, squashed under a heap of tumbled silver Mercedeses. When the trailer had jackknifed and finally struck the Pontiac, the impact had torn loose all of the new cars on the top level. Not all of them had fallen on the old Pontiac—Dar could see one new Mercedes upside down on the breakdown lane and another battered but on its wheels two hundred feet down the highway—but at least four of the heavy vehicles had dropped on the Firebird. Tow trucks and a small crane were carefully lifting the Mercedeses off the Pontiac. Firefighters and rescue crews were using the Jaws of Life to cut through the A-pillars of the smashed Firebird, and at least one medic was on all fours, shouting encouragement to someone still in the wreck. The occupants of the Firebird obviously had not yet been extricated.

Dar and Lawrence walked back to the cab of the trailer where the driver—a big man with a beard and beer belly who was shaking and weeping much harder than Sister Martha had been—was trying to talk to the CHP. The state patrolmen started to push Dar and Lawrence away, but CHP Sergeant Paul Cameron saw them and waved them forward. The trooper's face was set in grim lines as he leaned forward, gently patting the trucker's shoulder and waiting for more description. Dar looked beyond the accident scene and saw young Patrolman Elroy on his knees amidst the flares and all the broken glass, vomiting into the grass.

"...and I swear to Christ, I did everything I could to avoid the Pontiac," the trucker was saying, oblivious of his own shaking or the tears pouring down his sunburned cheeks. "I was just trying to get around the poor bastard, but there were cars on either side of me. Boxing me in. They didn't stop. Every time I changed lanes, the driver of the Firebird changed lanes...When I braked, he braked harder...We must have crossed five lanes like that. Then I hit him and jackknifed. Couldn't hold it...all the load...Jesus."

"How did you get out?" asked Sergeant Cameron, gripping the trucker's heaving shoulder tightly with his huge hand.

"The impact popped the windshield of the cab right out," said the trucker, pointing. "I crawled out onto the top of the wreckage and managed to get down...

That's when I heard all the screaming… the screaming…"

Cameron gripped harder. "You're sure it was the adult male who was driving, son?"

"Yeah," the trucker said, and lowered his eyes, his huge frame shaking.

Dar and Lawrence walked back to the wreckage, being careful to stay out of the way of the rescue workers. They had managed to pull all but one of the heaped Mercedeses off the flattened Firebird and now they were busy cutting away the A-pillars and peeling back the roof to get to the victims in the front seat.

The driver was still alive, but covered with blood as the paramedics gingerly lifted him out, immediately getting him strapped onto a litter and bracing his neck. He was an overweight Hispanic man, groaning and saying over and over, *"Los niños…los niños."*

His wife was dead in the front seat. It looked as if she had not been belted in but had curled up in a fetal position on the passenger seat. To Dar's eye, it looked as if impact concussion had killed her, not the crushing of the roof, which only came down to the level of the headrest in the front of the car.

The workers redoubled their efforts to get the last Mercedes lifted and pulled off as they continued peeling back the roof and cutting the B-pillars away. Actually, there were no real B-pillars left. As the last Mercedes was lifted off by chain and unceremoniously dumped into the grass, it was obvious that the rear of the Firebird had been crushed down to the level of the seat cushions by the terrible weight of the heaped cars. All of the Pontiac's tires had been blown and flattened. One paramedic was still on his knees, still calling encouragement to the victims in the back, even as the firefighters tore at the collapsed roof with their gloved hands, attempting to peel back the metal like the lid of a sardine can.

"There was a lot of screaming and crying for the first twenty minutes or so," Cameron said softly to Dar. "Nothing for the last few minutes."

"The wife maybe?" said Lawrence.

Cameron shook his head. He took his trooper hat off and wiped the sweatband. "Dead on impact. The driver…the father…he could just moan. The screaming was all coming from the…" He broke off as the power tools managed to tear the last of the roof of the Pontiac free, ripping the trunk lid off as it did so.

The two children were on the floor of the Firebird, beneath the level of the crushed roof. Both were dead. Both the girl and her little brother were cut and bruised, but none of the cuts or bruises looked serious. As the paramedics gently wiped away the blood, Dar saw how bloated their faces both were. The little girl's eyes were still open, very wide. Dar knew at once that they had survived the crash only to be asphyxiated by the weight of the vehicles pressing down on them. The dead little boy was still desperately clutching his older sister's right hand. Her left hand and arm were in a fresh cast. Both children's faces were blue and swollen.

"Fuck," said Sergeant Cameron softly. It was a prayer, of sorts.

The ambulance roared away with the father in the back. The rescue workers began the slow process of extricating the bodies.

"There's a baby," Dar said dully.

Lawrence and the CHP men around them turned their attention his way.

"I saw this family just a couple of days ago in the Los Angeles Medical Center," said Dar. "They had a baby with them. Somewhere there's a baby."

Cameron nodded to one of the CHP men, who began talking on his portable radio.

Lawrence, Dar, and Paul Cameron walked around to the back of the flattened Pontiac.

"Oh, goddammit," said the sergeant. "Goddamn them. Goddamn him. Goddamn them."

In the flattened trunk of the Firebird, Dar could see three sandbags and two fully inflated spare tires, still on their rims. A buffer for absorbing the shock of a rear-ending. Standard swoop-and-squat protection. A capper's guarantee to his recruited squat-car drivers that there would be no real injuries on their shortcut to big insurance payouts and riches in *los Estados Unidos*.

Dar turned abruptly and walked farther into the grass of the roadside.

"Dar?" called Lawrence.

Dar kept his back to the accident scene. He took a card out of his wallet and his Flip Phone out of his shirt pocket.

She answered on the second ring. "Olson here."

"Count me in," said Dar. He cut the connection and closed the phone.

15

"O IS FOR ORGANIZATSIYA"

Sydney Olson seemed to have taken over the entire basement of Dickweed's Justice Center. She had at least five more assistants working at an equal number of new computers and six more phone lines; her operation had spilled over from the single old interrogation room to the observation room behind the one-way glass, into two more unused interrogation rooms, and even out into the hallway where the male secretary now screened visitors. Dar wondered if the prisoners in the holding cells at the far end of the long corridor and their sullen guards were the only ones left in the basement not involved in this expanding empire.

The meeting started precisely at 8:00 A.M. on Friday morning. A long folding table had been set up in Syd's main office. The map of Southern California still took up most of the blank wall, but Dar noticed that there was an extra red pin—standing for a swoop-and-squat fatal accident—on the I-15 just outside the San Diego city limits, a new green pushpin where Esposito had died at the construction site, and a second yellow pin—a Dar assassination attempt—right on the hill in San Diego. Half a dozen more yellow pins still waited at the side of the map.

This was a serious operational meeting: neither Dickweed nor the local DA had been invited. Dar was surprised to see that Lawrence and Trudy had been.

"What?" said Lawrence when he saw Dar's quizzical expression. "You expect us not to be in on this?"

"Besides," Trudy had said, bringing Lawrence a Styrofoam cup of coffee from the big urn near the door, "the NICB is paying us."

Jeanette Poulsen, the attorney representing the National Insurance Crime Bureau, looked up and nodded at this.

While Syd was connecting her laptop computer to a projector, Dar looked at the other people taking their places at the table. Besides Larry, Trudy, and Poulsen from the NICB, there was also Tom Santana—sitting at Syd's right—and Santana's boss at the State Division of Insurance Fraud, Bob Gauss. Next to Gauss was Special Agent Jim Warren, and across the table from the FBI man sat Captain Tom Sutton from the CHP. The only other law enforcement officers present were Frank Hernandez from the San Diego detectives' bureau and a man whom Dar hadn't met before—a quiet, middle-aged, accountant-looking type whom Syd introduced as Lieutenant Byron Barr from the LAPD's Internal Affairs Division. Both Captains Hernandez and Sutton gave Barr the kind of suspicious, malignant squint that police reserve for all Internal Affairs officers. Syd kept it sharp and succinct, saying flatly that Lieutenant Barr was there because there was overwhelming evidence that some plainclothes detectives in the LAPD were involved in this conspiracy.

Dar saw Hernandez and Sutton exchange quick glances and nods. He interpreted this as *Oh, well, the LAPD, yeah, sure. Fuck 'em.*

"All right," said Syd, turning off all lights save for her computer and projector. She had a remote in her right hand. "Let's get started."

Suddenly the white screen at the far end of the table was illuminated with a color photograph of the pile of Mercedeses on the flattened Firebird.

"Most of you are aware that this accident occurred yesterday morning on the I-15 just beyond the city limits," Syd said softly.

More photos. The cars being lifted off. The driver being extricated. The bodies. Dar realized that these were Lawrence's photos, taken with his regular Nikon as they viewed the wreck, then scanned and sent to Syd via e-mail. The focus and detail were very clear.

"The only survivor of the crash was the driver, Ruben Angel Gomez, a thirty-one-year-old Mexican national with a temporary U.S. driver's license. His wife, Rubidia, and their children—Milagro and Marita—all died in the collision with a jackknifed car carrier under lease to the San Diego dealership of Kyle Baker Mercedes."

The close-up photos of the dead children clicked by. Syd stepped into the light of the projector. "There was a baby—seven-month-old Maria Gomez. We found her late last night in the care of a neighbor in the apartment complex where the Gomezes were living. Social services has taken charge."

Syd stepped back. The photos showed the trunk of the Firebird. She did not have to explain to this audience what the sandbags and extra wheels meant.

"Mr. Gomez is in critical but stable condition," said Syd. "He underwent two operations yesterday and still hasn't regained consciousness long enough to talk to investigators. At least this was the last I heard this morning..."

"He's still out of it," said Captain Frank Hernandez. "I called over there ten minutes ago. Keeps calling for his kids. They had to sedate him again. We have a Spanish-speaking uniformed officer there waiting for him to come out of it, but so far nothing."

"Is he in protective custody?" asked CHP Captain Sutton.

Hernandez shrugged. "To all intents and purposes," he said.

Syd went on with her briefing. The projected computer image now displayed a flow chart, in pyramidal form. The bottom dozen boxes were filled with the photos of the four Gomezes involved in the crash, Richard Kodiak, Mr. Phong—the man who had been impaled on the rebar—Mr. Hernandez—an earlier swoop-and-squat victim—and other faces and names, most of them Hispanic. The second tier of boxes in the pyramid included photos of Jorgé Murphy Esposito, Abraham Willis—an attorney also known to be a capper, who had died in a suspicious auto accident recently—and well-known Southern California injury-mill cappers: Bobby James Tucker from L.A., Roget Velliers from San Diego, Nicholas van Dervan from Orange County.

Above the cappers were several empty boxes over the word **Helpers**. Above that another long row labeled **Doctors**. Above the doctors' row, there were several empty frames labeled **Enforcers**. At the top of the pyramid were three boxes—two empty and one with a photo of Dallas Trace.

Dar saw the San Diego police captain and the CHP officer react with visible amazement. The others in the room, including Inspector Tom Santana, Special Agent Warren, Bob Gauss from the Insurance Fraud Division, and Counselor Poulsen from the NICB, seemed to be in on the news. If Lawrence and Trudy were surprised, they did not show it.

"Jesus Christ," said the CHP's Captain Sutton, "you can't be serious, Investigator. He's one of the most famous lawyers in the goddamned country. And one of the richest."

"That's where some of the seed money has come from for this expanded fraud operation," said Syd. Her computer remote included a laser pointer and now she put a red dot right on Counselor Trace's forehead. She clicked a button. A lean, expressionless man's face appeared in the **Enforcers** row of frames. It was a fuzzy photograph.

"This is Pavel Zuker," said Syd. "Ex–Red Army sniper. Ex-KGB. Ex–Russian mafia...although that title is probably still active. We found his fingerprint on the Tikka 595 Sporter that was used as a sniper weapon in the attack on Dr. Minor."

Captain Hernandez's dark complexion darkened further. "My forensics people went all over that weapon...They didn't find a thing."

Special Agent Warren folded his hands on the tabletop. "The Bureau lab at Quantico found a single print on the inside of the recoil lug mortise when they disassembled the weapon," he said softly. "It was very faint, but computer augmentation brought it out. We have a positive match on Zuker through the CIA data banks."

Syd clicked a button and a drawing appeared in the empty panel next to Pavel Zuker. It was a police artist's sketch of a man in a beard, labeled **Gregor Yaponchik**.

"The FBI has reason to believe that Yaponchik entered the country early this spring," said Syd. "At the same time Zuker did."

"Where did we get such information?" Captain Sutton asked. "Customs and Immigration?"

Syd hesitated.

"It came through channels from various Russian assets," said Special Agent Warren.

Sutton nodded, but the massive CHP officer also sat back and folded his arms across his chest as if expressing doubt.

"Yaponchik and Zuker were a sniper team in Afghanistan," said Syd. "They probably were working for the KGB even then, but they came to our various agencies' attention in the late eighties...right before the fall of the Soviet Union. After the dust settled, both were working for Chechnyan elements of the Russian mafia."

"Hit men?" said Lawrence.

"General enforcers," said Syd. "But in the end...yes, hit men. Both the Bureau and the CIA think that Yaponchik and

Zuker were directly involved in the Miles Graham affair."

Everyone in the room had heard about the millionaire entrepreneur Miles Graham. He had been the most famous of the capitalist wheelers and dealers shot to death in Moscow in recent years for not paying enough in bribes to the proper people.

Dar cleared his throat. He was reluctant to speak now, but also felt compelled to. "You say that Yaponchik and Zuker were in Afghanistan," he said softly, "as a sniper team? Americans and British use two-man sniper teams, but I seem to remember that the Soviets in Afghanistan were slow to deploy snipers, and when they finally did, it was a three-man section for every rifle squad."

Syd looked to Special Agent Warren. The FBI man nodded. He was holding a PDA with a dimly lit screen. From any angle other than his, the screen would be unreadable. He tapped at its buttons. "You're right," said Warren. "Three-man sniper squads were the rule, but this information says that Yaponchik and Zuker worked as a two-man team, more in the American style."

"Who was the shooter and who was the spotter?" asked Dar.

Special Agent Warren tapped at the handheld PDA and looked at the screen for a second. "According to the CIA field reports, both men were trained as snipers, but Yaponchik was an officer—a lieutenant in the army and then promoted in the KGB. Zuker was a sergeant."

"Then Yaponchik was the primary shooter," said Dar, who was thinking, *But Zuker, the number two man, was sent out to deal with me.* "Do you happen to have an assessment of the weapons the team used in Afghanistan?"

"The notes I received mention, quote, 'assumed to have utilized Dragunov SVD sniper rifles in Afghanistan and in training Serbian snipers near Sarajevo.'"

Dar nodded. "Old but reliable. *Snayperskaya Vintovka Dragunova.*"

Syd's head turned quickly. "I didn't know that you spoke Russian, Dar."

"I don't," said Dar. "Sorry for the interruption. Go ahead."

Syd said, "No, go on. You know something relevant here."

Dar shook his head. "When the American businessman in Moscow was killed...Graham...I remember reading that it was a double tap to the head from a distance of six hundred meters. A newspaper report said that the bullets recovered were 7.62-by-fifty-four-millimeter-rimmed. An SVD shoots that type of load and is accurate at that range. Barely."

Syd stared at him. "I thought that you didn't like guns."

"I don't," said Dar. "I don't like sharks, either. But I can tell the difference between a great white and a hammerhead."

Syd resumed her briefing in a concise but clear and unhurried voice. "Gentlemen, Jeanette, Trudy, we're officially authorized to extend and intensify this investigation. We have reasonable cause to believe that Counselor Dallas Trace is involved with the recent dramatic increase in staged highway and accident fatalities in Southern California and that a new network of fraudulent liability claims has been established by Mr. Trace and other prominent lawyers, as yet unidentified."

She clicked on another picture, this one of an elderly priest, smiling above his Roman collar. "This is Father Roberto Martin. Father Martin is retired now, but for years he was pastor of St. Agnes Church in Chavez Ravine—the Latino neighborhood near Dodger Stadium. Father Martin is a compassionate man and looked out for his mostly Hispanic parishioners. As long ago as the 1970s, Father Martin dreamt of founding a charity organization which would help the poor Mexican and Latin American immigrants. He helped raise money through the diocese and various L.A. businesses willing to donate to such a hypothetical charity—Father Martin had come up with the name long ago, Helpers of the Helpless—but to get the foundation organized, he turned to this man..."

A photo appeared of a plump, vaguely Hispanic-looking man with perfect hair, a smile as broad as Father Martin's, and an obviously expensive suit and tie. "This is the attorney Father Martin turned his dream over to," said Syd. "Counselor William Rogers...You probably know his name, an important attorney with several offices in East L.A. and impeccable political connections. Rogers is a well-known fund-raiser and was the number two man in the election efforts of L.A.'s current mayor. Father Martin hoped that Attorney Rogers would head up the Helpers of the Helpless and keep the charity going after he—Father Martin—retired."

"Did Mr. Rogers agree?" asked Lawrence.

"Not quite," said Syd. "Rogers set up a codirectorship, with his wife, Maria, sharing the leadership with a community activist and one of Rogers's own investigators, Juan Barriga."

Barriga's photo joined that of Rogers on the **Helpers** row of the pyramid. The men and women around the table nodded. They all knew that investigators working for attorneys who specialized in liability cases all too often found insurance fraud irresistible, these men and women spent their lives and careers interviewing slip-and-fall artists, swoop-and-squat experts, cappers, Medicaid cheats, flop artists, accident gangs, unethical doctors, professional whiplash victims, and fraudulent claimants of every sort. More important, the investigators invariably saw how quickly most insurance companies settled with these claimants to avoid more costly litigation.

"Juan Barriga has spent the past three years setting up a network of attorneys and doctors to work with those referred from Helpers of the Helpless. Both Bill and Maria Rogers select the Helpers volunteers personally. In addition, the Helpers of the Helpless receive referrals from the Mexican, Colombian, El Salvadoran, Costa Rican, Panamanian, and other consulates, as well as from Catholic parishes and various Protestant churches from all over the state."

Photos of some of these attorneys and

doctors appeared in the pyramidal flow-chart. Some of the attorneys were familiar, Esposito and the late Abraham Willis among them, but some of the others— Robert Armann, a former deputy district attorney now known as the most effective and popular member of the Beverly Hills City Council; Hanop Semerdjian, a re-spected civil rights attorney and spokes-man for Southern California's Armenian community; and Harry Elmore, a former U.S.C. football hero who went on to med-ical school and then to open free clinics in the worst sections of San Diego and L.A.—were faces that everyone stared at in shocked silence.

"Is your task force blowing smoke here, Investigator Olson?" CHP Captain Tom Sutton asked bluntly. "This looks more like a grab for media attention than a seri-ous investigation."

Syd turned away from the screen and met the big CHP captain's gaze without showing any rancor. "It does seem that way, doesn't it, Tom? But it's real. We've had a grand jury sitting for three months and we're going to get indictments...all the way up to Mr. Dallas Trace."

"Why are you telling us this now?" asked Frank Hernandez.

Syd turned off the projector and flipped on the overhead lights. She remained standing. "Because our investigation is moving into high gear and it will be on your turf, gentlemen. This is confidential information—"

"There are several ongoing investigations, and not just within the LAPD," said Lieutenant Barr from Internal Affairs. "Any leaking of this information would be...most unfortunate."

While the law enforcement officers glared at Lieutenant Barr, Syd said, "This...Alliance...backed up by Yaponchik, Zuker, and other muscle imported from the Russian *Organizatsiya*...is doing to the fraud business what the Colombians brought to drug sales more than twenty years ago in this country—serious organization, huge profits, and an almost unbelievable level of violence."

"So what do you want from us?" asked

Hernandez. "You've got the state re-
sources behind you...as well as the NICB
and FBI. What can we peons offer?"

"Liaison," said Syd. "Communications
when necessary. Access to forensic labs
and personnel when speed and location
demand a local response. Cooperation, so
that we don't end up working against one
another...or shooting at one another."

Hernandez pulled a cigarette from a pack
in his sport-coat pocket, glowered at the
ubiquitous No Smoking sign near the door,
and let the unlit cigarette dangle from his
lip. "OK. What's your plan?"

"I'm going to be going undercover
again," said Tom Santana. "I'll create a
cover story of being an illegal, get into the
system via one of the medical centers, and
check out the Helpers of the Helpless
from the inside."

Despite himself, Dar said, "Is that wise,
Tom? After the publicity on your busts of
the Asian gangs a few years ago..."

Santana smiled. His boss, Bob Gauss,
said, "That's what I told him, Dr. Minor.
But Tom thinks that hoodlums have a

short memory. And because he's technically task force commander of FIST, I can't
order him not to do it."

Dar started to speak again but shut up instead. He looked at Sydney. She was looking at Santana and seemed to be worried,
but she went on with the end of her briefing. "Tom will infiltrate the Helpers. We're
trying to follow the Russian trail through
the attempts on Dar Minor's life. Meanwhile, Dr. Minor and Mr. and Mrs. Stewart
are going to loan us their expertise to prove
that several of these fatal accidents were
either staged or actual acts of murder.
Their information, analysis, surveillance
data, and accident reconstruction will flow
through us to the NICB and then to the
grand jury."

A media cart in the corner held a TV
monitor and VCR. Now Syd picked up a
second remote control and turned on the
monitor and rolled a video. She kept the
sound muted. It was a tape of a recent airing of Dallas Trace's weekly CNN show,
Objection Sustained.

"Sometimes Trace tapes in New York,"

said Sydney Olson, "but usually it's more convenient for him to broadcast from his office in L.A. Before this year is out, I want our people to walk in front of those cameras...while they're live...and arrest that supercilious son of a bitch. I want his TV series to end with him being led away in handcuffs." She flicked the other remote and the computer projector showed the faces of the dead Gomez children on the screen while Dallas Trace's silent image laughed.

After the meeting, Dar wanted to talk to Syd, but she had a scheduled meeting with Poulsen and Warren, so he walked into the old courthouse part of the Justice Center with Lawrence and Trudy. Lawrence was still testifying at a liability claims trial that was starting in a few minutes, and Trudy needed to get back to the office in Escondido.

Before they parted ways, Dar said, "Are you guys sure you want to be part of this task force?"

"We already are," said Lawrence. "We

were involved in both the Esposito and Richard Kodiak investigations; we might as well keep going."

"Plus the NICB is putting us on retainer," Trudy said again.

"I'm surprised you changed your mind, though, Dar," said Lawrence. "You've seen dead kids at accident scenes before."

"More than I could count," said Dar. "But that was no accident, and I can't just walk away from a multiple murder after I've seen the victims being set up."

"I was talking to Tom Sutton," said Trudy. "We're going to depose the truck driver of the car carrier later today, but they've already interviewed him pretty extensively. There were three swoop cars involved, but the driver didn't really get a look at any of the drivers or license tags. He was too busy trying to avoid the Gomez car ahead of him."

"Three swoop cars?" said Dar. Rarely were there more than one or two swoop cars.

Trudy nodded. "Two to box in the truck. One to brake hard in front of the Gomezes.

All the truck driver could remember about the cars blocking him was that they were American-made, possibly a Chevy to his right, that he thinks they were driven by white guys, and that the cars were at least ten years old."

"They're almost certainly abandoned or chopped by now," said Dar. "But if white guys were driving, it could be our Russians and not just the cappers or their stooges."

"We'll give you a call later," said Lawrence, and the three went their different ways.

Dar had things he had to do, but he found himself wandering the hallways of the Old Courthouse for a while, and considered "catching up on his soaps." Syd would be free by 10:00 A.M. Just then, he saw W.D.D. Du Bois, Stewart Investigations's attorney, coming quickly down the hall toward him. The man walked with a cane, but his stride was still brisk.

"Good morning, sir."

"Good morning, Dr. Minor," said Du Bois. "You're precisely the man I wanted to see. We need to talk in private." Du Bois led Dar to an empty witness waiting room and locked the door.

The lawyer sat at the end of the table and made a small ceremony of setting his cane, battered briefcase, and hat in place. Dar took a seat on Du Bois's left. "Am I in some sort of legal trouble?" asked Dar.

"Well, other than Dickweed still wanting to prosecute you on vehicular manslaughter, not that I know of," said W.D.D. Du Bois. "But you are in danger, my friend."

Dar waited.

"Before you join Investigator Olson's task force," continued Du Bois, "I have to counsel you, Darwin—not only as your attorney but as your friend—that this is very dangerous business. Very dangerous."

Dar tried not to show his surprise. Syd's meeting had not been over for more than twenty minutes—had word spread so quickly? So much for Internal Affairs Lieutenant Barr's dire warnings to everyone. Aloud Dar said, "The bastards have tried to kill me twice. What more can they do?"

"Succeed," said Attorney Du Bois. The

lawyer's heavily lined face usually showed merriment, or at least bemused irony, but the lines were grimly set today.

"Do you know something about this conspiracy that would help the task force?" asked Dar.

Du Bois slowly shook his head. "Remember, Darwin, I am also an agent of the court. If I knew specifics, I would have already approached the FBI or Ms. Olson. All I hear are rumors. But they are very persistent and ugly rumors."

"And what do they say?" said Dar.

Du Bois locked his anxious brown-eyed gaze on Dar's. "They say that this is very, very serious and that these new cappers are deadly. They say that getting in their way is like crossing the old Colombian drug lords. They say that it is a new era in fraud in this country, and that the small businessman is being pushed out as sure as new Wal-Marts in an area will shut down the mom-and-pop hardware and dry-goods stores."

"Shut down the way Attorney Esposito was shut down?" asked Dar.

Du Bois opened his lined and gnarled hands in an expressive gesture. "All the old rules no longer apply," he said. "Or at least this is what I hear on the street."

"All the more reason to nail these bastards," said Dar.

Du Bois sighed, gathered his cane and briefcase, set his fedora on his head, and clamped his hand firmly on Dar's shoulder as the two stood. "Be very careful, Darwin. Very careful."

Dar returned to Syd's main office just as her meeting with Poulsen and Warren was breaking up.

"Just the man we wanted to see," said the FBI agent.

Dar was getting leery of this greeting.

"We were talking to Captain Hernandez earlier," said Syd. "He was bitching about the San Diego police overtime involved in watching you twenty-four hours a day, and we were bitching about how poor the protection has been."

Dar waited for the punch line.

"So the Bureau will be taking over

the protective duties," said Special Agent Warren, softly, but with authority. "We'll have at least a dozen people assigned to you full-time, so the protection will be both more intense yet much more subtle."

"No," said Dar. Syd, Jeanette Poulsen, and Jim Warren looked at him.

"The only condition for my continued involvement in this project," said Dar, speaking directly to Sydney, "is that we drop the twenty-four-hour protection stuff. I want you to call off all the bodyguards. Agreed?"

"You didn't say that there would be conditions to your joining the task force," said Syd.

"There are now. Just that one," said Dar. "Nonnegotiable."

Warren shook his head. "You're going to have to trust us on this, Dr. Minor. We're experts at witness protection and—"

"No," said Dar. "I'm serious about this. If we're going to work together, I need as much freedom as the rest of you. Besides, we all know that no number of bodyguards can protect against a talented sniper or someone willing to trade his life for the kill."

There was a silence. Finally Syd said, "We'll have to honor that...demand, Dar. But only because we realize that what you say is essentially true. Who was it—President Kennedy, wasn't it—who said, 'If the twentieth century has taught us anything, it's that anyone can be killed.'"

"Not Kennedy..." said Jim Warren.

"Michael Corleone..." continued Dar.

"In *Godfather Two*," finished the FBI man.

"God, you men and the *Godfather* movies," said Jeanette Poulsen. "That movie a few years ago...whatchamacallit...with Meg Ryan and Tom Hanks was right. You guys think everything in the universe can be summed up by dialogue from the three *Godfather* movies."

"Just the first two," said Dar.

"The third one was a mess," said Warren.

"Didn't count," said Dar.

"We pretend it was never made," said Warren.

"Are you two finished?" asked Syd. "Or do you have any other pertinent dialogue from the first two *Godfather*s for this situation?"

Dar ran his hand through his short hair so it spiked up a bit and put on his best, husky Al Pacino voice and arm gestures. "Just when I thought I was *out*, they pull me back *in*."

"Hey," said the NICB woman, "no fair. That's from *Godfather III*."

"That line is exempt from the rule," said Special Agent Warren.

"Good-bye, boys," said Syd.

"Notice how they can call us boys but it's literally a federal offense if we call them girls?" Dar asked the FBI man.

Warren sighed. "I just make it a practice never to call a female wearing a Sig nine-millimeter semiauto on her hip 'girl.'" He glanced at his watch. "You want to catch some lunch together, Dr. Minor? I hear there's a great Kansas City–type barbecue place near here."

"There is and I would," said Dar. He waved good-bye to the two women standing there like elementary teachers with their arms crossed in mature disapproval.

"Hey," said the perfectly groomed, soft-spoken Special Agent Warren in a good imitation of Fat Clemenza's voice. "Leave the gun—bring the cannoli."

16

"P IS FOR PERTINENCE"

Downtown San Diego was already emptying out in a lemming rush for the suburbs by the time Dar finished his lunch with the FBI man.

At one point, Warren said, "The Bureau will do anything it can to help you."

"I'd like to have copies of all the dossiers available on Pavel Zuker and Gregor Yaponchik," said Dar. "Not just FBI files, but CIA, NSA, Interpol, Mossad, NDA—any that are out there."

Warren looked dubious. "I doubt if I could get clearance to show you even the Bureau's limited files. What makes you think we could come up with Israeli documents?"

Dar answered him with silence and a poker face.

"Why would a civilian need this stuff?" asked Warren.

"The only civilian who would need it is the civilian who's been attacked twice by these two Russian gentlemen," Dar said softly. "That information might keep the aforementioned civilian alive, rather than dead."

The special agent looked like he had swallowed an olive pit, but he eventually nodded. "All right," he said. "I'll try to get you copies of whatever is available."

"Great," said Dar.

"Anything else you'd like?" said Warren lightly. "A helicopter, perhaps...or access to some of the different agencies' spy satellites?"

"Sure," said Dar, "but what I really want is the loan of a McMillan M1987R."

Special Agent Warren laughed good-naturedly before realizing that Dar was serious. "It's impossible."

"It's important," said Dar.

"It's illegal for a civilian even to own one," said Warren.

"I don't want to *own* one," Dar said patiently. "Just borrow one."

They ended the lunch with Warren still shaking his head. "I'll try for the files, but the McMillan..."

"Or its equivalent," said Dar.

"No chance of that whatsoever," said Warren.

Dar shrugged. He gave the special agent his card with all of his phone, fax, and e-mail numbers on it; he even scribbled in the cabin number that he had given to no one but Larry and Syd. "Let me know about the files as soon as possible," he said. He did not offer to pick up the check.

Leaving the metro area in his Land Cruiser, Dar called Trudy. "What's the most recent word on the Esposito investigation?"

"Thanks to you and the ME, it's being listed as a probable homicide," she said. "I interviewed the architect—the one who was talking to the foreman, Vargas?—and he's willing to testify that he and Vargas were very focused on referring to blue-prints for several minutes right at the time of the accident... or murder."

"So someone had time to keep Esposito under the lift—probably at gunpoint—and pull the hydraulic plug without being seen," said Dar. "Interesting."

"Both the LAPD and San Diego detec-tives are hunting for Paulie Satchel...the claimant who was supposed to have been meeting Esposito there."

"Good," said Dar. "I hope they find him before this string of accidents continues in his direction."

"You don't think that Paulie was the one who killed Esposito?"

"Nope," said Dar, relaxing as the traffic stopped completely. He checked in his mirror. The same car had been following him since he left the Justice Center. He would have been alarmed, but he recog-nized Syd's Taurus and her mop of blonde-brown hair. For a chief investigator, she did a lousy job of covert surveillance. "I know Paulie," said Dar. "He's a small-time liability claimant...he's had more disability claims than most people have had head colds. He's not the hit man."

"If you say so," replied Trudy. "I'll keep you informed. Is your phone going to be on?"

"Later," said Dar. "Right now I'm going shopping."

Dar's shopping was more efficient than Syd's surreptitious tailing. He stopped at a downtown Sears and bought an inexpensive but rugged sewing machine. He drove to an army surplus store that catered to hunters and bought three old two-piece sets of camouflage fatigues and a wide-brimmed boonie hat. He also found a mosquito-netting rig for his head and shoulders—"strong enough to keep out Alaskan 'skeeters," said the clerk, a one-eyed Vietnam vet, "but fine-mesh enough to keep out the fucking black flies." He had to try two more outdoors stores before finding the larger netting he needed in the quantity he required.

Dar had to go to several fabric stores and

another outdoor store before finding all the tough canvas and hessian and burlap fabric he wanted in the colors he needed. He had the last fabric store he visited cut the canvas into patch-sized segments, and the rolls of dun-colored fabric into literally hundreds of irregular strips and bits. At one point he had four clerks and the manager cutting and ripping and slicing. The woman who ran the store looked at him as if he were crazy, but she took his money.

Carrying the huge bags of fabric fragments back to his truck, Dar paused when Syd got out of her car, parked in the same lot, and walked over to him. "I give up," she said. "I don't have the faintest, foggiest, fucking idea what you're doing."

"Good," said Dar.

"Will you tell me?"

"Sure," said Dar, unlocking his truck and dropping the bags in. "I'm making a ghillie suit."

Syd shook her head. "What's that?"

"You'll have to look it up, Investigator. Are you going to keep following me?"

Syd bit her lip. "Dar, I know you don't like it, but I feel responsible for—"

"Fuck 'responsible,' " said Dar softly. "You've got a job to do and so do I. Neither one of us is going to get it done if you're following me all the time."

Syd hesitated. Dar touched her bare forearm. "Let's not work against one another," he said. "My best bet for staying alive is if you succeed in putting Dallas Trace and his shooters away quickly. Let's do that."

Syd nodded but said, "Will you answer one question for me?"

"Sure," said Dar, "if you'll give me an honest response to a question in return."

"All right," said Syd. "Where are you going to be tonight…this weekend?"

"I'm driving up to the cabin from here," said Dar, "but not staying the night. I'll drive back to the condo late. As for this weekend…well, I may go camping on Sunday and take a day or two off."

"Camping," Syd said dubiously.

"Sort of," said Dar.

"Will your phone be on while you're… camping?"

"No," said Dar. "But I promise you one thing, Investigator. I'll be someplace where neither Dallas Trace nor any of his minions would think to hunt for me."

"Minions," said Syd softly. "All right. I'll get off your tail. For now."

"My turn," said Dar. He looked around. They were alone in the parking lot. The evening shadows were getting longer. "What was that charade of a meeting this morning?" he said.

"What do you mean?"

"You know damned well what I mean," said Dar, with no anger in his voice. He leaned against his Land Cruiser and waited.

"There have been serious leaks," said Syd, "during the past month. We're certain that Trace and the others in the Alliance are getting our plans even before we put them in motion."

"The grand jury?" said Dar.

Syd shook her head. "This is operational stuff. It's being passed along by someone in the task force or someone privy to much of our information. So I had today's meeting and we'll be instigating some phone taps."

"On Hernandez or Sutton?" said Dar, surprised. "Unless you suspect Lawrence and Trudy and me and are going to tap our phones as well."

"Nope," said Syd. "This stuff was being leaked long before you and the Stewarts got involved."

"Are you tapping Special Agent Warren's lines as well?"

Syd made a face. "The Bureau's doing the tapping, moron."

"Typical," said Dar. Then, in a more serious voice, "I can't believe that your friend Santana's going back undercover and that you both let the information out when you *know* there's a leak."

Syd frowned. "My 'friend' Santana knows what he's doing, Dar. We mentioned it deliberately. He knows that there's a good chance of his being made even if there weren't a leak. The official story is that he'll be operating alone, but actually there will be three Latino agents going in as illegals at the same time."

"Fraud Division?" asked Dar.

"FBI," said Syd. "We're into the major leagues now. Tom knows exactly what he's doing and he'll make sure that his back is covered. Why does your voice get funny every time you talk about Santana?"

Dar said nothing.

The traffic was very heavy on Interstate 8 headed east, San Diego breathing out its week's worth of tired day workers. Dar kept the windows closed, the air-conditioning on, and played a CD of Bernstein's Berlin recording of the *"Freiheit"* Ninth while he relaxed. The traffic was much less dense on Highway 79 headed north and no one had exited the interstate behind him. He had not seen Syd's Taurus during the commute, and as far as he could tell, no one else was following.

The shadows were growing longer and merging as he drove up to his cabin. He checked his usual little telltales to make sure that no one had come through the front door since he had last left, and then he let himself in and locked the door behind him.

From the outside, there was no hint that the cabin had a basement: no basement windows, no outside entrance. But it did. Dar rolled back the red Persian rug on the far side of his bed, found the faint seam in the floor, opened it, and used another key to unlatch the trapdoor. The basement light went on automatically as the door was lifted and latched in place.

Dar went down the steep ladder and shivered slightly in the cave-coolness of the narrow corridor. There was nothing in this cement-block hallway except the steel door at the end. This required two keys to open and Dar fumbled for the second one.

The room beyond was only a third the size of the huge living space upstairs, but it was large enough for Dar's purposes. He had to snap on the lights here, but once they were on, there were no shadows in the neatly arranged stacks of boxes, crates, shelves, and drawers. The temperature in this room was regulated and the air dehumidified. The cinder-block walls were lined on the inside by a contained-asbestos layer and a thin wall of aluminum. The room was essentially a large safe-deposit box, safe from fire, tornado, or distant nuclear blast. Dar smiled at the irony of how much this rarely visited room had cost him.

On the far wall was a padlocked grille that opened to an oversized air shaft. It ran 122 feet to the abandoned mine shaft of a gold mine more than a century old; the mine shaft itself ran another 208 feet to its small opening in the steep gully. The shaft ended more than a hundred meters east of the sheep wagon. This air shaft—padlocked on both ends—had cost Dar almost as much to dig and install as it had to build the entire rest of the house.

He walked the narrow path between the storage boxes. As always, he glanced at his "go bag"—the black suitcase that had always been packed and ready when he worked for the NTSB. As always, without his thinking about it, his hand passed over the large green crate that held all of Barbara's clothes, all of their photographs from that time, and David's baby clothes. As always, Dar did not open the crate.

There was an unconcealed wall safe at the rear of the room, and Dar turned the dial quickly. He knew it was foolish to use David's birth-date numerals as his combination, but anyone who had come this far wouldn't be deterred by a mere combination lock.

It was a large safe, deep, with several metal shelves holding documents and computer disks and photographs. Dar ignored these and pulled out a walnut box with a carrying handle.

He closed the safe, set the thin walnut box on top of a crate, and clicked it open. Inside, laid carefully in green felt with sections packed in Cosmoline-filled plastic wrap, was a disassembled M40 Sniper Rifle—a military version of the classic, bolt-action Remington 700 sporting rifle.

Dar ran his fingers over the wooden stock of the rifle and then removed the 3–9 variable-power Redfield Accu-Range telescopic sight from its creche. He glanced once through the sight and then set it back in its place. He was clicking shut the locks on the carrying case when he heard a distant but loud banging from upstairs.

Dar took the gun case with him as he left, locked the storeroom, and climbed the steep ladder. Someone was banging loudly at the front door. Dar secured the trapdoor and the carpet, considered assembling the rifle as the banging at the door became a pounding, but kept the gun case closed as he peered out the front window.

Dar sighed, slid the gun case onto a lower shelf of books, and went to open the door.

"Are you all right?" asked Syd. She was holding her nine-millimeter Sig Pro in her right hand. All that banging on the door had been with just her left hand. Her knuckles on that hand were red.

"Sure," said Dar, standing aside so she could come in.

"Then why didn't you answer the door?"

"I was in the bathroom," said Dar.

"No you weren't," said Syd. "I walked around and peeked in that window. I couldn't see you anywhere."

Dar knew that the trapdoor, even locked open, was out of the line of sight of any of the windows. "Two hours ago you said you wouldn't follow me," said Dar. "Now you're peeking in my bathroom window."

Syd's face was flushed. It grew redder as she reholstered the semi-automatic and pulled her linen jacket closed. "I didn't follow you. I tried to call your cell phone, but it wasn't on. I tried to call your cabin number, but you didn't answer."

"I just got here a few minutes ago," said Dar. "What's happened? Is something wrong?"

Syd's eyes darted around the room. "Could I have a glass of Scotch?"

"We're both driving," said Dar. "I'm headed back tonight, remember? I was just going to leave in a few minutes."

"I know what a ghillie suit is now," said Syd, rather breathlessly, as if she had run from her car to the cabin. "And I know about Dalat."

17

"Q IS FOR QUAGMIRE"

I *never told Barbara about Dalat*, thought Dar as he poured the drinks and rounded up the spaghetti-making equipment. *As close as we were, I never talked about any of it. Not to her. Not to Larry. Never to anyone.*

Things are different now, he argued with himself. *A Russian sniper tried to kill you the other day.*

All right. Dar clinked glasses with Syd and they drank good Scotch while he began preparing the meal in a mutual silence filled with the turmoil of too much thought.

Dalat was and is a highland Vietnamese city located at the foot of Lang Biang Mountain, some fifty miles from the coast.

In 1962 President Kennedy and the United States government showed its solidarity with whatever South Vietnamese regime was in power at the time—Dar could not recall the strongman's name—by transferring plutonium and other radioactive materials to the South Vietnamese and helping to set up a working nuclear reactor at Dalat. The reactor was used to produce radioisotopes for research and medical purposes, but more important, it was a status symbol for the South Vietnamese and a gesture of America's cooperation and friendship.

Cut to March of 1975. Nixon and Kissinger had successfully "Vietnamized" the war. The soldiers who had been equipped to take the place of the six hundred thousand American grunts, Marines, Air Force personnel, and others who had been withdrawn were in full retreat. The Viet Cong and the regular North Vietnamese Army were busy overrunning and occupying every former American base, stronghold, and Vietnamese city. Saigon was ten days away from being overrun, and the situation at the American embassy—where only a token force of U.S. Marine guards were left—was, to put it in the Marine argot of the day, pure clusterfuck. A huge naval armada stood offshore, ready and waiting to haul away the last of the fleeing diplomats, dependents, and Marine guards.

In the middle of all the confusion—burning files, fleeing families, abandoned equipment, thousands of Vietnamese "helpers" petitioning to be flown out—two South Vietnamese technicians showed up at the U.S. embassy and diffidently reminded the Americans that the Dalat reactor was still up and running, and that weapons-grade plutonium was stored there. The ambassador and the top-ranking military man were finally briefed about this in the midst of all the confusion, and they immediately ordered the Vietnamese technicians to return to Dalat posthaste and to scram the reactor—perform an emergency shutdown procedure. They were ordered to then bring all of the vital radioactive material, *especially* the plutonium, to Saigon, where it would be flown out to the waiting armada.

The Vietnamese technicians allowed that they would very much like to do that, but respectfully reminded the general and the ambassador that Dalat was in the process of being overrun by both Viet Cong and NVA units, that all of the roads and railroad lines to Saigon and the coast had been interdicted by the enemy, and that all scheduled flights in and out of Dalat's tiny airport had been canceled because of the proximity of NVA soldiers. All of the other reactor personnel had fled, and the reactor itself was at that moment humming along unmanned. The two technicians described how they had flown out—through heavy small-arms fire—in a light plane belonging to the younger technician's brother, who just happened to be a captain in the South Vietnamese Air Force and who had dropped them at Saigon, landing in rough field along the chaos of the National Road and then had immediately taken off to fly on toward Thailand alone, and while the two technicians would be most happy to go back to Dalat to help their dear American friends, they were actually quite low level technicians who had no idea how to scram a reactor, and besides, having risked their lives to bring word of the Dalat reactor dilemma, perhaps they'd already earned their trip to the United States and a new life.

"Do we have any nuclear eggheads around?" asked the ambassador. "Any sailor or anyone who happens to know how to shut down a reactor and handle plutonium?"

As it turned out, they did. On board a nuclear aircraft carrier standing offshore were two American members of the U.S. Atomic Energy Commission as well as the International Atomic Energy Agency: one Wally Henderson and a John Halloran. Neither of them was military; both of the men were affable, easygoing academics, and neither had ever heard of Dalat or even of the existence of a South Vietnamese reactor. They happened to be off the coast of Vietnam because several of the warships in the evacuation armada were carrying scores of nuclear weapons, others were chugging along in harm's way via their nuclear-reactor power plants, and the Defense Department had thought it prudent amidst all the confusion to have someone around— someone above the level of technician or Navy-trained nuclear engineer—who knew how the weapons and shipboard reactors actually worked. Just in case.

Wally Henderson and John Halloran were promptly helicoptered in to the scurrying anthill that was Saigon, briefed, and flown into Dalat with twelve Marines. The briefing—to both the scientists and the Marines—was fairly simple: shut down the reactor, don't let it explode or whatever reactors do when they're being shelled by the enemy, rescue as much of the radioactive isotope material as you can, retrieve the approximately eighty grams of plutonium at the reactor, and fly back to Saigon. If the airfield is overrun, try walking the fifty miles through jungle to the coast where they could radio for pickup. At all costs, bring the plutonium along.

Of the twelve Marines, four were

snipers. Dar Minor, nineteen years old, a precocious college graduate with a degree in physics—which no one in the military or at the embassy knew of or cared about at the time of his assignment to Dalat—was one of those snipers. When they landed in Dalat in an ancient commercial DC-3, made all the less flyable by a lead-lined storage facility quickly jury-rigged to hold the radioactive materials, eight of the Marines, including the commanding officer—a lieutenant—stayed behind to guard the airfield from the North Vietnamese while Dar and three others accompanied Wally and John to the reactor. It was just after 0700 hours and the morning mists were burning off.

The reactor was abandoned, the elite ARVN guards had fled, and the guard gates and main doors were literally standing open. But the enemy had not yet arrived. To young Dar Minor, the facility reminded him of the mock-up of Fort Knox he had seen in the movie *Goldfinger* when he was eight years old: A huge, heavily reinforced and domed concrete structure on a low hill,

the Dalat reactor was surrounded by almost a kilometer and a half of grassy slope
in all directions. There were three rows of
barbed-wire perimeter fences, one within
the other at hundred-meter intervals, and
the four Marines had the presence of mind
to lock the gates of each as they drove their
Jeep and the two excited scientists to the
main reactor building. In three directions
lay thick jungle, in the fourth the open
road to Dalat. The reactor commanded the
high ground for that open kilometer and
a half. To a sniper—even to an untested
sniper like nineteen-year-old Dar—it was
obviously the ultimate killing zone.

Although unblooded, Dar was the leader
of his two-man team. Snipers had been formally a part of the Marine Corps only since
1968, when divisional orders had recognized their importance in the war and ap-
proved the organization and formation of
sniper platoons within each regiment's
headquarters company, as well as in the
headquarters and service company of each
reconnaissance battalion. Formally, the
sniper platoon consisted of three squads of

five two-man teams and a squad leader for each team, plus a senior NCO, and an armorer and an officer, bringing total platoon strength to one officer and thirty-five enlisted men. Formally, the reconnaissance battalion had a slightly different configuration adding up to a total strength of one officer and thirty enlisted men In reality, Marine snipers operated—as they had throughout this war, Korea, and two World Wars—in teams of two, both of them marksmen but the team leader literally calling the shots, with his number two acting as spotter.

During the Dalat mission, Dar was leader of Team Two, and as the team leader, he carried a 7.62-millimeter Remington 700 bolt-action sporting rifle, modified and renamed the M40 by the Marines, while his spotter was armed with an accurized M-14. The earlier Marine spotters in Vietnam-era sniper teams had been issued standard M-16s for rapid fire, but the Marines had discovered the hard way that the M-16s lacked the necessary long-range accuracy and had reverted to the accurized M-14s.

For this mission, the two sniper teams had literally brought more weapons and ammunition than they could carry. Dar had assumed that with the war over, the U.S. was leaving tens of billions of dollars of equipment behind; what would a few more weapons on this mission matter? The second Jeep was filled with four extra M40 Sniper Rifles, two extra M-14s, one extra M40 barrel for each team, and crates of ammunition. Each of the four Marines carried his own set of binoculars and personal short-range radio, while the two teams shared a large PRC-45 radio for calling in artillery or air strikes. In addition to the binoculars, each spotter carried a twenty-power scout telescope. To add to their observation power, the second Jeep hauled in two heavy NODs—Night Observation Devices—and four smaller AN/PVS2 Starlight scopes mounted on the two extra accurized M-14s. One of the large NODs was mounted on a tripod, but the other was mounted on the pièce de résistance of their arsenal, a .50-caliber M2 Browning machine gun specially modified to function as a single-shot sniper weapon. Also included for the M2 was a massive Unertl telescopic sight for daylight use.

Dar's spotter was a twenty-two-year-old black fellow corporal from Alabama named Ned. Ned had actually outscored Dar—very slightly—on marksmanship proficiency—but Dar had come out of his 205 hours of formal sniper instruction, 62 hours of marksmanship practice, 53 hours of field training, and 85 hours of tactical field exercises with the higher total score. The real top shot of the two squads was Sergeant Carlos, an old man—thirty-two years old—the only one of the four Marines who had seen combat. Carlos's spotter was another nineteen-year-old named Chuck, from Palo Alto.

Dar and the others parked the Jeeps out of sight in one of the several empty outbuildings, had a quick look at the eerily empty reactor control room as the two nuclear scientists got to work, and then went up onto the parapets to stand guard for the next forty-eight hours. Carlos was delighted at the reactor's layout in terms of being a shooting stand. There were two 360-degree, cement-walled balconies around the main reactor building, one at a four-story height and the other just below the dome at sixty feet up. The walls on both balconies were slightly tessellated in the sense that every twenty paces or so, the concrete was raised three feet above the average four-foot wall height. This turned the parapet into a battlement, according to Sergeant Carlos. To make it even more of a battlement, the four Marines quickly humped more than eighty sandbags from the abandoned guard posts below to create shielded shooting stands and revetments.

The reinforced walls of the seven-story containment structure were twelve feet thick; the parapet walls were four feet thick. Although a few low outbuildings were clustered near the base of the reactor building, the parapets were high enough that their field of fire was unobstructed in all directions. Access to the two levels and the main control room was via internal corridors and ladders. There were no windows.

"Shi-iit," said Sergeant Carlos when they finished their strenuous sandbagging job. "If Davy Crockett, Jim Bowie, Colonel Travis, and the rest of those crackers had this place and these weapons instead of the shitty old Alamo, my ancestors never would have killed their asses and captured the place."

It took Wally and John forty-two hours to shut down the reactor, locate and load the various isotopes, and find the marked canister reported to contain eighty grams of weapons-grade plutonium. The enemy arrived at the Dalat reactor three hours after the Marines.

An hour after Dar's arrival, Lieutenant Hale radioed from the airport. The eight Marines there—also outfitted with serious weaponry—were in a firefight with what appeared to be a battalion of VC. Half an hour after that, Lieutenant Hale's radio man reported that half the Marines were dead—including the lieutenant—and that the remaining Marines were attempting to hold off what appeared to be a full mechanized company of North Vietnamese regulars. The DC-3 had flown out, leaving them behind. Hale's men had called for dust-off, but gunships and evac choppers were unable to approach the air-port terminal because of massive anti-aircraft fire from the surrounding tree lines.

For another hour, Dar and the other three Marines on the reactor parapets lis-tened to the distant rattle of small-arms fire: the distinctive bursts from M-16s and M60s, the even more distinctive rattle of Kalashnikov AK-47s, the crump of mortars, and the blast of tank cannon. Sergeant Car-los said that this was the first time in three tours in Vietnam that he had ever heard enemy tank fire.

Then the shooting stopped. The silence was so terrible that Dar was actually re-lieved when the first Viet Cong appeared in commandeered ARVN Jeeps, a few light armored vehicles, and a line of trucks coming up the main road from Dalat.

"Watch this," said Sergeant Carlos.

The .50-caliber M2 with a special Unertl scope had been set up on the wide wall between the sandbags. While Chuck and

Ned spotted with their twenty-power scopes, Sergeant Carlos opened fire on the VC column at a shooting distance of twenty-two hundred yards—more than a mile away. The first bullet turned the head of the Jeep's driver into a balloon of red mist. The second bullet—an explosive round—ignited the Jeep's gas tank and blew the vehicle fifty feet into the air. Carlos's third shot penetrated the light armor of the vehicle behind the lead Jeep and must have killed the driver, for the armored vehicle veered to the right and splashed into a deep irrigation ditch. The sergeant's fourth shot blasted through the engine block of the third vehicle in line—a deuce-and-a-half-heavy truck— freezing its engine and stalling the entire convoy. Troops jumped out of the trucks and began running for the jungle on each side.

Sergeant Carlos continued his leisurely shooting while the other three men watched through spotting scopes. Every time Carlos fired, a human being died. Then the trucks were empty, as the Viet

Cong moved through the jungle toward them and called for NVA support. For good measure, Sergeant Carlos blew up three more trucks with explosive rounds. The flames and smoke drifted high into the morning air.

"You see, having your pals get picked off from more than a mile away hurts morale," said Sergeant Carlos. He let the .50-caliber weapon cool while he assigned Dar's team to the lower parapet and went off to prepare his own bolt-action M40 Sniper Rifle for "close-in" work of eight hundred yards or less.

Dar had always heard that war stories grow in memory and in retelling, but he had never told the story of those forty-eight hours at Dalat. His memory of them had always been as solid and unchanging as a stone in his soul.

The VC scouts had begun to return fire and send out probes from the tree line about twenty minutes after Sergeant Carlos had stopped their first convoy. Carlos and Dar used their 7.62-caliber M40s to kill the VC whenever they came out of the jungle shadows or showed themselves by muzzle flashes.

With the exception of the AK-47 rounds hitting outbuildings or gravel below, and a few reaching and barely chipping the reactor containment building itself, it was very quiet. Dar heard little except for the leisurely bark of the M40s and the softly spoken "Hit...hit...down but still moving...kill...hit" of Ned, his spotter.

Early that afternoon, about a hundred VC broke cover and assaulted the reactor complex. Dar and Carlos first killed the VC snipers who were giving the infantry what cover they could with their less accurate K-44 rifles—actually the old Soviet 7.62-millimeter M1891/30 Mosin-Nagant sniper rifles used by the Red Army in World War II. When they were finished with the snipers—always another sniper's number one priority—they shot the sappers carrying their bangalore torpedoes to blow the fences. When the sappers had all fallen, Dar and Sergeant Carlos turned their attention to all of the NVA officers that they could identify. As soon as any man in a green uniform and pith helmet shouted an order or urged the other soldiers on or brandished a pistol rather than the usual AK-47, he was shot. When the thinned assault line came within eight hundred yards, still two hundred yards from the outer fence, Ned and Chuck opened up with rapid fire from their accurized M-14s.

The line broke. The VC ran for the jungle. A few made it.

The NVA regulars showed up a few minutes later. Watching through the spotter scope, Dar was amazed. He had never seen a Russian T-55 tank before, much less been taught how to kill it. The two lead tanks seemed to have the plan to drive straight up the road, smash down the gate, and drive straight into the reactor complex. They did not fire their seventy-two-millimeter cannons. All four of the Marines realized that there would be no mortar or artillery fire coming from the Communists. Evidently, some commander up the line had made the decision that the Dalat reactor must be captured without damage to the containment building. It was a stupid decision, Dar knew, because well-aimed mortar rounds would have killed the four Marines and only chipped and pock-marked the massive concrete walls. Wally and John, working deep in the control room, reported later that they had heard none of the shooting. Luckily for the Marines, the NVA command structure seemed to know even less about nuclear reactors than had the U.S. ambassador.

When the lead tank got within one thousand yards, Sergeant Carlos began firing explosive .50-caliber bullets at the vision slits.

"You have to be shitting me," yelled Ned over the din. "You can't kill a fucking tank with a sniper rifle."

"Those vision slits are bulletproof," said Sergeant Carlos between shots, "but not shatterproof. It's hard to drive when you can't see worth shit."

It took eight rounds, but eventually the tank just stopped. A minute later, the crew bailed out and began running for the distant tree line. Dar and Sergeant Carlos killed them. The second tank took twelve explosive rounds around and into its vision ports before it veered suddenly to the right and stopped. The crew stayed inside until long after dark. When they ran for the tree line sometime after midnight, Dar killed three of them with his Starlight scope. The third tank turned around and clanked back into the jungle, but not before it let off a cannon round seemingly out of sheer frustration. The round blew a three-foot round hole in the outer perimeter fence and exploded on the grassy slope. The T-55 driver had made the mistake of turning around for maximum speed rather than backing away. One of Sergeant Carlos's twelve-hundred-meter shots ignited the extra fuel canister on the right side and the tank drove into the jungle with flames leaping from its rear deck.

There were two more serious infantry flanking assaults before sunset. Now the Marine shooting teams were moving from level to level, revetment to revetment, firing in all directions. They had to be careful not to slide and fall on all the spent brass on the parapet concrete floors. The VC reached and blew the outer fence on the last rush before twilight. Thirty men got into the zone between the outer and secondary fences.

"Did the ARVN lay mines?" Chuck asked hopefully.

"Naw," said Sergeant Carlos. "It's the only fucking place in fucking South Vietnam with no mines."

The thirty-man infantry shouted a victory cry, raised the North Vietnamese flag, and ran for the second fence. The four Marines killed them.

It was after midnight when the VC and the NVA began crawling out of the jungle toward the outer wire. In training, Dar had been taught that the new generation of passive image-intensifying devices— night scopes—were the Vietnam-era equivalent of World War II's Norden bombsight: top-secret technology. In the early years of the Vietnam conflict, the saying had been "Charlie owns the night." Now the Marines owned the night.

Twenty-five years after Dalat, Dar would see an ad in L.L. Bean or some other outdoor catalog for six-hundred-dollar night-vision goggles and he would have to smile. The priceless, die-before-letting-it-be-captured night-vision miracle had become catalogue item #NP14328, available for next-day delivery via FedEx. In recent years he had actually ordered such a pair of night-vision goggles and found them not only lighter and more effective than his old Starlight scope, but the price was much more reasonable.

Ned used the tripod-mounted Night Observation Device to sight the enemy at distances up to fourteen hundred yards and alert Dar and Chuck for their Starlight scope shots at eight hundred yards or less with the M-14s. Sergeant Carlos used the other NOD mounted on the .50-caliber M2 to cut down enemy soldiers at fifteen hundred yards the instant they moved in the midnight shadows.

Unusual for Vietnam at that time of year, the skies remained clear all that long night.

There was no moon, but the stars were very beautiful.

Shortly after sunrise of the second day, six brand-new T-72 tanks and six T-55s began clanking purposefully toward the Dalat reactor. Infantry moved close behind them, and NVA snipers maintained covering fire from the tree line.

"I didn't know the fucking North Vietnamese had that many tanks in their whole fucking army," commented Sergeant Carlos, punctuating the soft words with a spit of his chewing tobacco.

Deep in the bowels of the building, Wally and John had slept an hour each. While one slept, the other had driven radioactive materials around on a forklift. None of the four Marines had slept at all.

Sergeant Carlos watched the tanks approaching the outer wire. He had been busy since predawn, talking on the PRC-45—their so-called Prick 45 command radio. Just before the circle of tanks reached the outer wire, a flight of five fast movers—F-4 Phantoms in this case—roared in at two hundred feet and dropped their ordnance, high-explosive shaped charges. Dar watched with fatigue-tinged disbelief as the turret of the lead T-72 blew three hundred feet straight into the air, higher than the F-4s had flown, the tank gunner's charred legs clearly visible dangling and kicking from the tumbling turret.

Several of the tanks survived the air assault and churned around in confusion, some running over their own infantry in the smoke and flame. Thirty seconds later, a follow-up strike mission of three Navy A-4D Skyhawks flying off the U.S.S. *Kitty Hawk* laid down napalm on three sides of the reactor complex. The resulting smoke and flame made it very difficult for Dar and the others to kill the fleeing survivors, but there were few survivors.

The second twenty-four hours were far less clear in Dar's memory, though even more indelible.

Something happened to time; that was the only explanation for it. Time was distorted, stretched completely out of shape—

almost to infinity or eternity was his impression—yet folded back on itself with moments and hours and events overlapping and coexisting. It was as if Dar had dropped below the event horizon of one of the black holes he would study in his doctorate work in the years to come.

There were several more all-out infantry assaults on the morning of that second day. During one of them, the Navy air strikes were delayed by half an hour and several hundred NVA regulars—no VC in black pajamas here, but well-fed, uniformed, superbly well armed crack troops, the pride of General Giap of the North—reached the inner fence. In a normal situation, Dar and the others would have called in artillery fire missions from fire bases nearby, but all of the American artillery had packed up and left the country, and all of the ARVN artillery in the province had been overrun. The only thing that saved their little Alamo was the fact that Giap obviously wanted to take the reactor intact.

Dar remembered that it was during one of those attacks on the morning of the sec-

ond day that the barrel of his original M40
melted and he had to switch to the backup
sniper rifle. Ned was killed by NVA coun-
tersniper fire just before that last morning
attack—or perhaps just after. Dar could
not remember with certainty. But he did
remember the sequence of deaths. Ned
was shot in the eye while using the
twenty-power scope around midday.
Sergeant Carlos was hit in the chest and
throat sometime during the evening's
fusillade, and died just as the sun set red
and full behind Lang Biang mountain.
Chuck was killed by a volley of bullets just
seconds before they were to board the Sea
Stallion.

During the last night—Wally and John
still working and loading and using wal-
does, remote handlers, deep in the building—Chuck and Dar talked about Plan B.
Plan B was walking the fifty miles to the
coast. Both Marines knew it was now impossible. It was not just that there were
now at least two battalions of NVA mechanized infantry and perhaps three companies of VC in the jungle on all sides of

them. Marines could deal with that. But with Ned and Sergeant Carlos dead, Dar and Chuck could never make it to the coast carrying the two bodies, while helping the scientists with their hundreds of pounds of radioactive isotopes and plutonium and what all. And Marines did not leave their dead behind.

Dar had always thought this policy the height of obscenity—trading more human lives for dead bodies—but he also knew that he was not going to be the one to break the tradition and leave Carlos and Ned for the enemy.

When the last attack of the day came and the last air strike was called in, it was napalm again, dropped from four F-4 fast movers. Some of the ordnance burned the outbuildings, the Jeeps, and the base of the containment building itself. Dar would never forget the smell of frying human flesh, nor his shame at the fact that in his hunger, the smell made him salivate. He had not eaten in twenty hours. The screams seemed to come from just a few feet away instead of fifty yards away. Dar clearly remembered cowering on the parapet floor, covering his scoped sniper's rifle with his body as if protecting a child from harm, as flames rose two hundred feet high all around the reactor building and the air became too hot to inhale.

Chuck and Dar spent the second night moving from position to position, using the Starlight scopes on the M-14s and the NOD on the .50-caliber to spot and shoot the scores of sappers and troops crawling from all directions.

"Did you ever see *Beau Geste*?" Dar had called to Chuck during a lull in the shooting.

"What?" said the Marine from the higher parapet.

"Never mind," shouted Dar.

The NVA was laying down smoke by this time—which was smart because even image-intensifying night scopes could not see through smoke—but there was already so much smoke in the air that it worked against the NVA coverfire snipers as well. Usually, when a trooper got within one hundred yards, either Chuck or Dar

would catch a glimpse of greenish movement through the hellish curtains of smoke
and white-blob glare of the open flames,
and then one of them would kill him with
a single shot. When they were shooting
from the same side of the building, the
two Marines worked efficiently, yelling,
"Mine! I've got it!" like Little League
outfielders calling for a catch.

At 2:00 A.M. of that second night, Wally
and John staggered to the parapets to announce that everything was loaded on pal-
let trucks and they could leave in the Jeeps
now. While Dar explained that the plans
had changed, the enemy kept up constant
harassing fire. Thousands of bullets were
striking the parapets. The sandbags were
shot to pieces and the sound of bullets
striking them was as steady as a heavy rain
on a canvas tent roof. The ricochets were
the dangerous element. Both Marines
were bleeding freely from impacts from
flying masonry and spent bullets.

Dar remembered Wally cleaning his
glasses—the scientist's eyes red with fatigue but also wide in shock at Dar's

bloody and battered appearance—and saying, "Has there been shooting while we were working?"

The PRC-45 radio was destroyed shortly after Wally and John finished their work, but Dar had already requested two air strikes at 0400 hours. The original plan called for a slick to slip in to pick up the two Marines, the two bodies, the two scientists, and their half ton of radioactive material. They'd be covered by massive use of napalm and cluster bombs, to be followed by Huey gunships rocketing the tree line all around the perimeter. But the Navy was dubious that an Army Huey could lift that load, and two slicks trying to land close together in all that smoke and fire was courting disaster. Finally the Navy said that they would see if they could free up a much larger search-and-rescue chopper—a Sea Stallion—from its duties ferrying important Vietnamese politicians and their families and luggage and possessions from Saigon to the carrier task force.

The hour of 0400 came and went and there was no air strike, no gunships, no

Sea Stallion rescue chopper... Dar felt that there would be no hope for air evacuation after first light, as the NVA had serious antiaircraft guns and shoulder-launched SAMs all around Dalat by now. By 0540 hours, Dar had groggily swapped his remaining M-14 and Starlight scope for his M40 Sniper Rifle with its daylight Redfield scope. He remembered wiping blood off the lens, although whose blood it was, he could not tell. For the first time, as that second Dalat dawn set forth its rosy fingertips—the Homeric phrase kept echoing through his head—Dar felt the approach of *katalepsis*. He felt himself begin to surrender to both fear and bloodlust; he felt the loss of control he had spent his short life trying to master.

The fast movers roared in at 0645, six Phantom F-4s laying down so much napalm that Dar lost his eyebrows and most of his hair. The gunships came in before the deafening sound of the jets had faded, the Hueys rocketing and minigunning the tree lines in all directions. NVA shoulder-launched missiles flew out of the jungle by the score, leaving crisscrossing smoke trails like some elaborate Fourth of July fireworks display. But the gunships came in low and skimmed just a meter or so above the grass and flattened fences, actually passing through the walls of flames before opening fire with their miniguns, risking the massive amount of small-arms fire, rather than keep altitude and be brought down by a missile.

And then the Sea Stallion came in, blowing the smoke into complicated spirals that mesmerized the exhausted-beyond-numbness Darwin Minor. He almost forgot to move, so fascinated was he by the intricate spirals and vortexes of smoke created by the huge rotor blades. Years later, Dar used chaos mathematics to study the fractal variations of that phenomenon.

But of the events at 0645 hours on that second day, he only dimly remembered Chuck pulling him away from the parapet, carrying Sergeant Carlos's body to the waiting chopper while Chuck carried Ned's limp form, and then going back to help the scientists hump the isotopes and other trophies out into the light.

The lead-lined container of 80 grams of priceless weapons-grade plutonium had absolute priority—just like the contingency moonrocks the Apollo astronauts had grabbed as soon as they came out of their lunar module a few years before—and Chuck lifted it and jogged toward the Sea Stallion while Dar was pulling the last crate of reactor crap out the doorway.

Dar still retained a perfectly clear image of Chuck being struck by a dozen bullets as the smoke cleared enough for advancing snipers to fire from the inner fence. Dar had frozen in place. Wally and John were in the Sea Stallion, but Dar was outside, less than a hundred yards from the twenty-five or so NVA marksmen who had just cut Chuck to bloody ribbons. As warped as time seemed at that moment, Dar knew that he had no time to grab his rifle or to run for cover. He watched the AK-47 muzzles swing in his direction as if everything had been choreographed in slow motion. Then a Huey gunship seemed to drift over them, also in slow motion, its Gatling gun revolving and firing in a silence only Dar could hear, empty cartridges flying and dropping by the hundreds, by the thousands, dropping away and catching the light from the rising sun. It was a beautiful sight simply from an aesthetic point of view—the sunlight glinting on all that expended brass. Suddenly the entire mass of NVA snipers was enveloped by dust and then tumbled down and back, as if simply slapped away by the invisible backhand of God.

Dar threw Chuck's body over his shoulder, grabbed the priceless plutonium cylinder, and ran for the Sea Stallion.

To this day, Dar remembered nothing of the flight out to the waiting carrier except for his last glimpse of the Dalat reactor through the swirling smoke. The entire six-story building was cratered by bullets. Dar could not have spread his hand on any part of the wall without encountering more than one pockmark. The sandbags were completely gone—shot to pieces, and the pieces then shot away.

Later, Dar could not remember the landing on the carrier. He vaguely remembered the confusion on board as he was carried to the crowded infirmary. The Navy surgeon asked, "How bad are you hit?"

"Not hit," Dar had said. "Just cut up from ricochets and concrete chips."

They had cut off his boots, cut away his filthy, bloody blouse and trousers, and sponged his bloody flesh. "Sorry, son," the middle-aged surgeon had said. "You're wrong. You have at least three AK-47 rounds in you."

Even as they sedated him, Dar was not concerned. He had carried Sergeant Carlos to the chopper. He could not be badly hurt. The AK-47 slugs had probably spent most of their kinetic energy in striking the reactor wall or passing through a half-empty sandbag before striking him. He did not even remember being shot.

When he finally awoke after surgery and four days of unconsciousness, he was told that the huge carrier was now so overloaded with refugees that aircraft on deck—including the gunships and Sea

Stallion that had saved them—were being pushed overboard into the sea to make room for more choppers carrying VIPs from Saigon.

Dar slept again. When he next awoke, the city had fallen, and Saigon was now Ho Chi Minh City. The last diplomats and CIA personnel had filed onto the roof of the U.S. embassy and been flown out by slicks while thousands of Vietnamese allies had been held back by the final circles of Marines. Then the Marines were airlifted out under heavy fire.

The carrier task force headed for home. The important South Vietnamese politicians were sleeping in officers' quarters below, while hundreds of displaced Marines and sailors literally slept on the deck, crowding under the remaining choppers and A-6 Intruders, exhausted men trying to keep out of the rain that now fell constantly.

Dar had agreed to tell Syd about Dalat, but had suggested he make them dinner first.

"That was good pasta," said Syd when she'd finished.

Dar nodded.

Syd raised her coffee cup in both hands. "Will you tell me about Dalat now? I only know the barest facts."

"There's not that much to tell," said Dar. "I was only there for forty-eight hours in 1975. But I went back a few years ago—in 1997. There's a six-day tour leaving from Ho Chi Minh City that ends up in Dalat. Americans are discouraged from traveling in Vietnam, but it's not illegal. You can fly from Bangkok for just two hundred seventy dollars on Vietnam Airline, or three hundred twenty on the more comfortable Thai Airway. In Dalat you can stay in a bug-ridden hostel named Hotel Dalat, or a fleabag hotel called the Minh Tam, or in a Vietnamese version of a luxury resort named the Anh Doa. I stayed at the Anh Doa. It even has a pool."

"I thought you don't fly as a passenger," said Syd.

"This was a rare exception," said Dar. "Anyway, it's a pretty tour. The tour bus goes along the National Road Number Twenty from Ho Chi Minh City past Bao

Loc, Di Linh, and Duc Trong—mostly huge tea and coffee plantations in that area, very green—and then climbs up the Pren Pass onto the south end of the Lang Biang plateau to get to the city of Dalat."

Syd listened.

"Dalat is famous for its lakes," continued Dar. "They have names like Xuan Huong, Than Tho, Da Thien, Van Kiep, Me Linh...lovely names and pretty lakes, except for some industrial pollution."

Syd waited.

"There's some jungle," said Dar, "but above the city, it's mostly pine forests. Even the forests and valleys have magical names—Ai An, which means Passion Forest, and Tinh Yeu, which translates to Love Valley."

Syd put down her coffee cup. "Thank you for the tour, Dar, but I don't give a damn about how Dalat looked in 1997. Will you tell me what happened there in 1975? It's all still classified in the dossiers, but I know that you came out of there with a Silver Star and a Purple Heart."

"They gave decorations to everyone who

was there at the end," said Dar, sipping his coffee. "It's what countries and armies do when they're defeated—they hand out medals."

Syd waited.

"OK," said Dar. "To tell you the truth, the Dalat mission is still technically classified—but it's no longer secret. In January of 1997 a little paper called the *Tri-City Herald* broke the story and it got reprinted in the back pages of several other papers. I didn't see it, but the travel agent told me about it when I was booking my tour."

Syd sipped her coffee.

"Not too much of a story," repeated Dar. His voice sounded ragged even to himself. Perhaps he was coming down with a cold. "In the last days before the big bugout from Saigon, the South Vietnamese reminded us that we'd built them a reactor at Dalat. There was some radioactive material there—including eighty grams of plutonium—that the U.S. officials didn't want falling into the hands of the Communists. So they rounded up two heroic scientists named Wally and John and flew them into Dalat to grab the material before the VC and NVA overran the place. The scientists succeeded."

"And you went with them as a Marine sniper," said Syd. "And then?"

"And then, really, nothing," said Dar. "Wally and John did all of the work finding and extracting the stuff they were supposed to find." He managed a smile. "They knew how to shut down a nuclear reactor and use those remote handlers, but they had to teach themselves how to drive a forklift. Anyway, we took the isotopes and the canister marked plutonium and hightailed it out of there."

"But there was fighting?" said Syd.

Dar went over to pour more coffee, realized that the pot was empty, and sat down. After a minute he said, "Sure. There always is in a war. Even in a lame-duck war like the one in 1975."

"And you fired your rifle in anger," said Syd. It was a question.

"No, actually, I didn't," said Dar. "I fired my weapon, but I wasn't angry at anyone, except maybe at the assholes who had forgotten the damned reactor stuff in the first place. That's the truth."

Syd sighed. "Dr. Dar Minor as a Marine sniper...nineteen years old...It just doesn't fit the person I know...sort of know."

Dar waited.

"Will you at least tell me why you became a Marine?" asked Syd. "And a sniper of all things?"

"Yes," said Dar, feeling his heart suddenly thud against his rib cage as he realized he was telling the truth. He *would* tell her. And in many ways, that was much more personal than the details of Dalat.

He glanced at his watch. "But it's getting late right now, Investigator. Can we take a rain check on that part of the show-and-tell? I have some work to do before turning in tonight."

Syd bit her lip and looked around the room—she had closed the curtains and shutters before they'd turned on the first lamp—but now the shadows were as rich as the orange lamp glow. For a wild second

Dar thought that she was going to suggest that they spend the night—both of them—here in the cabin. His pulse was still racing.

"All right," said Syd. "I'll help you clear the dishes and we'll hit the road. But you promise that you'll tell me soon why you became a Marine?"

"I promise," Dar heard himself say.

They were outside in the dark, heading for their respective vehicles, when Dar said, "The Dalat story has a punch line, sort of. It's the main reason they kept it all classified, I think. Do you want to hear it?"

"Sure," said Syd.

"Remember I said that the mission was really about retrieving that priceless eighty grams of weapons-grade plutonium?"

"Yes."

Dar jingled his car keys in his right hand. He was carrying the gun case in his left. "Well, Wally and John found the lead-lined canister marked plutonium," he said. "We got it out. The Feds, in their wisdom, sent it under guard to the big nuclear facility at Hanford, Idaho, where they carefully stored it along with thousands of other canisters of the stuff."

"Yes?" prompted Syd.

"Well, four years after my first visit to Dalat, in 1979, someone finally got around to looking at it."

Syd waited in the pine-scented dark.

"It wasn't plutonium at all," said Dar. "We went to all that trouble to retrieve eighty grams of polonium."

"What's the difference?" said Syd.

"Plutonium makes atomic and hydrogen bombs work," said Dar. "Polonium doesn't do much of anything."

"How could they—Wally and George or whatever—make that kind of mistake?"

"Wally and John didn't," said Dar. "One of the Vietnamese reactor techs must have slapped the wrong symbol on the canister."

"So what happened to the plutonium?"

"According to another report in the reliable *Tri-City Herald* on January 19, 1997," said Dar, "the Republic of Vietnam's spokesman said, and I quote, 'The Dalat Nuclear Research Institute is currently preserving the amount of plutonium left behind by the Americans as required by technical necessity.' "

Dar had said this lightly, but Syd's silence seemed heavy. Finally she said, "You mean the reactor is up and running again?"

"The Russian scientists helped the North Vietnamese get it operational a month after they won the war," he said.

18

"R IS FOR RECON"

Dar, the merciless ex-Marine sniper, spent the rest of Friday night and all day Saturday sewing and going through his back issues of *Architectural Digest*.

Some years ago, when Lawrence was poking around amidst Dar's shelves, the adjuster had come across several years' worth of the white-spined interior design magazines, and said, "Who the hell do *these* belong to?" Dar had made the mistake of trying to explain why he liked reading such home interior design magazines—how the pictured worlds without humans were so static, so perfect, so...*minded*... how that frozen-forever-perfection always translated in the prose to a couple, gay or straight, living in a timeless, clutterless, decision-free universe since everything was in its place, every pillow fluffed and creased to perfection. In reality the *Architectural Digest* edition was usually off the stand less than three months before the director and movie star who had built their perfect palace announced their divorce. The irony of the great gap between the perfectly designed, perfectly photographed homes and the chaos of real life amused Dar. Besides, it made good bed and bathroom reading.

"You're nuts," Lawrence had suggested.

Now Dar thumbed through almost two years of back issues before coming across the article he remembered.

Dallas Trace's $6 million home had been built from scratch in a crowded neighborhood just below the crest of Mulholland Drive along the Valley side. The neighborhood—Coy Drive, Dar found out, although not through the magazine article, of course—was comprised of relatively modest ($1 million and up) 1960s-era ranch houses, but Attorney Trace had bought three of the properties, had the homes bulldozed, and hired one of America's stranger architects to build him a Luxor-like post-postmodernist cement, rusted iron, and glass…thing…clinging to the hillside and dwarfing all of the other homes on the ridgeline.

Dar read and reread the article, concentrating on three pages of photographs and memorizing which of the huge windows looked out from which room. There was a small insert of the thinly smiling Counselor Trace—"The World's Best Legal Mind" was the caption—sitting in an uncomfortable-looking Barcelona chair. His bride, Imogene, the big-breasted then twenty-three-year-old Miss Brazil (second runner-up in that year's Miss Universe competition) whom Dallas Trace had legally renamed Destiny (because it was her destiny to marry the famous lawyer), perched on the even-less-comfortable-looking metal arm of the chair.

Dar thought that the house itself was an abomination—all postmodernist walls going nowhere, show-off knife-edge cornices, pretentious forty-foot-high living room ceilings, industrial materials with bolts and hinges and catwalks jutting everywhere, rusting iron "wings" that did or signified nothing, a strip of swimming pool narrow enough to step across—but he was delighted to read about the architect's decision "...not to bother with such bourgeois amenities as drapes or blinds, since the tall, magnificent windows, many coming together glass-to-glass at sharp angles overhanging the wild ravine, served to destroy any distinction between 'outside' and 'inside' and to pull the magnificent wilderness into each of the bright and varied living areas."

This "magnificent wilderness," Dar knew from studying his Thomas Guide and topo maps of the area, was actually the only undeveloped ridge in the area, one saved from the bulldozers by the discovery of multiple Indian artifacts and the relentless lobbying of some of Coy Drive's more stubborn residents—including Leonard Nimoy and a writer named Harlan Ellison.

Sewing the ghillie suit was a pain in the ass. Dar had to take the oversized, two-piece camouflage overalls, attach netting to the whole damn thing, reinforce the front of the suit with heavy canvas—also camouflage-patterned—and then sew on more tough canvas to the elbows and knees.

Dar then took the several hundred irregularly cut strips of hessian/burlap and "garnished" the suit—a seven-hour job of sewing the bastardly bits of cloth to every part of the net, which in turn had been sewn to the outer coveralls. The front of the ghillie suit was only lightly garnished, but Dar had to apply enough strips to the back of the suit for the floppy pieces of fabric to hang down to drape on the ground whenever he was in a prone position. The wide-brimmed boonie hat he had purchased was similarly garnished, only here the Alaskan mosquito-netting outfit came in handy.

Dar had never worn or made himself a ghillie suit in his training for Vietnam— Marines had humped into the jungle and fought in their green or camouflage fatigues, often using branches and greenery

for camouflage while waiting for the enemy, or occasionally excavating a dug-out
and camouflage-covered so-called belly-
hide fire position. Ghillie suits were just
too damned hot and clumsy for jungle
fighting. But in the mid-1970s at Camp
Pendleton just up the road from San
Diego, Dar had been taught the history of
the ghillie suit.

Ghillies had been Scottish gamekeepers
in the 1800s who developed such man-
made camouflage outfits for stalking
game—and poachers—on the great Highland estates. German snipers had started
the trend toward the modern ghillie suit
in World War I when they discarded their
issued, oversized, hooded, stiff and cum-
bersome canvas greatcoats and constructed
their own camouflage robes for use when
crawling around in No Man's Land. They
had soon discovered the usefulness of
adding a camouflaged hood that could be
pulled over the head, leaving only a small
slit with a gauze eyepiece for vision.
Snipers also soon learned that the human
eye—especially in a battlefield environ-

ment—is exceptionally sensitive to both unusual movement—say, a bush crawling along under its own propulsion—and to the slightest glimpse of the outline of a human face. The sight of a rifle barrel also tended to catch a soldier's or counter-sniper's attention very, very quickly.

And so the sniper's ghillie suit had evolved this century through a harsh but very efficient process of natural selection. Today, in sniper schools such as the Royal Marines' school at Lympstone in Devon or the U.S. Marines' Scout Sniper Schools in Quantico, Virginia, or Camp Lejeune and Camp Pendleton, it is common practice for the Marine NCOs to take visiting officers from other services out onto the training field and explain the theoretical advantages of camouflage in the profession of sniping. At the end of the short lecture, five to thirty-five ghillie-suited snipers stand up—usually none of them farther than twenty paces from the startled Army officers, and many of them literally within touching distance. The rule in making a successful ghillie suit is that if someone can see it before he steps on it, it's back to the sewing machine or forward to the grave.

Dar was pleased in some obscure way that even today, the Marines' Sniper School students were expected to make their own ghillie suits during their spare time. Some of the products, Dar knew from visiting Camp Pendleton in recent years, were quite original.

This reminded him. He stopped sewing and cussing for a few minutes and called Camp Pendleton, making an appointment to see Captain Butler there late on Tuesday afternoon. Returning to his worktable, Dar was glad that he would not be bringing his own ghillie suit along for inspection. Marines can be very insensitive sometimes.

Dar finished the ghillie suit about dinnertime. He tried it on—slipping into the fatigues, buttoning everything up, pulling on the boonie hat with its three feet of netting and mosquito-screen camouflage attachments—and then went to stand in front of the full-length closet mirror to see how he looked.

There was no full-length mirror—only its frame and two bullet holes.

Dar went into the bathroom and stood on the edge of the tub to check out his new suit. The bathroom cabinet gave him only a partial view, but it was ridiculous enough to make him just want to lie down in the tub and take a nap until everything—including Dallas Trace and his Alliance and his Russian enforcers—just went away.

Dar thought that he looked like some low-budget, Roger Corman, 1961 horror-movie monster—a shapeless sheepdog mass with hundreds of irregular dun and tan and soft green tatters hanging from it. He could not see his own eyes through the mosquito-netting veil, and accompanying camo-strips. His hands were concealed by the overhanging sleeves, netting, and strips of hessian/burlap. He was no longer a human shape, merely a raggedy-ass blob looking like a pile of ambulatory hound dog ears.

"Boo!" he said to his reflection. The blob in the mirror did not react.

Lawrence agreed to give him a twilight ride to a trailhead so that Dar could go camping. The ghillie suit and everything else Dar needed—theoretically—was crammed into his oversized rucksack.

When Dar had called with the request, about 7:00 P.M. that Saturday evening, Lawrence had said, "Well, sure, I'll drive you to where you want to go camping... but what happened to that nine-ton Land Crusher you used to own? It seems to me that would do the job."

"I don't want to leave it on the road where I'm hiking in," Dar said truthfully. "I'd worry about it."

Lawrence certainly understood that. It was a running joke between Trudy and Dar how Lawrence invariably parked in the most distant edge of any parking lot, and then with the curb and shrubs and cacti on one side if he could—anything to avoid dings. When Larry's car got dings, Larry's car got sold.

"Sure, I'll drop you off," Lawrence had said. "I wasn't up to anything except watching a video tonight."

"Which one?"

"*Ernest Goes to Camp*," said Lawrence. "But that's OK, I've seen it."

Two hundred and thirty-six times, thought Dar. Aloud, he said, "I appreciate this, Larry."

"Lawrence," said Lawrence. "You want to leave your Crusher here or shall I come pick you up in town?"

"I'll drive out to your place," said Dar.

Now, on the way out from Escondido in Lawrence's Trooper, the bulging rucksack loaded in the backseat, Lawrence said, "Where you headed? Borrego Desert State Park? Cleveland National Forest? Or are we going as far as Joshua Tree or someplace?"

"Mulholland Drive," said Dar.

Lawrence almost drove off the road. "Mul…hol…land…Drive? As in L.A.?"

"Yeah," said Dar.

Lawrence squinted at him. "For camping."

"Yep," said Dar. "Probably two days' worth. I've got my cell phone, so I'll give you a call when I need to be picked up."

"Eight-thirty on a Saturday night, it'll be after midnight when we get there, and you're going camping somewhere off Mulholland Drive."

"Right," said Dar. "Just off Beverly Glen Boulevard, actually. You don't have to drive on Mulholland, just through Beverly Hills and up Beverly Glen to just over the ridge-line...on the Valley side."

Lawrence squinted at him and then slammed on the brakes, kicked up dust in a turnout, and turned the Trooper around, headed back toward his home.

"You're not going to take me?" said Dar.

"Sure, I'll take you," growled his friend. "But if I'm going into goddamned Los Angeles on a Saturday night and going through goddamned Beverly Hills, and stopping on Mulholland after midnight, I'm going home to get my .38." He glanced suspiciously at Dar. "Are you armed?"

"No," Dar said truthfully.

"You're nuts," said Lawrence.

*   *   *

Dar asked Lawrence to stop once, on Ventura Boulevard. It had taken Dar three minutes on the Internet to track down Dallas Trace's unlisted phone number, and now he used a pay phone to call that number. A woman's voice answered in a Latina accent—not sultry Brazilian, but no-nonsense Central American housekeeperese.

"Mr. John Cochran calling for Mr. Trace," he said in his softest male-secretary voice.

"Just a minute," said the woman. A minute later, Dallas Trace's fake West Texas drawl boomed on the line. "Johnny! What's up, amigo?"

It was Dar's turn to turn on a fake dialect. Speaking through his red bandana, he growled in his best East L.A. gang voice, "Chew're what's up, you honky motherfucker turf-jumping chickenshit bastard. If chew thing you can off Esposito that way and cut us all out—I mean, fuck your Russian fucking mafia, man—we know about Yaponchik and Zuker and we don't give a fuck, man. Those Commie fag bastards don't scare us, man. We comin' for *you*, homme."

Dar hung up and got back in the Trooper. Lawrence had been close enough to hear most of Dar's monologue.

"Calling your girlfriend?" said the adjuster.

"Yeah," said Dar.

Dar had Lawrence drop him off about two hundred yards east of the intersection of Beverly Glen Boulevard and Mulholland Drive. They waited for a car or two to pass, until the road was dark, and then Dar was out of the Trooper with his rucksack and moving quickly downhill into the tall weeds. He did not want to be arrested by Sherman Oaks police in the first five minutes of his mission. Lawrence drove off.

Dar reached into his heavy rucksack and found the carefully wrapped L. L. Bean night-vision goggles and the small box of camouflage color sticks. The ghillie suit was heavy, but most of the weight in his pack came from optical aids he had brought along and wrapped carefully in foam.

Dar was wearing black jeans, dark Mephisto boots, and a black Eddie Bauer cotton henley. Clicking on the battery-powered night-vision goggles, he saw that he had stopped just before running into a barbed-wire fence. The lights of the San Fernando Valley were so bright that it caused the goggles to flare every time Dar raised his gaze above the uninhabited ridge.

"The Counselor and his wife designed the house to take maximum advantage of the view of the city lights," the *Architectural Digest* article had read, "the same view that inspired their former neighbor, Steven, to create the unforgettable alien Mother Ship." It had taken Dar twenty minutes to figure out that the writer was talking about Steven Spielberg, who had lived in this neighborhood long ago when he was working on *Close Encounters of the Third Kind*. Right now that Mother Ship–shaped V of bright lights visible between the darker hills was just a pain in the ass—or to be more specific, a pain in the eyes.

Dar removed the night goggles and used the camo-sticks to paint his face and hands. The idea was to use light colors on those parts of the face where shadows were formed—under the cheeks and chin and nose, in the eye sockets—and darker colors on prominent features such as his nose and cheekbones, jaw and forehead. The important thing, both with the face and hands, was to create an irregular pattern that would keep the human brain from piecing together the outline of a human face or hands at a distance.

This was a point of no return. If a Sherman Oaks PD searchlight suddenly pinned him now, he would have a hell of a time explaining the face paint. Of course, he rationalized, the night goggles and rucksack full of ghillie suit might be a problem to explain as well. Then again, so far he had not trespassed.

Dar eliminated that technicality by climbing the barbed-wire fence and heading out onto the long ridge, passing through the few trees that ran along Mulholland and into the scrub grass and shrubs. The ridges on either side—each about two hundred yards away—were developed to capacity with homes, most with outside security lights. Between that glare and the moonlight, Dar realized that it was easier to slip along with the night-vision goggles up on his forehead.

It took him about ten minutes to hike to a place on the ridgeline directly opposite Dallas Trace's mansion. Dar knew from *Architectural Digest* that the huge home presented a fortress's blank face to the street: high walls, windowless concrete, a basement garage with automatic doors, no sight of the main door. It must be, Dar knew, a serious problem for the FBI, NICB, state's attorney's office, or anyone else who was trying to carry out legal surveillance of the place.

But the back of Defense Attorney Trace's home was a blaze of lights. Every room seemed to be lighted. Dar went to one knee, set the rucksack down carefully, and extracted his old Redfield Accu-Range telescopic sight. The scope was only 3–9 variable magnification, but it was easier to use than binoculars and had the advantage of showing only one set of optical lenses to the sun in the daylight.

Well, there was no doubt that this was the house. The four-foot-wide pool on its strip of coral-colored concrete that made up the backyard was brightly lit, as was the almost vertical strip of mowed grass below it. Dar could make out a security fence about twenty yards down the hill: razor wire atop an outward-slanted fence. The rear lights were bright enough to illuminate the hillside, but he could see extra motion-detector-activated lights on the wall and fence. Dar had no doubt that the fence and the lights, as well as the doors and the windows, were all hooked to state-of-the-art anti-intruder circuitry and that both the Sherman Oaks private security agency and the police would be notified if so much as an errant squirrel ended up in that yard. Mr. Dallas Trace's home was not an easy target for a lazy or careless burglar.

Dar could see no one moving in any of the rooms, nor anyone visible in couches or chairs, even though a sixty-four-inch high-definition projection TV was flickering away in one of the lower-level rooms. The magazine article had not exaggerated when it had raved about the forty-foot-high window walls on the main level; they jutted out like a ship's bow over the ravine to Dar's west. As always when confronted with such architectural monstrosities, Dar's thoughts were *Who the hell changes the light bulbs in the ceiling and washes those windows?* He had come to peace with the realization that he was a Philistine of practicality at heart.

Right now practicality demanded finding a good place to spend the next twenty-four hours or so. Once planted in a ghillie suit, a sniper did not move in daylight unless there was pressing need to. The idea was to stay prone in one place during all the hours of the day, observing. Dar knew from experience that it was difficult to do this if one staked out one's position on an anthill or a cactus or too many rocks or on the opening to a rattler's den.

Dar used the night goggles to search for a place just northeast of Trace's house—

where every window and room on this side was still within view—and found a relatively flat area below the crest of the ridge, tucked in between Spanish bayonet yucca and a large ottoman-sized boulder. Another boulder behind him would shield him from daylight view of anyone strolling idly along the ridgeline. Taller grass in front should make a good viewing blind. His ghillie suit should blend well with the tall but dry tan grass growing along this stretch of hillside. But to make sure, Dar flipped up his night-vision goggles, crouched with his back to the Trace house, and used a tiny, shielded penlight to study every inch of the position. Moving any stone larger than his fingernail— and knowing that even those tiny pebbles left would be well known by sunrise—he did his checklist: fire ants, no; cacti, no; snakes, no; gopher hole, no; dog shit, no; fox den, no; animal tracks, no (it was never smart to set your sniper position on a game trail); and finally, signs of humans—cigarette butts, shell casings, Dairy Queen cups, used condoms—no.

Dar sighed, pulled out his ghillie suit and wrestled himself into it with as little noise as possible, laid his rucksack under the extra camouflaged netting he had brought for that purpose, and lay prone, feeling the padding of the thick canvas on his elbows, knees, and belly, setting his camera with the huge four-hundred-millimeter lens under the ghillie suit next to him, and using the Redfield as his spotting scope. Thus the long night began.

During his training with the 7th Marine Regiment more than two and a half decades earlier, Darwin Minor had been taught how to keep a sniper's log. He had no pencil and paper with him now, but if he had, the log might have read something like this:

Date: 6/24 (Saturday)
Time: 2300
Place: Hill 1, Finger 1 (coord. 767502)
2310 First movement in house. Maid leaving.
2345 Mrs. Dallas Trace (Destiny) enters

main room accompanied by a man. The man is blonde, well tanned, a muscle-bound bodybuilder type. Not Mr. Trace. Probably not Yaponchik or Zuker. He looks more like the stereotype of a Beverly Hills pool maintenance man.

2350 Mrs. Trace and bodybuilder enter upstairs bedroom. Turn on one lamp. Engage in strenuous sexual intercourse.

6/25—Sunday A.M.

0005 Bodybuilder appears ready for nap. Mrs. Trace does not. Previously observed activity begins again.

0030 Mrs. Trace wakes up bodybuilder and ejects him from room.

0038 Dallas Trace enters downstairs main room one minute after Mr. Muscles leaves by kitchen door. Trace is accompanied by 4 bodyguards. Photographed everyone with Nikon using 400-mm lens and ultra-high-speed film. Bodyguards appear too young and stupid to be Yaponchik or Zuker.

0045 Bodyguards check backyard pool area, sweep area with night scope. Had worried about thermal imaging, but hoped that residual heat from boulders would muddy TI scan. Bodyguards use only image intensifiers. They carry Mac-10s.

0050 DT goes upstairs to check on Mrs. Trace. She is sleeping. Trace goes back downstairs to confer with guards.

0115 DT makes several phone calls.

0205 Bodyguards reenter house. DT goes to upstairs bedroom.

0210 Lights out in bedroom. Guards remain in main room and billiard room. Work in shifts of 2.

0300 Cramp in left leg only 4 hours into watch. Too old for this crap.

0450 Predawn light. Make sure ghillie suit and extra camo-cloth covers everything.

0521 Sunrise. Was freezing all night. Already beginning to get too hot.

0640 Pissed into small fissure next to boulder without moving. Violates training, but will be damned if I'm going to ruin these new coveralls this early. Glad I fasted and purged system all day Sat.

0715 No movement in DT house except change of guards. Using polarizers to see through reflection of rising sun. Partially successful.

0735 Female jogger runs up trail twenty meters above me. Hear her Walkman. Doberman with her. Dog came down to sniff, peed on me. Was called back by jogger.

0930 Redfield scope sees through kitchen window well enough to spot DT eating large breakfast the maid cooked for him. Mrs. DT still asleep.

1039 Mrs. DT joins husband in kitchen. DT on phone.

1115 DT dresses—jeans, cowboy boots, western blue silk shirt, bison vest.

1138 DT leaves home. 3 of 4 bodyguards go with him.

1222 Maid leaves. 4th bodyguard led upstairs by Mrs. DT. Strenuous sexual intercourse.

1250 Bodyguard returns to main room.

1300 Maid returns.

1430 Heat very intense. Using water judiciously, but finish second bottle. One left.

1440 Rattlesnake crawls over my right

leg and suns itself on boulder approx. 1 meter to my left.

1630 Snake leaves immediate area.

1645 Heavy rain. Visibility still acceptable.

1655 Last night's bodybuilder returns. He *is* the pool man. He hangs around under patio canopy to stay out of rain.

1710 Mrs. DT leaves with 4th bodyguard. Pool man is called into house by maid. Two engage in strenuous sexual intercourse in video room.

1820 Rain ends, but rivulets of water are pouring off boulders and through my position. Maid and pool man have left house. No movement visible.

2120 Last twilight gone because of clouds. Eyes very tired because of scope use. Eyedrops almost gone.

2210 DT returns with his 4 guards and 5 unidentified men. New men look foreign. 3 of them stay in main room with DT's regular bodyguards while 2 go upstairs with DT to office.

2245 Long conversation. DT sits with his back to the glass just like in his Century

City office. The 2 men continue standing during the discussion. Shoot 3 rolls of high-speed black-and-white film using bipod to steady 400-mm lens. This is the sniper team: Gregor Yaponchik and Pavel Zuker. Zuker even stands 3 paces back on Yaponchik's left during discussion, just as a spotter does for his master sniper. Cannot quite read the Russians' lips—although I can tell that they are speaking English—but I seem to make out the words "Latino" and "Mexican" several times. I assume they are discussing whether my phone call of the night before was a fraud.

2255 DT is showing the 2 men photographs of lawyer Esposito and me. The photos of me were obviously taken by a long lens—2 outside my San Diego condo and 1 at the Gomez wreck. Last 2 were taken at the cabin. Damn.

2300 Meeting breaking up. Clear images of Zuker and Yaponchik. The spotter looks nothing like the FBI photo of the man with the beard—he is tall, thin, and clean-shaven, with short-cropped black hair and deeply sunken eyes. He smokes a cigarette during the discussion; I can see the anger on DT's face as the lawyer gets up to find an ashtray.

Yaponchik is an older man, perhaps 2 to 3 years my senior. He reminds me of some Swedish actor...can't recall his name... Bergman movies. Short blonde hair, long, lined face, thin lips always seeming to be ready for an ironic smile, blue eyes, sculpted cheekbones and chin. Very large hands with long fingers. Dressed in a very expensive Italian suit. Does not look Russian. More Scandinavian.

2320 The 3 go back downstairs and talk to the 7 gathered bodyguards. I am certain that the 3 who came with Y and Z are foreign, Eastern European or Russian—their taste in suits has not yet evolved—while the original 4 appear to be American thugs, professional but not in the Russians' league.

2330 Rain starts again. Photographed all 10 men. Resisted urge to call Dallas Trace on my cell phone and ask for Yaponchik.

2340 Mrs. DT comes home and goes straight to bed.

2345 Yaponchik, Zuker, and 3 other Russians leave.

6/26—Monday

0015 DT makes three calls from his office.

0042 DT goes to bed. Mrs. DT sleeping. He tries to rouse her. Fails. DT watches TV in bedroom.

0150 TV off. Bedroom dark. Guards on 2 shifts.

0200 Remember his name—Max von Sydow. Yaponchik looks a lot like Max von Sydow.

0210 Two guards "sleeping" in extra downstairs bedroom engage in homosexual activity. Details not observed after initial foreplay.

0235 Phone to request extraction. Lawrence displeased.

0530 Extracted just after first light.

0540 Lawrence inquires if I have lost my fucking mind.

Dar slept two hours on Tuesday morning and then developed his rolls of film in the little darkroom off the loft's bathroom.

Some of the close-ups of the men were grainy, but all were clear enough.

Next Dar used his reverse L.A. phone directory to look up the names and addresses of the people Dallas Trace had called during the recon session—Dar had been able to see all the numbers punched except for one call when Trace's body had blocked the view through the scope. Several were unlisted, but he found those soon enough through Lawrence's Internet skip-chase service. Dar circled several locations in his L.A. County Thomas Guide.

Special Agent Warren had left two messages on Dar's machine, and when Dar called him back, the FBI man said that the files Dar had requested were available. Dar asked if they could be messengered over early that afternoon. Syd Olson had also left several messages. Dar called her at the Justice Center, assured her that he had enjoyed his camping trip, and made an appointment to see her at her office at an improbably early hour the next morning.

A young FBI agent personally delivered the dossiers, had Dar sign five forms, and still looked unhappy when he left. Dar almost wondered whether he should have tipped the young man.

Dar showered a third time, dressed in chinos and a blue Oxford-cloth shirt, and tried to wake up as he studied the dossiers before driving up to Camp Pendleton. Yaponchik's file was thicker than Zuker's, but most of it was official information obtained through tapping unclassified Soviet army sources. The KGB-related material was largely blacked out—Dar always loved that Freedom-of-Information-sort-of aspect to dossiers—but the outline was there for both men: Russian army snipers active in Afghanistan, KGB paramilitary during the last years of the regime, Russian mafia ties through the mid-1990s, no recent information. There was the blurry picture of Zuker—Dar was convinced that they had photographed the wrong man—and one labeled "Yaponchik and Zuker with rifle platoon," which appeared to have been taken in Afghanistan with an Instamatic camera from about a mile away. Even with enhancement, the photo was nothing but grain, the faces mere blobs.

Dar smiled at this page. The previous page would serve his purposes. Right now, he realized, his purpose was to get his ass up to Camp Pendleton before he was late for the appointment.

Odds were that the U.S. Marines would entertain you on the drive up the I-5 beyond Oceanside, and today was no different. Light Marine tanks and Bradley fighting vehicles—followed by the occasional dune buggy with a .60-caliber mounted machine gun—roared along the camp side of the fence to the east of the interstate, kicking up dust before following ruts back into the barren hills. On the ocean side, landing craft were standing a mile or two offshore while hovercraft filled with Marines roared toward the beaches, up the beaches, and then into the dunes and scrubby woods beyond the dunes.

There were no interstate exits between Oceanside and San Clemente beyond the northern end of the huge base, but Dar had exited at the Hill Street/Camp Pendleton exit and used one of the southern entrances to the base. Before he reached the administration complex, he had been stopped three times: twice at gates complete with pop-up steel and concrete obstacles where it was confirmed that he had a 3:00 P.M. appointment with Captain Butler, and once by a Marine traffic cop who held him up a minute while three tanks roared across the access road at forty miles per hour and disappeared back into the dunes.

There were more security checks in the admin building, but by the time Dar strolled toward the last set of undistinguished concrete office huts, he was wearing his visitor badge and stepping a bit more lightly than usual.

The U.S. Marine captain did not keep Dar waiting. The secretary showed him in and Captain Butler, a tall, thin black man in desert camo-fatigues that were starched to a razor's edge, jumped up from his desk and gave Dar an uninhibited bear hug that was very much non-Marinelike.

"Damn, it's good to see you, Darwin," said the captain, grinning broadly. "We've missed a few of our monthly nights on the town."

"Too many," agreed Dar. "It's good to see you, Ned."

The captain always kept a cool pitcher of iced tea and a bowl of freshly picked lemons in his office—his one self-indulgence, Dar knew—and they went through the ice-clanking, pouring, lemon-cutting, and toasting ritual.

"Absent friends," said Ned.

They both drank and then took their seats—Dar on the worn leather couch, Captain Butler in the even more worn leather chair near it. Ned's grin remained.

After Dalat, when Dar had been rotated stateside, he used his first leave to visit his spotter's widow and two-year-old toddler in Greenville, Alabama. He had met Edwina before, during the long training when Ned Sr. and Dar had fought each other for every point in marksmanship and fieldcraft. This time Dar simply showed up and said that anything either of them ever needed, he would try to provide.

At first Edwina had thought it was just a gesture, but when she'd phoned to tell Dar she was moving with the baby to California to be closer to her family, it was Dar who paid for air tickets and a moving van rather than let them travel by bus. When Ned showed an early aptitude for math, it was Dar who quietly arranged for enrollment in a private school in Bakersfield, where they lived. When Dar had moved to California after Barbara and the baby's death, it was Edwina and the high-school-aged Ned whom he'd spent several weeks with before getting on with his life. Dar had been ready, willing, and able to help Ned—whose SAT scores were phenomenal—get into any college or university in the country. Dar had been thinking Princeton. Ned had been thinking Marines.

Ned Jr. had won three battle ribbons during the Gulf War, leading a recon platoon ashore while the Iraqis waited for the massive Marine invasion from the sea that never came. General Schwarzkopf had used the thousands of Marines poised for amphibious assault as a bluff, a distraction, holding the rapt attention of the hundreds of thousands of occupying Iraqi troops. Meanwhile hundreds of thousands of coalition army troops and tanks did their amazing two-hundred-mile left lateral shift, without enemy detection, before beginning the "Hail Mary pass" of an offensive that broke the back of the Iraqi army.

Ned Jr. had turned nineteen during the 1991 Gulf War, precisely the age his father had been at Dalat.

Since the rising young officer's posting to Camp Pendleton five years ago, Dar and Ned tried to have drinks and dinner together at least once a month. It had been Ned's frequent deployments to places unmentioned that had interfered in recent months, not Dar's schedule.

They talked a few minutes about family and mutual friends. Finally Ned set down his iced tea and said, "To what do I owe the honor of this visit?"

Dar briefed the captain quickly and succinctly on the Alliance, Dallas Trace, and

the Russian snipers, and then, uncharac-
teristically, found himself unable to finish.
Even though Ned had not taken up his father's specialty in the Marines, he waited
now with a sniper's patience.

"If you do me the favor I'm about to ask,
it may endanger your entire career, Ned,"
said Dar. "I will not only understand if you
say no, I'm almost hoping that you'll say
no. It's not just an unusual request, it's illegal."

Ned smiled very slightly. "Disclaimer
noted, Corporal," said the captain. "Three
good friends—you've met them all—and
I have some leave time coming. Whom do
you want us to kill and how much do you
want them to hurt first?"

Dar laughed politely and then realized
that Ned was not joking. "No, no," he said
hurriedly, "I was just hoping that I could
unofficially borrow some hardware. I can
return it before it goes missing on anyone's
manifest."

The captain nodded slowly. "We don't
have any extra Abrams M1A1 battle tanks
here," he said, "but would a Bradley ar-

mored fighting vehicle do?" Ned smiled when he said this, but it was the smile of a carnivore, not a jokester.

Dar sighed. "I was thinking of a rifle."

Ned nodded again. "It seems to me that despite regulations way back then, you came home from that Vietnam fracas with a rifle as a gift of the 7th Marine Regiment."

"The Remington 700," said Dar. "Yes. I still have it."

"Does it still fire?" said Ned.

"It's been a few months since I had it on the range, but it was still able to put five rounds into the five-and-a-half-inch-square target head at six hundred fifty yards."

The captain frowned. "Six hundred fifty yards? What's wrong with the thousand-yard range?"

"I'm old," said Dar. "My eyes are old. I use glasses now when I read for long periods."

"Fuck that," Ned said, and added, "Sir." The captain ran his fingers along the knife edge of his fatigue trousers. "All right. This sniper attempt against you at home—what was the opposition using?"

Dar described the Tikka 595 Sporter.

Ned shrugged slightly. "It's not expensive, but it's a pretty good weapon. Domestic accurate high-power rifles like that tend to start at about $2,000—European sniper weapons run up from $8,000 or so—I think the Tikka retails at about $1,000. I don't think that would be the main guy's first choice in weapons."

Dar nodded in agreement. "They sent the spotter after me. I suspect that the weapon was meant to be disposable in case of problems."

Ned grinned again. "The spotter, huh? They don't think much of you, do they?"

"There are some brilliant spotters," Dar said softly. "I used to know one who was a better shot and braver man than any top shot I've ever met."

Ned looked at him for a minute. Then he gestured for Dar to follow.

The warehouse was huge. Somewhere off in the shadowy distance, a forklift was humming, but other than that, they were alone.

Ned opened a crate. "If you're looking to update your old M40, Darwin, this is a nice toy."

Dar reached in to touch the weapon set in its foam lining.

"H-S Precision HSP762/300," said Ned. "Comes with barrels and bolts for both calibers—regular NATO 7.62 rounds or .300 Winchester Magnums. The stock is made of Kevlar graphite and fiberglass, of course—no more splinters in Marines' cheeks, thank you—and it comes with a bipod and adjustable butt plate much like our updated M24s. Look here—see how the fluted barrel is locked into the receiver by an interrupted screw thread and matching bracket plate? You can pack this away in a light twenty-three-by-seventeen-inch carrying case and essentially have two different weapons on hand when you unpack it."

"Very nice," said Dar, "but I was thinking of using the old Remington 700 and Redfield scope for regular work."

Ned frowned slightly. "Why don't you just go buy a bow and a couple of arrows, Darwin?"

It was Dar's turn to grin. "Not a bad idea. I hear they're quieter and a lot cheaper than suppressors. No weapon is ever really obsolete."

The captain nodded at that. "Not if it still kills," he agreed. "You set for cutlery?"

"K-Bar," said Dar.

Ned closed the crate and repadlocked it. "OK, you use your antique M40 for regular work up to the limits of your failing old codger-vision...What did you say that was?"

"I didn't say," replied Dar, "but ten yards would be about right."

"Buy a shotgun," said Ned. "Or better yet, a big, mean dog."

"A lady friend gave me a nice Remington shotgun," said Dar. "Well, loaned me one..."

Ned's eyebrows shot up, not at the mention of the shotgun but at the phrase *lady friend*. Dar never spoke of lady friends. The captain said quietly, "All right, what was the special work you were interested in? Perhaps you were thinking of point-five-inch punch?"

"I've heard good things about the McMillan MI987R," said Dar.

"I've used it," said Ned, his voice serious now. "Very accurate. At twenty-five pounds it's one of the lightest .50-calibers around. It's got a recoil that would give an elephant hemorrhoids, but most of it's absorbed by a pepper-pot muzzle brake and lots of recoil pads. We even stock the U.S. Navy SEALs' 'Combo 50' variety with a folding stock. But it's a standard five-round magazine bolt action. Do you envision needing any rapid fire in addition to your Remington's slow work?"

Dar hesitated. Snipers were trained to think of one bullet, one kill. That was why the most modern Kevlar/fiberglass sniper rifles had largely reverted to single-shot bolt-action form that would be quite familiar to a sniper from the trenches of World War I. But he had the Remington for long-distance, light-caliber work... What would be his best choice for rapid fire? Ned's father had saved Dar's life several times in the forty-eight hours at Dalat with his accurized M-14 firing on full auto.

Ned put his arm around Dar's shoulder and walked deeper into the corridor of crates. "Would you like to see something my fire team used in the Gulf War? It turned out to be very handy."

"Sure."

Ned opened a long box. "We called it the 'Light Fifty' over there in the desert. Officially, it's the Barrett Model 82A1 Sniper Rifle...12.7-by-ninety-nine-mm Browning, just like the .50-calibers of old. It's got a short recoil—the barrel is actually sent back two inches every time it's fired and it has a huge muzzle brake. It weighs twenty-nine and a half pounds without a sight, comes with a ten-power Leupold and Stevens M3a Ultra scope, and—here's the important part, Dar—it has an eleven-round detachable box magazine. It's the only semiautomatic .50-caliber sniper rifle on the market."

"What would it cost me?" said Dar. "Out

the door, taxes, warranty, undercoating, and optional leather seats?"

Ned's eyes looked very much like his father's when he gave Dar a long, searching look. "You bring it—and yourself—back in one piece and it's yours. I'll even throw in a modern flak vest, three thousand rounds of regular ammo, and five hundred SLAPs."

"Holy shit," said Dar. "Three thousand rounds...and Saboted Light Armor Penetrators. Christ, Ned, I'm not going off to war."

"Aren't you?" Ned said, closed the long box, locked it, and lifting the box off the stack, handed Dar the key.

Dar was in heavy traffic on the I-5 heading back into town, wondering whether to stop and pick up a burger or just go straight home to sleep, when Lawrence rang him.

"They found Paulie Satchel, Dar."

"Good," said Dar. "Who's they?"

"Eventually the cops," said Lawrence, "but first it was the Hampton Quality Preprocessing people."

"Who the hell are the Hampton Quality Preprocessing people?" said Dar. "And can this wait?" He felt like a thief with the Light Fifty and boxes of ammo under a tarp in the back of the Land Cruiser. He had sweated through his Oxford-cloth blue shirt during the routine drive out of Pendleton and he still expected Marine guards to come roaring after him any second.

"No, it really can't wait," said Lawrence. "Can you meet me at this destination?" He gave an address in an industrial section on the south side of the downtown.

"I can be there in about thirty minutes in this traffic," said Dar. "If I absolutely have to." It was a shitty neighborhood and he had images of his Toyota Land Cruiser being stolen and the Bloods or Crips suddenly gaining .50-caliber semi-auto firepower.

"You have to," said Lawrence. "If you haven't eaten, don't."

19

"S IS FOR SATCHELBIGGIE"

It had been three hours since the "accident" and they had not extricated Paulie Satchel's body yet. After one quick look, Dar understood why.

Darwin had never given much thought as to how hamburgers were stamped out—he knew that they arrived frozen and pre-shaped at all of the franchise burger places—but now he saw that Hampton Quality Preprocessing was the place. It was a large, clean, new plant in a crowded, dirty, old industrial neighborhood.

Dar showed his credentials to the people demanding it. Lawrence had already been at the scene earlier and led him on a five-cent tour through the plant. "Loading docks for the beef to arrive, that room's where it's cut and separated, grinding room there, this area's where the extruded raw hamburger is put on a five-foot-wide stainless-steel conveyor belt that runs through the wall into the stamping room."

The stamping room was where Paulie Satchel—the one possible witness to Attorney Jorgé Murphy Esposito's final moments—was entangled in the machinery.

Besides a medical examiner finishing some paperwork in one corner, there were two plainclothes detectives there—Dar knew Detective Eric Van Orden—and five other men wearing white coats over their business suits and surgical masks over their faces. Lawrence introduced them as three executive representatives of Hampton Preprocessing International, headquartered in Chicago, and two of their own insurance investigators.

"Nothing like this has ever happened in one of our plants, anywhere, never," said one of the men behind the masks. "Ever."

Dar nodded and he, Lawrence, and Detective Van Orden stepped closer to the body. What made the scene especially grisly—besides the fact that Paulie Satchel had been squeezed headfirst through a three-inch maw of a hamburger press—was the river of raw hamburger meat, no longer so fresh, that surrounded his sprawled body like a river current of raw flesh.

"He's been working here for three months under the name of Paul Drake," said Detective Van Orden.

"Perry Mason's chief investigator on the old shows," said Dar.

"Yeah," agreed the cop. "Satchel was a little weasel with a lot of TV-watching time on his hands between liability claims. He always got some shit job to tide him over until the insurance checks arrived. We've got aliases on him as Joe Cartwright, Richard Kimble, Matt Dillon, Rob Petry, and Wire Palladin."

"Wire Palladin?" said Lawrence.

Van Orden gave a twitch of a smile. "Yeah, remember Richard Boone in the old *Palladin* series? The gunfighter all in black?"

"Sure," said Lawrence. "Palladin, Palladin, where do you roam…" he sang.

"Well," said Van Orden, "the card that the gunfighter used to hand out on the show read 'Wire Palladin, San Francisco.' Paulie was never exactly rocket-scientist material. He must've thought that Wire was Palladin's first name."

Lawrence gave the headless, armless body a reproving glance. "Everybody knows that Palladin didn't have a first name," he said to the corpse.

One of the company insurance men came over and began to speak urgently through his mask. "We know of you, Dr. Minor…know your work…and we don't know who has called you in on this, but you should know right now that although this plant was highly au-tomated—Mr. Drake should have been the only person in the room at the time of the accident—there are at least eight mechanical safeguards against such an accident occurring while the employee was cleaning the input orifice of the stamping container."

"He was cleaning the stamping container?" said Dar.

"It was on his schedule for early this afternoon, when the acccident occurred," said Van Orden.

"Eight safeguards," repeated the insurance man. "As soon as that T-eleven restraining grate was lifted, the entire line was programmed to automatically shut down."

Dar ignored the split infinitive and said, "How about the other seven...safeguards?"

"No way that he could stop the line and lift that gate and open the compression claws to clean the stamping container without the failsafe devices shutting it down," said a company executive who had joined the insurance man. "You can imagine our shock when we found all of these built-in safeguards either bypassed or eliminated from the machinery."

The detective sighed and pointed to the mass of machinery and maze of circuitry inside the opened stamping-press panel. "This wasn't new," he said. "Paulie was too stupid to bypass these things, and the murderer certainly didn't spend hours tinkering with the machinery before starting the press on Paulie."

The company man and the insurance man took a horrified step back when they heard the word *murderer.* Perhaps it was the first time the detective had used it.

Lawrence pointed to the Rube Goldberg rewiring. "This has been like this for years," he said. "The fail-safes obviously slowed down the process too much, so they just bypassed all this crap and had the operator—Paulie in this case—shut off the power back there." Lawrence pointed to a huge red button at the far end of the line. "And then he could clean the stamping press entrance five times as fast and they could get back to production."

"Can someone turn the line and the press back on from *outside* this room?" asked Dar.

The five company people shook their masked heads so vigorously that sweat actually flew through the air.

"And Paulie was supposed to be working alone?" said Dar.

"He was working alone today," said Van Orden. "Signed in at one P.M. as usual. Would have ended his shift at nine."

"Other workers been interviewed?" said Dar.

Van Orden nodded. "The line shut down at the usual time when Paulie cleaned the press. There are only five other workers in the building... it really is highly automated... and four of them were all outside together, taking a smoke break, when the... event... occurred."

"What about the fifth man?" asked Dar.

"He was working in the back room there and has a perfect alibi," said Lawrence.

"None of these guys saw anyone enter the building," said Dar.

"Of course not," said Van Orden. "That would make our job too easy, wouldn't it? But there are three other doors where someone could have come in from the opposite street side or the alley without being seen. None of them were locked."

Dar turned and looked at the river of raw

hamburger and the big red button at the head of the line. "So all the killer had to do was push that button."

Lawrence folded his arms. "But you notice where the button is by the door. Even with Paulie's head lowered and close to the press, he would have heard and seen a person entering the room. Yet he stayed near the press."

"Either someone made him stay there," said Van Orden, "or..."

"Or he knew the person and trusted him," said Dar.

Lawrence pointed to the slit where Paulie's body was still embedded; there were only about three inches of space between the steel runway and the serrated maw of the press entrance. Paulie's shoulders were visibly compressed into that tiny area. Hamburger had flowed by on either side. It looked like an obscene cartoon.

"This would have been a slow death, Dar," said Lawrence. "Whoever it was who started the line did so when just Paulie's fingers were in the press entrance. But you see these sort of flippers on the side...

They mash the line of raw hamburger into the maw."

"So Paulie wasn't stamped all at once?" said Dar, seeing the real horror of the death fully for the first time.

"These guys who built the machine estimate that it must have taken about ten minutes for him to be dragged in—and stuffed in by those two big hydraulic compression claws—far enough for his body to jam the works," said Detective Van Orden. "First his fingers, then hands, then both arms..."

"With hamburger flowing around him and past him and getting stamped into patties with him the whole time," said Lawrence.

Not for the first time, Dar wished that he did not possess such a visual imagination. "He must have screamed himself hoarse," he said.

Van Orden nodded. "But the machinery was still on in other parts of the factory—it's damned loud in the rendering and sorting room—and four of the other five guys were out front smoking. The fifth guy was out back on the stacking and loading deck, and we interviewed the trucker who was with him. Neither of them heard anything over the diesel engine of the truck running and the other noise back there."

"And then, finally, Paulie's head would have been pulled in," said Lawrence. "The last few minutes would have been silent."

All five of the company people had backed as far away as they could at this point. Dar felt like taking pity on them and telling them that Paulie Satchel had no family—no one to sue them. He had been a lonely little weasel of a small-time con artist. Now he was...hamburger.

The flies were beginning to buzz en masse.

"Let's go out this door to the alley," suggested Detective Van Orden. "Get some air."

"Is there any question that this is a wrongful death?" asked Dar when the three of them stood in the relatively fresh air of the alley.

Eric Van Orden actually laughed. "No...
I know about your investigation into the
scissors-lift accident and so forth, but
there's no doubt that this is going to be
pursued by Homicide."

"Why are all the company people allowed to hover around a crime scene?" Dar
asked the detective. "I mean, I understand
giving the insurance guys some access,
but..."

Van Orden looked at Lawrence. "You
didn't tell him about the lawsuit problem?"

Lawrence shook his head.

"Paulie doesn't have any friend or family," said Dar. "I doubt there will be a
suit."

Van Orden was shaking his head while
giving that ironic cop smile. "No, no, we're
talking about a class-action lawsuit here,
Dar."

Dar did not understand.

"The hamburger line runs to the stacking room back here. The last guy sorts the
patties onto trays with wax paper, then
slides the trays into a stacked carrier—"

"Oh, damn," said Dar, seeing where this was going.

"—and then they slide the racked carriers into a freezer truck...one truck every two hours...for fresh and efficient delivery."

"You interviewed the driver," said Dar. "That meant a delivery truck was here. The patties were loaded after...Jesus, did he drive off with them?"

"Twenty carriers of four hundred patties each," said Van Orden. "Eight thousand patties."

"They were delivered to Burger Biggies all over the metro area," Lawrence said glumly. Burger Biggy was a client of Stewart Investigations. Usually the claims against the chain were no more serious than the usual obvious slip-and-falls, although there was one nasty case in which a woman sued for half a million dollars because she was raped while in her car in the drive-through waiting for her order.

"How many of the patties had part of...contained bits of..." began Dar.

Both Lawrence and the detective shrugged.

"That's what the company guys are trying to determine," said Van Orden.

"I assume there's been a recall," said Dar.

"It's under way as we speak," said Lawrence.

Dar skipped dinner that Tuesday evening and went to bed early. The next morning he was at the Justice Center at 7:30 A.M. only to find Syd hard at work in her basement office. He was not surprised.

Syd asked, "How was your camping trip? I wish I could have gone along."

Dar felt a tingle of the pleasant sexual tension he had felt earlier around the chief investigator. Then he made himself remember the easiness—almost visible intimacy—between Syd and Tom Santana, and throttled back his stupid, adolescent imagination.

"You wouldn't have liked it," he said. "It rained." He tossed the three FBI dossiers on her desk and said, "I've finished reading these, and wondered if you could give them back to Special Agent Warren when you see him."

Syd shrugged. "Sure. I'm sorry there's not more in those reports on Yaponchik and Zuker."

"The photographs of them helped," said Dar.

Syd did a slow double take. "Photographs? You mean that useless Polaroid of the Afghanistan sniper platoon? I couldn't make anything out."

"No," said Dar, picking up the CIA dossier, "I mean *these* photographs." He opened the folder to the photos from his stakeout, which he'd inserted.

Syd looked at the close-ups. "Holy shit. I don't remember…" She stopped and squinted at Dar. "Wait a minute."

Dar had not played poker since the Marines, so he gave Syd his best chess face.

"You realize, Dr. Minor, that any illegal surveillance photographs entered into evidence would be reason enough for the defense to have the indictments—much less a verdict—thrown out." She had not stated it as a question.

Dar looked puzzled. "What do you mean?

You think the CIA photos were taken illegally?"

Still squinting, she looked again at the grainy close-ups of Yaponchik and Zuker. Dar had used the same font as the CIA had used to label each photograph before photocopying them several generations to get the fuzzy look he wanted.

Syd looked at him for a minute, bit her lip, looked at the photos again, and said, "Well, it's always possible that I missed these, I guess. We'll get these in circulation right away. For all the grain, they're good photographs. Those CIA boys know their business."

Dar waited.

"Yaponchik, the older KGB guy, looks like someone..." she mused.

"Max von Sydow?" said Dar.

Syd shook her head. "No, no. Maximilian Schell. I've always thought that Maximilian Schell looked sexy, in a dangerous, sinister sort of way."

Dar snorted. "Great. He tried to kill me and you think he looks sexy, in a dangerous, sinister sort of way."

Syd looked at Dar. "Well, I think *you* look sexy in a dangerous, sinister sort of way."

Dar did not know what to say to that. After a minute he said, "So how's the investigation going?"

"Wonderfully," said Syd. "I guess you've heard about Paulie Satchel."

"I saw Paulie Satchel," said Dar. "How does he…that…translate to wonderful?"

"Now we have four obvious murders," said Syd, as happy as Martha Stewart with a new blend of paint. "The police and FBI are finally completely on board."

"Four?" said Dar. "Esposito, Satchel…"

"And Donald Borden and Gennie Smiley," said Syd. "Oakland PD got word last night that a scavenger working in a landfill near the Bay found two big garbage bags that had been uncovered by a dozer. They were leaking…"

"Both Richard and Gennie?" said Dar.

"We've only got the dental records confirmed on Borden, but the other corpse was a female."

"Cause of death?" said Dar.

"Double tap to the head for each of them," said Syd. Her phone rang. Before picking it up, she said, "22R...probably from a Ruger Mark II Target. Short range. Very professional." Then, "Good morning, Olson here."

Dar looked at the photographs of Yaponchik and Zuker, studying them as if he had not already been memorizing them for twenty-four hours. Syd said, "Hmmm-mmm, really? Where was it mailed from? Uh-huh? Did you have your lab dust it for prints? Uh-huh? You have a match on all of them already? Uh-huh. Well, I guess sometimes we just get lucky. In fact, Dar and I got lucky with one of these old CIA files. Yeah, I'll bring them over and show you in an hour or two. Yeah. 'Bye."

She hung up and looked at Dar with a heavy gaze that many suspects had felt in this very same interrogation room over the decades. "You'll never guess what Special Agent Warren received in the mail."

Dar closed the CIA dossier and waited, showing mild interest.

"An envelope—no return address, no

prints—mailed from Oceanside yesterday..."

"Yes?" said Dar.

"Photographs," said Syd. "Glossy eight-by-tens. Pretty good resolution. Seven men. At least four of them are seen talking to Dallas Trace in the photos. Five of the men have been identified already."

Dar showed his interest.

"Two Russian mafia whom we didn't know were in the country," said Syd. "One of them a known ex-KGB strongman who worked with Yaponchik in the good old Soviet days..."

"The others?" said Dar.

"Three of the other four are known mercenary bodyguards and hit men," said Syd. "They all have rap sheets. One of them was a made guy until he killed one of his boss's friends."

Dar whistled. "That brings the organized crime task force and RICO into this, doesn't it?"

Syd ignored the question. "Quite a lucky break. First finding these lost CIA photos. Then this..."

Dar nodded agreement.

Syd leaned back in her chair, and said, "OK, where were we?"

"How the investigation is going," said Dar.

Syd nodded toward a tall stack of reports, videocassettes, audiotapes, and files. "Tom and the three FBI people have made contact with the Helpers of the Helpless through coyotes and various emergency rooms. They came into the net by different ways, but are in the same group of recruits now. The Helpers run a sort of swoop-and-squat training school. We already have a dozen names and it's only been a few days."

"Great," said Dar.

"And you know about the special AIU?"

"AIU?" said Dar dubiously.

"The task force's special Accident Investigation Unit," said Syd in her no-nonsense voice. "You're on it. In fact, you're the head of it."

"Oh," said Dar.

"It's headquartered at Lawrence and Trudy's place," said Syd. "I'll meet you guys out there later this afternoon when I get a break from working on these new photos."

"I should know what the IUD is investigating," said Dar.

Syd sighed. "Just a string of little accidents that seem to be murders," she said. "Esposito. Paulie Satchel. Abraham Willis."

"Willis?" said Dar. "Oh, the capper attorney who died up near Carmel."

"The Gomezes," continued Syd. "Mr. Phong. Dickie Kodiak aka Dickie Trace."

"I guess I'd better get up to Escondido," said Dar. "It sounds like I'm pretty busy."

"I'll see you later this afternoon," said Syd.

Lawrence and Trudy were devoting afternoons to task force business. Their dining room had been turned into an extension of Syd's task force headquarters, with cork boards all around the long table, a white board, projectors, a VCR with a small monitor, and a Gateway laptop with a dedicated modem line just for constant updates on the data and graphics related to the accidents under investigation.

Dar, Lawrence, and Trudy quickly divvied up investigations according to who had done the most work on the original. Lawrence took the Phong, Satchel, and Gomez cases because his clients had involvement in two of them. Dar planned to reopen the Richard Kodiak file and continue investigating Esposito's scissors-lift death. He told Lawrence and Trudy about the various photographs that had come to light.

"Interesting," said Lawrence. "Do you have copies of these photos by any chance?"

"I just happen to," said Dar.

"Doesn't Dallas Trace live up on Coy Drive near Mulholland and Beverly Glen?" said Lawrence.

"I wouldn't really know," said Dar.

"Well, I do. I looked it up the other night after dropping you off on your field trip," said Lawrence. "All right, let's see these bad guys."

They all studied the photos for a while.

Dar knew that neither Lawrence nor
Trudy ever forgot a face after studying it
for a case.

Eventually they decided to start work on
the Abraham Willis case because none of
them had been involved with it. The CHP
and Carmel police had e-mailed and faxed
their full files to Syd, and Syd had added
her task force investigation materials to the
four-inch-thick file before giving it to
Lawrence and Trudy.

For a while the three read in silence,
looking at photos and accident-scene
sketches, passing materials around. The
accident seemed straightforward enough.

Counselor Abraham Willis—a San
Diego–based lawyer who lent his name to
injury-mill cases and capper referrals—
had left his office early on a Friday afternoon to drive up to Carmel for the weekend. Witnesses interviewed in Santa Barbara said that he had dinner and several
drinks there, and the owner of an inn near
Big Sur was able to identify Willis as someone who had stopped in late that evening
and had another drink before driving on to

Carmel. Willis had been alone in both the Santa Barbara restaurant and the Big Sur tavern.

A little before 10:00 P.M. on that same Friday night, Willis had evidently pulled his 1998 Camry off the road into a turnout at a scenic view on a cliff between Point Lobo and Carmel. There was no one else at the turnout at that time.

"We know that turnout," said Lawrence. "It has a gorgeous view north toward Carmel."

"Couldn't have been much of a view at ten P.M.," said Trudy.

"Maybe he had to take a leak," said Lawrence.

"Or just wanted to get some ocean air…to shake off the effect of the drinks," said Dar.

"Didn't work," said Lawrence.

According to the CHP reconstruction, Willis had then climbed back in his Camry, put it in drive rather than reverse, crashed through a small wooden fence at the apex of the turnout—and plummeted, car and all, sixty feet to the boulders below.

"Why no guardrail?" asked Dar.

Trudy sketched the scenic turnout on a napkin. "See, there's guardrail on both sides of the turnout, then the parking spaces between with low concrete wedges, then thirty feet or so of grass with a gravel path, then this low wood fence with a row of reflectors... It's just to warn pedestrians not to walk beyond there to the cliff's edge."

"How far from the fence to the cliff's edge?" asked Dar.

"About another thirty feet to the actual cliff overhang, then a sheer drop. But there are a couple of boulders there. Notice that Willis's Camry struck one of them—the driver's-side door was found up there, on the clifftop, not on the boulders below."

"I noticed that," said Dar. "It doesn't make any sense."

"The NICB investigator agreed with the CHP investigator that Willis couldn't stop the car and was trying to jump when the car door hit the boulder," said Lawrence. "The impact knocked him back into the passenger seat and then the car went over the edge."

"Why couldn't Willis stop the car?" said Dar. "Even if he hit the accelerator rather than the brake initially, he had almost sixty feet in which to stop."

"Drunk," said Trudy.

"Spontaneous acceleration followed by brake failure," said Lawrence.

Trudy and Dar gave him sarcastic looks. Spontaneous acceleration only occurred on TV magazine "exposés," and total brake failure was almost as rare as fatal meteor strikes.

The CHP photographs of the body were suitably grisly. Willis had been thrown from the car upon the initial impact with the sea rocks, and the car had rolled over him before finally coming to rest. The Camry was also in pretty bad shape. Someone had reported the smashed fence at about midnight and the CHP found the wreck and body a little after 1:00 A.M. The crabs had gotten to Counselor Willis, but not so badly that his secretary could not identify the body. Willis had been married but divorced years before, in New York State, and no family had claimed the body.

"OK," said Trudy, "let's look at occupant loading on the restraint system."

They went through the CHP report. They went through the Carmel police officer's report and the sheriff's report. They looked at the NICB investigator's report. They studied the photographs.

Syd showed up then. The chief investigator looked exhausted but happy. She noticed the intense concentration of the group and said nothing after the initial greetings.

Finally Trudy held up a black-and-white photo of the interior of the '98 Camry. The car had struck the boulders hood-first, so the incursion into the passenger area was total—the crumpled steering wheel and dashboard actually ramming the passenger seats, the windshield completely gone and the roof crumpled down on the driver's side almost to seat height.

"What's wrong with this photo?" said Trudy.

"Only one air bag deployed," said Lawrence.

"On the passenger side," Dar said, and grinned. *Got them.*

Syd was frowning. "I don't get it."

Lawrence was on the phone immediately, calling the Carmel sheriff. Willis's Camry was still being held as evidence, unceremoniously stacked out behind an autobody shop in town. "Carmel doesn't have anything as mundane as a junkyard," said Trudy, as Lawrence began talking quickly with the sheriff.

"Well then, can you send a deputy or someone over to look at it?" Lawrence was saying. "We need this information now."

Lawrence listened and nodded. "Have him take a cell phone so that we can talk to him directly. What? OK, then...I'll hold." Lawrence covered the mouthpiece with his hand and said, "The deputy doesn't have a cell phone, but they'll patch through his radio call. I guess the body shop is about two hundred meters from the sheriff's office."

"I don't get it," Syd said again. "What are we looking for?"

"Occupant loading on the restraint system," said Trudy.

Syd shook her head. "There wasn't any," she said. "I read all of the reports. They're sure that Willis wasn't buckled in when he went over. He was actually catapulted out through where the windshield would have been if it hadn't popped out at the same time."

"But look at the photo," said Dar, sliding it over to the chief investigator. "One air bag deployed."

Syd looked at it. "On the passenger side," she said. "But I'm not sure what that proves…probably an air-bag sensor malfunction, don't you think?"

Trudy shook her head. "Sensor malfunctions are so statistically rare that we can almost rule it out," she said. She paused while Lawrence spoke with the deputy via their radio patch-through.

"OK…yes, hi, Deputy Soames…Lawrence Stewart here, Stewart Investigations. Are you standing by the Willis Camry? OK, good. Yeah, I bet it is. Uh-huh. That's a good one, Deputy." Lawrence rolled his eyes. "Deputy, would you look at the driver's-side seat for me and—"

Lawrence listened a moment. "Yes, Deputy, I know it's all smashed to hell and squashed and bloody on that side, I'm not asking you to get *in* the driver's seat. The driver's-side door should be missing…It is? Well, good, we're talking about the same car then."

Dar slid more photos in front of Syd. She looked at the one of the Camry's left front door lying by the boulder on the clifftop and bit her lip.

"Now please look down at the base of the seat, Deputy. Yes, right where the seat belt is attached to the frame there. There's a small enclosure there…see it? Good. Is there a red tag sticking up?"

Lawrence listened a few seconds. "A red tag," he repeated. "It should be quite visible. It would read 'Replace seat belt.' " He listened. "You're sure? Thank you, Deputy."

Lawrence returned to the table. "No tag."

"If Mr. Willis had been belted in, the restraint system would have undergone a one-point-seven-g load," said Trudy. "We could see the effects on the harness and the inertial reel, of course, but Toyota also has that little tag that pops up to remind the repair people to replace the belt restraint system after an accident."

Syd still looked puzzled. "But both the CHP investigator and our people knew that Willis wasn't belted in," she said.

Dar lifted a transcript. "His secretary said in an interview that Willis always belted up. He told her more than once that he'd seen too many cripples and highway KIAs."

"But he was drunk that night," said Syd.

"Legally, but certainly not falling-down stupid drunk," said Trudy. "Not drunk enough to mistake reverse gear for drive, or his accelerator for a brake pedal. Plus, even when you're drunk, you do things out of habit. He would have buckled up even if it took him two or three fumbles."

Syd rubbed her chin. "But I still don't

see the significance of the passenger-seat airbag deploying."

"There had to be weight on the passenger seat for the airbag sensor to deploy that airbag," said Lawrence, looking at the photo of the crushed interior and the single deflated airbag.

"During the fall he must have fallen over against that seat," Syd said, saw the fault in the statement, and immediately added, "No…"

"Right," said Dar. "During the fall from the cliff, Mr. Willis was in free-fall with the rest of the Camry. He wasn't buckled in, so he was essentially levitating…floating above the seat like a shuttle astronaut in orbit…"

"No weight on the seat, so the sensor doesn't deploy the airbag," said Lawrence. "Not even during the terrible impact on the boulders."

"But the airbag *did* deploy," mused Syd.

"On the passenger side," said Trudy with a grim smile. "But not during the impact with the sea rocks…"

"The wooden fence," said Syd, getting

the entire picture now. "But if Mr. Willis was in the passenger seat when the Camry hit the flimsy fence doing just thirty-five miles an hour as the CHP analyzed..."

"Why didn't the driver's-side airbag deploy?" Dar finished for her. "Someone had to be driving. Unless..."

"Unless the driver bailed out before the impact with the fence," said Syd, speaking to herself. "Someone rapped Willis on the head, knowing that the injuries would not be sorted out from the traumas of the fall, propped him on the passenger side, drove the Camry at the little wooden barrier, then jumped out on the grass just before the car hit the fence, knowing that the Camry would keep going to the cliff's edge."

"So the driver's airbag didn't deploy during the initial impact with the wooden barrier because the sensors knew that there was no one on the driver's seat," said Lawrence. "The same reason the driver's-side bag didn't deploy during the impact with the rocks below. It's not just because Willis was in free-fall as the other investigators reasoned; he was floating around on the passenger side."

"But he was ejected through the driver's side of the missing windshield," said Syd.

Dar nodded. "I'll have to do a computerized graphic reenactment, but the ballistics math looks consistent with the initial impact of the left front of the Camry on the boulder. Because of the principal-direction-of-force vector, the occupant— not belted in, airbag already deflated— would have been launched tangentially across and out, passing over the hood on the driver's side. Whereas if the passenger-side airbag had deployed on impact with the rocks..."

"He probably would have been pinned in the wreckage," said Syd, seeing the whole thing now.

"Which explains why the Camry's driver-side door hit the rock up above before going over the cliff edge," said Trudy. "It wasn't Willis trying to get out. The door was just still swinging open after the murderer jumped out on the grassy berm before the impact with the wooden railing."

Syd was looking at the grisly photos. "Those arrogant bastards. They're so arrogant they're just stupid."

Syd's cell phone rang. She got up from the table as she answered, listened, then came back to the table. She was sheet white. Even her lips were bloodless. She grasped the table edge and literally dropped into her chair. Her hands were trembling. Dar and Lawrence leaned closer. Trudy hurried out to get a glass of water for the investigator.

"What?" said Dar.

"Tom Santana and the three FBI agents who went undercover with him," said Syd, forcing out each word. "That was Special Agent Warren. The CHP found...all four bodies...crammed into the trunk of an abandoned Pontiac just half an hour ago." She took the glass of water from Trudy and sipped it with shaking hands.

"How..." began Dar.

"All four shot twice by a rifle," said Syd, her voice steadier but her face still pale. "One head shot or one heart shot each— probably medium range."

"Good Christ," said Lawrence. "Who in his right mind shoots three FBI agents and a State Fraud Division investigator?"

"No one in his right mind," said Dar.

"Those miserable, arrogant fucks," said Syd, her hand shaking again, the water in the glass spilling. Dar knew that now the shaking was from pure fury. "But now we know who tipped Trace and his shooters," she said.

"Who?" said Trudy.

There were tears in Sydney Olson's eyes, but she actually attempted a smile. "Come to my task force meeting tomorrow morning at eight," she said, her voice a whisper. "You'll find out then."

20

"T IS FOR SYMPATHY"

Syd's Thursday morning task force gathering was one of the more efficient meetings that Dar could ever remember attending.

She'd insisted on leaving immediately after the call the previous afternoon. Dar had agreed to stay for dinner, but before he ate, he walked the perimeter to make sure they were safe from snipers. He thought that they were. The Stewarts' sprawling home was on a steep hillside above the road, with open pasture and then a dense woods below them to the south. It was more than 800 yards to the tree line, and even from there, the angle was very bad for a shooter. The only way people in the house would be visible to the south would be if they walked far out on the overhang-

ing patio, and the three of them had already discussed the inadvisability of doing
that. The house was set lower than the
street to the north, but there the houses
were tightly packed and heavily land-
scaped, the traffic brisk on the street outside—and Larry and Trudy had adequate
security on their doors and shutters on
their north-facing windows—so that offered no opportunity for a sniper.

Still, after dinner, Dar had driven around
the neighborhood at twilight, making sure
that everything looked and felt right, before heading home.

Nothing looked or felt right during the
8:00 A.M. task force meeting. Syd herself
looked exhausted, and the others all
seemed sad or distracted or irritated for being gathered so early.

It was pretty much the same group as
in the previous Friday's meeting—Syd,
Poulsen, Special Agent Warren and another FBI man, and Bob Gauss, who had
once been Santana's boss. Next to Warren
sat Lieutenant Barr from LAPD Internal

Affairs. Larry and Trudy sat to the right of Dar across the table from this group, Lieutenant Frank Hernandez and the CHP's Captain Sutton sat on Dar's left, and at the far end of the table was a new face—District Attorney William Restanzo. Restanzo looked every inch the blow-dried, white-haired, firm-jawed once and future politician he was.

Syd opened the meeting without preamble.

"You all know that four people working for this task force were murdered yesterday," she said. "Investigator Tom Santana, Special Agent Don Garcia, Special Agent Bill Sanchez, and Special Agent in Charge Rita Foxworth. All four were lured to a remote place in the county—under pretext of training for swoop-and-squat accident fraud—and shot from concealment by a high-powered rifle."

Syd paused and took a breath. "The details of the murders are not pertinent to this task force meeting and the investigation is ongoing under the supervision of Special Agent in Charge Warren."

Detective Hernandez looked around the group. "If the details aren't pertinent, why were we summoned here, Investigator Olson?"

Syd met the officer's stare. "To arrest the person responsible for those murders," she said.

No one spoke. Dar saw Lawrence shift slightly, and knew he was making his holster more accessible—perhaps unconsciously.

"We knew there was a leak from high up months ago," continued Syd, "but it was Tom's idea to announce his going undercover to this group. We tapped the phones of most of you..."

Syd waited for protest, but there was just a general clenching of fists, squinting of eyes, and thinning of lips. No one spoke.

"And what did the wiretaps reveal?" Captain Sutton asked, his smoker's voice a rasp this morning.

"Nothing, directly," said Syd. "The person who had been paid off must have suspected that he or she was under suspicion. There was no illegal activity heard or recorded under the wiretap surveillance authorized."

"Then how…" began Hernandez.

"The person under surveillance avoided even local pay phones," continued Syd, "which was wise, because pay phones near this suspect's apartment had been tapped. What the suspect *did* use was a special cell phone purchased by agents of the fraud Alliance and registered under a fictitious name. We believe there were several of these phones given to the suspect, to be used for emergency contacts."

Syd unbuttoned her blazer and Dar could see the 9mm Sig-Sauer holstered on her belt. Then she turned toward the NICB attorney, Poulsen. "What you didn't think of, Jeanette, is that we wanted this person bad enough to follow all of the major suspects with cell-phone scanners." Syd stabbed a button down on a tape recorder.

Poulsen's voice could be heard, static-lashed and tinny but quite recognizable: "Santana from Fraud Division and three FBI agents have gone undercover to make contact with your Helpers of the Help-less."

A man's deep voice said something unin-telligible.

"No, I don't know the agents' names," came Poulsen's voice, "but it's two men and a woman and they should be coming into the country via the same coyote and contacting the Helpers at the same time Santana does. That's all I can tell you now."

The man's voice rattled again, but this time the words "money" and "transfer" and "usual amount" could be heard.

Attorney Poulsen shot up out of her chair as if propelled by a huge spring. Her face was deep red and the cords stood out on her pretty neck. "I don't have to listen to this shit. This is nonsense. You can't get any real information to your fucking grand jury after six months, so now you're fram-ing me with this…" She started striding past Syd toward the door. "You'll have to reach me through my attorney."

Syd grabbed the taller woman by the arm, spun her around, and slammed Poulsen's upper body down onto the conference table while she pinned both arms behind her. Syd swept a pair of cuffs off her belt and had the woman handcuffed before Poulsen could lift her head from the table.

"You have the right to remain silent—" began Syd.

"Fuck you—" began Poulsen, but Syd grabbed a hank of her hair and slammed her face back onto the tabletop.

"Anything you say can and will be held against you in a court of law," continued Syd in a calm voice. "You have the right to an attorney…" She pulled Poulsen's handcuffed wrists high above and behind her, causing the woman to gasp and shut up.

"We'll take over here, Chief Investigator," said Warren. He and the FBI man next to him each took the now-weeping Poulsen by an arm and led her out of the room, still reading the NICB attorney her rights.

When the door was closed behind them, Syd wiped her hands on her linen slacks as if they were dirty. "We've traced one hundred and fifteen thousand dollars transferred to a secret account that Attorney Poulsen set up eight months ago," she said.

Syd's voice had stayed steady during all of this, but now she paused long enough to draw a breath. "Our regular task force meeting will be held a week from tomorrow. District Attorney Restanzo has agreed to join the task force and will be present at our next meeting. I hope to be able to announce some real developments by then."

Syd looked around the table. "Some of you knew Investigator Santana—I've known him and been close friends with him, his wife, Mary, and their two children for four years. Tom's funeral will be held tomorrow, ten A.M., in Los Angeles, at the Trinity Catholic Church in Northridge, just off Reseda Boulevard near the State University campus. We'll let you know about the arrangements for Special Agents Garcia, Sanchez, and Foxworth."

During Santana's funeral, Dar realized that he had not been in a Catholic church since the funeral for David and Barbara.

Afterward, people milled in the sunlight outside the church for a while. There would be a private graveside ceremony, and Syd asked if she could talk to Dar afterward. Dar nodded, seeing his dark suit and glinting sunglasses reflected in her dark glasses. She had not cried during the funeral, nor when she'd hugged and spoken to Mary Santana and the two children.

"Name a place and time," said Dar.

"Lawrence and Trudy want us at the Esposito accident site by four for a demonstration," said Syd. "After that? Your condo?"

"I'll be there."

Lawrence's cell phone rang as Dar and the adjuster drove back to San Diego in the newly repaired NSX. "Bingo," said Lawrence.

"One of the photos?" said Dar.

"Yep. I showed them to the few guys who were working the construction site that Sunday—not Vargas, the foreman, he didn't want to cooperate, but to the other guys—and two of them made a positive ID. They each saw this guy walking around with a hard hat. They hadn't recognized him, but figured he must be some contract laborer for that weekend."

"One of the Russians?" asked Dar.

"No. The New Jersey ex-mafia guy, Tony Constanza."

"Will they testify in court?"

"Who knows?" said Lawrence. "I didn't tell them that this was a murder case with ex-mafia hit men involved, I just showed them the pictures. If I knew what it was all about, *I* wouldn't testify."

District Attorney Restanzo was standing on the construction site with three of his underlings, and none of them seemed very happy about getting their wing tips muddy. Two uniformed police officers had cordoned off the area around the scissors lift and were standing guard, holding the curious construction workers at bay, while Lieutenant Hernandez stood with arms folded. Trudy had the video cam set on a sturdy tripod. Lawrence was standing under the raised scissors lift precisely where Jorgé Murphy Esposito had been standing when he was killed. As during the original accident, there was a quarter ton of lumber on the massive lift bed thirty-six feet up.

Hernandez was explaining. "There's been controversy over whether this was an accident or should be added to the wrongful-death files already involved in this Alliance case. Mr. Stewart has the answer." He gestured toward Lawrence, who nodded at Trudy. The red light on the camera came on.

Lawrence cleared his throat. "All right. We all know that autopsy evidence and circumstantial evidence surrounding the death of Attorney Esposito suggest that he could not have pulled the hydraulic screw loose on the pillar there and died as he did, in under two seconds, without the front of his torso being sprayed by hydraulic fluid. The coroner's photographs show clearly that only the cuffs of Mr. Esposito's trousers and the soles of his shoes were sprayed with the fluid. Several workers on the site here have identified photographs of a man they say was present on the Sunday Mr. Esposito died. That man is a certain Tony Constanza, a former mafia informer now in the employ of Attorney Dallas Trace."

"I don't like the term 'mafia,'" said District Attorney Restanzo. "Mafia equates with Italian and Sicilian and is a slur on a specific ethnic group. Everyone knows that the so-called Syndicate has long since moved away from dominance by any single ethnic group. We prefer the term 'organized crime.'"

"All right," said Lawrence. "For the record, Mr. Tony Constanza used to be a member of that wing of the multiethnic, multiracial, equal-opportunity organized crime syndicate which, even today, is composed primarily of Sicilian- and Italian-Americans and is commonly known as the mafia.

"All right," continued Lawrence, looking at the district attorney, "if you're going to prosecute this, you need proof that it was murder, not an accident. I'd like to show you that proof. I'm currently standing where Mr. Esposito was two seconds before this scissors lift lost all hydraulic pressure and collapsed on him, crushing him in the scissors' mechanism. Would anyone like to join me here while we reenact the accident?"

For a minute no one moved. Then Dar stepped under the platform next to Lawrence. He had no idea what his friend was up to, but he trusted his professionalism. Dar's black Bally shoes and the cuffs of his Armani suit trousers were getting splattered with mud, but that did not bother him. He knew how to spit-shine shoes.

"Mr. District Attorney, would you like to loosen and remove the hydraulic adjustment screw?" said Lawrence. The huge platform loomed thirty feet above his head...and above Dar's.

"It's muddy over there," said Restanzo, who was obviously still pissed off at the mafia thing.

"I'll do it," said Lieutenant Hernandez. He squished through the mud to a spot just outside the shadow of the platform, next to the main hydraulic post.

Lawrence paused as Syd Olson crossed

the lot in a quick walk. "Sorry I'm late," she said, a bit out of breath.

"We were just going to show how this works," said Lawrence. "Lieutenant, would you please unscrew and remove the hydraulic adjustment screw?"

Dar flicked a glance at Lawrence. The two men were standing casually enough, arms folded, the mass of platform weight a palpable presence above them, but Dar was mentally figuring if he would have time to grab Larry and throw both of them out from under the falling scissors lift in time. It was a simple equation with a simple answer. No.

Hernandez shrugged and began turning the massive screw counterclockwise. It moved, there was a gurgle of hydraulic fluid, and the platform shifted six inches downward.

"Oh, shit," said Hernandez, jumping away.

"All the way out, please," said Lawrence.

The homicide lieutenant approached the post as if it were a live rattlesnake. Ever so gingerly he put his arm around it and touched the screw. He turned it another half notch. The platform seemed to quiver in anticipation of its massive collapse.

"All the way out, please," repeated Lawrence.

The screw stopped turning. Hernandez leaned on the massive lug nut, changed hands, tried harder. Then he tried both hands.

"The fucking thing…excuse me, Mr. Restanzo…the thing won't budge."

Lawrence walked over to the post and Dar followed, happy to be out of the death zone. Lawrence put his hand on the massive bolt and screw and waited for Trudy to zoom in.

"Mr. District Attorney, Chief Investigator Olson, Lieutenant Hernandez, gentlemen…this screw is in its regular setting, just as it was on the day that Attorney Jorgé Murphy Esposito died. There is no chance that Counselor Esposito removed the hydraulic screw by accident. As you've seen, the screw was designed to be adjusted slightly by hand, but beyond two turns, it requires at least a medium-sized wrench to be turned further. Basic engineering."

Lawrence turned and looked at Syd and the district attorney. "Whoever killed Mr. Esposito—and we have witnesses who will place the former mafia hit man Tony Constanza here at the time of Esposito's murder—must have held a gun on Mr. Esposito while removing this screw with a wrench."

"We didn't find any wrench at the accident scene," said Hernandez.

"Exactly," said Lawrence. He signaled for Trudy to shut off the video and he walked out of the shadow of the scissors lift with Dar following.

Trudy and Lawrence dropped by Dar's condo for a drink before heading back to Escondido. Syd seemed to be in no hurry for the talk she had asked for after Tom Santana's funeral.

"OK, we have the Esposito thing nailed with Constanza as the man," said Trudy. "The Willis case up at Carmel has been reopened and the FBI have taken possession of the Camry...They're going to use every forensic trick they know to find a print or fiber or something."

"Warren is going all out on this one," said Syd.

"Three field agents dead," said Lawrence. "I wouldn't wonder."

"Is Dallas Trace just crazy?" asked Trudy. "He's been a defense counsel for thirty years...Doesn't he know that the one thing you don't get away with in this country is killing law enforcement people?"

Dar cleared his throat. "I don't think Trace is running things anymore—if he ever was," he said.

The other three looked at him.

"This behavior is Russian," continued Dar. "Their crime bosses run the country. If government bureaucrats or police get in the way, they murder them. That simple."

"That's true," said Syd. "They have no RICO statutes over there, or anything similar that allows federal or local police to really crack down on the bastards. The Russian mob owns and runs the distribution of coal, natural gas, alcohol, half the foods available, and electric energy."

Trudy said, "So you're saying that the Alliance brought in the Russians to organize things, but that now the *Organizatsiya* is calling the shots?"

"That's my bet," said Dar. "I think Dallas Trace and the others who wanted to get in on the capper business climbed onto a tiger—or maybe I should say onto a bear—and now it's all they can do to hang on and not get eaten."

"It's too late for that," said Syd, her gaze distant. "They've gone too far. They're all going to get eaten, even the Russian bear...and slowly, I hope."

"So what would you like to talk about?" asked Dar when the Stewarts had left. Syd sat on the sofa across from Dar's chair, lost in thought.

Her head came up and she met Dar's eyes with that intelligent, blue-eyed, attentive gaze that had first called to Dar. "Actually, I don't want to just talk," she said. "I wanted to make a suggestion."

"Yes?" said Dar.

"I want to come up to the cabin with you this weekend," said Syd. "Not to play bodyguard and not for a strategy session. Just you and me getting away together."

Dar felt the words jolt him. He hesitated. "It might not be very safe around..." He had been going to say "me," but he said, "...the cabin."

Syd smiled. "Where is it safe if they keep coming after us, Dar? If you don't want to go away with me, it's OK, but let's not worry about being safe right now."

Dar understood that the sentence had more than one meaning for her. "Do you need to drive back to the hotel to get your stuff?"

Syd kicked the small duffel bag she'd carried in with her earlier. "I'm already packed," she said.

While driving out of town together in the Land Cruiser, his old rifle and the loaned weapon and ammunition under tarps in the back, a few groceries—steaks, fresh salad, a bottle of wine—in the backseat, Dar suddenly had a thought. Perhaps he was being presumptuous, but if she felt the way he did, she might not be spending the night in the sheep wagon. *Damn*, thought Dar, *I should have stopped at a drugstore before we left town*. He suddenly blushed. For years he'd been totally faithful to Barbara, and then there had been no one.

Syd touched his arm lightly. He looked over at her.

"Do you believe in telepathy?" she said. She was smiling again.

"No," said Dar.

"Me either," said the chief investigator. "But can I pretend that it exists for a minute?"

"Sure," said Dar, returning his gaze to the road and hoping that his neck and cheeks were not as red as they felt.

"We may be in the same dilemma here, Dar," she said, "not being young and modern enough to think out all the implications of this. But there's a certain advantage."

Dar kept his eyes on the road.

"I led a really dull life as an FBI trainee

before marrying Kevin," she said, "and Kevin and I were faithful to each other, we just didn't work out. And for a bunch of reasons, there's been no one since."

"Barbara and I...were like that," said Dar. "I haven't...I mean I've chosen not to..."

She put her hand on his arm again. "You don't have to say anything, Dar. I'm just saying that it's your call. We're not kids. Maybe all this stupid abstinence on both our parts gives us something special to share in this day and age."

Dar glanced at her. "You keep doing this sort of thing," he said, "and I will believe in telepathy."

They arrived at the cabin just at dusk. The light was thick and golden even through the nearly closed shutters.

"Do you want to have a drink and dinner now?" said Dar.

"No," said Syd. She took her holster off her belt, removed three clips of ammunition in their neat leather belt holders, and set them on the dresser.

It had been so long since Dar had helped undress a woman that he had almost forgotten that the buttons were backward. Out of her clothes, Syd looked all gold and white in her plain underpants and bra. They kissed. Dar remembered how hooks and eyes worked and he unfastened them without fumbling. Syd's breasts were full and heavy, her hips wide: a grown woman.

"Your turn," she said, helping him pull his T-shirt over his head. She unfastened his belt buckle. "I've been wondering since I met you," she whispered after another kiss, her breasts compressing against his bare chest. "Are you a boxer shorts or Jockey shorts kind of guy?" She unzipped his fly and helped him step out of his chinos.

"Oh my," she said.

"Habit I picked up way back in Vietnam days," said Dar. "No one wore underwear in the jungle."

"How romantic," Syd said with a smile, but this time as she hugged him her right hand went lower and found him.

The sheets were cool. Syd swept the pillows aside. Dar kissed her mouth, kissed the pulse throbbing at the base of her throat, kissed her breasts and long nipples. Their fingers interlaced even before they began making love.

Syd kissed him deeply and long. Their fingers intermeshed more tightly as her arms spread above her head, his palms against hers, his arms pressing hers down into the sheets, every square inch of his flesh aware of hers.

They had dinner at around 11:00 P.M. Dar grilled the steaks outside, wearing only his bathrobe, while Syd tossed the salad, fried some potato wedges—they were too impatient to wait for baked potatoes—and let the cabernet sauvignon breathe. Dar was hungry as they sat down to eat. Syd was obviously ravenous.

He had forgotten—it was that simple. Of course, he remembered the pleasure of sex—that was impossible to forget—but he had forgotten the thousands of small pleasures of intimacy with a woman. Of lying naked with her in dim light and talk-

ing before sheer, physical imperative reasserted itself; of showering together and
turning the simple act of washing each
other's hair into a pure form of lovemaking;
of laughing while walking around in
bathrobes and bare feet, starving, rushing
to get dinner ready. Of being happy in the
moment.

They each had a glass of Macallan single-
malt for dessert and sipped it in front of
the fire. The night was warm and the
screens were open, letting in the rustle and
scent of the pines and the occasional noise
of night birds or yip of distant coyotes, but
they had lit a fire anyway. Then the Scotch
was left only half consumed on the side
table and they were in bed again, more
passionate than before, Syd crying out at
the same instant Dar did, each of them
abandoning the boundaries of self at the
same instant.

They lay touching then in the sweat-
soaked sheets, the air rich with the combined sexual scent of themselves.

"All right, it's time to tell me," Syd said
softly.

Dar propped himself up on one elbow. "All right," he said. "Tell you what?"

"Why you joined the Marines and became a sniper." Syd's eyes were bright in the dying firelight.

Dar actually laughed. He had been expecting something a bit more...romantic?

Syd's voice was soft but serious. "I want to know why someone as intelligent and sensitive as young Darwin Minor joined the Marines and became a sniper."

Dar lay on his back and looked at the ceiling. He found himself strangely unprepared to explain this because he never had before. Not even to Barbara.

"I've already told you I was interested in the Spartans. But I didn't really tell you why." He paused. "I was scared," he said at last. "I was a scared kid. At age seven...I remember the day, the afternoon, where I was, the curb I sat on, when the realization hit me...At age seven I realized, *knew*, that I was going to die someday. I was already an atheist. I knew there was no afterlife. The thought scared the shit out of me."

"Most of us encounter that sooner or

later," Syd whispered. "But usually not that young."

Dar shook his head. "The fear wouldn't go away. I had night terrors. I began wetting the bed. I was afraid to be separated from my parents, even to go to school. I was aware that not only did I have to die, but so did *they*. What if they died while I was away in Miss Howe's third-grade class?"

Syd did not laugh. After a minute she said, "So you joined the Marines to find courage...to get over that fear?"

"No," said Dar. "Not really. I graduated from high school early, finished college in three years with a degree in physics, but all the time, what I was really interested in was death and fear and control. That's when I started studying the Spartans and their ideas about controlling fear." He rolled over to look at her. "The Vietnam war had started..."

Syd set her palm flat on Dar's chest. He could feel the coolness of her fingers. "And so," she said very softly, "the U.S. Marines."

Dar shrugged slightly. "Yeah."

"Thinking that perhaps the Marines would still know the secret science of controlling fear."

"Something like that," said Dar, realizing how stupid all of this sounded.

"Did they?"

He chewed his lip a moment in thought. "No," he said at last. "They had preserved a lot of the disciplines started by the Spartans—tried to live up to their ideals—but had lost most of the science and philosophy which lay behind and beneath the Spartan mind-set."

"But...a sniper," said Syd. "The only snipers I've met are on SWAT and FBI tactical teams, but they seem to be outcasts..."

"Always have been," said Dar. "That's probably why I gravitated in that direction. Whereas even Marines are taught to be part of a bigger organism, snipers work alone—or in teams of two. Everything has to be factored in: terrain, wind velocity, distance, light—everything. Nothing can be ignored."

"I can see why you would gravitate to that," whispered Syd. "Always thinking."

"The guy who set up and ran my sniper school was a Marine captain named Jim Land," said Dar. "After the war, I read something that Land wrote for a little sniper instruction manual called *One Shoot—One Kill*. Want to hear it?"

"Yes," whispered Syd. "More sweet nothings, please."

Dar smiled. "Captain Land wrote: 'It takes a special kind of courage to be alone—to be alone with your fears, to be alone with your doubts. There is no one from whom you can draw strength, except yourself. This courage is not the often seen, superficial brand, stimulated by the flow of adrenaline. And neither is it the courage that comes from the fear that others might think you are a coward.' "

"*Katalepsis*," whispered Syd. "You told me about that before."

"Yes," Dar said, and continued. "'For the sniper there is no hate of the enemy, only respect of him or her as a quarry. Psychologically, the only motive that will sustain the sniper is knowing he is doing a necessary job and having the confidence that he is the best person to do it. On the battlefield, hate will destroy any man—especially a sniper. Killing for revenge will ultimately twist his mind.

" 'When you look through that scope, the first thing you see is the eyes. There is a lot of difference between shooting at a shadow, shooting at an outline, and shooting at a pair of eyes. It is amazing when you put that scope on somebody, the first thing that pops out at you is the eyes. Many men can't do it…' "

"But you did it," said Syd. "At Dalat. You looked into human eyes and still squeezed a trigger. And that's been your survival secret for all these years."

"What's that?" said Dar.

"Control," said Syd. "The constant pursuit of *aphobia*—avoiding possession at all costs."

"Maybe," said Dar, uncomfortable with the psychoanalysis and all his blabbing that led to it. "I haven't always succeeded."

"The .410 shell with the firing-pin imprint," said Syd.

"A misfire," agreed Dar. "That was eleven months after Barbara and the baby died. It seemed...logical...at the time."

"And now?"

"Not so logical," he said. He turned and took her in his arms. They kissed. Then Syd pulled her face back far enough to focus her gaze on his.

"Will you do something for me tomorrow, Dar? Something special...just for me?"

"Yes," he said.

"Will you take me soaring?"

Dar chewed his lip again. "You've been flying. You were up in Steve's sailplane... You know mine only has one seat and—"

"Will you take me soaring tomorrow, Dar?"

"Yes," said Dar.

21

"U IS FOR UPDRAFT"

First, there was the silence.

The high-performance, two-person Twin Astir glided through the air as silently and purposefully as a red-tailed hawk soaring and lifting on unseen thermals. The only external sound was the soft rush of air over the metal-and-canvas skin of the craft, and since their airspeed was low, that was hardly any sound at all. When they had passed eight thousand feet of altitude, Dar had had them both put on their oxygen masks—he had leaned forward to check that Syd's was working properly—and because of the masks, they did not speak. Only the soft hiss of oxygen acted as undertone to the movement of air outside.

Second, there was the sunlight.

It was a brilliant day, blue sky, only a

few stacked lenticular clouds over the lee slopes of the high peaks, visibility otherwise unlimited. Sunlight prismed on the clean canopy which gave them a 360-degree view from twelve thousand feet. To the west, beyond the ridges and mountains and deep-running faults, gleamed the Pacific. To the south and east burned the brightness of high desert and the Salton Sea. Easily visible to the north was the smog bank held in by the hills east of Los Angeles, and the great red expanse of the Baja flowed south beyond the smog banks over Tijuana and Ensenada.

Third, there was the closeness.

If it had not been for his five-point harness straps, Dar could have leaned forward over the low rear instrument console and wrapped both of his arms around Syd. Dar could smell the shampoo that he'd lathered into Syd's hair that morning. He remembered the water and shampoo running down over her shoulders and breasts when he had rinsed her hair, squeezing the water out, the soap bubbles glinting on her breasts and nipples in the morning sunlight...

Dar shook his head and concentrated on flying the aircraft.

When they had arrived at Warner Springs gliderport that morning, Steve had been surprised but happy to loan Dar his Twin Astir—he would not accept a rental fee—and Ken had been surprised to see Darwin Minor there with a woman.

Dar had done a long preflight inspection of the high-performance two-seater, and then he and Syd had gone over the parachute procedures for the third time.

"Steve didn't make me wear a parachute," said Syd.

"I know," said Dar. "But if you fly with me, you wear one of these."

His older parachute had been freshly repacked and now he had cinched and tightened and adjusted until it fit Syd perfectly. The morning grew later and hotter as Dar went over and over the instructions on kicking free of the plane and pulling the rip cord, controlling the risers, spilling air from the chute to change direction, bending knees on landing, and other anxiety-producing details.

Finally Syd had said, "Have you ever bailed out of a glider?"

"Never," said Dar.

"Have you ever *used* a parachute?"

"Just once, about ten years ago," said Dar. "Just a regular sky dive to make sure I could do it if I had to."

"And?"

"It scared the everlasting shit out of me," Dar said truthfully, and then began going through the instructions again.

They had argued briefly about Syd bringing along her Sig semiautomatic and the magazine clips on her belt. Dar pointed out that there was no need for handguns in a sailplane trip and that the holster, weapon, and three leather-wrapped extra magazines would just get in the way of the parachute harness and re-straint belts. Syd had pointed out that she was a law officer and it was her legal duty to have the weapon with her at all times. Dar gave up that argument, warning her that the weapons would become a literal pain in the ass half an hour into the flight.

He had brought the oxygen because of

Ken and Steve's enthusiasm over the day's prospects of wave soaring—a glider's most dramatic means of gaining real altitude—and it took several more minutes for him to instruct Syd on how to stow the small oxygen canister and use hand signals to communicate when the mask prevented conversation.

"One important item," Dar had said as Ken's towplane began pulling them west into the breeze. "If we go to oxygen, don't throw up in the mask."

"What do I do if I get sick?"

"There's a little bag tucked into the right side of your seat there. Take the mask off, throw up in the bag, put the mask back on."

"Wonderful," Syd had said as the Twin Astir lifted off. "You're really making me look forward to this flight."

Syd had not shown any signs of sickness during the flight. In fact, she'd shown only exhilaration as they were towed west toward the mountains into the so-called foehn gap—a whirling rotor of upward-spiralling air—between the stack of lenticulars and the mountains, and released on the upwind side of it. Dar had soared them around and back, working the rotor like a ski-slope lift, flying across the invisible elevator of lift in repeated sweeps.

He had been careful to point out that even on a beautiful, clear day such as this, there might be a lot of turbulence upon entering the rotor. "Are the wings *supposed* to do that?" she had asked over her shoulder, looking dubiously as the Twin Astir seemed to be imitating a snow goose trying to get airborne.

"Absolutely," said Dar. "If they don't flex like that, they break. Much better to flex."

Having mapped the wave front through successive approximation, Dar flew through the turbulence of the outer waves again and found the true center of lift. After that, the ride was silky and soundless and breath-taking.

"My God," Syd had cried. "It's like we're in an elevator."

"We are," said Dar.

"It doesn't seem like we're moving at all in relation to the ground, the mountain," said Syd.

"We aren't right now," agreed Dar. "The wind's strong enough to give us great lift right now, but our ground speed is zero. I'll have to make another turn and pass in a minute or we'll be blown back toward those lenticulars and lose the rotor…but for now, we're in perfect balance."

Syd had answered by putting her hand back over her seat and Dar's low console. He hesitated only a second before reaching out and holding it, squeezing it.

At eight thousand feet he had them dutifully go to oxygen, just to be cautious.

They continued the smooth soar and climb, circling to the right, then hanging on the lift like a hawk balanced on an invisible pillar of a thermal, watching the sky get bluer and the horizon grow.

Dar held a mental three-dimensional map of the controlled and uncontrolled airspaces in this part of California, ranging from Class A to Class G, and he knew that they were well within an "E" space. This meant they were within controlled airspace but nowhere near a control tower, flying on visual flight rules. They could fly up to a ceiling of 18,000 feet above mean sea level, which was where the jet routes and commercial lanes began. He leveled the sailplane by flying out of the rotor at 14,500 MSL and widened their circles while increasing their airspeed to keep altitude.

Dar had Syd take the front stick and control the aircraft for a while, showing her how to take slow turns without stalling or losing too much altitude.

Syd loosened her mask and asked, "Can we do some acrobatics?"

Dar frowned but lowered his mask again, feeling the bite of cold in the air. "Do you mean *aerobatics?*"

"Whatever," said Syd. "Steve told me that you can do loops, rolls, all sorts of things in this special kind of glider."

"I don't think you'd like those," said Dar.

"Yes, I would!" said Syd.

"Put your mask back on," said Dar. "You're getting hypoxic, I think." But he added, "And hang on . . . but not to the stick. Keep your feet away from the pedals."

They were still in the lift zone, crabbing fairly dramatically as Dar kept the Twin Astir's nose to the breeze, and now he put the nose down to gain some airspeed. Without shouting another warning through his mask, he used the ailerons to put the sailplane through a snap roll, while simultaneously using the rudder and elevators to keep the Twin Astir's nose aimed at a point just above the horizon. The sailplane recovered perfectly, aimed exactly where it had been headed.

"Wow!" shouted Syd. "Again!"

Dar shook his head. But then, aware that he was showing off (*for a girl*, he thought), he banked right, dropped the nose below the horizon line to gain some airspeed, applied continuous up elevator while fine-tuning the aileron and rudder, and put the Twin Astir through a 360-degree barrel roll while flying a descending helix around their invisible horizontal axis. The sky and earth traded places, once, twice, three, four times.

Dar leveled off, checking his real altitude, glancing at control surfaces, and fiddling with the MacCready Speed Ring bezel around the variometer to estimate his best transit time to the next thermal.

"More!" shouted Syd.

Dar brought the nose up until the glider lost lift at its angle of attack and they stalled. The effect was roughly the same as stepping into an empty elevator shaft. The nose dropped and the Twin Astir plunged directly toward the earth, now some ten thousand feet below them. It was as if someone had cut the strings that held them aloft and the elegant sailplane had turned into so much dead metal and useless fabric, falling like an aluminum coffin dropped out of a cargo plane.

Syd screamed and Dar felt guilty for a minute until he recognized the scream as one of pure joy rather than terror. He loosened his mask and said, "You'll have to save us from this."

"How?"

"Push the stick forward."

"Forward?" cried Syd through her mask. "Not back?"

"Most assuredly not back," said Dar. "Forward. Gently at first."

Syd pushed the stick forward, the wing surfaces began finding lift, and slowly, under Dar's guidance, she pulled them out of the stall until the variometer told them that they were no longer losing altitude.

"This stupid stunt is called a wing-over," said Dar. He took the controls, told Syd to hang on, and then pulled the nose to an impossible steep-pitch attitude. Their speed dropped precipitously. Just before they reached true stall speed, Dar applied full rudder to the yaw, slewed the Twin Astir around 180 degrees, pointed the nose almost straight down to pick up airspeed, and finally brought the plane to its normal, sedate glide attitude.

"Again!" said Syd.

"No, I don't think so," said Dar. He removed his mask and shut off the regulator. "All this horsing around has got us down to eight thousand feet. You can take your mask off and shut off the O-two."

Syd did, but said, "Let's loop."

"You wouldn't like a loop," said Dar,

knowing perfectly well that she would love it.

"Please."

Before Dar could respond, a white Bell Ranger helicopter roared up to within fifty feet of them on their starboard side and leveled off at their same altitude.

"Idiot!" Dar began, and then silenced himself as he saw that the rear doors were missing and that a man in a dark suit was crouching in the opening. Then a muzzle flashed, and bullets struck the sailplane just behind the cockpit.

Dar had listened to countless cockpit voice recorders—the fifteen-minute loop tape in the orange so-called "black box"—and in the vast majority of fatal air crashes, the pilot's or co-pilot's final words were "Shit!" or some other choice epithet. Dar knew from the tone that the obscenities were not outcries against imminent death, but a professional's final exclamation of outrage and frustration at his or her own stupidity—at getting into the problem or not being able to solve it. At killing everyone aboard.

"Shit," Dar said as he put the nose down and rolled the glider hard left, losing altitude as he rolled. He leveled off several hundred feet below the chopper, but the helicopter flew ahead and buzzed around a full 180 degrees, roaring back within fifty feet of the Twin Astir, the man in the back firing as the aircraft passed. Dar had hit the air brakes and now the Twin Astir stalled—simply dropped—and the bullets passed just over the cockpit.

Syd had managed to extricate her 9mm Sig-Sauer from the straps and harnesses and was trying to get it in the tiny sliding portal that worked as a wind vent. "Goddammit!" she said as the helicopter zoomed past them and whirled around to attack from the rear. "That guy in the back has an AK-47!" she shouted.

Syd slid the right vent panel open. "I can't aim from these stupid little vents without unstrapping!"

"Don't unstrap!" said Dar. He was desperately trying to think, to find an advantage. *What advantage does a high-performance sailplane have over a two-hundred-mile-per-*

hour helicopter? The glider could perform a loop and no helicopter could...*Big damned deal*, thought Dar. The Twin Astir could do a nice slow-motion loop while the Bell Ranger flew circles around it, shooting it to bits.

Anything else?

Well, thought Dar, *we can fly one hell of a lot slower than they can.*

They can hover, dipshit.

The Bell Ranger was coming past on their left side again. Dar could see that there were only two occupants—the pilot on the right side in front, and the man in the suit with, yes, an AK-47 assault rifle, in the back with both doors removed. The man appeared to have some sort of safety strap attached and he slid easily along the rear bench from one open door of the chopper to the other.

Dar waited until the last possible second, dived for speed, and looped the Twin Astir as they entered the turbulence of the foehn gap rotor of vertical air.

Too late, thought Dar as he heard at least another two hits somewhere behind him.

As they went up and over the loop, Syd holding her semi-automatic in both hands, Dar wondered how badly they were hit. None of the bullets had penetrated the cockpit yet. The sailplane had no engine to destroy, no fuel tank to ignite, no hydraulic links to cut, but its very simplicity meant that any hit on a control cable would disable them. A bullet in the ailerons could cause Dar to lose all control. Even the slugs that seemed to have passed harmlessly through the fuselage behind him were already spoiling the airflow over the glider's smooth surface, hindering control.

Dar rolled during the loop, seeing the Bell Ranger hovering a hundred meters to the west, waiting for them to resume level flight. Instead of pulling out of the loop, Dar kept the nose down and dived for the earth.

Mistake, he thought, watching the altimeter unwind with startling speed. His instinct had been to get the sailplane down into those canyons and gulleys, using the ridges for lift, trying to put something—a hill, a mountain, trees—between them and the shooter. But as soon as he saw the altitude drop below a thousand feet, he knew that he had made an error—possibly a fatal one.

This was no regular aircraft chasing them. The damned thing could turn on its own axis while flying straight ahead, bank as steeply as the Twin Astir, and hover when the glider would reach stalling speeds.

But Dar had committed himself. He glanced over his shoulder.

The Bell Ranger was hovering above and behind, a bird of prey waiting for its victim to end its contortions before pouncing.

Dar was just beginning his contortions. He came low across a wide valley, looking for a place to set the Twin Astir down, sure that they would have a better chance on foot than in the air. No meadows. No open mountainsides. All trees and boulders and ridgeline.

The helicopter nosed forward in a screaming dive behind them, rotors glinting.

"Can we open this canopy?" shouted Syd. "I need to get a shot."

"No," said Dar. He flew the glider directly at a rock wall, found the heated ridge-lift thermal less than fifty feet from the rock, and banked hard left, climbing on the thermal.

The helicopter easily made the turn, matched climb rates, and flew with them just beyond rotor distance. Dar could see the man in the back grinning as he raised the AK-47.

"Tony Constanza!" said Syd. She had loosened her harness enough to lean forward and get the muzzle of her Sig-Sauer out the open ventilation panel.

Constanza fired on full automatic even as Dar put the nose down, aiming for the ridgeline.

A bullet struck the nose of the Twin Astir. Another smashed the canopy, passed through between Dar's and Syd's heads, and exited through the Plexiglas on the right.

"Are you all right?" shouted Dar.

Before Syd could answer, Dar drove the nose of the sailplane inches above the Douglas firs, knocking needles off the treetops, and then banked hard right down the narrow valley.

The Bell Ranger gained altitude, clearing the ridgeline by yards instead of inches, and then roared above and past them headed south, Constanza's assault rifle firing on full automatic.

Dar flew lower than the trees, following a small river running down the center of the narrow gully. Ahead of them, the helicopter slewed, swerved, and stopped directly in their path, hovering with its open door facing them and the AK-47 muzzle already flashing.

Dar banked hard left and felt two impacts on the right wing. Then he was through the gap in the east ridge he had noted from above. There was lift here, but he could not afford the airspeed to utilize it fully as he kept the nose down and flew down this even narrower gully, the Twin Astir's wingtips less than two meters from rock walls on either side.

The Bell Ranger roared in behind them.

"I need to get a shot," cried Syd again, swiveling wildly in her seat. Her harness had been loose enough that she had been thrown back and forth during the hard banks and choppy recovery.

"No," said Dar. "We're already beginning to handle poorly. If we open the canopy, our aerodynamics aren't worth shit."

The helicopter roared overhead at four times the glider's speed. Constanza was leaning out, spraying slugs in their direction, but he had a bad angle.

The sailplane came into a wider valley just at the edge of the major uplift, almost back to the stacks of lenticular clouds, and Dar banked up and left. The glider lurched from the thermals flowing up and off the rock and they were over the ridge, soaring a thousand feet above a wider, descending valley.

"This isn't going to work down here," Dar said to Syd. "We need altitude."

"We *had* altitude," said Syd, still holding the 9mm pistol in both hands. "Then you came down here."

"I know," said Dar. "I fucked up."

Dar worked the glider into the powerful

vertical currents closer to the ridge just as the Bell Ranger made another sweep. Constanza was leaning out against his safety strap, blazing away, ejected brass glinting in the sunlight. Slugs struck the Twin Astir's tail and Dar felt control go sluggish. Another bullet shattered the canopy just behind Dar's head. He pitched the nose up steeply—trading speed for altitude as he entered the turbulent borders of the lift column—and another bullet ripped through his seat cushion.

Or was it through my parachute? Dar wondered, knowing then what he was going to do.

"Are you all right?" he called again to Syd as they spiraled up, the altimeter and variometer spinning clockwise as they gained altitude rapidly in the lift rotor. The sailplane's ground speed dropped to almost nothing as they headed back west into the strength of the wind, climbing like a panicked sparrow while the helicopter roared up and around them in a carefully choreographed helix.

Dar's eyes were on the instruments. He

needed at least five thousand feet above ground level for his plan—if he could call it a plan—to have any chance of working. It was obvious that the chopper was not going to give them that kind of time. The Bell Ranger crabbed closer, the shooter leaning out the left side this time, both aircraft climbing in a slow left spiral.

Syd loosened her harness further, leaned forward so she could get an angle through the narrow air vent, and fired five times at the helicopter.

Dar saw sparks fly on the forward fuselage and then watched as Tony Constanza ducked back into the shadows of the backseat. Dar could see the heavyset gunman shouting at the pilot.

The Bell Ranger banked right and roared above them in a counterclockwise spiral; they knew that Dar would have to level off at some point. Then they could come in from the rear or from above—at some angle where Syd could not fire without shooting through the Twin Astir's own canopy.

"Tighten your straps!" Dar shouted,

then explained to her what they were going to do.

Syd's head swiveled around. Her mouth hung open. "You're shitting me."

Dar shook his head. "Hang on."

The sailplane swept right into the outer edge of the foehn gap rotor thermal. The winds were stronger and the heat of midday had added to the powerful thermal updraft, but Dar could not be sure whether the increased turbulence they encountered was from the lift or from damage to the fuselage and control surfaces of his aircraft. It did not matter. Steve's beautiful high-performance two-seater only had to hold together for another few minutes.

The Bell Ranger moved in to shooting range, sliding sideways as if it were on rails.

Dar dived to pick up speed and then looped the sailplane. As they passed the helicopter, bullets rained onto the aft part of the fuselage like pellets of hail. Dar felt the right rudder go slack, but he still had some control.

The helicopter stayed where it was: the pilot knew that Dar would have to complete the loop.

He did so, climbing into another, broader inside loop. Syd fired twice from the front seat. Slugs from the AK-47 slammed into Dar's instrument console, shattering the instruments, punched four holes in the top of the canopy inches above their heads, and struck the nose hard enough to slew the glider to the left as he tried to climb into his second loop.

The Bell Ranger held its place, waiting for Dar to pass by again.

Just before the top of their loop, perhaps five hundred feet above the helicopter, Dar rolled the sluggish Twin Astir until they were performing an outside loop. He felt the negative g's trying to force him up and out of the aircraft—the pressure of the restraint harness on his shoulders was painful—and he heard Syd gasp. Dar's vision dimmed and then turned red for an instant before he forced the balking sailplane into level flight and then raised the nose again.

There was no more lift. The Twin Astir stalled and fell out of the sky.

Dar put the nose down enough to keep some control. The helicopter pilot must have been watching their insane aerobatics, for he pitched the nose of the Bell Ranger down and accelerated up the valley.

Too late. Dar's airspeed was approaching the sailplane's terminal velocity. For a precious few seconds, he could match the chopper's airspeed. He did so, attacking the right rear flank of the white-blue-and-red chopper as if the shaking, bucking Twin Astir were a P-51 coming in for the kill. Of course, Syd could not fire forward because of the canopy, and if she waited until they were close to the chopper and alongside it, Constanza's semiautomatic assault rifle would cut them to pieces. Neither aircraft offered a stable gun platform, but at least Dallas Trace's ex-mafia hit man had the advantage of being able to spray bullets all over the sky.

Dar was not going to give him that chance again.

What do we have that they don't? he thought

again for the twentieth time. And for the twentieth time he came up with the same answer. *Parachutes*. Of course, his parachute might have been cut to shreds by the bullet that had passed under him. He would find out.

What glider pilots fear more than anything else is a midair collision. Now he had to cause one.

Dar, Syd, and their fragile, wounded Twin Astir swooped from above—the sparrow attacking the hawk. If he continued on this glide path, he would overtake the chopper for an instant just as they flew into the fifty-foot buzz saw of the rotor blades. That would be fatal for everyone. At the last second, Dar dropped the nose of the Twin Astir, opened his speed brakes, matched velocities as best he could, and banked left.

The glider's left wing banged against the protected rotor assembly. Part of the wing cracked and bent.

Dar kicked hard right, fighting the stick and rudders. He had perhaps three more seconds of control.

The sailplane slewed left again. This time the torn wing threaded the rotor assembly like a plank of wood going into the hungry maw of a circular saw. The rotor blade made contact with the wing, sliced through it, chewed up chunks of the wing, and then began to tear itself and its jammed rotor assembly apart.

Responding to Newtonian imperatives, the glider was spun violently counterclockwise and tumbled into a flat spin. Dar knew that no pilot in the world could recover from such a flat spin. The sailplane, a work of aerodynamic perfection a few minutes earlier, was now just tangled junk falling straight out of the sky. Dar lost sight of the helicopter and tried to focus on the instruments, but between the bullets that had passed through the console and the rate of deadly spin, he saw nothing intelligible. The horizon, mountains, ridges, desert, were spinning by at unbelievable speed, but because Dar and Syd were still in the center of the swirling mass, there was very little sense of centrifugal force. Dar had no idea whether they were three thousand feet high or thirty feet above the impact point. There was no noise except for ice-cracking sounds as the left wing continued to break up.

Syd was wrestling with the canopy lock, but it seemed to be jammed. Dar slammed his five-point-harness buckle free, shook off the straps, and stood in the wildly spinning plane. He knew that they just had seconds in which to act because already the spin was turning into a tumble in the direction of the shattered wing. He leaned over Syd's left shoulder and threw his weight against the second canopy latch. The broken Plexiglas flew open and suddenly the wind was cool and rushing against Dar's face and upper body, trying to pluck him up and out of the little cockpit. He held on to the low instrument console in front of him while he leaned forward to help Syd get free of her harness.

"No, not those straps!" he shouted over the wind as she continued, wildly, to unbuckle and uncinch. "That's your parachute."

She stopped and stood. He saw that she

had taken time to shove the pistol back in her belt holster and to secure the strap over it.

He grabbed her right hand where it clutched the edge of the cockpit. "Jump when I count to two," he shouted. "Push hard against the fuselage…We *have* to get clear! One…two!"

They hurtled into space. For a second Dar saw Syd's arms go out like wings and his blood ran cold as he wondered if she would forget to pull the rip cord. But she was just diving away from the wreckage— the Twin Astir had now started tumbling about its axis and had turned into a huge eggbeater thirty feet behind them—and several seconds later he saw her sport chute blossom. He pulled his rip cord a second later.

Only after the spine-jarring shaking of the canopy opening did Dar look up. He saw no holes in the fabric, no torn risers. His hands went to the riser controls and he spun the chute around just as he heard the noise of the Bell Ranger's descent toward them. If the pilot had kept control of the helicopter, Dar knew he and Syd were dead.

But the helicopter was not under power or control—at least not under much control. The vertical tail rotor blade was essentially gone, and what was left of it was chewing up the rotor assembly in great gulps. The pilot had cut the engine—which appeared to be smoking, perhaps from one of Syd's wild shots, more likely from chunks of shrapnel thrown forward from the runaway tail rotor—and was trying to autorotate down to safety, allowing the freewheeling main rotors to give them enough lift to survive a crash landing.

The helicopter was headed straight for Syd and him.

It took only an instant for Dar to realize that this was not another murder attempt. He was sure that the pilot did not want a second collision—especially with bodies and parachute fabric fouling up his rotors—but there was very little the pilot could do but ride the autorotating helicopter down in its mad death spiral toward the ground.

There was a noise above and behind him and Dar twisted in his harness to look. He realized then that whether he was destined to live another thirty seconds or another fifty years, he would never forget the image he saw then.

Syd had taken her hands off the riser controls and had the 9mm semiautomatic held firmly in both hands. Her legs were apart in the proper shooting stance—just a thousand feet too high—and she was emptying the Sig's entire second clip into the Plexiglas windshield of the Bell Ranger.

The helicopter missed Dar, but not by so much that he did not literally pull his legs up to avoid the rush of the rotors. Then the heavy machine continued to spiral down faster and faster.

Syd's pistol had locked open. Dar watched her drop the empty magazine, pull the last one from her belt, and slap it into place, even as her orange-and-white parachute swirled her around in spirals above him. She was just a bit too far away for shouting, so all that Dar could do was point toward the risers, pull on the right one to spill enough air to send him dipping and spiraling in that direction, and then point to an open meadow area.

Syd nodded, holstered the weapon, and began tugging her riser D-rings, attempting to follow Dar into the clearing. Then both of them quit struggling and watched the Bell Ranger's last seconds four hundred feet below them.

The pilot was good, but not quite good enough. A helicopter in autorotation is essentially so much dead weight controlled by a mostly dead stick, but the pilot managed to time the death spiral so he missed the trees and came around into a clearing and lined up, more or less, with the thirty-degree slope. If Dar had been piloting a sailplane, he would have followed the rules for off-field glider landings and attempted to land going uphill, both to reduce his roll-out and to use the last bit of lift the hillside offered. But the hillside offered nothing to the massive Bell Ranger, and the pilot had no choice but to land headed downhill, at a good clip, and let the skids slide along the ground like the runners on a bobsled.

Even from several hundred feet up, the meadow looked smooth enough. Dar was wise to the lie of that appearance: there would be large rocks and small boulders, gullies and rock-dense shrubs, and probably larger obstacles. Whatever the Bell Ranger hit, it hit hard, the front of the skids digging in and the helicopter going nose over in an instant, the free-wheeling rotors slamming into the earth one second later and sending a cloud of dust a hundred feet into the air.

Through that dust Dar could make out the Bell Ranger tumbling end over end, the tail boom ripping free, the cockpit bubble smashing inward. The sound was audible and terrible even from two hundred feet above it all. Then the mass of twisted fuselage came to a stop against two larger boulders about a hundred yards downhill. There was a lesser noise to the south and Dar twisted just in time to see the folded mass of the Twin Astir disappear into the tall pine trees several hundred yards away.

Dar concentrated on trying to land gently, showing Syd how to do it by example. It was not much of an example. He ended up hitting a thick willow crotch first and catapulting head over heels into the weeds, coming to rest on his back with the chute dragging him across the slope. Syd landed gently fifty feet uphill…on her feet. She took two hops and stood there, apparently dazed but certainly in one piece.

Dar struggled out of his harness and jumped to his feet to help her out of her gear before the wind came up and started dragging her back up the slope. Suddenly everything began to spin again. He decided to sit down for a second until the movement stopped, and he had no sooner flopped on his butt than Syd was there— free of her harness and helping him disentangle his feet from the chute fabric billowing all around him.

"Come on," she said, and the two of them started moving down the hill toward the debris field of the Bell Ranger.

Syd paused to look at the tail boom

and mangled rotor—pieces of their sailplane's wing still entangled—but Dar
stupidly jogged the last hundred feet. He
could smell the raw stink of aviation fuel
in the breeze and knew that if anything
ignited the passenger cabin, anyone surviving the crash would have done so in
vain.

The cockpit was completely smashed in.
The pilot was dead—still in his harness
and seat—eviscerated and almost decap-
itated by the twisted Plexiglas and metal
floor. Dar could not see in the back. Fuel
was running freely from the wreck. He
pulled himself up the skids of the toppled
machine and stood on the main cabin,
looking down into the backseat. Constanza
was not there.

"Dar!" Syd shouted from seventy-five
feet uphill, and then froze.

Tony Constanza had just staggered from
behind the larger of the two boulders. He
was battered and bloody, his suit jacket
and shirt almost torn off, but he was pointing the AK-47 assault rifle at Dar.

"Freeze!" shouted Syd, going into a

crouching stance and aiming the little Sig-Sauer.

Constanza gave her a fleeting glance. He was not eight feet from Dar and the Kalashnikov automatic weapon was aimed at Dar's chest.

I can jump him, Dar thought muddily. *No, you can't, asshole*, was the more clear mental reply.

"You going to shoot me with that little thing from way back there, bitch?" shouted Constanza. "Not before I cut this motherfucker in two. Drop your gun, cunt."

Hearing that word almost made Dar leap. The AK-47 kept him standing in place.

Syd lowered her weapon.

"No!" shouted Dar.

"I said *drop it*, bitch," screamed Constanza, raising the assault rifle's muzzle toward Dar's face.

Syd brought the Sig-Sauer back up and fired three times, the shots so close together that they sounded like one continuous hammering to Dar. The first bullet blew Tony Constanza's left knee into a flap of red meat and white gristle; the second struck him high in the left leg; the third hit him in the left buttock and swung him around.

The AK-47 emptied half its banana clip into the dirt.

Dar jumped down and kicked the weapon away. Syd bounded down the hill in great strides, keeping her pistol trained on the screaming, rolling man the whole way.

"Help me, Jesus fuck," said Constanza as she slid to a stop next to him. "You shot my balls off, you bitch."

"Not likely," said Syd. She kicked him over on his belly, held the pistol to the back of his head as she expertly patted him down, and then pulled his wrists behind him and cuffed him.

"Syd," said Dar softly, "didn't they train you at Quantico to shoot for center body mass at that pistol distance?"

"Of course they did," said the chief investigator. "But we need this guy alive." She holstered her weapon. "Is this the only way you know how to deal with felons?" she said. "By crashing into them?"

Dar shrugged. "It's what I know best." He knelt next to the whining man. "He's going to bleed to death from that thigh wound," said Dar, "if we don't do something."

"Yes," agreed Syd, with no emotion visible on her face.

Dar held Constanza still while Syd removed the man's belt and lashed it tight high on his upper thigh, using it as a tourniquet. He screamed when Syd put full pressure on the belt, and then he fainted.

Dar sat heavily on the dry grass. "He's still going to bleed to death before anyone finds us. It'll be hours before Steve or Ken gets worried."

Syd shook her head. "Sometimes, Darwin, my dear, you are such a Luddite." She took her cell phone out of her vest pocket and punched a speed-dial number. "Warren," she said. "Jim…Syd Olson here. Yeah. Well, we've got Tony Constanza with us, but he's hurt pretty bad. If he's going to be our star witness, you'd better get a medevac helicopter to…" She lowered the phone. "Where the hell are we, Dar?"

"East face of Mount Palomar," said Dar. "About the four-thousand-foot level. The helicopter has a box of colored flares in the back...Tell Warren that we'll pop smoke when we hear the dust-off chopper."

"Did you get all that, Jim?" said Syd. "OK. Yeah...we'll sit tight." She looked at Dar. "They're sending a Marine medical chopper from Twenty-nine Palms."

"Tell him that this area is thick with rattlesnakes," said Dar.

"We'll sit tight," repeated Syd, "but Dar says that this hill is rife with rattlesnakes, so please tell the Marines to move their asses if you want your witness and his captors alive." She rang off.

They looked at each other, at the unconscious gunman, and then at each other again. They were both wet with sweat, blue with bruises, red from blood flowing from small cuts and gashes, and sticky with dust. Suddenly they grinned at each other.

"God, you're beautiful," said Syd.

"I was just going to say that to you," said Dar.

Then they were holding each other and kissing so passionately that a stray boot almost woke up the moaning but still unconscious hit man.

Almost but not quite.

22

"V IS FOR VINCIBLE"

Dar was invited to be in on the arrests, but he declined. He had work to do. He heard the details later.

In England, Syd explained later, the police prefer to wait for a suspect to enter his or her home before making an arrest. There is less chance of violence and of innocent by-standers being hurt that way. In America, of course, exactly the opposite is true. A home, all too frequently in America, is an arsenal and fortress. American cops prefer to make arrests in semipublic but controlled places, where the suspect can be—at the very least—outgunned. The exception in this case was to be the ranch house where the five Russians—including Zuker and Yaponchik—were known to be hiding out and where the FBI wanted to hit them with surprise and overwhelming force.

The FBI claimed precedence and jurisdiction on the Thursday morning raids, and because of the death of three of their agents, no one argued. Los Angeles–based Special Agent in Charge Howard Faber personally led the tactical team of eighteen helmeted, Kevlar-vested, submachine-gun-toting special agents into the Century City tower at 6:48 A.M. Pacific time. SAC James Warren would have liked to have been there, but he had taken charge of the stakeout and raid on the Russian mafia men's isolated ranch house near the Santa Anita Racetrack. Chief Investigator Sydney Olson, also decked out in a Kevlar vest labeled "FBI" in bright yellow, was second in command to SAC Faber on the Trace assault. Like the others, she carried a Heckler & Koch MP-10 submachine gun.

Dallas Trace was on the air live, his CNN *Objection Sustained* program airing at its usual 10:00 A.M. Eastern time. Special Agent in Charge Faber and each of his tactical team leaders carried a tiny TV monitor and they watched as the show's titles rolled, the intro music ended, and the New York anchor—another ex–defense lawyer—announced the day's topic and welcomed her friend and colleague from California, famous defense counselor Dallas Trace. The silver-haired attorney was at his usual post at his desk, slouched back in his leather chair, wearing his usual buffalo-hide leather vest, the windows behind him showing a smoggy early L.A. morning.

Ten of the FBI tactical team agents swept through the offices, herding early-bird legal secretaries, young lawyers, secretaries, and receptionists out of their rooms and cubicles, corralling them in the outer reception room where two agents in black Kevlar stood guard. Having secured the hallways and offices, two of the agents then kicked open the door to the conference room that served as the "greenroom" during the television broadcasts. Three of Counselor Trace's four American body-guards were sitting in there, watching the monitor, drinking coffee, and wolfing down donuts. They looked at the tactical team in openmouthed surprise and then they were down on the floor, hands behind their heads, being brusquely frisked by the FBI team members. Each of the bodyguards was carrying at least one firearm, and the biggest and meanest of the bunch was carrying a second pistol in his back belt and a tiny revolver in an ankle holster. Two of the three also carried long-bladed folding knives that were illegal for street use.

Watching their portable monitor, sure that none of the disturbance had been heard in Trace's office, Faber, three of his agents with H&K MP-10s, and Syd waited just outside the lawyer's office.

Dallas Trace was just drawling, "...an' if ah had been the defense attorney for these poor, prosecuted, persecuted, and harried parents—who are obviously innocent of theah daughtah's tragic death—I would be bringing lawsuits against the city of—" when the FBI kicked in the door and the four agents and Syd came in with guns drawn.

The two cameramen and the single sound man looked to their floor producer for guidance. The producer hesitated two microseconds and then she gave the finger-spinning gesture for "keep rolling." Dallas Trace merely looked up at the intruders with his mouth wide open.

"Counselor Dallas Trace, you are under arrest for conspiracy to commit murder and conspiracy to defraud," said Special Agent in Charge Faber. "Stand up."

Trace continued sitting. He tried to speak, obviously finding it difficult to switch gears from the mythical lawsuit he was about to announce for the poor, per-secuted, and prosecuted parents of the murdered child, but before he could make a sound, two of the FBI men in black grabbed the attorney's arms and dragged him to his feet. His arms were pinned behind him, and Syd snapped on the cuffs.

After what probably had been the long-est period of speechlessness in Dallas Trace's adult life, he found his voice—in fact, he roared. "What the *hell* do you think you're doing? Do you have *any* goddamn idea who I am?"

"Defense Attorney Dallas Trace," Special Agent in Charge Faber said again. "And you are under arrest. You have the right to remain silent—"

"Silent my *ass!*" screamed Dallas Trace, his western drawl magically replaced by a nasal New Jersey accent. "Tell that sowbitch to get those cuffs off me."

Later polling showed that it was this comment, aired live on a popular CNN program, that most alienated potential female jurors.

"Anything you say can and will be held against you in a court of law," continued SAC Faber as the two men in black Kevlar stripped the lawyer of his lavalier microphone, belt-pack, and wiring, and then guided Trace out from behind his desk. "You have the right to an attorney—"

"I *am* an attorney, you dipshit!" shouted Dallas Trace, spittle flying. "I am *the* foremost defense attorney in the United States of—"

"If you cannot afford an attorney, one will be provided for you," continued Faber, calmly, as the five of them—three agents, Trace, and Syd—shoved past the goggling floor producer. Both cameramen were grinning broadly as they panned the lenses around to the door where the other tactical-team agents waited with their weapons at parade rest.

Dallas Trace looked back over his shoulder at the cameras. "Greta!" he cried, calling to his New York CNN cohost. "You *saw* this. You *saw* what they did to me..."

And then Trace was gone.

The line producer lunged for the still live lavalier mike and thrust it in Syd's face.

"Why this outrageous arrest in the middle of—" began the producer, before Syd interrupted with, "No comment." She and the two agents walked out the door.

On that same Thursday morning, six FBI men and five Sherman Oaks plainclothes officers raided Dallas Trace's home. There was no resistance. The bodyguard who had been left behind to guard Mrs. Trace happened to be in bed with her at the time the black-garbed FBI tactical team kicked open the bedroom door.

The bodyguard disentangled himself from Destiny Trace's enveloping and unyielding legs, rolled over, looked at his shoulder holster and pistol on the chair twenty feet away, looked into four suppressed H&K muzzles with laser sights dancing small red dots across his forehead, and held up his hands.

Mrs. Trace sat up in bed, apparently resisting any impulse to cover her bare breasts. One of the FBI men's attention must have strayed for an instant, because a laser dot flickered across Mrs. Trace's bouncing breasts, before returning to the bodyguard's forehead.

Destiny Trace frowned, pursed her lips, and looked at the hulking man in bed with her, looked at the crowding FBI agents in their storm-trooper helmets, goggles, and flak jackets, looked at the Sherman Oaks detectives in their Kevlar vests, frowned again and suddenly shouted, "Help! Rape!

Thank God you're here, Officers... This man was assaulting me!"

The Monday before the Thursday raids, Lawrence spent most of the day helping Dar set up the new surveillance cameras.

"This is costing you a shitload—with overnight delivery and everything," volunteered Lawrence as they carried the first video unit, its battery, cables, and waterproof camouflage tarp from the Trooper into the trees along the road to the cabin. "If you'd given me a couple of weeks, I could have saved you about a thousand bucks on this stuff."

"I won't need it in a couple of weeks," said Dar.

They positioned the first camera in a tree along the side of the gravel driveway about one half kilometer from the cabin. It was a sophisticated video unit—not much larger than a paperback book—with zoom lenses and a remote controlled motor that allowed it to pan and swivel. Thin cables ran to its own triple-lithium battery pack and the tiny transmitter, which were both easily concealed in the base of the rotted-out birch. The remote controlled camera had two lenses: one for daylight use and the other for electronic light amplification after dark. It and the other gear had indeed cost Dar a metaphorical shitload.

When the camera was properly situated, Dar drove up to the cabin and sat in his Land Cruiser while he used the remote unit to swivel, pan, zoom, and switch lenses. He practiced turning the unit on and off. He checked the reception on his portable receiving and control unit with its three-inch black-and-white monitor. Then he called Lawrence on his cell phone.

"Works fine, Larry."

"Lawrence."

"Come on up to the cabin and I'll fix us some coffee before we mount the other cameras. Also, I'll show you something I found in the woods."

After coffee, Dar left the boxed video equipment in the cabin and took Lawrence for a stroll. They headed east toward the sheep wagon but then cut uphill from the trail, through boulders, toward the high ridge above the cabin. From there they bushwhacked downhill until they came to a Douglas fir about thirty meters above the cabin itself. Dar silently pointed to a bulky video camera set in a camouflaged nook in the tree. The camera's lens was aimed at the cabin.

Lawrence said nothing, but inspected the thing as carefully as a munitions expert would inspect a land mine. Finally Lawrence said, "No microphone. No pan or scan or zoom or night-vision capability. It's just a fixed lens—wide angle—but it gives a good view of your parking area and cabin entrance. Plus, it has one hell of a strong battery, an extra-long-play recorder, almost certainly a time-stamp feature, and the whip antenna is way the hell up there. Whoever's monitoring you can call up several days' worth of video and fast-forward through it to see who's in the cabin and when they arrived."

"Yeah," said Dar.

"With that powerful a transmitter and the antenna way up there, it could be broadcast for several miles," said Lawrence.

"Yeah," agreed Dar.

Lawrence crawled up the sap-covered lower trunk and inspected the instrument again. "It's not FBI technology, Dar. Foreign...Czech, I think...crude but tough. My guess is that it's transmitting on a PAL format."

"That's what I thought," said Dar.

"The Russians?" said Lawrence.

"Almost certainly," said Dar.

"Want me to disable it?"

"I want them to know where I am," said Dar. "I just wanted to show this to you so that we don't reveal anything about our work while we're in front of this lens."

"Are there others?" asked Lawrence, squinting suspiciously into the dappled daylight of the forest.

"None that I've found."

"I'll take a look for you," said Lawrence.

"I'd appreciate that, Larry." Dar had great respect for his electronic surveillance expertise.

"Lawrence," said Lawrence, sliding back down the tree like a noisy bear.

Tony Constanza had sung like a canary after coming out of sedation for surgery on the previous Saturday afternoon. Even though his hospital room was guarded by half a dozen FBI agents, he was obviously terrified that the *Organizatsiya* hit men would come after him as soon as they learned that he was alive. Constanza must have figured that his best chance was to squeal and to squeal quickly, before Yaponchik, Zuker, and the others discovered where he was being guarded. He obviously had a healthy respect for their lethal capabilities. He also had some enthusiasm for being in the Witness Protection Program and living—he was quite specific about this—in Bozeman, Montana.

Constanza said that he didn't know exactly where the Russians were holed up, but that it was "like a ranch house, you know, all by itself, somewhere out beyond Santa Anita Racetrack somewhere past

Sierra Madre Boulevard...up in the brown hills there with all that tumbleweed shit." The FBI had already received such an address from an anonymous mailing—it was the address of one of the phone numbers that Dar had seen Dallas Trace dial during his overnight surveillance of Trace's house. Now the FBI's own surveillance pinpointed the house and confirmed the presence of the five Russians.

SAC James Warren assigned twenty-three FBI agents to carry out constant surveillance on the location—a Mediterranean-style ranch house set half a mile from its nearest neighbor—from that Saturday evening. He told Sydney Olson that he would have preferred to move in immediately, but that it would take several days to obtain search and arrest warrants for the others now being incriminated by Constanza, and any premature arrest of the Russians would have tipped everyone else. In the meantime, every move the Russians made was being followed carefully by FBI agents in vans, via undercover roles as phone-company and street-repair people, by video surveillance, and by helicopter. The phone line into the house was not only tapped, it was trapped. Warren had twenty more agents with tactical assault training available at a minute's notice. Pasadena, Glendale, Burbank, and LAPD SWAT teams were volunteering to help, even though they knew no details of the operation.

The first arrests took place Sunday morning when LAPD Detectives Fairchild and Ventura were called into separate offices by Internal Affairs Divisions, told to surrender their shields, weapons, clips, and IDs, and told that they were to be formally charged with accessory to fraud and conspiracy to murder the four FBI agents. Ventura was informed that IAD and the FBI knew about the secret transfer of funds to his newly established offshore accounts—installments of $85,000, $15,000, and $23,000. No bank transfers had been found in Detective Fairchild's name, but the officer was informed that the investigation was still ongoing. Both detectives were interrogated.

Detective Ventura hung tough, but Detective Fairchild folded. He not only admitted that Ventura had gotten him involved in the cover-up of the murder of Richard Kodiak, but said that it was Ventura who had traced Donald Borden's and Gennie Smiley's whereabouts in the Bay Area, and fingered them both to Trace's Russians for the professional double taps to the head. According to Detective Fairchild, Ventura had even bragged that "for another twenty thousand I would have dumped the fucking bodies myself, and done a better job of it than those assholes." Fairchild admitted in a signed deposition that Ventura had referred to Dallas Trace as "the goose who was going to lay them both a lot of golden eggs" and that further dealings with the fraud Alliance had been planned. Fairchild said that Ventura had threatened to murder *him* if he opened his mouth about the conspiracy.

Both police officers were taken into custody. Fairchild negotiated a deal with the district attorney for leniency in exchange for turning state's evidence. Neither the

FBI nor the LAPD made any announcement of the arrests—the men were being kept in an FBI safe house in Malibu for extensive interrogation—and anyone calling the precinct and asking for either detective was told that they were "working undercover and unavailable" while the phone calls were traced. Two of the calls came from Trace's American bodyguards, and one of them was traced to the Russians' Santa Anita house.

Syd expressed her concern about Dar's safety to him during the five days before the projected arrests of the main players, but Dar had answered easily—"What's to be afraid of? The FBI are all over the Russians, Trace's American thugs are being followed...I'm safer than ever before." Syd was too busy preparing for the raids to spend time at the cabin with Dar, but she did not seem reassured.

That Monday before the raids, Dar and Lawrence had also rigged fiber-optic cameras in the cabin. Dar chose two positions, both on the south interior wall, so that the two lenses would cover everything in the large, single-room cabin except the closets and the one bathroom.

Dar used his key to unlock the hidden trapdoor, led Lawrence down the steep stairs, and then unlocked the door to the storeroom.

"Holy shit," said Lawrence, "trapdoors, secret rooms... You a spy, Dar? A spook?"

"No," said Dar, embarrassed that he had kept this place a secret. "I just needed a safe place to store some stuff. You understand."

"Not really," said Lawrence. He looked around the room again. "My God, it looks like the last scene in that first Indiana Jones movie... that big warehouse full of crates. You got a sled named Rosebud in here somewhere?"

"No," said Dar quietly. "I had to burn that one winter when I ran out of firewood." He led his friend through the corridors between crates and showed him the padlocked air-vent grille. "If you ever need to get out of here, just unlock this and crawl, Larry. It's about two hundred feet to that old gold mine I told you about once. It eventually comes out in the steep gully east of here."

Lawrence shook his head. "I don't think it'd do me any good."

"There are extra keys upstairs," said Dar. "Keys for the trapdoor, the door to this room, and the grille padlocks... They're in a leather case under the ice tray in the fridge."

Lawrence shook his head again. "OK, but that's not what I meant. I just don't think I'd fit in that particular air shaft."

Dar looked at the vent, then looked at Lawrence, and nodded. "Well, if you were ever trapped down here when things were... unpleasant... upstairs, just bolt the steel door and stay here. The room's shielded and fireproof and the air is drawn in from the cave, so even if the cabin burns down above you, this place would be safe."

"Uh-huh," said Lawrence, obviously un-convinced. "Trudy and I are going to be at our condo in Palm Springs the rest of this week," he said. "Unless you need me here, I mean."

Dar shook his head. "No. And be careful in Palm Springs until we hear that Trace and the Russians and all the rest are behind bars."

Lawrence only grunted and patted the pistol in his shoulder holster.

They hooked the two fiber-optic cables and their transmitter to the cabin's power supply, and then to the auxiliary generator as backup. Then they ran antenna wire up through the wall and onto the roof of the cabin. After that, they hiked downhill from the cabin—keeping the cabin between them and the viewing field of the Czech video camera up the hill—and set up the second outdoor camera in the burned-out stump of a huge old Douglas fir just where the grassy, open hillside began. Then Lawrence returned to the cabin while Dar took the receiver/monitor—concealed in his tan rucksack—and hiked several hundred yards up the hill.

"Got a picture?" came Lawrence's voice over the cell phone.

"Yes," said Dar. He switched back and forth between cameras two and three. The wide-angle lenses each gave a bug-eyed view of the room, but every part of the cabin except the bathroom and the inside of the closets was clearly visible on the tiny monitor screen. These lenses had no pan or zoom controls, but were effective in very low light conditions.

"Now I know what you're up to," said Lawrence on the phone.

"You do?"

"Yeah," said the private investigator/adjuster. "You're planning a huge orgy up here and you want to get it all on tape."

Dar tried camera four. It panned up and down the slope, showing the entire approach to the south side of the cabin. With the wide-angle lens he could see miles across the valley to the south and zoom in on objects up to a hundred yards away.

On the same Thursday morning that saw the arrest of Dallas Trace, Attorney William Rogers—the East L.A. lawyer who had helped Father Martin create the Helpers of the Helpless—was pulled over to the side of the road on his way to work.

As the attorney stepped out of his vehicle, joking with the state patrol officers in their CHP car about not seeing the stop sign, FBI agents, sheriff's deputies, and LAPD officers converged on the site.

Rogers was handcuffed, read his rights, and loaded into one of the cars. Syd was told by the agent in charge that Rogers began weeping and demanding to call his wife, Maria. The agents did not tell the attorney that his wife had been arrested moments before at her office headquarters for the Helpers of the Helpless.

In hospitals all over Southern California, local police and FBI agents accompanied by INS officials began their sweep, interrogating and eventually arresting more than sixty Helpers from a group of more than a thousand detained. All hospitals and medical centers in California barred their doors to the Helpers that same day. In the files at Maria Rogers's Helpers of the Helpless Headquarters in East Los Angeles, the names of more than a hundred insurance-fraud cappers, doctors, attorneys, and facilitators were gathered.

* * *

Dar sited the fifth video camera on his property on Tuesday. For several hours he hiked the hundreds of acres of property he knew so well. Finally he decided on the best sniper nest above the cabin—a small, level, grassy area shielded by low boulders on two sides and by huge boulders behind it. Lying there with his old M40 Sniper Rifle and Redfield scope, Dar found that the range—a little under two hundred yards—was almost as perfect as the view. There were clear shots between the scattered trees of the cabin, the entrance to the cabin, and the parking area west of the cabin. The roost was protected by the overhang of rock ledges behind it and by steep slopes on either side. It was perfect; too perfect.

Dar went looking for a less obvious site. He found it less than seventy yards to the northwest of the first one. This second site was also tucked against large boulders, but offered only a narrow gap between slabs of rocks, the shooting site overgrown with prickly bushes, in which a sniper and his spotter could both lie prone. The site was higher than the first and offered a slightly better view while being even harder to approach from any angle without exposure. The extra seventy yards or so of range would not be a problem for the kind of modernized *Dragunov* SVD sniper rifle used to kill Tom Santana and the three FBI agents.

It took Dar almost three hours to retreat from the site without leaving any footprints, hike all the way around the ridge to the steep rear approach to the boulders of the ridgeline, and free-climb the near-vertical rock wall more than a hundred feet to a point on the larger boulder above the second sniper's nest. There he had to secure a Perlon climbing rope around a boulder in order to rappel down the steep arc of the rock face to a shrub-filled ledge where he could set up the video camera, conceal it, its battery, and its transmitter with the waterproof camouflage tarp, and then hide the long broadcast antenna by running it up cracks in the rock face to the summit.

Dar then returned to the cabin and

tested the monitor. The picture was not as clear as the transmission from the other four cameras, but he could clearly see the second sniper's nest from above and zoom in on the original site he had found lower down.

Dar spent the rest of the morning hiking the rocky ridges and steep ravines to the northeast of the two sites he had found. He was not satisfied until nearly noon.

Syd explained that the FBI's primary concern was the Russians. They had shown their ruthlessness and their ability to kill at long range. Several FBI tactical team world-class snipers and assault experts were flown in from Quantico. At night, with no muss or fuss, eight of the surrounding houses in the Santa Anita hills above Sierra Madre Boulevard were evacuated and taken over as observation or command and control centers for Special Agent Warren's task force.

Every movement the Russians made was followed—tail cars and lead cars changing off, helicopters at 8,000 feet watching through powerful optics — and by the time the five Russians drove their two Mercedeses back to the ranch house on Wednesday evening, the tac-team had grown to sixty-two. By this time, FBI snipers in ghillie suits had laboriously crawled to within 150 yards of the house on all sides.

The FBI shooters were armed with the most modern equipment available — modified De Lisle Mark 5 sniper rifles firing 7.62 mm rounds in either standard or subsonic combinations. The rifles were descended from Dar's venerable Remington 700 bolt-action model, but had evolved about as far as space shuttle pilots had from the first African australopithecine hominids. The weapons utilized heavy match barrels with integral suppressors — "silencers" to the layman — which, when combined with subsonic ammunition, allowed for accuracy at ranges of more than two hundred yards. The rifles made no sound, not even the smack of a bullet breaking the sound barrier.

Mounted on each De Lisle Mark 5 was a

single, lightweight, integrated sight which combined a powerful telescopic sight with an image-intensifying night sight, an infrared range finder, and a thermal imager. The FBI snipers could kill at two hundred yards in the rain on a starless night through light fog or smoke.

The rest of the FBI assault teams were outfitted with Kevlar helmets, full body armor, gas masks, infrared goggles, fully suppressed submachine guns with laser sights, .45-caliber fully automatic pistols, and stun grenades known in the trade as "flash bangs." For the 5:00 A.M. assault on Thursday, the lead team would go in behind a barrage of tear gas projectiles fired through all the windows and use a man-carried hydraulic battering ram to take down the front door. Then the first three tac teams would enter the building by all available first-floor windows and doors. Waiting in the garage of the nearest house was a fully armored tactical assault vehicle with its own battering ram. Five helicopters were tasked to the assault, and each of them carried master marksmen. Two of the helicopters were equipped to drop men on lines for rapid assault from the air.

"Hardly seems like a fair fight," Syd Olson suggested to Special Agent in Charge Warren on Wednesday afternoon.

Warren had given her the slightest of smiles. "If it becomes anything near a fair fight," he said, "I deserve to be fired."

Syd had nodded and called Dar at his condo to see how he was doing.

Dar was doing fine by Wednesday afternoon. He had used the morning to catch up on work in his warehouse apartment— documenting the fatal Gomez swoop-and-squat and preparing a computer-animated reenactment of Attorney Esposito's death by scissors lift. He chatted with Syd a few minutes, telling her that he was going up to his cabin to get a good night's sleep while she and her colleagues did all the hard work the next day. He asked her to be careful, promised to see her on Thursday, and wished her luck.

Dar had spent all of the previous afternoon and evening zeroing his two weapons. Using the ravine to the east of the cabin—it was sixty feet wide where the gold mine opened into it, narrowing to less than twenty feet in width up the hill parallel to where Dar had found the potential sniper roosts—he fired off several hundred rounds of ammunition from both his old M40 bolt-action and the loaner Light Fifty.

Dar used a new purchase—a $3,295 pair of new Leica Geovid BDII range-finding binoculars—to double-check the range with the Leica's built-in laser range finder as he set out targets at distances of 100 yards, 300 yards, 650 yards, and 1,000 yards. Dar was capable of thinking in meters, but like most old-time snipers, he did range-finding calculations in yards. He was pleased that his visual estimates of target distance in each case fell within five feet of the laser's readout. The Leica's range finder itself was guaranteed to be accurate to within three feet at 1,100 yards.

Although Dar had fired the M40—the old modified Remington 700 hunting rifle—occasionally on shooting ranges in the past few years, he still had to reacquaint himself with the weapon. When he had been trained as a young Marine, it was discovered that Dar had 20/10 vision, which meant simply that what was perfectly clear for a person with 20/20 vision at one hundred yards was just as clear to Dar at two hundred yards. Even before Dar had decided for certain on becoming an outcast through advanced sniper training, he had qualified as an "expert rifleman" at Parris Island boot camp. In the time-honored tradition of the Corps, riflemen could qualify in three categories—marksman, sharpshooter, and—very, very rarely—expert rifleman. Dar had qualified as expert rifleman on Record Day with 317 points out of a possible 330, a distinction that was rare enough that his commanding officer had told him that only a dozen Marines had equaled it going back to World War II. The first 317 score had been made by a Marine who went on to be a famous writer and biographer.

The qualities that went into superb marksmanship included the control of breathing that was so important, extraordinary eyesight, patience, the ability to fire a weapon from several positions, and the ability to factor in distance, gravity, wind, and the weapon's unique quirks with every shot. Another important—and underrated—requirement was cleverness with adjusting the rifle's sling, a skill difficult to teach but which had come naturally to young Dar. Now, almost thirty years later, Dar knew that his eyesight had deteriorated to a mere 20/20 for distance shooting, but the comfort with the weapon, the ability to adjust the sling properly without thinking about it, the sense of proper range and ability to zero the weapon, the ability to fire easily and accurately from a prone, kneeling, sitting, and standing position—all these remained.

Dar took great care that Tuesday afternoon to zero the M40. His modified Redfield scope was fitted with mil-dot reticles as well as elevation and windage turrets. He adjusted the elevation turret according to the different ranges he was firing, and clicked the windage turret left to right to compensate for the lateral effects of wind on the bullet. The "zero" of the weapon was simply the setting required to put a shot exactly on target center at any given range with no wind blowing. Here the ravine came in handy because it blocked the prevailing winds from the west and allowed Dar to zero the weapon at all distances during lulls when there was no breeze whatsoever.

During advanced sniper training at Quantico and again in Vietnam, Dar had set his own accuracy requirements. Firing match-grade ammunition such as he was using now, Dar was not satisfied unless he could group his shots within a diameter of 20 millimeters at a range of one hundred yards, 125 millimeters at six hundred yards, and 300 millimeters—regularly—at one thousand yards. The final goal was not as generous as it sounded, Dar knew, because it took a bullet fired from his M40 approximately one second to travel six hundred yards, but a full two seconds to travel one thousand yards. Two seconds is an eternity in ballistics. Wind variations come into play over such a huge amount of time, and if the target is moving... forget it.

Dar spent five hours on Tuesday firing the M40 from all four positions—prone, sitting, kneeling, and standing. He would assume the position, feeling the sling snug tight and right, the stock tight against his cheek, a "spot weld" of contact between his cheek and his thumb on the small of the wooden stock, trigger finger positioned on the trigger with no contact with the side of the stock, his breathing so calm as to be imperceptible. And then he would close his eyes for several seconds. If, when he opened his eyes, the crosshairs in the scope were still precisely on his previous aiming point, he knew that he had obtained a so-called natural point of aim.

The hardest thing for Dar to recapture was trigger control. This had come natural to him in the Marines, but he knew from firing-range practice that he had to work to find it now. Trigger control was nothing more complicated than taking up the slack at precisely the correct point in his breathing cycle while he fine-tuned his aim, then squeezing the trigger the extra millimeter needed without moving the rifle in any way. It was not complicated, but it took mental focus, muscle control, and breathing control.

Having zeroed the M40, Dar took targets down into the open field below the cabin and fired scores of rounds in actual wind conditions. Tuesday was a windy day, and in a steady 15-mph wind, the 7.62 mm bullet would drift 4.5 inches off target at two hundred yards, a disturbing 20 inches off target zero at six hundred yards, and a ridiculous 48 inches off target at six hundred yards. Of course, the wind was almost never steady.

Dar knew that the new generation of snipers went into battle with pocket calculators or—in the more sophisticated weapon systems—minicomputers in the actual scope with electronic wind sensors attached.

Dar thought that this was a waste of human brainpower and basic senses. He had been well trained to gauge the wind. Less than 3 mph and one can hardly tell if the wind is blowing, but smoke drifts. Gusts of 5 to 8 mph will keep tree leaves in a constant motion, and Dar had long since learned the sound of different wind values in the ponderosa pines and Douglas firs that surrounded his cabin. Any wind between 8 and 12 mph kicks up dust and grit, blows loose leaves, and can be seen in swirls and dust devils. Between 12 and 15 mph the tiny birch trees in the field would be constantly swaying.

Dar had instinctively known, even as a young Marine sniper trainee, that the wind's speed is only a small part of the equation. The wind direction must also be properly sensed and factored in. Any wind blowing at right angles to his direction of fire—from eight-, nine-, ten-, and two-, three-, four-o'clock positions—was a full-value wind. Any oblique wind—one, five, seven, eleven o'clock—would be accorded only half value, so a 7-mph breeze from his nine-o'clock position would be rated as a 3.5-mph wind when he made his lateral adjustments to the scope. Finally, if the wind was blowing directly at his firing position or from the rear—six or twelve o'clock—Dar would factor in only minimal effect on the bullet: a slight drop in velocity firing into the wind; a corresponding rise in velocity with a tail wind. Being a sailplane pilot had honed his skill in sensing wind velocity and direction.

Once these factors of range and wind were taken into account—preferably in microseconds—then Dar just used the old Marine marksman formula of range, expressed in hundreds of yards, multiplied by wind velocity expressed in miles per hour, and divided by fifteen. Dar could perform this calculation instantly and instinctively even after all these years.

Lying and kneeling out in that long, grassy field all Tuesday afternoon, Dar kept the small video monitor tuned to camera one activated beside him—making sure that no one was driving up to the cabin while he was practicing. Sometimes wearing his ghillie suit, sometimes in his green slacks and field shirt, Dar fired at regular range targets and Paladin targets and concentrated on achieving m.o.a. and sub-m.o.a. groups. Even after he was achieving these groupings regularly—in slightly gusty conditions and at all of his preset ranges—Dar reminded himself of one crucial point.

These targets are only paper.

On Wednesday evening, just before dusk, all of the FBI men on the Russians' ranch-house perimeter came to full alert. By this time, eight tactical team snipers in ghillie suits had wormed their way to within 150 yards of the house and all three sides of the property bordering the street. Three of the snipers were in the tall grass less than five yards from the manicured lawn.

At 4:30 P.M. the only telephone call of the day came in. It was trapped and played back on the FBI tape recorders.

Voice: *Your dry cleaning is ready, Mr. Yale.*

Voice thought to be Gregor Yaponchik: *All right.*

The FBI traced the call within seconds—it had come from a Pasadena dry-cleaning establishment. Warren had an agent call the place and ask if Mr. Yale's dry cleaning was ready yet. The manager said that it was and confirmed that he had just called to inform Mr. Yale of that. The manager apologized for not being able to deliver the dry cleaning, but explained that the unincorporated area north of Pasadena was outside their normal delivery area. The agent calling assured the manager that this was all right.

At 8:10 P.M. a white van pulled up and three Hispanic men in gray shirts and work pants got out. The van had a yard-service ad on its side and Special Agent in Charge Warren had his people on the phone within ten seconds, checking with the company to see if this was a legitimate visit. It certainly did not seem kosher at this hour.

It was. The yard-service people assured the special agents that this was the weekly service and that it had been held up because of van problems and "complexities" at the previous customer's home. Syd later explained that Warren was tempted to tell the service company to call their people and to get them the hell out of there *now*, but the three yard men had already begun their work—mowing the yard, clipping the shrubs, and cutting up a small, dead tree—and the FBI man decided that it would draw less attention to let them finish. It was almost dark.

One of the workmen went to the front door, and agents in the house a quarter of a mile from the Russians' place got a clear photograph of Pavel Zuker talking brusquely to the quickly nodding yard worker. Zuker closed the door and a second later the garage door went up. In the dim light the FBI people could make out heaps of leaf bags next to the two Mercedeses in the garage.

The workers were fast—racing true darkness—and they mowed the lawn in a rush, coming within feet of the face-down and flattened FBI snipers in the higher grass. Once, one of the yard men stopped his mower, picked up what looked like a metal horseshoe, and tossed it into the high grass beyond the yard, almost braining an FBI marksman.

It was almost full dark when the mowing

and pruning was done, and the FBI watched carefully as the three workmen disappeared into the garage and reappeared a moment later, carrying the bulky leaf bags.

"Count them," commanded SAC Warren over the radio link.

"The leaf bags?" said some unfortunate special agent.

"No, you moron, the workers. Make sure that only the three who went into that garage get into the van."

"Roger that," came the confirmation from observers and marksmen.

The three went in and came out, tossing the leaf bags in the back of the van and stowing other detritus. The porch light and small driveway lights came on automatically. Lights in the house switched on as the van drove away.

"Shall we intercept them?" asked the special agent at the outer perimeter.

"Negative," said Warren. "Their boss said that they're working overtime and they're headed home from here. Let them go."

The snipers in the grass and the observers in the houses and passing high-altitude helicopters switched to night vision. Everyone there would have preferred planning the assault for 3:30 A.M., when the Russians would be at their groggiest—or better yet, all asleep—but because of the timing of the other arrests, it had been decided that the assault could commence no earlier than five A.M. Warren and Syd and the others had decided that it would be worth the extra risk of a dawn assault just to make sure that Dallas Trace and the others targeted for arrest that morning heard nothing on the morning news.

Dar had also fired the Barrett Light Fifty for several hours into Tuesday evening. That was a fascinating experience. The rifle came with a bipod, but it was still a beast to manhandle around—weighing twenty-nine and a half pounds without the telescope and measuring an inch more than five feet long. A monster. Adding the M3a Ultra telescopic sight and a few cartridge boxes to the load reminded Dar that he had a bad back.

On Wednesday Dar did his work at the condo, talked to Syd briefly in late afternoon, took the Remington Model 870 shotgun out from under the bed, loaded it, filled his pocket with some extra shells; and carried his overnight bag to the Land Cruiser. He looked around carefully in the basement parking garage before walking to his vehicle. It would be embarrassing to go through all this preparation and then have a pissed-off Russian shoot him with a .22 pistol in his own parking garage.

None did.

Dar drove out through Wednesday traffic. He wanted to arrive at the cabin well before dark, and he did. Stopping on the long gravel driveway to the cabin, he activated the various video cameras one by one. Nothing on the road ahead. No one in the sniper points high above the cabin. No one immediately visible in the field below the cabin. No one in the cabin.

Dar drove the rest of the way, carried in his bags and some groceries, and made dinner. He thought about calling Syd, but knew that she would be busy at the tactical command center all that evening.

What the hell, he thought. *I'll hear about it on the radio tomorrow and read about it in the evening paper.*

He sipped some coffee. *I hope.*

Somewhere around midnight, he double-checked that the cabin doors were locked and turned off the lights. A fire still burned in his fireplace, filling the warm room with flickering light, and he left a soft light on in the kitchen and another next to the bed.

Instead of going to bed, Dar took the shotgun and the receiver/monitor, moved the strip of carpet slightly, unlocked the trapdoor, and went down into his basement. The lights came on automatically. He left the shotgun propped up against the outer wall, unlocked the steel door, and crossed the storeroom to the ventilator grille. Unlocking the heavy padlock there, he inspected the dusty vent with his flashlight and then crawled on his elbows and knees the 220 feet—breathing much more heavily than he liked—until he came to the second grille. He unlocked it, slipped out into the old gold mine, and found his plastic-wrapped M40 rifle and the heavy rucksack right where he had left them the day before.

He pulled on the Marine-issue flak vest stored in the pack, hefted the heavy rucksack, and slung the rifle comfortably on his right shoulder. Water dripped in the old mine shaft. Puddles were everywhere and often six inches deep. Dar splashed through them, still using the flashlight for illumination. He was wearing waterproof hiking boots and his green slacks and camouflage field shirt loose over the heavy vest. On his web belt was the black-steel K-Bar knife in its scabbard. His cell phone was in his shirt pocket, but it was turned off.

Once he reached the entrance to the mine, he doused the flashlight and stowed it, pulling out the L.L. Bean night goggles. There was no moon and the ravine was filled with shadows, but Dar let his eyes adapt naturally and kept the night-vision goggles raised on his forehead as he found his way up the ravine, up the narrow path on the east face of the gully, and continued climbing toward his preselected spot.

It was a beautiful night—a few clouds, cooler than most summer nights, but perfect for a hike.

The FBI assault team battered down the front door of the Santa Anita ranch house at precisely 5:00 A.M. Agents fired tear-gas projectiles through all of the windows. Other agents at the door tossed flash bangs into the living room and lunged inside, laser beams stabbing for targets through the smoke.

Living room empty. Agents held ladders while other agents threw themselves through the bedroom windows as the FBI snipers covered them. No one in the bedrooms.

Special Agent Warren led the first assault team from room to room on the ground floor, and then up the stairway to the second floor. Two helicopters landed on the lawn while two more hovered overhead, brilliant searchlights shining down through the dissipating smoke and the brightening twilight. FBI men in the choppers fired more tear gas through the second-story windows.

No one on the second floor. No one in the kitchen. No one in the basement.

It was one of the last teams to reach the building who radioed in the report. Dead bodies in the garage.

Warren and a dozen others, everyone bulky in their body armor and helmets, goggles and gas masks dangling, converged there within twenty seconds.

The three dead Hispanic men were stripped to their underwear. Each had been shot once in the head.

"But only three got in the van last night..." began a young special agent.

"The goddamned leaf bags," said Special Agent Warren.

"Shall we expand the perimeter?" asked a helmeted figure.

Warren sagged back against the doorframe, clicking the safety on his suppressed H&K MP-10. "They could be in Mexico by now," he said dully.

Nonetheless, Warren was on the radio a second later, alerting headquarters, authorizing helicopter and ground searches for the yard-service van, confirming that the CHP, LAPD, and other agencies had to be briefed immediately, and authorizing a national manhunt.

A message was relayed from the Malibu safe house where Detectives Ventura and Fairchild were being kept. It seemed that Fairchild, who was cooperating with the investigators, had been allowed to go for a brief, escorted walk on the beach the previous afternoon. The FBI agents had not known that there was a pay phone just off the beach, but Fairchild had been allowed out of sight for several seconds to urinate in the bushes, and this morning one of the agents took a walk on the beach and found the phone. He immediately checked to see if there had been any outgoing calls from it.

There had. One of fifteen seconds' duration had been made at 4:30 P.M. The call was to Detective Fairchild's brother-in-law, who ran a dry-cleaning establishment in Pasadena.

"Damn," said one of the agents.

"Damn, heck, and spit," said another.

"Fuck me," said Special Agent in Charge Warren, who had no immediate Bureau supervisors on the scene. "I bet Fairchild got more money than Ventura—he just hid it better."

"Shall we tell Special Agent Faber and Investigator Olson about the Russians?" asked the primary dispatcher.

Warren looked at his watch. It was 5:22 A.M. The Dallas Trace assault was still more than ninety minutes away. "Faber and his people are in position and on radio silence," he said. "I'll call Cassio, the agent in charge of the Century City security perimeter covering the assault team's backs, and tell him that we're sending another dozen tac-team agents to reinforce him."

"Do you think the Russians will try to rescue Dallas Trace?" asked a goggly agent next to Warren.

The special agent in charge actually laughed. "Not a chance in hell. These guys know that the balloon has gone up.

They're not going to drive from one ambush into another one. We'll tell Faber and the rest of the assault team after they do their thing." Warren's voice lost all traces of humor then and he said something most un-Bureau-like. "And I want that LAPD cop—Fairchild—castrated."

Syd received the page eight minutes after the FBI had driven Dallas Trace and his three bodyguards away in separate vehicles. She was standing on the street outside the Century City office tower, busy shaking the sweat out of her hair and ripping the Velcro tabs loose on her bulletproof vest, but she stopped everything when she saw the number on the pager.

Warren explained the situation in two sentences.

"Dar!" said Syd, looking at her watch.

"Investigator Olson," said Special Agent Warren, "these Russians aren't amateurs. They have a ten-hour head start on us. They're not going to waste it on some stupid revenge attempt. They're probably in Mexico by now."

Whatever he said next was lost as Syd shouted, "Get two FBI choppers with tac teams out to Dar's cabin—*now!*" and then flipped shut the phone, picked up her submachine gun, and ran full speed for her parked Taurus. She had no idea that her cell-phone transmission had been garbled and that Special Agent Warren had understood none of it.

23

"W IS FOR WAIT"

It seemed like a long night to Dar. He told himself that perhaps this was because he was not used to lying on a cold stone ledge all night waiting for a group of strangers to come try to kill him. *Nope,* he reassured himself, *that couldn't be the reason.*

The position he had chosen was a rocky outcrop on the east side of the wooded ravine. The slabs of rock on which he lay were about 260 yards above the cabin—with a clear view of the parking area and entrance through gaps in the trees—and even more important, at approximately the same elevation as the two sniper's roosts he had identified to the west. The slab he had chosen—the very word *slab* disturbed him a bit—lay in a natural fissure in the rock with two shooting channels: one looking downhill toward the cabin and the parking area, and the other offering a small slot in the rocks that was perfect for direct fire against the sniper positions. The bad news was that the stones to the east and north of him were higher than his roost and angled downward, which would create a nasty ricochet problem if someone actually started shooting at him from either of the obvious sniper's roosts to the west. He hoped that it would not come to that.

Dar had stored the Barrett .50-caliber in the rock niche under a waterproof tarp, and now he was lying on that tarp, wishing he'd brought a closed-cell foam pad. The twenty-five-pound bulletproof vest he was wearing over his blouse was thicker than a police-issue Kevlar vest. It was modern Marine-issue and incorporated a thick ceramic chest protector that could stop a 7.62mm rifle bullet at medium range, but that also made it extra stiff and uncomfortable. *I'm getting old*, he thought.

The Barrett Light Fifty was on its bipod on the slightly down-tilting slab, leaving room next to his position for extra ammo, the Leica range-finding binoculars, and the receiver/monitor. His old M40 Sniper Rifle lay under camocover and waterproof plastic in the other gap to his right, ready to be used in an instant if he had to fire on the other sniper positions.

Dar figured that if the Russians did not come that night, they would not be coming at all.

His plan was relatively simple and it did not include any real heroics. If, by any chance, the Russians showed up at his cabin before the FBI nabbed them, Dar had his cell phone charged and pro-grammed with Special Agent Warren's and Syd's numbers. Dar always thought of his cabin as being at the edge of the world out here, but the line-of-sight cell phone re-ception was excellent. This was, after all, Southern California. None of the people who had built expensive cabins out here to get away from it all could afford to be out of touch for even an hour.

Dar hoped that there would be no shoot-ing—that he would just lie low in his duck blind while the Russians waited for him to come out of the cabin—until the FBI helicopters roared in with the real professionals. But if he was detected, he was ready to return fire and at least keep the Russians occupied until the cavalry arrived. His position was almost as strong defensively as the reactor at Dalat had been so many years ago—moated by the ravine, impossible to approach unseen from the west or south in the direction of the road and cabin, and difficult to climb to from the east. Dar had brought along his ghillie suit so that if the Russians' "return fire" got too nasty—and Dar considered *any* return fire nasty—he would slip into the camouflage suit and head for the fields below the tree line to the east. By the time the Russians reached this side of the ravine, Dar should be all but invisible below and the FBI should have arrived in force.

I'm absolutely paranoid, thought Dar, soon after beginning his post-midnight vigil. *Why the hell would the Russians come after me again?*

But in his heart, he knew why. Both Gregor Yaponchik and Pavel Zuker had been trained and had operated as snipers. Dar knew that of all the soldiers on earth, only snipers are specifically trained to stalk another individual. Marines and Army grunts might end up with small units stalking small units, or even a single enemy, but only the sniper is trained to use stealth, concealment, and ambush at long range to kill another specific individual. And always first on the sniper's kill list was the most dangerous threat—the enemy sniper.

Dar did not know if the Russians or their American employers had access to his Marine file, but he could not risk assuming they did *not* know he had been a sniper once. More than that, Yaponchik and Zuker had been tasked to kill him three times, and three times they had failed. If Dar knew anything about a sniper's mentality—and he did—he knew that someone like Yaponchik would have an intense feeling of frustration at leaving this particular job unfinished.

Dar remembered a cartoon he'd once seen of a king sitting on his throne. *I'm paranoid*, the king had thought. *But am I paranoid enough?*

The night passed slowly. Making sure that there was no glow to reveal him, Dar switched the monitor from video camera to video camera, using the night lenses for the outdoor cameras. No movement on the road. No movement—or at least none detectable—in the broad fields down the hill from the cabin. No one at the sniper's nests three hundred yards opposite him. No uninvited guests in the cabin.

Dar found one channel of his brain mulling things over. He allowed it to mull as long as it did not disrupt his focus.

He thought about his years reading the Stoic philosophers. He knew that the average person thought of the Stoics—if he thought of them at all—as proponents of a "stiff upper lip" and "don't whine" philosophy. But the average person, Dar knew, was only half a bubble off moron-center.

He and Syd had talked about it. She understood the complexity of the Stoics' writings—Epictetus and Marcus Aurelius.

She understood dividing life between those things that one had no control over—and where the maximum courage was called for—and those elements that one could and should control, and in which caution was prudent. This had been part of Dar's life and thinking for so many years that he found it surprising that he was reviewing and critiquing it on this night of all nights.

No longer talk at all about the kind of man that a good man ought to be, but be such, wrote Marcus Aurelius. Dar had tried to live this maxim.

What else had Marcus Aurelius taught? Dar's nearly photographic memory brought back a passage. *Let this always be plain to thee, that this piece of land is like any other; and that all things here are the same with things on the top of a mountain, or on the seashore, or wherever thou choosest to be. For thou wilt find just what Plato says, Dwelling within the walls of a city as in a shepherd's fold on a mountain.*

Well, here he was dwelling literally within a fold on a mountain. But now he thought of the sentiment behind the statements—both Plato's and Marcus Aurelius's—and he knew in his heart that he did not agree with the core of it. After Barbara and the baby's death, Dar could no longer live in Colorado. It had taken a while to accept, but soon enough it had become that simple. This place—this mountain, this place near the seashore—had been a new beginning for Dar.

And now it had been violated. The Russians had tried to kill Syd and him not far from here, and they had taken pictures of him at this very place.

Dar felt no fury, no approaching *katalepsis*. He had damped his feelings down for so many years—turning to the humor found only in irony for his salvation—that he felt no anger controlling him now. But as he lay on the mountainside waiting—he had to admit that his *hope* was that the Russians might come for him. Despite all logic to the contrary, the hope burned in him like a cold fire.

Every time Dar had ever visited an accident scene, he had thought of Epictetus. *Tell me where I can escape death: discover for me the country, show me the men to whom I must go, whom death does not visit. Discover to me a charm against death. If I have not one, what do you wish me to do? I cannot escape from death, but shall I die lamenting and trembling? ... Therefore if I am able to change externals according to my wish, I change them: but if I cannot, I am ready to tear the eyes out of him who hinders me.*

Epictetus might have scorned the impulse, but Dar had to admit that he was quite ready to tear the eyes out of the Russians if they came at him again. Thinking this, he felt the long K-Bar knife in its sheath on his belt. He had spent an hour honing that knife the previous evening and another hour spraying and coating it, even though the thought of sliding cold steel into another human being's body made him want to throw up on the spot.

Some person asked, "How then shall every man among us perceive what is suitable to his character?" How, he replied, does the bull alone, when the lion has attacked, discover his own powers and put himself forward in defense of the whole herd?

Damn Epictetus anyway. Dar did not consider himself a brave man...nor a bull. And he had no herd to protect from the lion.

Syd, came the thought, unbidden. But he had to smile at that. Even as he lay here, hiding in his nook in the rocks in the middle of the night, forty miles from the city and danger, Syd was preparing to assault the bad guys. It was she who was protecting the herd from the lion.

Dar spent the hours shifting to get comfortable, keeping watch through his goggles and monitor, listening to the breeze stir the pines (while instinctively estimating the wind velocity), and generally deconstructing the philosophy upon which he had based his entire life.

Thou art a little soul bearing about a corpse, Epictetus had taught. Having seen so many fresh corpses in his life, Dar could hardly argue. But during the last few weeks—during the moments with Syd—he had not felt so much the corpse animated by only a little spark of soul. He had to admit to himself...he had felt alive.

By 5:00 A.M., tired and sore but still wide-awake, Dar had reviewed all of his onto-logical and epistemological underpinnings and realized that he was an idiot.

Be like the promontory against which the waves continually break, Epictetus had taught, *but it stands firm and tames the fury of the water around it.*

Well, fuck that, thought Dar. Didn't Epictetus ever go to the seashore? Didn't he know that sooner or later every promontory gets battered down and washed away? Probably the Aegean did not have waves like the ones Dar watched every week at the edge of the Pacific. The sea always wins. Gravity always wins.

After more than ten years of trying to be a promontory, Dar was tired of it.

Predawn light crept over the hillside. Dar put away his night-vision goggles but kept toggling the camera views. The access road was empty. The cabin was empty. The field below was empty. The sniper sites were empty.

By 7:00 A.M., Dar felt a surge of relief mixed with a strange disappointment. The raids were all scheduled to have begun by now—Syd had told him that much—and he understood that the Russians were to be rounded up before the American civilians.

By 7:30 A.M., Dar was tempted to say the hell with it and just hike down the hill, prepare himself a big breakfast, call Syd, and get a few hours' sleep. He decided to wait a bit longer. Syd would still be busy now.

At 7:35 A.M., Camera One showed movement on the driveway. A huge, black Suburban with tinted windows moved slowly past the camera position, stopped, and then backed into the slight turnout across from the surveillance tree.

Five Russians got out. They all wore black sweaters and slacks, but Dar recognized Yaponchik and Zuker at once. The older Russian—he still reminded Dar of Max von Sydow—seemed almost sad as he handed out the weapons to the others. The three younger men headed down the road and out of immediate camera range carrying their AK-47 assault rifles. Even on the small video screen, Dar could see that they were also armed with knives and semiautomatic pistols on their belts.

Yaponchik and Zuker also had holstered sidearms, but they were the last to pull their weapons from the back of the van, two *Snayperskaya Vintovka Dragunova*— sniper rifles of the type that had killed Tom Santana and the three FBI agents.

Dar had to smile. Even with all their money, the Russians stuck with the weapons they knew best. *Sentimental*, he thought, feeling the wood stock of his own antediluvian sniper rifle. Dar saw that both weapons had ten-round detachable magazines and a combination flash suppressor and compensator to reduce muzzle jump and flash. He had noticed that the other three Russians' AK-47s were also fitted with suppressors. Evidently this group wanted to stop by, kill Dar Minor silently, and get on their way.

Dar knew that the SVD had some serious limitations as a sniper rifle. It was accurate enough out to a maximum range of six hundred meters, but at eight hundred meters, it had only a 50 percent chance of hitting a stationary, man-sized target. Theoretically, this gave Dar's longer-range M40 a great advantage. But unfortunately, it was only three hundred yards to the cabin and less than that between the two sniper roosts—his and the one Yaponchik and Zuker seemed headed for.

Dar used the cameras to watch the Russians deploy. One of the men with a submachine gun appeared on the southern slope below the cabin, crawling through the high grass. Two entered the woods above the cabin. Yaponchik and Zuker came into camera range high up on the hill...paused...and then selected the less obvious of the two sniper positions. Dar's video camera had a perfect view as the two older Russians settled into the tiny redoubt and ranged in their weapons and spotting gear.

Dar's heart was pounding wildly. *Time to call in the cavalry*, he thought. He pulled out his cell phone, checked that the charge was good—he had brought an extra battery—and lifted his thumb to punch Special Agent Warren's preprogrammed emergency number. That was when more movement on the video screen caught his eye.

Dar had set the monitor to cycle through the five camera positions. Now he could see Syd Olson's Taurus driving past the parked Suburban, pausing, and then driving on to the cabin. Right toward the waiting Russians.

24

"X IS FOR TERMINATE"

Dar immediately tapped the preprogrammed number for Syd's cell phone. She did not answer. He let it keep ringing while he slid forward and studied the area around the cabin with the gyrostabilized Leica DBII glasses.

There she was.

Syd had gotten out of the Taurus with a Heckler & Koch submachine gun raised and ready, her shoulder bag slung behind her. She was approaching the cabin stealthily, and Dar guessed that she had muted her phone or turned the damned thing off. She was still wearing a Kevlar vest from the FBI raid, but the black body armor was hanging loose, not tightened by the side Velcro. A perfect through-the-ribs heart shot at this range.

Dar felt his pulse racing and his mind going blank. He had lost track of the two Russians with their assault weapons—they were somewhere in the woods not far from Syd—and he could think of no way to warn her.

Concentrate, goddammit. Dar struggled to get his breathing and pulse rate under control. Syd was fifty feet from the cabin door now, visible through the trees for a second, and then obscured, and still he could not find the Russian gunners.

Dar popped his head up long enough to use the binoculars on Yaponchik and Zuker's sniper's position three hundred yards west of him. He could just see the top of Zuker's head and the barrel of Yaponchik's SVD. Zuker was spotting with binoculars. Dar had memorized the field of fire from both of those positions and knew that Syd would be visible and within perfect range in just a few more steps. Before Dar dropped back into his ledge slot, he saw Zuker whispering into a radio.

Shit. The Russians could communicate and Dar could not.

Syd came into the open, her attention focused on the cabin. She looked confused, as if she expected a different situation. She took a careful step, the H&K submachine gun with its diopter sight raised and ready, swiveling to look first at the wooded hillside to her left and then at the cabin door ahead and to her right.

It's locked, thought Dar, trying to send the information through the sheer force of will. *No extra key out there. It's locked, Syd.*

Dar pulled the M40 Sniper Rifle to him, started to peer through the scope in preparation of sending a warning shot in her direction, and then had a better idea. He lifted the binoculars instead.

Syd started toward the cabin door. If he had left the cabin unlocked, the Russians might have let her enter before coming in after her, trying to bag both of them. But once she tried the door and found it locked—once they realized that he was not inside—Dar had no doubt that they would cut her to ribbons.

Dar laid the M40 next to him—glanced at the monitor where camera three showed the third Russian closer on the south slope, less than thirty yards from the porch—and then sighted through the binoculars again.

The Leica was equipped with a Class One laser, but the device was meant for range-finding flashes, not for projecting a constant beam. Nonetheless, by tapping the red button atop the binoculars as quickly as he could, Dar sent a red laser dot flicking and dancing almost at Syd's feet.

She looked down in a long second of confusion. Dar hoped that none of the Russians could see the winking red spot on the pine needles. Just as Syd realized what she was looking at, he aimed the binoculars at her chest and continued tapping the red button. The range kept flashing in the digital display to one side of the viewfinder—264 yards, 263 yards, 262 yards—but Dar ignored it and kept the red dot winking on the black body armor directly above Syd's left breast.

She dropped and rolled as if a trapdoor

had opened up to swallow her. There were soft coughs from the forest, a slight noise from the ridge above, and bullets began to rip at the spot where Syd had been standing a second before. He held her in the binoculars long enough to see her roll behind a fallen Douglas fir trunk and then splinters and chunks of rotten wood were flying everywhere as the unseen gunmen in the woods continued firing with their suppressed AK-47s.

The lack of noise made the firefight seem unreal. A second later, reality reasserted itself as Syd lifted her H&K MP-10 above the level of the fallen tree and sprayed bullets at random into the woods. That noise was quite audible. The effect was negligible.

Move! Move! Don't stay in that spot. Yaponchik can fire through that rotten tree!

This time the telepathy seemed to work. Dar saw Syd roll just as the DVD bullets—the Russian sniper weapon could fire at semiautomatic rate—tore through the thirty-inch trunk as if it were made of papier mâché.

Dar decided that it was time to get in the fight. He rolled to the Barrett Light Fifty, sighted into the stand of pines, firs, and birch just uphill from Syd, and opened up. The noise was terrific. Dar had almost forgotten that the first five magazines he had laid out were loaded with SLAP rounds—saboted light armor penetrators—capable of punching through nineteen millimeters of steel plate at a range of twelve hundred meters. The effect on some of the trees was dramatic. One entire young ponderosa pine was clipped off about twelve feet above the ground and came to earth with a crash. A giant Douglas fir absorbed a heavy round, but the entire 200 feet of tree rocked back and forth as if in a high wind, while wood chips and sap flew everywhere.

The rapid fire did not throw off Dar's aim, although there was precious little to aim at. *I'm killing a lot of trees*, thought Dar. The automatically ejected brass, rattling and rolling on the slab next to Dar, offended his sniper sensibilities—he had been trained to police all his cartridges—

but he ignored the aesthetics of the situation, slapped in a second magazine—regular 12.7-by-99mm rounds this time, firing standard 709-grain bullets—and blasted away into the woods, trying to sense movement or muzzle flashes.

The heavy fire from above must have rattled the Russians; their firing stopped. Syd appeared to have run out of ammunition. For a second, all was silence except for the ringing in Dar's ears.

I fucked up, he realized, too late. *Totally fucked up.*

Dar swiveled the Barrett .50-caliber until the cabin's doorway filled the sight. He slapped in another magazine of SLAP rounds. The first shot tore a five-inch hole in the wood above the door handle. The second shot blew the lock to bits. The third shot blasted the door open and half off its hinges.

Go, go, go, he thought toward Syd, and then did something that should have been fatal: he went to his knees swinging the heavy Barrett 82A1 Light Fifty toward Yaponchik and Zuker, propping the long weapon on the rock. If they had already sighted and ranged him, Dar knew, he would die instantly.

He caught a glimpse of Zuker's head, binoculars trained twenty yards or so to Dar's right, still hunting, and then he loosed off the seven shots left in the magazine.

The armor-piercing shells seemed to explode around the Russians' niche in the boulder, throwing sparks and hunks of granite fifty feet into the air. One shot, too high, struck the boulder above the firing position and unleashed a small avalanche of pebbles and shards. But Dar was fairly certain he had not hit either Russian.

He dropped back into his own slot, could no longer find Syd in his sight, and flicked the monitor to the inside cameras.

Syd had made a successful dash for the cabin and was hunkered down near the bedroom window. The Russians near the cabin were spraying the building and window with automatic weapons fire, throwing glass shards across the bed, splintering wood, ripping into couch cushions, and making Syd flinch back to the corner. The door was still hanging open and ajar behind her. Dar saw at once that she had run out of ammo for her H&K MP-10 and had left the extra magazines outside with her shoulder bag. *And telephone*, he thought grimly. Syd was crouched with her 9mm Sig Pro pistol held in both hands, facing the opened door and obviously waiting for the first Russian to come through that opening.

Dar pulled his phone from his web belt and dialed the cabin number. There was no sound from the tiny TV monitor, but he saw Syd jump and look over at the phone.

Answer it, thought Dar. *Please, answer it*.

There came a brief lull in the Russians' fire and Syd lunged for the phone, pulled it off the table, and threw herself back into the corner. Dar kept shifting his vision from the small monitor to the Light Fifty's scope, ready to cut down the Russians if they made an assault on the open door.

"Syd!"

"Dar? Where are you?"

"Up the hill...Are you hit?"

"Negative."

"All right, listen. There's a trapdoor to the basement—the opening's right at the end of the long rug on the right side of the bed, about four meters from you—the keys are under the ice tray in the refrigerator..."

"Dar, how many—"

"You've got two of the Russians in the woods above you with suppressed AK-47s," said Dar. "Yaponchik and Zuker have sniper rifles farther up the hill. One guy south of the cabin..." Dar activated Camera Four on the south slope. The Russian was under the porch and moving to the side of the cabin, obviously ready to rush the back door. "Under the porch and ready to enter," finished Dar. "Get the keys! Go!"

He laid down covering fire into the trees as he watched Syd's tiny image dash through the room, throw the ice tray out of the refrigerator, grab the small leather case, and rush back to the side of the bed.

Yaponchik and Zuker both started firing. Dar could hear the cough of their inadequate suppressors, but more impressive was the splintering of the north wall as the 7.62mm rounds slammed through the thin wood where Syd had been crouched in the corner a moment before. The slugs blew Dar's favorite lamp to pieces and ripped into the hardwood floor.

Dar wanted to lay down cover fire— knowing well that the two snipers would be lying out of sight—but he had to see if Syd made it into the basement.

She was fumbling with the keys, dragging the phone across the floor to her as she did so.

"I can't get the fucking—"

"The narrow key," said Dar. "That's it."

The trapdoor came up and the basement light came on. Syd looked around her. The third Russian came in through the porch doorway and opened fire. Syd ducked behind the raised trapdoor, but the bullets struck the varnished wood and knocked her back and down. She dropped out of sight into the basement and Dar saw her 9mm pistol sliding across the floor, obviously knocked out of her hand by the force of the trapdoor hitting her. He could only pray that the metal-lined hardwood trapdoor had stopped the slugs.

The cabin cameras showed the other two Russians coming in the front door now, covering each other as one knelt and the other hovered above him, both weapons swiveling. The third Russian, standing near the trapdoor, gave the "all clear" signal and pointed toward the floor.

The Russian by the trapdoor removed something from his belt.

Shit, thought Dar. *Grenade of some sort.*

Before Dar could fire, the first Russian to enter the room had lifted the trapdoor, dropped his grenade in, and thrown himself away from the entrance. The blast blew open the trapdoor. Dar saw that the basement light had been knocked out—the entry was just a black square in the polished wood floor now—and then he saw the three Russians gather around the trapdoor and aim their weapons into that darkness.

Using the video monitor as his reference point, Dar aimed the Light Fifty and fired

off two SLAP rounds. The first one penetrated the wall just to the left of the window frame and struck the Russian who had
dropped the grenade. The armor-penetrating shell entered the small of the man's
back and blew his spine, internal organs,
and rib cage out through his chest, exiting
the cabin by blowing a wide hole through
the south-facing windows. The second
SLAP round struck the falling corpse's
head and exploded it.

He saw both of the other Russians flinch
and fall, one of them obviously struck in
his unarmored arms and face by skull fragments.

Dar shifted his aim to where the un-
wounded killer was lying in the corner—right where Syd had been a few
moments before—and he fired the three
remaining SLAP rounds in this magazine
through the wall there. Two of the
rounds missed—high, as the Russian
crouched into a tight fetal position—but
the third one struck him just above the
ankle, blowing his foot off and propelling
it and a shank of white bone across the

room, almost striking the last crouching Russian.

Dar slapped in another magazine and only then realized that he himself was under heavy fire.

Both Yaponchik and Zuker must have been firing. The heavy 7.62mm slugs were striking the rocks to the east, west, and north of him. Some of the better-aimed shots sent slugs down his east-west sniper trough and the bullets whined by inches below his boots before ricocheting up and out. The other ricochets—the ones from the tilted slabs above and behind him— were as bad as he'd feared.

Bullets ricocheted into his rucksack. Another slug struck his Leica binoculars and flung them far out over the ravine. Then one struck the back of his Marine flak vest, directly between his shoulder blades. The impact wasn't too bad, he thought. No worse than someone hitting you in the back with a small sledgehammer. It knocked the wind out of him for a full minute and dimmed his vision as red as a three-g loop in the sailplane.

Maybe it penetrated and severed my spine, he thought dully and distantly, feeling his back. There was a nice hole in his camouflage blouse, but the heavy vest he was wearing underneath was intact. He could actually feel the flattened slug in the ceramic and metallic fiber. *Jesus,* he thought respectfully, *and that's only a ricochet at 280 yards—with much of the slug's velocity depleted in the original strike.*

There were both physical and philosophical implications to consider, but before Dar could get his mind and body fully back on-line, other bullets whined around him. He checked the video monitor.

The last surviving—or at least the last functioning—Russian in the cabin had belly-crawled over to the open trapdoor and was now spraying the basement with his AK-47.

Dar did not see how Syd could have survived if she had been in the basement corridor rather than the locked storeroom, but he decided it still would be best if he killed that Russian.

The problem with that plan was that the

SLAP rounds might well penetrate the floor as well as the last Russian and kill Syd if she was lying wounded in that basement corridor. Dar's "safe room" was steel-lined, but the basement corridor had only regular flooring between it and his armor-penetrating shells. He removed the magazine of SLAP rounds, tapped a regular .50-caliber magazine twice on the rock next to him, and slapped it into the Light Fifty.

Ignoring the sniper fire that was ricocheting off rocks to his right and back into his niche from rocks above, Dar used the monitor to help him sight on the Russian as he controlled his breathing, steadied the crosshairs reticle on the patch of wall behind which the Russian was lying, and gently squeezed the trigger.

No good. The first three .50-caliber rounds penetrated the wall easily enough, but they were deflected slightly, striking around the Russian. Also, it looked to Dar as if the .50-caliber rounds were penetrating the floor. He would have to use the M40 and hope that he would get a shot through the window.

The Russian was distracted by the heavy-caliber shells striking around him and he looked over his shoulder at the perforated wall. Dar could see on the monitor that the Russian was calling to his comrade in the corner, but the man who had just lost his foot was curled in a ball and evidently quite unconscious. A dark pool was visible all around his leg.

As Dar grabbed the modified Remington 700 from its hiding place under the ledge of rock, a bullet ricocheted twice and cut across the back of his thighs just below his buttocks. Dar gritted his teeth rather than scream aloud and looked over his own shoulder. He couldn't see anything because of the bulky vest and loose camouflage blouse, but when he put his right hand back, it came away quite bloody. He decided that he would operate under the assumption that it was just a fat-and-muscle groove-wound with no serious arteries struck; he would know soon enough if he was wrong.

Dar sighted through the Redfield scope, still watching the TV monitor—which had miraculously survived the ricochets so far—with his open left eye. As with all scientists using a microscope or telescope, Dar had been taught as a sniper how to concentrate with his scope eye while keeping the other one open to aid in ranging and peripheral vision.

The Russian in the cabin appeared to have been distracted by the .50-caliber slugs. Now he got to one knee and peered into the dark basement opening, obviously hoping to see a body to report to Zuker and Yaponchik before hastily leaving the area.

The Russian leaned forward, peering down the ladder. Suddenly there was a flash and the gunman's white oval of a face on the monitor became an irregular patchwork of grays and blacks. The body flew backward and landed with arms open, AK-47 flying across the floor.

Dar held his fire and watched. Bullets whined above him and one ricocheted no more than a millimeter from his right ear. A calm part of Dar's mind was reporting to him that the sniper fire against him had lessened in volume. Obviously there was only one SVD firing against his position now—which meant that either Yaponchik or Zuker, probably Zuker, had moved out to flank him—but the main focus of Dar's attention at the moment was that black square on the video monitor.

Syd's head and shoulders came up quickly, a shotgun even more quickly. She swiveled, holding aim, seeing the three dead Russians but checking every visible corner of the cabin.

Dar had to grin. She had found the Remington 870 shotgun he had left in the hallway, probably opened the saferoom door and perhaps hidden in the room or at the very least behind the steel door during the grenade and AK-47 attack, and then had come out to meet her attacker.

Dar reached for the cell phone on his belt to call her. The cell phone had been shot away.

Shit.

He saw her run to the receiver of the phone still lying on the floor, but then he saw that the phone itself had been blasted to pieces by one of his .50-caliber rounds.

He watched her toss the receiver aside and then crawl over to the Russian with the missing foot. She pulled a radio from his belt and the microphone from where it was strapped high on his left shoulder. Dar could see her listening and he knew that she could speak Russian.

Good girl, he thought, glad that Syd could not hear the sexist comment. There was no way that he and she could communicate right now, but at least she might get some information on what the two surviving Russians were planning up the hill.

Which reminded Dar to abandon this position before Zuker showed up behind him and opened fire into the stone trench.

The SVD fire was still slamming off the rocks inches above Dar's head, and it was so wonderfully aimed that Dar instinctively felt that it was Yaponchik, the top shot, who had stayed behind, ordering his spotter to flank Dar.

Of course, Dar had taken some care to choose a position where he could not be flanked that easily. His field of view and easy killing zone still commanded the area near and above the north side of the cabin, so it was doubtful if Zuker would head downhill in that direction to cross the ravine where it shallowed out. There was zero chance that Zuker was going to climb down into the ravine and simply hope there was some way up its vertical east wall where Dar would not hear him coming. So Zuker had left the sniper roost and was working his way north and east, closer to the ridgeline, almost certainly moving very slowly through the thick forest and foliage there, hoping or knowing that there would be an easy crossing somewhere up there where the ravine narrowed and was at its deepest. Dar knew that the Russians had been here before, so he assumed that they had checked out the entire area; any decent sniper would have. That meant that they both knew about the fallen log that crossed the ravine near the waterfall—Reichenbach Falls, Dar had unofficially named it. The wide fir had fallen many years before, and was slippery with spray from the falls and overgrown with moss. The walls of the ravine opened onto it from small, thickly shrubbed gullies on either side. Dar estimated the ravine to be about sixty feet deep there, with overhanging ledges and nothing but ragged boulders below.

Tucking the Light Fifty under the ledge to protect it from Yaponchik's deliberate ricochets, Dar glanced a final time at the monitor—Syd was crouched near the window with the Remington shotgun at port arms, obviously awaiting developments. He took his M40 rifle and crawled slowly backward and out of the trench, sliding below the ridgeline and rocks there, out of Yaponchik's field of fire for the first time.

He spent ten seconds checking to see how badly wounded he was. The backs of his legs burned as if someone had branded him, but the blood was already coagulating—stiffening his ripped trousers—so it couldn't be a serious wound. A quick pat confirmed that it was indeed a groove-wound, shallow, deeper in his right leg than his left. He was also surprised to discover that the ricochet that had destroyed his cell phone had also passed through his web belt and embedded itself in his right side, directly under the skin above his hip-bone. It hurt no more than a bruise, but Dar knew that it had driven quite a bit of dirty fabric into him, so it would have to be cleaned and dressed and the slug removed if he was to avoid infection.

I'll deal with that later, Dar thought, and began running north through the woods, keeping his rifle ready, making as little sound as possible in such thick woods. He made sure that his head was always below both the rocks along the ravine and line of sight to Yaponchik. His legs burned and he realized that the groove-wound was as much along the cheeks of his ass as through the backs of his legs. *How undignified,* he thought. He listened to his own panting and to the jingling of extra magazines and M40 ammo in his camo-fatigue pants and blouse.

Dar knew that he was in a race for his life. If Zuker had jogged to the log bridge, he would have arrived first, found a good firing position, and could easily kill Dar as he came crashing uphill through the trees.

But Dar's subliminal memory confirmed that Yaponchik had not been firing solo for very long before Dar had noticed it and bailed from his position. Most important, snipers were trained for stealth and caution, and it took a fool to run blindly through the woods the way Dar was. Zuker, Dar knew, was nowhere near as desperate as Dar was at that moment, and odds were that he would not be moving so fast.

Dar reached the shallow gully—not more than a meter and a half deep, filled with ferns and brambles—which ran about four meters to the fallen tree over the ravine. He was alive. So far, so good. But he was panting so hard that he could not hear if anyone was in the weeds here with him. Dar undid the clasp on his K-Bar knife—feeling lucky that the knife scabbard had not been shot off his belt along with the cell phone—and began crawling toward the tree, rifle aimed.

There was no one else in the gully on this side. The log looked longer and narrower than Dar remembered it, and the ravine much deeper. Spray rose from the rocks below. Dar knew that this fissure, not as deep but still formidable, ran several hundred yards north, almost all the way to the ridgeline. To cross there, a sniper would have to come out of the trees and expose himself along that ridgeline.

Dar caught his breath and peered through the ferns at the twenty feet of fallen log. The mossy surface was wet. Only one old branch might serve as a handhold along the way, and Dar was certain that it was rotten and would not hold his weight if he went off. He had often noted this log in his hikes up the hill, but he had never crossed it. Why should he? It would be a profoundly stupid thing to do.

Dar got to his knees and exposed his head and shoulders, inviting a shot if Zuker was waiting somewhere across the ravine. That would have been Dar's strategy if he were up here alone—hide and wait for Zuker to cross the log. But he was not alone here. Syd was pinned down in the cabin, and Yaponchik could go after her at any time.

Ten seconds passed and there was no fatal shot. Dar slung the M40 across his back—difficult to get to but guaranteed not to fall into the ravine unless he did—and then jumped out onto the log and started the crossing.

Pavel Zuker, a slim, mean-faced man, jumped out onto the log at the same instant. Dar did not know which of them looked the more surprised. Zuker had not been able to see Dar from his waiting point in the opposite gully, and Dar certainly had not sighted the Russian before this.

Both men had slung their rifles similarly and there was neither time nor sufficient balance to go for them, so each went for the weapon at his belt. Dar pulled his K-Bar knife. Zuker pulled an ugly little semi-automatic pistol and aimed it at Dar's face. They had both come too far out to turn back and were now separated by only nine feet or so. Dar froze.

"Isn't this just like a stupid American?" said Zuker, his accent thick. "Bring a knife to a gunfight."

An old joke, thought Dar, crouching near

that one protruding branch. Still holding his K-Bar knife in his right hand, Dar used his right boot to give that branch a heavy kick just where it entered the trunk.

It broke off, just as Dar had thought it would, but not before rocking the entire tree twenty degrees to the right and then back.

Zuker fired twice, the second bullet passing an inch or so over Dar's head. Then the Russian dropped to straddle the log, hanging on with his left hand until the rocking stopped, trying to steady the pistol with his right arm. He fired again.

Dar had been ready for the sudden motion and kept his balance, even while jumping forward, knife coming around, left hand grabbing at Zuker's right wrist. The nine-millimeter slug hit him along his left side, sliding off his heavy body armor but knocking Dar off balance. He would have fallen then if he had not dropped and straddled the tree trunk as well.

The two men were inches apart now: Zuker grabbing and holding Dar's knife hand, Dar desperately gripping Zuker's gun hand, keeping the muzzle aim only inches away from his forehead. Zuker fired again. The bullet took a tiny slice out of Dar's left ear. The entire tree-bridge was rocking. Dar could hear the water hitting the sharp boulders sixty feet below and could feel the spray and sweat loosening his grip on the Russian's right wrist. They were face-to-face now. Dar could smell the smaller man's breath and easily see the customized, finger-grooved grip on the Kahr nine-millimeter, as well as the fluorescent yellow front sight and ugly orange paint on the rear sight.

The two struggled in sweaty silence. The cool, analytical part of Dar's mind sent the message—*the CAC Customs Arm Kahr has a 6.5-pound trigger pull*—while the adrenaline-filled majority of his brain told the useless analytical part to shut up, for Christ's sake. Dar realized that even though he was slightly stronger than the wiry Russian, Zuker was going to win this game. All the Russian sniper had to do was bend his wrist enough to get the muzzle aimed at Dar's head, while Dar had to turn the knife around and into full contact. Though he was ducking his head as far forward and out of range as he could, it was time for a strategy change.

Just as the black muzzle opening was rotating steadily toward Dar's temple, he threw his head and shoulders back instead of forward, ripping his right arm free by jerking it back violently. He almost dropped the knife, but managed to hang on to it as he leaned far back as Zuker fired, creasing Dar's scalp this time. Then Dar brought the knife around the side, low and fast under the Russian's blocking left arm, using more energy in the motion than he thought his body still possessed, stabbing toward the belly with a vertical blade and then tugging up as hard as he could, precisely as he had been taught at Parris Island more than two and a half decades earlier.

The Russian said, "Ooof," as the wind was knocked out of him, but then he smiled broadly, showing poorly cared for Russian teeth—mostly steel.

"Kevlar vest, American asshole," said

Pavel Zuker, and then, having the leverage over Dar in this awkward choreography, he rotated his weapon further. Dar's slick grasp slipped a little more, until the yellow forward sight was aimed directly at Dar's right eye.

Suddenly Zuker's smile faded and he looked thoughtful, perhaps a bit disappointed. Dar remembered the same look on the faces of childhood friends when they were being called in by their mothers just as the playing got good.

Zuker looked down at his belly and at the blood pumping and squirting out over the handle of the K-Bar knife and Dar's clenched fist. He was frowning in real confusion now.

Dar knocked the Kahr pistol out of Zuker's suddenly strengthless grip and then grabbed for the Russian's vest, but Zuker was already tilting, sliding, falling—gone. Dar caught a last glimpse of the Russian's eyes—still alert and asking an unspoken question even as the blood quit pumping to the sniper's brain—and then the man fell out of sight into the spray. Suddenly Dar was busy keeping his own balance as the tree-bridge rocked from the energy of Dar tugging the blade free of Zuker's midsection. Dar drove the knife into the center of the log and hung on with both hands until the rocking stopped.

Panting heavily, his body debating as to whether he should vomit now or later, Dar looked down through the mist at the broken form sixty feet below. The water ran thick and red downstream from the corpse. Zuker's pale face was still raised, the mouth open wide as if still trying to ask a question.

"Kevlar *doesn't* stop knife blades," panted Dar, answering Zuker's unspoken question. "Especially blades sprayed with Teflon."

Might be a good idea to get off the log, the banished analytical part of his mind suggested diffidently.

Dar crawled on all fours the last ten feet. Pulling himself into and up the shallow gully on the other side, seeing the boot-prints where Zuker had hidden behind a fold in the rock before attempting the crossing, Dar was acutely aware that his middle-aged body wanted to call it quits for the day.

He vetoed that idea and crawled slowly up and out of the gully, sheathing his K-Bar knife after wiping the blade on ferns, and then unslinging his M40.

There were four possibilities. He knew that Yaponchik would not be at the sniper's nest. He was either downhill finishing off Syd, or running for his Chevy Suburban, or in another good position and waiting to shoot Dar. Or executing some combination of the previous three.

Getting slowly to his feet, banishing the daemon of *katalepsis* that threatened to possess him, Dar held his rifle at port arms and began moving west through the woods.

25

"Y IS FOR YAPONCHIK"

Dar's sniper crawl westward was slow and stealthy and according to the manual. He kept his head down, his mental map of the terrain clear, staying aware of the sun's position, using every bit of cover and natural camouflage available, his rifle cradled in his arms as he slithered forward slowly on his elbows, belly, and knees. The hundred-yard-per-hour advance would have earned him high marks at Quantico, but Dar soon realized that at this professional rate, he would arrive at the cabin about three weeks after Yaponchik had shot Syd and driven off.

He paused to think about this, using the Redfield to scope the high ground to his right and the clearing to his left, when suddenly a burst of SVD fire and another, much quieter, cough of automatic weapons fire helped make up his mind.

For a second Dar thought that the unmistakable double-cough of the poorly suppressed AK-47 meant that there had been a sixth Russian there, but then he realized that he had underestimated Syd. She may have used up her H&K ammunition, but there were at least three AK-47s in the cabin with her, and the Russians had been carrying extra banana clips out the wazoo. Syd was loaded for bear and evidently she had flushed one.

Yaponchik's suppressed SVD sniper rifle fired again, soft stutters of three rounds each time, and Dar noted the location. Downhill and to his left about eighty yards. The AK-47 coughed loudly back from the direction of the cabin.

Dar actually closed his eyes a second as he visualized the last few minutes. Yaponchik had gone against Dar's expectations and had moved *downhill*—which made sense, Dar now realized. The expert Russian sniper had surrendered the high ground, but had put himself closer to his vehicle while choosing a spot that was probably perfect for picking off Dar as he crept along, paying more attention to the hill above him.

Dar knew that Yaponchik would not have revealed himself to Syd's view from the cabin doors or windows, which meant that Syd had moved outside the cabin—Dar's guess was that she had headed out the south door, down the hill, and then back up near the parking lot, probably concealing herself in the boulders there. She must have gotten a glimpse of Yaponchik through the AK-47's optics. Dar realized that he would not have been at all jealous if she had killed the Russian son of a bitch for him, but from the sound of the firefight, Yaponchik was still very much alive.

Dar stood up and ran like hell, crashing through underbrush, tripping and rolling once but never losing his rifle or knife, leaping downhill. He could see the boulder that was his destination and estimated that it was uphill and about fifty yards east of Yaponchik's position. From there he and

Syd could put the Russian in defilade and a cross-fire vector without endangering each other.

Dar slid belly-first behind the boulder as three SVD rounds slammed into the top of it. Yaponchik may not have seen him, but obviously had heard him coming. *Good.* Dar crouched behind the boulder, ready to fire around its west end if and when Yaponchik returned Syd's fire. But although the AK-47 coughed twice more, there was no response from the Russian's sniper rifle.

Shit, thought Dar. *He's disengaging.*

There came a burst of SVD suppressed fire from near the parking area, and Dar heard Syd shouting from the distance— "Dar, he's shooting up our truck and car"—and then more SVD coughs and then silence.

Dar was moving again, sliding downhill, keeping the thicker of the trees between him and the parking area, but trying to flank Yaponchik.

He reached the edge of the cabin clearing and assessed the situation quickly. All of the tires were shot out on the Land Cruiser and Taurus. He could see Syd just west of the cabin, curled behind a protective boulder, but there was no sight of Yaponchik. He whistled once.

Syd saw him and shouted, "He went down the road on foot. I was afraid to come out because I don't know the range of his weapon."

"Stay where you are!" shouted Dar. "Keep around the east side of the rock."

He went to her, moving from rock to tree to rock, sprinting and weaving and dodging through the open areas, hoping that Syd could get off a clean return shot if Yaponchik killed him now.

He made it without getting shot and slid behind the boulder next to Syd. He could see that her face and hands were cut and bleeding.

"You're hit!" they both said at the same time.

"I'm OK," they both answered simultaneously.

Dar shook his head and touched Syd's right arm, looking at the cuts on her wrists and hands. He realized that the lacerations on her face were also much more bloody than serious. "Shrapnel?" he said.

"Yeah. I was behind the door, but there was a lot of steel ricocheting around that corridor when that guy dropped the grenade," said Syd softly, still crouched low. "There's blood all over you, Dar."

Dar looked down at his body armor. "All of this belongs to Zuker," he said.

"Dead?"

Dar nodded.

"But your side and back," said Syd. "Turn around."

Dar did so, feeling the stabs of pain from his right side and the backs of both legs.

"That's not Zuker's blood," said Syd. "It looks like they shot your ass off."

"Great," said Dar, feeling suddenly queasy.

Syd actually peeled back some of the rags of his camouflage trousers to look at the wound. "Sorry. It's a deep graze. The bleeding's almost stopped. Your ear's a bloody mess. And what's with the blood on your side, under your armor?"

"Ricochet," said Dar. "Just under the skin. Not important. Let's concentrate on Yaponchik."

They peered around opposite ends of the boulder, jerking their heads back instantly. No shots. The Land Cruiser and Taurus looked sad sitting there on eight flat tires.

"I think he's disengaged," said Dar. "Heading for the Suburban."

"It's parked about a half mile down the road..." began Syd.

"I know." Dar rubbed his cheek, smelled blood, and looked at his hands. He rubbed his right palm against his trouser leg. That did not help.

"If we go after him—" began Syd again.

"Shhh. Give me a second," said Dar. He closed his eyes, remembering the access road and distances as well as he could. He doubted Yaponchik would be running down the road—the Russian would know that trucks and cars could be driven on their rims, for one thing. Most likely the sniper would be staging a careful, tactical withdrawal, moving from sniper point to sniper point, waiting for any pursuit.

Dar guessed that he still had a few minutes before Yaponchik got to the Suburban. After that, the sniper would be the FBI's problem. But...

There was one part of the access road visible to the cabin: a hard curve with a steep embankment on the northwest side and no trees on this side. It was about a mile down the driveway, not long before the access road met the highway. A vehicle would be visible in the gap for only a few seconds before turning right back into the trees and then onto the highway. He might have time.

Dar handed his M40 to Syd. "Use this rather than the AK-47 if he comes back." As he struggled out of his heavy vest, he noticed for the first time that she was carrying binoculars on a strap around her neck. "Where'd you get those?"

"From the Russian whose foot you shot off," said Syd.

"Is he dead?" The binoculars made sense to Dar now that he thought about it—Yaponchik would want to use as many of his colleagues as spotters as he could.

Syd shook her head. "He's unconscious and in shock, but I used my belt to tie off his stump. He lost a lot of blood. He'll be dead unless the good guys get here soon."

"We can't call—" Dar began, and then shut up as Syd held up her cell phone. Obviously she had taken time to retrieve her bag from in front of the cabin.

"Warren's on the way," she said.

Dar nodded. All the more reason just to hunker down and call it a day. Dropping his heavy flak vest on the ground, he said, "Stay alert. Use my bolt-action if Yaponchik comes back. I'll be back in a couple of minutes."

Dar ran like hell—learning that it hurt quite a bit to run with a 7.62mm groove in the back of his legs, more so now that the adrenaline rush had receded somewhat. It was especially painful as he slid down the grassy slope just beneath the cabin, ran under the long porch, climbed to find the trail past the sheep wagon, and slid down the steep hill above the gold-mine entrance to get to the ravine. He could feel fresh blood soaking his tattered fatigue pants as he wheezed and panted his way up the steep trail on the east side of the ravine and then jogged just below the rock-rim ledge to his previous sniper's roost.

Dar had to pause a second above the trough in the stone, not just to catch his breath but to wonder at the number of ricochets that had scarred the stone where he had been lying. The poncho and rucksack containing his handmade ghillie suit were shot to tatters. At least two of the Light Fifty magazines had been perforated like tin cans on a shooting range. His video monitor had been blasted to shards by a wayward ricochet—which ruled out Plan A. So much for watching to see when and if Yaponchik reached the Suburban.

Dar jumped into the slit and pulled the .50-caliber Barrett Model 82A1 out from under the rock overhang. The Light Fifty had not been hit. Dar quickly filled his oversized pockets with both SLAP and regular ammo magazines and then began jogging back along the rim to the base of the ravine.

He had forgotten how heavy and unwieldy this so-called Light Fifty was. The ten-power telescopic sight did not make it lighter. While in the Marines, Dar had always pitied the radio men and heavy-weapons guys humping their monsters—PRC-77 ass-kicker scrambler/descrambler radios, or their M60 machine guns or M79 "thumper" 40mm grenade launchers. He wondered if all of them—all of them who survived—had ended up with bad backs later in life.

By the time he scrabbled up the last slope from beneath the porch and joined Syd behind her boulder, he was not only bleeding freely again from both wounds but was soaked with sweat. At least he'd had the presence of mind to take the twenty-five-pound body armor off.

"No movement," reported Syd. "I've been using the glasses rather than the scope on your rifle."

Dar nodded his approval. "No sounds?"

"I haven't heard the Suburban start

up...but then it's way the hell down the road."

"But you're sure it hasn't passed that open spot?" said Dar.

"I said no movement, didn't I?" said Syd a bit crossly.

Dar took the Light Fifty and jogged to his left, down the slope a bit, keeping out of line of sight with the woods or road nearby, moving toward a flat-topped boulder just above the last little stand of fir trees before the hillside became grassy pasture. When he had successfully crossed the space without drawing fire, he gestured for Syd to join him.

Dar had set up the Light Fifty on the flat top of the boulder and was lying prone, reading the mil-dot scope reticles and adjusting the wind and elevation settings. The wind was a minor factor today—even out here in the open—with only slight gusts below three miles per hour. But at this distance, Dar knew, even the slightest factors had to be entered into the equation.

"You're shitting me," said Syd, staring at

the distant patch of open road through her borrowed pair of seven-by-fifty binoculars. "That has to be at least a mile away."

"I estimate about one thousand seven hundred yards," said Dar, still working with his settings. "So a little less than a mile." He tried to get comfortable with the weapon again, getting the spot weld of his thumb and cheek around the stock and slowing his breathing. In the far distance, they heard a V-8 engine roar to life.

"Good," said Dar. "Unless he's coming back here, we know where Yaponchik is now. And he has about half a mile to drive to that curve."

"You're not seriously thinking of—"

"Spot me," interrupted Dar. "I only have time for a couple of practice shots." He peered through the M3a Ultra scope. "I'm going to aim for that boulder on the cut just where the road turns right again."

"Which boulder? The dark one or the light?"

"The light," Dar said, and squeezed off a round. The unsuppressed blast and gas recoil made Syd jump.

"I'm sorry," she said. "I didn't see the hit point."

"That's all right," said Dar. "I think I missed the whole fucking hillside. Spot me." He fired two more rounds.

"I see the second strike," said Syd, excited now. "About thirty meters short of the road. Shall I use meters or yards?"

"Shit," said Dar, making more adjustments. "It doesn't matter—meters is fine," he said, sighting again. He had two rounds left in this clip and he knew that the Suburban would be appearing in seconds. He fired off the last two rounds, made no effort to spot their impact, ejected the clip, and clicked in another magazine of SLAP rounds.

"They both hit the cut," said Syd, working hard to keep her binoculars steady. "One about a meter to the right and the other about a meter and a half high and to the right of the light boulder."

"Got it," said Dar, making final adjustments. "Close enough for government work. Now I'm going to keep my eye in the scope, so you tell me as soon as the hood of the Suburban appears."

"You'll only have a second or two to—"

"I know," said Dar. "Don't speak until it appears. Just say 'now.' "

Syd was silent, looking through her optics while Dar blinked away fuzziness in his right eye, found the correct eye relief—that is, the perfect distance of about 2½ inches between his eye and the glass of the scope—forced his left eye to stay open, and concentrated on the crosshairs. At this range he would have to lead the truck, and to do that, he had to estimate its speed. The road was bad and the curve was sharp, but Dar doubted if Yaponchik would be driving slowly to save wear and tear on the Suburban's suspension. If he were Yaponchik, he'd try to take the turn at thirty-some miles per hour. There would be a lot of dust as the Suburban braked to make the curve.

The image in Dar's scope was blurred by near-vertical, shimmering waves. Dar knew this phenomenon as a "boiling mirage" which was created by heat waves rising across the great distance; it helped him figure wind velocity. If the parallel ripples had been leaning just a bit more to the left, Dar knew that on a day with eighty-degree Fahrenheit weather such as this, the wind would be moving the mirage waves at a speed of three to five miles per hour. Since they were almost vertical, it meant that there was no appreciable wind at that instant. Also, Dar knew instinctively that the higher temperature was going to increase the muzzle velocity of the Light Fifty slugs—already leaving the barrel at a minimum velocity of twenty-eight hundred feet per second—and that meant that each bullet would strike a bit higher than usual on the target. But the day had turned muggy—Dar guessed about 65 percent humidity—and the added moisture made the air denser, which offered more resistance, which would slow the bullet some. Dar added these factors into his elementary equation of the range—1,760 yards was his final estimate, all the while wishing that he had his Leica with the laser rangefinder back—times a wind velocity of 1.5

miles per hour, divided by fifteen. He made a half-click adjustment to his elevation sights and waited.

In the second or two left before engagement, Dar realized the absurdity of the situation. At this range, with this ammunition, factoring in for gravity alone meant that his aiming point was more than sixteen feet above the window level of the vehicle. The target would be moving almost at right angles to Dar's field of fire—which was good—but if Yaponchik was braking to only thirty miles per hour for the sharp curve, Dar would have to lead the moving vehicle by twenty-some feet. Dar had already estimated that he only had about thirty-five feet from the time the Suburban became visible before it would pass his aiming point. He could not track this target, so he would have to "trap" it—which meant that the Suburban and the SLAP rounds had to arrive at the aiming point at the same time. Luckily, the Suburban was one big fucker. All right, factor in the time it would take for Syd to give the warning and—

"Now!" said Syd.

Dar was just at the end of his breathing cycle and now he held his breath and gently squeezed the trigger once. Trying to ignore the recoil while resetting the crosshair of the reticle on precisely the same part of the boulder, he fired again, sighted, fired again, sighted, fired again, sighted—something dark entering his peripheral field of vision now—and fired again.

"Hit!" said Syd.

"Just one?" asked Dar, jumping to his feet and using the Redfield scope on the lighter M40 for his own viewing.

The Chevy Suburban had lurched to the right and embedded its right front quarter panel in the road cut just beyond the boulder that had been Dar's aiming point. Through the scope, it looked to Dar as if he had missed the cab but put two armor-piercing rounds into or through the massive V-8 engine block. The hood had been blown off and the windshield was a mass of fracture lines. A third slug appeared to have shredded the left rear wheel—and probably the axle beyond, as well, Dar guessed—and there was the shimmer of fire rising from the back of the truck. There had been no massive and instant explosion, but Dar knew that if he had ignited the Suburban's gargantuan fuel tank, the truck would burn very nicely.

The flames became visible then. Dar kept the scope on the passenger-side door, knowing that the doors on the right of the big truck were wedged against the dirt-and-rock cut.

For a moment Dar was certain that Gregor Yaponchik was going to burn to death—black smoke was already rising into the morning air from the now freely burning back of the vehicle—but then the door opened and Yaponchik stepped out casually. He was carrying a weapon, but the shape did not look right—not even through the mirage shimmer and distortion—to be the suppressed SVD he had been using above the cabin.

"He has a rifle," said Syd just as Dar dropped to his knees, lay prone, and used the ten-power Ultra scope on the Light Fifty to get a better look.

"Shit," Dar said very softly. Yaponchik's face was still a blur through the mirage ripples, but Dar could recognize the make of the rifle by a glimpse of its unusual five-round rotating-spool magazine. *"Scharf-schutzengewehr Neun-und-sechsig,"* he muttered to himself.

"What?" said Syd, lowering her binoculars.

"Austrian-made SSG 69 sniper rifle," said Dar, watching the Russian walk off the road and down the steep hillside toward the near mile of field that separated them. "Much better than the Russian rifle he was using near the cabin. This baby is accurate to more than eight hundred meters."

Syd looked at him, and out of the corner of his eye, Dar saw the concern on her face. "But your fifty-caliber has a better range, doesn't it?"

"Yeah," said Dar, standing again and studying the advancing man through his Redfield scope. He was a tiny figure rippled by heat waves.

"You can kill him long before we're in range of his rifle, right?" said Syd.

"Right," said Dar. Yaponchik had entered the sunflowers and high grass of the meadow and was walking straight toward them across the broad, brown expanse. Dar began slinging his M40 rifle to a proper support. He emptied his pockets of everything but three magazines of 7.62mm ammo and jumped off the boulder. He began walking down toward the field.

Syd ran after him.

"Go on back to the boulder," Dar said softly.

"Fuck you," said Syd, although without heat. "What is this, some sort of machismo bullshit?"

Dar was silent for a second. Then he said, "Yeah, maybe. Or maybe Yaponchik is just coming this way to surrender. He could have run into the woods going west, you know."

Syd looked at Dar as if he had turned into an alien life form. "So you think he's bringing along this SSG 69 or whatever rifle to aid in his surrender? To give you as a victory gift, maybe?"

"No," said Dar. "I think he wants to get in range so he can kill me."

"Us," said Syd.

Dar shook his head, glancing over his shoulder at the Russian walking toward them. Yaponchik was about fourteen hundred yards away now. "Go on back to the rocks, please, Syd."

"I said fuck that," repeated Syd. "Shall I get the AK-47?"

"It's useless at these ranges," said Dar.

Syd shook her head. "If I knew how to adjust the sights on that fifty-caliber up there, I'd blow Yaponchik's head off. He killed Tom Santana."

"I know," said Dar softly. He turned and continued down the slope to the field, pausing only when he realized that Syd was still coming with him.

"Please, Syd."

"No, Dar."

Dar sighed. "All right. Will you be my spotter?"

"What do I do?"

"Just what you did up on the rock. Stay about three paces behind me and to my left. Keep him in your glasses. Let me know where my shots are hitting."

Syd nodded grimly and the two slid down the steep and pebbly slope to the beginning of the meadow. Dar lifted his old M40 and gauged distance through the Redfield reticles. His guess at Yaponchik's height had been about five eleven, so that would put his current range at twelve hundred yards and closing.

He and Syd began walking through the high grass. The brown stalks slapped softly against their legs and left seeds on the cotton of their trousers. Dar reached a point about fifty yards from their boulder and stopped.

"We'll let him come to us," he said softly.

Syd was watching the Russian through her glasses. "That's a nasty-looking weapon," she said.

Dar nodded. "The Steyr Company developed it for the Austrian Army," he said. "Synthetic polymer stock…It has a customized butt made adjustable with spacers."

"I always wanted one of those," said Syd.

Dar glanced at her, astounded at her grace under pressure. "I think he's mounted a Kahles ZF 69 sight on it," he said at last.

"Is that important?" asked Syd.

"Only because the ZF 69 sight is graduated for very accurate firing out to eight hundred meters," said Dar. "So we might expect him to take his first shots about then."

"What's his range now?" asked Syd, looking through her binoculars again.

"About a thousand meters." Dar raised his M40, slung it tight, and began clicking the elevation settings.

"He's coming slow enough," said Syd. "He's sure as hell in no hurry."

"It's a nice day," said Dar, seeing Yaponchik's face clearly for the first time.

At that moment Yaponchik lifted his SSG 69 to port arms and then raised it to sight through the oversized scope. He was still walking.

"Turn sideways," said Dar. He glanced behind him. "No, not to the left...I have to stand this way because I shoot right-eyed and right-handed, but you turn the other way, so your right side is to him."

Syd did so, but said, "What the hell is this, some eighteenth-century duel? Is the idea that my ribs are going to stop the black-powder pistol ball?"

Dar had nothing to say to that. Yaponchik had stopped and was ranging them. Dar checked the reticles in his sight and figured the range at about one thousand yards.

Syd said, "Tell me that your rifle is a far superior piece of American engineering than his, Dar."

"My rifle is a Vietnam-era piece of shit compared to his," admitted Dar. "But I'm used to it."

"OK," said Syd in a tone that said all banter was over for the day. "Ready to spot you."

Dar adjusted his eye to the sight again. He could see Yaponchik's face at this range. It should not be possible, he knew, not from a thousand yards, but he could swear that he could see the Russian's cold, blue eyes.

Yaponchik's muzzle flashed.

There came a ripping sound from the grass five yards in front of Dar. A puff of dust rose. An instant later two loud cracks echoed across the wide field—the sonic boom of the bullet and then the second part of a double clap, the unsuppressed sound of the rifle firing. Dar watched as the older man smoothly operated the bolt action. Dar could actually see the spool magazine rotate as the next bullet was chambered. *How many rounds did a Steyr SSG 69 spool magazine hold? Five or ten?* Dar knew that he would find out. He watched as Yaponchik removed the spent cartridge by hand and carefully set it in his trouser pocket just below his black body armor.

Dar suddenly realized that he was not wearing his own vest. *Fuck it,* he thought, and sighted.

The Russian began walking forward again.

Dar waited. Shooting at a moving target smaller than a Chevy Suburban was rarely a good idea at such a range. When Yaponchik stopped and raised his rifle again, Dar stopped his breathing and squeezed the trigger.

"I didn't see it hit," said Syd from her place behind him. "I'm sorry, I didn't see the—"

"Did you see a puff of dust anywhere ahead of him?" asked Dar as he worked the bolt action, retrieved the cartridge, and set it in his blouse pocket.

"No."

"Then I was high," said Dar. Yaponchik's muzzle flashed again.

Dar heard the whine of the slug passing his right ear before the double-crack of the shot itself. Dar had to admit that Yaponchik was ranging him fairly well. And the Russian did not require a head shot since Dar had no vest.

Dar banished the thought and concentrated on vision and calculation.

Yaponchik fired again. The bullet struck halfway between Dar and Syd, throwing pebbles and dust four feet in the air. Dar kept his stance, blinked away shimmers, and lowered his aim slightly. He had to be impressed by the professional fluidity with which Yaponchik worked the bolt action, pocketed the cartridge out of old habit, and resumed his perfect sniper stance without lifting his face from the ZF 69 sight.

Dar fired. The recoil made him lose Yaponchik for a second.

"Short—" cried Syd.

"How much?"

But Syd was already providing the information. "About a meter short. Right on line, though."

Dar nodded and lifted his sights. He heard rather than saw the wind come up as the grass rustled and his torn blouse lifted slightly in the breeze. He adjusted his sight two clicks to the left.

Yaponchik had already squeezed the trigger. *Only one bullet left in that magazine,* thought Dar. *I hope.*

The slug threw up a geyser of dust a foot in front of Syd. She did not flinch. Luckily there had been no rock for the bullet to ricochet from.

Dar heard and felt the breeze strengthen slightly, saw the rippling mirage lines tilt a little farther to the left and then a little more, not quite horizontal but close to it. He estimated the wind at six and a half miles per hour, gave his elevation screw another half click left, reached his exhale spot on his breathing cycle, held his breath, and fired.

"Hit!" cried Syd. "I think…"

Dar did not have to think. He knew it had not been a clean head shot—he could still see Yaponchik's face and cold blue eyes staring—but there had been a spray of red mist.

The instant seemed to drag on for long minutes, although only a second or two elapsed. Dar had time to action the cartridge out and chamber the next round, his eye never leaving the sight, before Yaponchik fell.

Unlike the movies in which humans are thrown violently backward for many yards from even a pistol shot, Dar had never seen a shooting victim do anything more dramatic than crumple. That was what Yaponchik did now, still holding his sniper rifle at port arms.

"Neck, I think," said Syd, her voice thick.

"I saw it," said Dar. "Right at the base of the throat. Just above the vest-line."

They began walking toward the downed man, Syd removing her 9mm semiautomatic from its holster, when Dar suddenly stopped.

"What?" said Syd, sounding slightly alarmed.

"Nothing," said Dar. He had slung his M40 over his shoulder. Out of curiosity, he extended his right hand. Then his left. There was no shaking whatsoever. "Nothing," he said again, feeling a great hollowness rise within him and threaten to carry him away. "Nothing."

They began walking again. Yaponchik's crumpled form did not stir.

Syd and Dar were only thirty yards away and could actually see the red spray of arterial blood on the grass and the Russian's head tilted back at an impossible angle when the skies above them filled with noise.

Both stopped and looked up.

Two of the helicopters had Marine markings and the third one had "FBI" lettered on the side. The FBI chopper landed between them and Yaponchik's body.

Dar turned, ripped the Velcro off Syd's vest, lifted the Kevlar over her head, and held her in his arms. All around them, the grasses swayed wildly from the madness of the rotors' blast.

"I love you, Dar," said Syd, her words lost in the engine roar, but perfectly understandable.

"Yes," Dar said, and kissed her softly.

26

"Z IS FOR ZOOLOGICAL"

It was ten days later, a Sunday morning, when Dar's condo phone rang at 5:30 A.M.

"Shit," muttered Dar sleepily.

"Ditto," said Syd, propping herself up on one elbow.

"Excuse me," said Dar, grunting slightly with pain as the stitches in his side stretched. He reached across Syd's bare breasts to get the phone, and felt clumsy as he lay on his belly to answer it. He had never learned to sleep on his stomach, but the slowly healing wound just below his backside gave him little choice. Syd claimed that she did not mind when Dar forgot in the night, rolled over on his back or side, and awoke shouting and cursing.

The bullet in his side had been no problem. The emergency-room medic had given Dar a local anesthetic and dug the slug out in fifteen seconds. "Hardly worth coming inside for," the medic had said. "Should have just used the drive-through."

Oddly enough, it was his ear that still gave him the most problems. There was still some plastic surgery in the future for that.

Lying on his stomach, using the wrong ear, he answered the phone. "Dar Minor here."

"Lawrence Stewart here," came Larry's happy voice. "Dar, you've got to see this."

"No, I don't," said Dar.

Trudy got on the line. It sounded like their cell phone. "Yes, you do, Dar. Trust us. This is going to be a tricky reconstruction job. Bring both your regular camera and your digital."

Dar sighed. Syd pulled the blanket over her head and sighed even more heavily. "Where are you?" said Dar. If it was more than ten miles away, they could forget it.

"The San Diego Zoo," said Lawrence, obviously pulling the phone back.

"The zoo?"

Syd lifted her face above the covers and silently mouthed a word. *Zoo?*

"The zoo," said Lawrence. "Trust me, you'll never forgive yourself if you miss this one."

Dar sighed again.

"Hurry," said Lawrence. "And say good morning to Syd and invite her along, too." The adjuster broke the connection.

Dar looked at Syd. She shrugged—Dar always thought that her shoulders were cute—and said, "Why not? We're awake now."

"It's Sunday," Dar reminded her. "We have a tradition of spending Sunday mornings a little…differently."

Syd laughed. "Tradition," she said. "One precedent. Some tradition."

He touched her cheek. "*I* think it's a tradition," he said softly. "Shall we shower together?"

"I heard Lawrence say we needed to hurry," said Syd.

"Okay," said Dar. "I'll shower first."

* * *

They stopped by a Dunkin' Donuts to get coffee and sustenance. The cups were hot—napkins around them did not help much—and Dar was doing quite a balancing act, moving the cup from hand to hand while shifting. Syd just tried to keep from spilling her own coffee. She knew by now how picky Dar was when it came to the NSX's leather upholstery.

"Have you decided yet?" she asked as they took the zoo exit.

"Decided what?"

"You know what. You said you'd give me an answer by Sunday. Today's Sunday." She tried to sip the hot coffee without spilling it as the black sports car zoomed up the curling exit ramp.

Dar sighed again. "I don't know..." he said.

"Come on," urged Syd. "You've seen the depositions from Dallas Trace and Constanza and that surviving Russian..."

"The one you saved with the belt tourniquet," said Dar nostalgically.

"Yep," said Syd. "Anyway, you've read their testimony. This fraud group—the

Alliance—is even bigger than we thought. We're going after the New York boys and girls next...and then the Miami area."

"You don't need me," said Dar. There were police cruisers at the open gate to the zoo. The patrolman glanced in, saluted Dar, and waved them on.

"No, we don't need you," agreed Syd, "but now that this is a joint NICB/FBI operation, nationwide, it would sure be fun to have you along. Just try it for a year."

"I hate handguns," said Dar, turning in to the parking lot. He could see the Stewarts' Isuzu Trooper parked by a coroner's ambulance and five more police vehicles.

"You wouldn't have to carry just because you're on the task force," said Syd. "Just stay home—wherever that will be—and work on your analyses and computer reconstructions while I'm out in the field. And then, in the evening, I'll hang my shoulder holster on the headboard and we'll make love before dinner—"

"You don't wear a shoulder holster," pointed out Dar.

"Damn it, Dar. You can be such a pain sometimes."

Dar parked and they got out into the warm July air and began walking toward the distant glare of yellow accident-scene tape.

"Syd," he said softly, "why didn't you tell me that I almost fucked up the whole investigation for you guys?"

Syd drank the last of her coffee, tossed the cup in a receptacle, and looked at him. "The photos, you mean? And tracing the Russians' phone number? It doesn't matter, Dar. The photograph of Constanza that Lawrence used to identify Esposito's killer was taken by the FBI guys in their observation post across from Dallas Trace's place."

"Why didn't you tell me about that and—"

Syd touched his arm. "It doesn't matter, Dar," she said softly. "The defense could use that if it had been a real factor in the arrests, but they'll never hear about the illegally taken photos or the phone number. The FBI got all the same stuff legally anyway—"

"But I almost screwed everything up..."

Syd stopped. Dar was surprised to find her smiling at him. "Look at it this way, Dr. Minor. Now you don't have to testify in any of these trials...just send a few reconstruction videos to Lawrence. That means you'll be free to head back east with the task force and me in August."

"New York in August," said Dar, realizing as he said it that he was deciding to go.

Syd squeezed his hand and they walked past the yellow tape and through the door to the large-animal enclosure where the police were gathered.

The zoo's assistant curator was trying to explain. "Carl's taken care of Emma for fifteen years...more than fifteen years," she said between sobs. Her face was red and she kept wiping the mucus from her reddened nose. "Carl really loved Emma. He's been so worried about her the last two weeks. Constipation in an elephant can be fatal, you know..."

"Emma's the elephant," confirmed Lieutenant Hernandez.

"Of course Emma's the elephant!" said

the assistant between sobs. She was wearing long, yellow rubber gloves. In the next enclosure, the elephant in question gave a trumpet that sounded as sad as Dumbo's mother calling to her baby. "And now... now...they'll probably have to destroy her," said the assistant, her shoulders heaving with sorrow.

Hernandez patted the distraught woman on the back.

Lawrence, Trudy, Dar, Syd, and half a dozen uniformed police officers were gathered around the three-foot-high and seven-foot-long heap of elephant excrement. A pair of human legs protruded from the near end of the heap. The trousers were well creased and the same khaki green as the other zookeepers' uniforms.

"It reminds me a little bit of that scene from the first *Jurassic Park* movie," said one of the cops in soft but amused tones.

"It reminds me of the 'Chuckles the Clown' episode of the old *Mary Tyler Moore Show*," said another cop, hitching up his gunbelt. "What did Murray Slaughter say in that episode? Something like... 'We're lucky nobody else died. You know how hard it is to stop with just one....' "

"That's because Chuckles was dressed as a peanut in a parade when the elephant shelled him," said the first cop. "This zoo guy wasn't in a peanut costume."

"No, but..." said the second cop, lamely trying to save his joke.

"Shut up," said Dar. To the kneeling medical examiner, who so far had studied only the deceased's feet and legs, Dar said, "When did this happen?"

"We think a little after midnight," said the ME.

"And *how* could it happen?" asked Syd.

The medical examiner got to his feet with a groan. "Ms. Haywood there says that Carl—that's Emma's keeper here— had been worried about the elephant's constipation for days. Evidently, last night about three hours after closing time, he mixed Emma a serious laxative mixed with oats and various grains. He overdid it on the laxative part, though."

"Boy, did he," said a third cop.

"Jesus," said the youngest cop. "I've

heard of projectile vomiting, but I've never seen a case of projectile—"

"Shut up," Dar said again. All of the cops glared at him. They were having a good time.

Trudy was shooting photographs. Lawrence was measuring the long trail of dung. "Seven feet and eight inches long," he said as if reading off skid marks. "Five and a half feet wide. A little over three feet deep in the middle."

Dar went to one knee near the two legs protruding from the heap. Syd looked at him curiously. Dar touched the dead zookeeper's polished shoe. "He must have been pushed backward hard enough to be knocked unconscious when his head hit the concrete," Dar said dully. "Then asphyxiated. He probably just never regained consciousness."

"Better for him, probably," said the young cop with a grin. "Imagine having this on your record…"

Dar moved so fast that the young cop took two steps back and actually set his right hand on his pistol in alarm.

"I told you to shut the fuck up and I mean *shut the fuck up*," snarled Dar, his finger almost in the young cop's eye.

The officer tried to show a smile of contempt, but the effect was spoiled when his lips quivered.

"No more pictures, Trudy," said Dar. "Not yet. Please."

Syd watched as Dar walked over to the sobbing assistant curator, borrowed her long, yellow gloves, came back to the pile of dung, and begin digging carefully, almost reverently, at the far end.

Dar was weeping silently. Tears coursed down his cheeks and his shoulders were shaking.

The cops looked at one another and then took several steps back in embarrassment. Lawrence looked at Trudy.

"Larry, would you give me that hose, please?" said Dar, his shoulders still shaking slightly. His fingers were visibly trembling in the yellow gloves.

"Lawrence," said Lawrence, but he brought the trickling hose.

Dar used the water and his fingers to

wash the dung off the dead man's face as best he could. Syd stepped closer. The dead zookeeper had been a very handsome man, in his late fifties. His graying hair was short and curly. He looked asleep—more natural and simply at rest than most corpses laid out in funeral homes for public viewing. Dar ran more water over the face and gently brushed away the last of the dung.

"Ms. Haywood," he said to the assistant curator, "what was his name?"

Emma the elephant trumpeted sadly from the next enclosure. The noise was like an inconsolable woman weeping.

"Carl," said Ms. Haywood.

Dar shook his head. "His whole name."

"Carl Richardson," said the assistant curator. "He has no family...His grown daughter died in an accident near a Hawaiian volcano last year. Emma was his only...He always tried to..." Ms. Haywood broke down again. "He was only a month away from retirement," she managed to say. "He was very worried about how Emma would get along without him."

Dar nodded and looked at Lawrence and Trudy. "You can take the pictures now," he said. "But let's get the man's name right. Mr. Carl Richardson."

Lawrence nodded and began taking more photos.

Dar stood and pulled off the gloves, dropping them on the concrete. "Names are important," he said as if to himself. "A name is—"

"An instrument of teaching," said Syd, "and of distinguishing natures."

"Socrates," said Dar as if in final benediction. He turned his back on the group and walked to a nearby restroom to wash up.

Syd waited for him outside. When Dar finally emerged, his sleeves were rolled up and his hands, arms, face, and neck smelled of liquid soap.

"Sorry," he said when he came close to Syd.

"Hush," said Syd. "It's a pretty Sunday morning and the zoo isn't open yet. Can we walk a bit before we head home? The only thing I don't like about zoos is the crowds."

Dar nodded. Syd took his hand and they started walking down the wide and curving asphalt path. The bright summer sun made the tropical foliage here an almost impossible green. Somewhere a lion or tiger coughed.

"Hesma phobou," Syd said after a while. They paused in the shade of a wildly branched tree with tiny leaves. On a nearby island, small monkeys were leaping from branch to branch in perfectly silent balletic arcs.

"What?" said Dar, looking at her strangely.

"Hesma phobou," repeated Syd. "I've been reading up on your Spartans. The weeping after a battle...falling to their knees...shaking, trembling. *Hesma phobou* — 'fear shedding.'"

"Yes," said Dar.

"It wasn't considered a weakness," continued Syd. "It was considered necessary. Another way — after the battle — of ridding themselves of the worst sort of possessing-fear daemon. The daemon of indifference."

Dar nodded.

"It's been too long, my dear," she said, and squeezed Dar's hand.

"And they never forgot the names of their fallen," said Dar. He hesitated only a few seconds before he spoke again. "My wife's name was Barbara and my son's name was David."

Syd kissed him.

"It is a pretty day," said Dar. "Let's enjoy the zoo awhile and then come back and get Lawrence and Trudy. We can have breakfast outside somewhere with them."

"Lawrence," said Syd.

Dar raised his eyebrows slightly.

"You called him Lawrence," said Syd. "Not Larry."

"A name is important," he said.

Syd smiled. "Let's take that walk, shall we?"

They had not walked more than ten paces before an explosion of noise behind them made them turn.

One of the smaller monkeys had miscalculated slightly and leapt for too small a branch, the branch had broken, and the little primate had fallen at least forty feet, using his hands and feet to grab at undersized branches and leaves every inch of the way down. The branches had all torn free but had softened his fall enough that he looked only shaken and embarrassed as he huddled on the concrete base of the monkey island and trembled, sitting on his haunches but curled almost into a fetal position. He was sucking his thumb for comfort. The sunlight glowed red through his ears, and his skin twitched.

Around him, more leaves and twigs continued to fall in a steady shower of debris. Above him, all of the other monkeys were chattering, screeching, gibbering...It sounded like wild and mindless laughter. Other animals picked up the noise and roared, growled, coughed, and whinnied in unison until the entire zoo sounded like a giant echo chamber. Only Emma the elephant's infinitely sad trumpeting raised itself in lonely counterpoint to the chaos and chorus of hysterics.

Dar looked at Syd. She took his hand, smiled, shrugged, and shook her head.

Questions unanswered but some riddles solved, the two walked down the path from shade to sunlight and then back again.

ACKNOWLEDGMENTS

The author would like to acknowledge the help and advice of Wayne A. Simmons and Trudy Simmons in researching this novel. Thanks also go to the Warner Springs gliderport for letting me test my theories on aerial combat in one of their high-performance sailplanes, to *The Accident Reconstruction Journal*, to the United States Marines' Scout Sniper School in Quantico, Virginia, and to Camp Pendleton in California. Acknowledgment should also be given to the writings of Stephen Pressfield on the Greek theories of *phobologia*—the study of fear and its mastery—and to Jim Land, whose sniper instruction manual may be the definitive work on the topic. To the artist in the Acura division of the Honda Motor Corporation who assembled the engine of my Acura NSX by hand, I can say only *"Dōmo arigatō gozaimasu—Shūri o onegai dekimasu ka?"*

All of the accidents investigated in *Darwin's Blade* are based upon real accident reconstruction files but each is a composite—the combination of several investigations into one reconstruction used for fictional purposes. My thanks go to all of the accident investigators and accident reconstruction experts whose professionalism, research, and bizarre sense of humor have illuminated this novel. Any accuracy or verisimilitude in this book is due to them; the mistakes, unfortunately, are the author's alone.